The Shadow of the Lynx

Born Ele..... ...., ... Holt was one of Britain's most prolific writers of historical romance, writing 183 books over the course of her career. Always determined to keep her birth date and private life a closely guarded secret Holt wrote under many pseudonyms – Jean Plaidy was one of her most popular, and was created when she lived near Plaidy Beach in Cornwall. She decided to be a novelist at an early age but did not publish her first book, *Beyond the Blue Mountains*, until 1947. Having written over ninety historical romances, she then began a new series of Gothic romances, the first of which, *Mistress of Mellyn*, appeared in 1961. *The Shadow of the Lynx* was first published in 1971 as part of the same series. She died at sea in January 1993, somewhere between Greece and Port Said, Egypt.

Visit www.AuthorTracker.co.uk for exclusive updates on your favourite HarperCollins authors.

VICTORIA HOLT

The Shadow of the Lynx

Lynx

HARPER

This novel is entirely a work of fiction. The names, characters
and incidents portrayed in it are the work of the author's
imagination. Any resemblance to actual persons, living
or dead, events or localities is entirely coincidental.

Harper
An imprint of HarperCollins*Publishers*
77–85 Fulham Palace Road,
Hammersmith, London W6 8JB

www.harpercollins.co.uk

This paperback edition 2006
1

First published in Great Britain by
William Collins 1971

ISBN-13 978 0 00 723553 7
ISBN-10 0 00 723553 4

Typeset in Sabon by Palimpsest Book Production Limited,
Grangemouth, Stirlingshire
Printed and bound in Great Britain by
Clays Ltd, St Ives plc

Nora

Chapter One

$\mathscr{E}$ven as I stood on the deck and the *Carron Star* slipped away from the dockside I had to keep assuring myself that I was really leaving England, that I was making a clean break with the old life, and was in fact sailing away into the unknown. There I stood in my tartan cape, which flapped open in the breeze to show a serviceable skirt of the same material, my straw hat tied on with a long grey chiffon scarf, seventeen years old, travelling to the other side of the world with a man whom, a month ago, I had never seen and of whose existence I had been unaware.

On the wharf people were waving handkerchiefs, many of them surreptitiously wiping their eyes as they smiled bravely. There was no one to wave goodbye to me.

A middle-aged man with bold eyes and mutton-chop whiskers sidled close – too close.

'Any friends over there?' He was surveying me speculatively.

'No,' I replied.

He was smiling in a familiar fashion. 'Travelling alone?'

A voice behind me said: 'My ward is travelling with me.' And there was Stirling, his greenish eyes glinting derisively, his voice with the faint Australian accent clearly demanding to know why a stranger should dare to address *his* ward.

The man moved away awkwardly. Stirling did not speak to me. He merely stood beside me, leaning on the rail, and I was aware of a warm, happy feeling of security: I knew in that moment that I had taken a step away from the all-enveloping misery in which I had been living during the past weeks. I had lost the one I loved beyond everyone and every-thing; but here was Stirling and he was beside me – 'my guardian' as he called himself. It was not strictly true; but I liked it.

I think it was at that moment that I began to feel that Stirling and I were meant for each other.

But that is not the beginning. I should perhaps start when I was born, since that is where all stories start; but they really begin even before that. I often wondered about the prelude to my birth. I tried to picture my parents together – which was difficult because I never saw my mother. It was not a fact which worried me particularly, because there was my father, Thomas Tamasin – and possessing such a father, why should I fret because I had no mother?

She had 'gone away' as he put it when I was a year old. It was not until I was six years old that I understood what that meant.

Life was amusing lived with Thomas Tamasin. I believed that the two of us were enough. Why should we have wanted a third person? Even a mother would have been an intruder.

We had a series of housekeepers whose duty was to look after me; and it was not until I was six that I heard the word 'abandoned'. It was used by the housekeeper to a friend who had called to see her at our house which was then in north London. (We were constantly moving about to suit my

4

father's enterprises, which were numerous.) I was sitting beneath the kitchen window, which was wide open, watching ants purposefully marching back and forth on the crazy paving.

'Poor mite!' said the housekeeper. 'What she misses is a mother.'

'And him?'

'Oh . . . him!' Laughter followed.

Then: 'She left him, didn't she?'

'So I've heard. She was a fast piece of goods. On the stage or something.'

'Oh . . . an actress!'

'No good anyway. Young Nora was not much more than twelve months old when she went off. There's something wrong with a woman who'll abandon a child at that age. He ought to have married again.'

'That what you tell him?'

'Go on with you!'

Abandon! I thought. And the child who had been abandoned was myself.

'What's abandoned?' I asked my father when he came home.

'Left. Run away from.'

'It's not a nice thing to be, is it?'

He agreed it wasn't.

'People would only abandon what they didn't like,' I commented.

He admitted this was probably so, and I didn't tell him that I knew I had been abandoned because it would have hurt him. I was always careful not to hurt him, just as he was not to hurt me. In any case, having him, what did I care that I was abandoned?

We never talked about my mother. There were so many other things to talk about. There were his plans for making a fortune – though not so much making it as spending it. There was always some project afoot. At one time he was going to put an invention on the market which would revolutionize the daily life of millions of people. I liked invention times because then he stayed at home working in the room at the top of the house and it was comforting to have him near. I would sit close to his work bench and we would talk for hours of what we would do when his genius was recognized and the world was profiting from it. 'Ourselves included,' he would say with that laugh of his which was like water running down a drainpipe and which always made me laugh too. He made a spring lock which didn't work as it was intended to; he made mechanical toys which never quite achieved their purpose, except one which was a boy on a seat which swung over the top of a rail, but even he used to get stuck up there sometimes. He sold a few of these and we had a saying: 'Remember the boy on the swing?' It was his great success; but it was not the fortune he was after. He tried market gardening, and for a period we lived in the country; but he wanted to experiment all the time, to produce something different; an ordinary living was not good enough for him.

'When my ship comes home . . .' he would say, and that was the prelude to our favourite game. We sailed round the world in our imaginations; we found places on the map and said, 'We'll go there.' We were always together in these imaginary journeys; we had adventures in which we met sea monsters more awe-inspiring than anything encountered by Sinbad. Sometimes he wrote them down and he sold one or two to a magazine. Our fortunes were made, he declared. Why hadn't he realized that he was a literary man? But that didn't work either. He wanted to get rich quickly.

He had inherited a little money and this he set aside for my education. That was an indication of his care for me.

However improvident he might be in all else, he was determined that I should be secure. He wanted me to go to the best schools, he told me. I said I wanted only to be with him. So I should, he assured me, but while he was making our fortune I had to go to school. I went to several and learned quickly – the sooner to get away from it all.

It was just after my fifteenth birthday that he decided to go after gold. This was the greatest opportunity; this was the miracle. His life had been strewn with great chances which so far had proved to be mirages, but this was different. This would in truth make our fortunes.

'Gold!' he said, his eyes smouldering. 'We'll be millionaires, Nora. How would you like to be a millionaire?'

I thought I should like it very much, but where did we get this gold?

'It's there in the earth, waiting to be picked up. All you have to do is take it.'

'Then why isn't everyone a millionaire?'

'There speaks my practical daughter. It's a good question and there's a simple answer. It's because they're not as wise as we are going to be. We're going out to get it.'

'Where is it?'

'It's in Australia. They're finding it all over the place.'

'When do we start?'

'Well, Nora, just at first I'll have to go alone. It's no place for a girl who has to get educated.'

That was the moment of fear and the blank despair in my face must have frightened him.

'You have to learn the three Rs; you have to talk and act like a lady if you're going to be a millionaire.'

I reminded him that I was already acquainted with the three Rs. I also knew how to talk and act like a lady and did so except when I lost my temper.

'Well, you see Nora, you're too young just as yet. You

stay behind for a while. I've found a good school where they'll look after you and in next to no time I'll be back. We'll be millionaires and start enjoying life. What would you like to do? Where would you like to go? There's no limit. We can start making plans without delay. The fortune is as good as in our pockets.'

He convinced me as he always could and he persuaded me to go to Danesworth House. 'Only a few months, Nora. Then . . . all the money in the world. Everything you can wish for. Now what will you have to start with?'

I said: 'There are lots of people looking for this gold. Suppose it takes years for you to find it?'

'I tell you, Nora, I have the Midas touch.'

'I could be your housekeeper. I could cook for you, look after you.'

'What! My millionaire daughter! No. We're going to have someone to look after us . . . for ever more. No more partings. No more intruders. That'll be the day. And all you have to do is wait awhile at Danesworth House while I go and get the gold.'

That was how he talked, forcefully, persuasively and so vividly that we were able to live in our imaginations through all the extravaganza he planned for us.

So I went to school and he sailed across the world; and every day I waited for the letter which would tell me that he had found his fortune and that we were millionaires.

School was just a tiresome bore. I was less in awe of Miss Emily and Miss Grainger than most of their pupils. I was good at my work; I avoided trouble; I was not interested in schoolgirl mischief. I only lived for the summons. I used to picture how it would come. In a letter perhaps: 'Come to Australia at once.' Or perhaps he, who loved surprises, would come to the school to take me away. There would be a summons to the study; and there in that cold arid room he

8

would be standing; he would catch me up in his arms to the astonished disapproval of Miss Emily or Miss Grainger – for which he would care nothing – and he would shout: 'Pack your bags, Nora. You're leaving. We're millionaires.'

The letters came regularly. I knew that tired as he was with the day's work he always remembered how I would be waiting and watching for the posts.

There were letters from the ship posted at various ports of call. He described his fellow passengers amusingly for my benefit. I was terrified that his ship would run into a storm which would be dangerous and I was very uneasy until he wrote telling me that he had arrived.

He wrote vividly and I had a clear picture of those early days, and although he wrote with the utmost optimism, I understood the hardships he had to endure. I pictured his setting out with the tools he would need: pickaxes; the cradle he used for puddling; his billy-can; his rations. I pictured the field on which he worked – a desolate place it must have been with the trees chopped down and the tents pitched there. I imagined their sitting round the fire at night exchanging stories of their finds and most of all their hopes. He would be in the centre; he would have more colourful tales than anyone; and of course there was his charm and his way with words. Somehow he made me see those unkempt men, their backs aching as they bent over their cradles watching the water run through the soil that could reveal the longed-for golden streaks. I could see their grim faces and on all was the lust for gold – the longing, the yearning – for they would all see in the yellow dust the gateway to fortune.

He loved the life, I sensed that. If I could have been with him he would have been perfectly happy. I believe now that had he made his fortune he could not have enjoyed life half as much as he did when he was endeavouring to find it. I should have been there with him. I could have cooked the food while they worked on the diggings; I saw myself as the little mother of the colony. Had I been there I was sure I should never have wanted them to find gold in any quantity. I should have wanted them to go on forever searching for it.

The months passed; he had moved to another field. He had found nothing but a little dust. Never mind. The new field was rich, he was sure; and one must have experience.

His optimism never flagged; he was always on the verge of great discovery. As to myself I must have seemed strange to my fellow pupils. I was aloof; I was not interested in school affairs but I managed to satisfy my teachers and I was left a good deal to myself. I was that 'odd Nora Tamasin whose father was a gold miner in Australia'. They had wormed that much out of me.

Then the tone of the letters changed. He met the Lynx.

'The Lynx is the most unusual man I have ever met. We were drawn to each other from the first. I have decided to join him. He knows this country inside out. He's been here for thirty-four years. If you could see him you'd know why they call him Lynx. He's got a pair of eyes that see everything. They're blue – not azure blue, not like the tropical seas, oh no! They're like steel or ice. I never knew a man who could so quell with a look. He's the big man round here. His name is Charles Herrick. He came out as a convict and now owns most of the place I'm in. He's a man in a million. It's going to be different from now on. I'm going into business in a big way. No more working overworked plots. It's all different and all because of Lynx.'

I thought a great deal about the Lynx. I was a little jealous of him because my father's letters were full of him. He admired him so much. And now, through those letters, I understood what hardships he had suffered. The stories of camp-fire gaiety, the songs they sang by firelight, the comradeship of the diggings were only half the story. I now sensed the apprehension, the careful rationing of food, the preservation of the precious water, the terrible despair when day after day the cradles revealed nothing but the worthless dust.

'Lynx is going to strike gold in a big way, Nora, and when he does I'll be with him. He's a man of experience. Besides a sizeable property he owns the local store and a hotel in Melbourne. He has hundreds of men working for him and he knows all there is to know about gold. He can't fail. I've told Lynx about you. He thinks that you should come out when you're educated. But I'll be home before then.'

I pictured Lynx – a pair of piercing eyes, a convict! Thirty-four years ago people had been sent out to Australia when they had been found guilty of some misdemeanour. Of what had Lynx been guilty? I wondered. Something political perhaps. I was sure he was not a thief or a murderer. I wanted to hear more of him.

'Lynx is a sort of king, magistrate, employer, dictator . . . the head of things. He is just, but he'll have his own way. I've never felt such friendship as I do for him. It was a lucky day when I met him. I've thrown in all I have with him. He's certain that we'll find a rich vein of gold. We're going to work as secretly as possible. If we don't keep it dark we'll have diggers here from all over the place. The rumour only has to get round and they come in their thousands. Lynx is wily and we're in this together.'

Letters had been coming more or less regularly. Sometimes I would get several together. My father would explain that there had been floods which had made it impossible to get letters down to Melbourne, or an expected ship had not arrived on time. There was always an explanation for delays and he never failed to give it. The message which came to me through all the letters was that however hard he was working, whatever was happening, he never forgot me and the ultimate goal, which was for us to be together.

And then no letters came. At first, though disappointed, I was not unduly alarmed. It was the floods or a delayed ship and there would be several when they did come. But they did not come and the weeks went on and there was still no news.

Two months passed. I was frantic with anxiety; and one day Miss Emily sent for me to come to the study. It was an arid place with its polished floor, its reverent silence broken only by the ticking of the ormolu clock on the macramé-draped mantelpiece. Miss Emily was seated at the desk, her expression one of pain which suggested, erroneously, that what was to follow hurt her more than it hurt me. Parents thought Miss Emily very kind and gratefully entrusted their children to her; they felt she would protect their darlings from the harsher rule of Miss Grainger. In fact it was mild-seeming Miss Emily who was really in charge, but she liked it to be believed that the unpopular rules and regulations were made by her sister.

'I am sure,' she said, her elbows resting on the desk, the tips of her fingers pressed together while she regarded me with some severity, 'I am *quite* sure that you would not wish for charity. It is now two months since we heard from your father and while Miss Grainger is always prepared to be reasonable, she cannot be expected to feed and clothe you, at the same time giving you an education fit for the daughter of a gentleman.'

'I am convinced that a letter from my father is on the way.'

Miss Emily coughed. 'It is a long time coming.'

'He is in Australia, Miss Emily. Posts are delayed.'

'Those were exactly Miss Grainger's words in the beginning. Now three months' school bills are outstanding.'

'But I am sure it will be all right. Something has delayed the letters. I am certain of it.'

'I wish I could be . . . for your sake. Miss Grainger is distressed but she has decided she can wait no longer. She cannot continue to support you – feed you, clothe you, educate you . . .' She made each item sound like a labour of Hercules. 'But, however, she does not wish to turn you out.'

'Perhaps,' I said haughtily, 'it would be better if I left.'

'That is a rather foolish statement, I fear. Where would you go, pray?'

When Miss Emily 'prayed' it meant that she was really annoyed; but I was too apprehensive for caution. My fears for my father's safety – because I knew that only if something dreadful had happened to him could those letters have failed to arrive – made the wrath of Miss Emily comparatively unimportant to me.

'I could do something, I suppose,' I said spiritedly.

'You have no knowledge of the world. You, a girl of what is it? Sixteen?'

'Seventeen next month, Miss Emily.'

'Well, Miss Grainger is going to be very generous. She is not going to turn you adrift. She has a proposition and of course you will wish to accept it. Indeed you can do nothing else when you consider the alternative.'

Miss Emily's smile was pious; the palms of her hands were now pressed together and she turned her eyes up to the ceiling. 'You may stay at the school as one of our pupil teachers. That will go a *little* way towards earning your keep.'

So I became a pupil teacher and knew utter despair. It was not because of my position in the school but because with every passing day, when no letter came, my fears increased. I had never been so miserable in the whole of my life. Every day I would tell myself that a letter must come; and every night when I lay in my little attic bed – for I had been moved from the dormitory – I asked myself whether it ever would. Should I live the rest of my life at Danesworth House waiting for news? I should grow old and fusty like Miss Graeme whose hair resembled a bird's nest made of grey-brown fluff; I should become pale and wan like Miss Carter; I should peer myopically like Mademoiselle and worry because I could not control the girls.

In the meantime I was less important than they were. I joined Mary Farrow in the attic bedroom with its bare boards and rush mats. Mary had been an orphan in the care of her grandmother and when Mary was sixteen the grandmother had died and Mary was left penniless. Miss Grainger had been magnanimous as with me, and Mary had become a pupil teacher. She was as colourless in her character as in her complexion, and was resigned to her future as I never could be.

We fared worse than the servants. They at least were not constantly reminded that they owed their position to Miss Grainger's charity. They were more useful than we were, too. We were apprentices and our board and lodgings were our only payment. We must not only give the younger children their lessons but act as nursemaids to them; we must keep our attic clean and be prepared to perform any task that might be imposed on us by Miss Emily or Miss Grainger – and they saw that there were plenty.

The mistresses despised us – as did the servants; even the children realized that they might take liberties in our classes which they dared take in no others. Miss Emily had a way of coming silently into a classroom – always when it was most unruly – and standing and listening with her gentle smile before she delivered a reproof in front of the children which made them more certain than ever that they could plague us. Poor Mary suffered more from them than I did. She was meek; I had a fiery temper and I think they were just a little in awe of me.

Sometimes I would lie in my narrow bed at one end of the attic waiting for the ghostly touch of the chestnut tree as the wind moved gently through its branches, and I would say to myself: 'Abandoned! This is the second time in your life. Why is it that people abandon you? There must be a reason for it. Twice in one lifetime.'

But my father would never abandon me. He would come back. I could not face a world without him. I had known such contentment merely to be with him and, until recently, the greatest gift to childhood – security. Not monetary security, but the only kind which is important to the child – the security of being loved.

I had been a pupil teacher for barely a month – though it seemed more like a year – when the news came.

I was reading to my class that morning, but I was not really attending. It was a warm spring day. A bee was now crawling up the window, now flying off in exasperation to return and fling itself against the glass in a desperate effort to free itself. It was trapped. There was no way out; but the window on the other side of the room was open and the foolish creature would not go there. He continued to buzz frantically up and down. Caught! Like myself.

The door opened suddenly and there was Miss Graeme

looking at me oddly. I noticed that the breeze from the open door sent the bee in the opposite direction. He found the open window and flew out.

'You are wanted in the study,' said Miss Graeme.

My first thought was: There is news of him. Perhaps when I reach the study he will be there.

I turned to the door.

'You should leave your class some work,' reproved Miss Graeme.

I told them to go on reading; then I fled past Miss Graeme, up the stairs to the study. I knocked at the door and waited for the response. Miss Emily was seated at the desk, a letter before her.

'You may sit down, Nora. I have a letter here. There has been some delay in the posts owing to the floods in Australia.' I sat, keeping my eyes on her face. 'You will have to be brave, my dear,' she went on gently.

I felt sick with apprehension. It must be very bad news since she called me 'my dear'. It was. There could be nothing more terrible.

'The reason we have not heard from your father is that he is dead.'

I stumbled up to my attic and lay on my bed. The leaves of the chestnut tree lightly touched the window; the breeze made a soft moaning noise and the sunshine threw dancing patterns on the wall.

I should never see him again. There would be no fortune, no travels, no being together – only utter desolation. He was buried on the other side of the world, and all the time I had been waiting for a letter from him he had been lying in a coffin with the earth on top of him. Even Miss Emily was sorry for me.

'Go to your room,' she had said. 'You will need to recover from the shock of this.'

I had come blindly up to my room. I had not listened to what she was saying. Words came back to me as I lay there. 'It has settled your future.' I did not care for the future; I was only concerned with the misery of the present. I kept seeing him, remembering his laughing eyes, hearing his booming voice. 'When my ship comes home . . .'

And the terrible truth was that his ship would never come home. It had foundered on the rocks of death.

He had written to me as he was dying. How like him! The letter had come by way of his solicitors with the news of his death. Miss Emily had withheld it for a few hours to give me, as she said, a little time to recover from the initial shock.

'Don't grieve for me. We had a happy time together.
Don't let any sadness touch your memories of me,
Nora. I'd rather you forgot me altogether than
thinking of me should make you sad. It was an accident . . . and it's finished me, but you're going to be all
right, Nora. My good friend has promised me that.
Lynx is a man of his word, and he has given me that
word so that I can die happy. He is going to take care
of you, Nora, and he'll do it better than I could. When
you read this I'll be gone, but you'll not be alone. . . .'

The writing was scarcely legible. The last words were: 'Be happy' and they were only just decipherable. I pictured the pen falling from his hands as he wrote them. To the end all his love and concern had been for me.

I read the letter again and again. I would carry it with me always.

And I lay numbly on my bed, unable to think of what the future held, unable to think of anything but that he had gone.

Miss Emily sent for me. Miss Grainger was with her in the study and with them was a man in black with a white cravat and a very solemn expression. I thought he was my new guardian, but he could never be the man my father had described as Lynx.

'This is Nora Tamasin,' said Miss Emily. 'Nora, this is Mr Marlin of Marlin Sons and Barlow – your father's solicitors.'

I sat down and listened without taking everything in; I was still numb with misery. But I gathered that everything had been legally arranged and I was to be given into the care of Mr Charles Herrick, the man whom my father had appointed as my guardian.

'Mr Herrick naturally wishes to take you into his home and you are to join him there as soon as possible. This is in Australia and your father's last wish was that you should do this. Mr Herrick is unable to come to England but a member of his family will come to escort you to your new home. Mr Herrick is anxious that you should not travel alone.'

I nodded, thinking: My father would have wanted that. He must have asked the Lynx – it was difficult to think of him with such a mild name as Mr Herrick – to take great care of me.

It was expected that in a few weeks' time my guardian's emissary would arrive in England. I should in the meantime prepare myself to depart.

Mr Marlin took his leave and Miss Emily said that everything was now most satisfactorily settled, by which I knew she meant that outstanding bills had been paid. The next few weeks I could utilize in preparation for my departure.

There might be one or two things I needed to buy. I might do this – within reason – and Miss Emily would graciously allow one of the teachers to accompany me to the town and advise me on my purchases. Perhaps I would like to work at my books. Indeed I might feel that work was the best antidote to sorrow and might wish to continue to act as a pupil teacher for which work – although this had not been mentioned before – I seemed to have an aptitude.

'No, thank you, Miss Emily,' I said. 'I will prepare myself to meet whoever is coming for me and do what shopping I consider necessary.'

Miss Emily bowed her head.

I stayed in my attic quarters. Poor Mary was envious. She only saw that a new and exciting life stretched out before me; she did not realize what grief had led me to it. I shopped. I bought the tartan cape and skirt and strong boots which I thought would be needed where I was going. I had little interest in these purchases, nor in anything. I could think of nothing but the fact that my father was dead.

And at last I was once more summoned to the study.

'You will travel in the company of Miss Herrick, who is I gather your guardian's daughter – a lady of responsible years. You are to meet her at the Falcon Inn which is some five or six miles from the town of Canterbury. For some reason the lady is there. There is a mention of business which has to be performed. It seems a little inconvenient as I suppose you will be sailing from Gravesend or Tilbury. However, those are the instructions. At Canterbury a fly will be waiting to conduct you to the Falcon Inn. Miss Graeme will accompany you to London and see you safely on to the Canterbury train. You will be all right from there on.'

'Of course, Miss Emily.'

'After Miss Graeme has left you, you must on no account speak to strangers,' said Miss Grainger.

'I certainly should not, Miss Grainger.'

'So there is no difficulty. On Thursday morning at nine o'clock you will leave Danesworth House. The fly will take you to the station. The train leaves at nine-thirty. Cook will pack a sandwich for you.'

'I am sure there is no need for Miss Graeme to accompany me. I could easily change trains when I get to London.'

'That is quite out of the question,' said Miss Emily. 'You would have to get across London by yourself. Unthinkable! Why Canterbury should have been chosen, I can't imagine. But that is the case; and we have been requested by your guardian – through the solicitors – that you should be accompanied until you are safely on the Canterbury train. Therefore it is unthinkable that it could be otherwise.'

So Lynx's despotic rule could touch even Miss Emily.

I packed my bags; I waited; the girls and mistresses gave me their respectful interest. I was the sort of person to whom strange things happened. I might have enjoyed my new importance if I could have forgotten my father's death.

At last the day came and Miss Graeme and I left Danesworth House. We boarded the London train and sat side by side looking out at the green fields and the wheat which was turning to gold. Gold! I thought angrily. If he had never gone to look for gold he would be here now.

My eyes filled with angry tears. Why had he not been content to be an ordinary person! But then he would not have been himself. Miss Graeme touched my arm lightly and I saw that there were tears in her eyes. She started to tell me that sorrow came to us all and we had to 'bear up' and go on with our lives. There was 'someone' who had 'never spoken' but who had intended to and would have done so if he had come home from the war, but he died unnecessarily and cruelly on the battlefield. In the Crimea, I supposed; and so, instead of being a buxom and happy mother, she was a wizened grey-brown mouse of a school teacher.

I listened and tried to show my sympathy; then we ate our sandwiches and in due course arrived at the London station. Flustered and aware of her responsibilities, Miss Graeme hailed a cab and we went to Charing Cross station where finally I was put into the train.

The last I saw of Miss Graeme was her spare figure in the brown coat and skirt and the hat with the brown veil, looking forlorn and wistful as the train carried me away.

Now I began to feel apprehensive. The new life had begun and I was on my own. I could run away now if I liked. I had a little money – very little; I could take a post as governess. I had my teacher's experience. But my father had wanted me to go to the Lynx, so I was given no choice. Suppose I arrived in Australia and hated it. Suppose they did not want me. I knew so little of what lay before me. I had not asked enough questions. I had been submerged by my misery; and now suddenly, here I was, speeding along to Canterbury, looking out at the orchards of apples and pears which would not be ready for picking for almost another two months and then I should be far away. We went past the hop fields which in another month would be alive with the activities of the pickers; cowled tops of oast houses dominated the scene. I wanted to cry to the train driver: Stop. I am rushing towards the unknown. I want a little time to think.

Perhaps in that moment my grief had receded a little since I could feel this misgiving for the future when previously I had felt nothing but the tragedy of the present. But the train rushed on relentlessly. We were at the station. I alighted and the porter took my bags. The fly which was to take me to the Falcon Inn was waiting for me.

We drove away from the station, past the ancient walls of the town and out into the country.

'Is it far to the Falcon Inn?' I asked the driver.

'Well, it's some little way out, miss. Most people stay in the town.'

I wondered why Miss Herrick who had come to England to collect me should have arranged for the meeting to take place at this spot. It was as Miss Emily had remarked 'unusual'. Perhaps the Lynx had ordained it.

The countryside was lusciously green; we passed through several villages clustered round the church – village greens and ancient inns; and at length we came to the village of Widegates with its old church and row of houses, most of them Tudor, some earlier still. I caught a glimpse in the distance of grey towers and asked what they were.

'That would be Whiteladies, miss. It's the big house round here.'

'Whiteladies. Why is it called that?'

'It was a convent once and the nuns wore white habits, so the saying goes. Some of it still stands. The family built the house there keeping what was left of the convent.'

'Who are the family?'

'Their name is Cardew. The family's been there for three hundred years or more.'

We had pulled up at the Falcon Inn. The stone steps which led to the door were worn away in the middle; the sign on which was depicted a falcon was freshly painted and over the door was the date 1418.

The driver brought in my bags. 'Everything's settled, miss,' he said. So I went to the reception desk and told them who I was.

'Ah yes,' said the receptionist. 'I'll have you shown to your room. There is a message for you. Will you go down to the parlour when you are ready.'

I went to my room which was large but rather dark because of the leaded windows; the floor sloped slightly and the wooden beams proclaimed its age. There was water in the ewer so I hastily washed and combed my thick dark hair.

When I was ready I went down to the inn parlour to which I was directed by a maid. There was no woman there but a man rose as I entered. He put his hands behind his back and watched me. I remembered Miss Emily's injunctions not to speak to strangers. I certainly should not speak to this one if I could help it for his look struck me as being a trifle insolent.

But he spoke to me. 'You are looking for someone?' His accent was faintly unusual; he himself was tall and lean; his face was weathered brown as far as I could see, for he was standing with his back to the light and there was not much of it in any case as the windows were similar to those in my bedroom.

I nodded coolly.

'Perhaps I can help you.'

'Thank you. I don't need any help.'

'Oh, I can see you are very self-sufficient.'

I turned away. Perhaps I should go to the desk and ask for Miss Herrick. I felt Miss Emily would not approve of my waiting in this room with a rather forward stranger; and although I did not intend to allow Miss Emily's judgments to rule my life, in this instance I was in agreement with her.

'I am sure I *can* help you,' he said.

'I don't see how.'

'Then I will enlighten you. You are looking for a Miss Herrick.'

I looked startled and he laughed. It was very irritating laughter. He was truculent, very sure of himself.

'That happens to be so,' I said primly.

'Well, you won't find Miss Herrick here.'

'What do you mean?'

'What I say. I always say what I mean.'

'Are you mistaking me for someone else?'

'You know very well I'm not. You are Nora Tamasin. Right.'

I was annoyed by the manner in which he answered his own question. Also I was bewildered. How could he know so much about me?

'And you have come here to meet Miss Herrick. She is not here.'

'How do you know?'

'Because I know where she is.'

'Where is she?'

'About forty miles north of Melbourne.'

'You are mistaken. The Miss Herrick I have come to meet is here in this inn. She sent a fly to meet me at the station.'

'I sent that fly.'

'You!'

'I reckon I should have introduced myself a little earlier. I just liked teasing you a bit because you looked so haughty. Adelaide, my sister, hasn't come. There was too much for her to do at home so my father thought I should be the one to come for you. Besides he wanted me to see a bit of England. So I'm here to take you back. Stirling Herrick, named after the Stirling River, just as Adelaide, my sister, is named after the town. It was my father's tribute to the country of his adoption.'

'Your father is Charles Herrick?'

'You've hit the nail right on the head, as they say. I've come to take you back. You're looking doubtful. You want to see my credentials? Right. Now here's a letter from that firm of solicitors, Marlin something . . . and I can prove to you over and over again that I am who I am.'

'This is all very strange.'

'It's all very simple. My father has promised to look after you so you're coming home with me. I'm a sort of brother. You're not looking very pleased about that.'

I said: 'I can't understand why he should have sent you.'

'Perfectly simple. He wanted me to come to England. I've been having talks about marketing our wool.'

'Here in Canterbury?'

'Oh yes. My business takes me all over the country. I had to ask you to come here so that we could have a day to get to know each other before you were rushed on to the ship. Now I am going to suggest we send for tea and over that we'll talk.'

He pulled the bell and when the maid came ordered tea. When I saw the thin bread and butter and scones with cream and strawberry jam, I realized I was hungry. He watched me while I poured out and there was amusement in his eyes, which were an unusual shade of green; they almost disappeared when he laughed and he looked as though he were accustomed to screwing them up against the strong light – which was very likely. I guessed he was in his twenties – about eight years my senior perhaps – and I thought it very unconventional that a young man should have been sent to be my travelling companion. Very different from the Miss Herrick I was expecting. I was sure Miss Emily would disapprove and that pleased me. I felt better than I had since I had received the news of my father's death.

'Why was I told that *Miss* Herrick would be waiting for me?' I demanded.

'It was arranged that she should come at the start, but Lynx decided that the house could not be run without Adelaide. He could spare me better.'

Lynx! The magic name. It was the first time he had used

it so I said interrogatively: 'Lynx?' wanting to hear more of that strange man.

'That's my father. People often call him that. It means he has sharp eyes.'

'I gathered that.'

'You are really smart, I can see.' His smile was ironical.

I said: 'Does he really want me . . . this Lynx?'

'He's promised your father to look after you so of course he wants you.'

'He might feel he must do it from a sense of duty because his conscience would worry him if he didn't.'

'He doesn't have any sense of duty . . . nor conscience either. He does what he wants, and he wants you to live with us.'

'Why?'

'No one ever questions his motives. He knows what he wants and that's about all there is to say.'

'He sounds an impossible sort of person.'

'Lynx *is* possible, although you might doubt it until you know him.'

'You talk of him as though he's some sort of god.'

'Well, I reckon that's not a bad description.'

'Does everyone have to be as reverent as his son?'

That made him laugh. 'You have a sharp tongue, Nora Tamasin.'

'Do you think it will help to protect me against this Lynx?'

'You've got it wrong. He's the one who is going to protect you.'

'If I don't want to stay I shall come back here.'

He bowed his head.

'There would be ways and means, I am sure,' I added.

'And you'd find them, I reckon.'

I had eaten one scone; he finished the entire plateful. He folded his arms and smiled at me as though he found me amusing. I was not sure what to make of him. Of one thing I was certain. Messrs Marlin Sons and Barlow could not have known that he had come alone to take me back with him for they, like Miss Emily, would surely consider this rather improper.

'But,' I said, speaking my thoughts aloud, 'I suppose you are a sort of brother.'

He laughed. 'I reckon so, Sister Nora. And that makes everything all right. You don't think so.'

'You have a habit of attempting to read people's thoughts . . . not always correctly.'

'But you are pleased.'

'It's too soon to answer that question. I hardly know you.'

'We're pleased to have a new sister.'

I was silent for a while; then I said, 'How did my father die?'

'Haven't they told you?'

'They merely said it was an accident.'

'An accident? He should have handed over the gold, then they wouldn't have shot him.'

'*They* shot him! Who?'

'No one knows who. He'd been out to the mine and was on his way back on the dray, bringing gold with him. There was a hold-up. They were waylaid. It often happens. Those fellows have a nose for gold. They know when it's being carried. So they held up the dray five miles out of Cradle Creek. Your father wouldn't give it up so they shot him.'

I felt bewildered. I had imagined his falling from a tree or being thrown from his horse. I had never thought of murder.

'So,' I said slowly, 'someone killed him.'

Stirling nodded. 'It happens now and then. It's a wild country and life's cheaper there than it is over here.'

'This was my *father*!' I felt furiously angry because someone had come along with a gun and wantonly taken

27

that precious life. There was a new emotion to supersede my grief – anger against my father's murderer.

'If he had given up the gold he wouldn't have died,' said Stirling.

'Gold!' I said angrily.

'That's what they are all after. It's what they all want.'

'And this . . . Lynx . . . he does too?'

Stirling smiled. 'He wants it. He's determined to find it one day – so he will.'

'How I wish my father had never got this idea into his head! If he hadn't he would be here now.'

It was too much to contemplate. I turned away, determined that he should not see my intense emotion.

'It's like a fever,' he said. 'It gets into your brain. You think of everything you want in life and if you find gold . . . real gold . . . thousands of nuggets . . . you can have it.'

'Everything?' I said.

'Everything you can think of.'

'My father found gold, it seems, and lost his life preserving it, and I lost him.'

'You're upset. You wait till you get out there. You'll understand then. It's a great life. You never know when you'll make a strike. It's a constant challenge, a constant hope.'

'And when you do someone kills you for it.'

'That's the life out there. Your father had bad luck.'

'It's . . . hateful.'

'It's life. I've upset you. I should have broken it gently. The only thing that matters is that it happened.'

He stood up. 'You go back to your room. You rest awhile; and then we'll have some dinner together and talk some more. It's the best thing.'

I went up to my room, leaving him in the inn parlour. Was there to be no end to the shocks I was receiving, I asked myself. So he had been murdered. Killed in cold blood. It was fantastic. I pictured the dray lumbering along the road, the masked figure hiding under the trees and then 'Stand and deliver. Forfeit your gold or your life.' In my imagination I could see him clearly, the gold in bags about his waist perhaps. And he would say to himself: 'No, this is my gold . . . mine and Nora's.' Perhaps he was planning to bring me out to him so that I could share in the fortune, if fortune it was. So when the gun was pointing at him he refused to give up his gold, and so he gave up his life.

'I hate gold,' I said aloud. 'I wish it had never been discovered.' I thought in fury of the glittering eyes behind the mask, of a trigger that was coolly pulled, and a report that had put an end to all my happiness. Oh, how I hated my father's murderer!

He had not died immediately. They were able to take him to Lynx and he wrote his last letter to me. But he was dying then. And it need never have happened.

Stirling was right. I needed to be alone. This was almost as great a shock as the news of my father's death had been. It had not been an accident. It was deliberate murder.

I went to the window and looked out. Below me was the street with its ancient houses. I could see the spire of the church and the towers of the house they called Whiteladies. It had once been a convent, I remembered; the nuns had worn white habits; and this inn would have been there at the time. The pilgrims on their way to Canterbury would have stopped here – the last halt before they reached their goal. Looking down on the street I could so easily picture them, weary and footsore, yet relieved because the host of the Falcon Inn was waiting to welcome them and offer them food and shelter before they went on to Canterbury.

As I stood at the window I saw Stirling come out of the inn. I watched him walk purposefully down the street taking long strides, and looking as though he knew exactly where he was going.

So stunned had I been by first finding that he had come instead of Miss Herrick to take me to Australia and then by his revelations about my father's death that I had not had time to consider him. So . . . he was the son of that man Lynx who was fast becoming a symbol in my mind. The all-powerful Lynx of whom people spoke with awe and the utmost respect. Why had Lynx not sent his daughter? Perhaps he did not care that she should travel alone. I had imagined her to be a middle-aged lady. But why had they said Miss Herrick would come and then sent a young man? It was all very strange.

Stirling had turned off the main street. I wondered where he had gone. His appearing like that had disturbed my train of thought. The sunlit street looked inviting. I could think better out of doors, I assured myself; so I put on my cape and went out. There were few people about. A lady with a parasol strolled by on the other side; a dog lay sleeping in a doorway. I walked down the street, glancing as I passed at the shop window where behind bottle glass wools, ribbons, hats and dresses were displayed. There was nothing there to interest me, so I went on and came to the turning which Stirling had taken. It led up a hill and there was a signpost which said: 'To Whiteladies'.

As I mounted the hill the grey walls came into sight; and when I reached the top I could look down and see the house in all its splendour. I knew that I should never forget it. I told myself afterwards that I knew even then what an impor-tant part it was to play in my life. I was spell-bound, bewitched, and in that moment forgot everything else but the magic of those towers, the ambience of monastic seclu-sion, the mullioned windows, the curved arches, the turrets and the tower, the sun shining on flinty grey walls. One almost expected to hear the sound of bells calling the nuns to prayer and to see white-clad figures emerging from the cloister.

I had an overwhelming desire to see more. I started to run downhill and I did not stop until I stood before the tall wrought-iron gate. This gate in itself was fascinating. I studied the intricate scrolls and mouldings; some white metal had been inlaid on the iron work on either side. I looked closer and saw that the decoration represented nuns. White Ladies, I thought; and I wondered whether it was the original gate which had stood there when there was a convent beyond it, long before the present house had been built. The grey stone wall stretched out on either side of the gates. Moss and lichen grew on it. How I should have loved to open the gate and walk into those magic precincts. This was more than a passing fancy; it was an urge which I had great difficulty in restraining. But how could one walk into someone's private house simply because it seemed the most fascinating place one had ever seen! I looked about me. There was a deep stillness everywhere. I felt completely alone. I remembered that Stirling had come this way. He would probably have passed this house without noticing it. I had decided that he would be lacking in imagination, and to him this would merely be a grey stone building; he would not think it exciting because centuries ago nuns in white robes had lived here. I wondered what it felt like to be shut away from the world; and I was suddenly interested and relieved to find that my thoughts had turned temporarily from my personal tragedy.

The wall was frustratingly high and as I walked along beside it I could only see the tower projecting above it. The view from the hilltop was much more revealing – only from that vantage point there was a sense of remoteness. Here one might be closer but the wall shut one out.

It seemed strange that when I was on the verge of going

to a new country I should be so intrigued by an old house which I had never seen before and it seemed unlikely I should ever see again. Perhaps it was because I had been indifferent to everything for so long that I seized on this and believed I was more interested than I actually was.

As I walked beside the wall I heard voices.

'Ellen has brought out the tea, Lucie.' It was a clear high voice, very pleasant and I longed to see its owner.

'I will see if Lady Cardew is ready,' said another voice, deeper, slightly husky.

They went on talking but their voices were lowered and I could not hear what they were saying. What sort of people, I wondered, lived in this house? I *must* discover. I was in such a strange mood that I had almost convinced myself that if I could see on the other side of the wall I would find two white-robed nuns – ghosts from the past.

An enormous oak tree spread its branches over the walls. Its acorns would surely fall on Whiteladies' land. I studied the tree speculatively. I had not climbed a tree for some time. Such activities had not been encouraged at Danesworth House; but there was a fork which would make an adequate if not comfortable seat. I could not climb a tree. It was too undignified. Besides, what bad manners to spy on people. I fingered the soft silk scarf which my father had given me before he went to Australia; it was a soft shade of green and I loved it for itself in addition to the fact that it was one of his last gifts. I am sure he would have climbed the tree. Miss Emily would be horrified. That decided me – particularly as I heard the voices again.

'Are you feeling better, Mamma?' That was the clear young voice.

So I climbed to the fork of the tree which was just high enough to permit me to see over.

It was a beautiful scene. The grass was like green velvet,

32

soft and smooth with an air of having been well tended through the centuries; there were flower beds containing roses and lavender; a fountain was throwing its silver spray over a white statue; the green shrubs had been cut into the shape of birds; a peacock strutted across the lawn displaying his magnificent tail while a plain little peahen followed in his glorious wake. It was a scene of utter peace. Close to the pond was a table laid for tea over which a big blue and white sunshade had been set; and seated at the table was a girl of about my age. She looked as though she were tall; she was certainly slender, a dainty Dresden figure. Her honey-coloured hair hung in long ringlets down her back; her gown was of pale blue with white lace collar and cuffs. She fitted the scene perfectly. There was another woman; she must be Lucie, I decided. She was about ten years older than the girl; and in a bath chair was a woman whom I guessed to be 'Mamma', fair-haired like the girl, delicate and fragile-looking with the same Dresden quality.

'It's pleasant in the shade, Mamma,' said the girl.

'I do hope so.' The voice was a little peevish. 'You know how the heat upsets me. Lucie, where are my smelling salts?'

I watched them talking together. Lucie had brought the chair closer to the girl who rose to make sure that the cushion behind Mamma's head was in the best place. Lucie went across the lawn presumably to fetch the smelling salts. I imagined her to be a companion, a higher servant, perhaps a poor relation. Poor Lucie!

They were talking but I only heard their voices when the breeze carried them to me. This breeze, which could be strong when it blew, was intermittent. What happened next was due to it. The scarf about my neck had become loosened during my climb. I had not noticed this and as I leaned forward to see and hear better, it caught in a branch and was dragged from my neck. It hung lightly suspended on the tree but as I was about to take it a stronger gust of wind caught it and, snatching it from me, carried it over the wall mischievously as though to punish me for eaves-dropping. It fluttered across the grass and came to rest close to the group at the tea table but they did not seem to see it.

I was dismayed, thinking of the occasion when my father had given it to me. I either had to call to them and ask them to give it to me or to lose it.

I made up my mind that I could not shout to them from the tree. I would call at the house and concoct some story about its blowing over my head – which it had done – and I certainly would not tell them that inquisitiveness had made me climb a tree to spy on them.

I slid down to the foot of the tree and in my haste grazed my hand which started to bleed a little. While I was staring at it ruefully Stirling came towards me.

'Oak trees have their uses,' he said.

'What do you mean?'

'You know very well. You were spying on the tea party.'

'How could you know that unless you were spying too?'

'It's less shocking for men to climb trees than girls, you know.'

'So you were spying on them.'

'No. Like you I was merely taking a polite look.'

'You were interested enough to climb a tree and look over the wall!'

'Let's say my motives were similar to yours. But we have to retrieve the scarf. Come on. I'll go with you. As your deputy-guardian I can't allow you to enter a strange house alone.'

'How can we go in there?'

'Simple. You ask to see Lady Cardew and tell her that your scarf is lying on her beautiful lawn.'

34

'Do you think we should ask to see her? Perhaps we could tell one of the servants.'

'You are too retiring. No. We'll go in boldly and ask for Lady Cardew.'

We had reached the gates. Stirling opened them and we went into a cobbled courtyard at the end of which was an archway. Stirling went through this; I followed. We were on the lawn.

I felt uneasy. This was most unconventional, but Stirling was unconventional and unused to our formal manners; and as we crossed the grass towards the party at the tea table and they looked up in blank astonishment, I realized how very extraordinary our intrusion must seem.

'Good afternoon,' said Stirling. 'I hope we don't disturb you. We have come to retrieve my ward's scarf.'

The girl looked bewildered. 'Scarf?' she repeated.

'Oddly enough,' I said, trying to bring some normality into the scene, 'it blew from my neck over your wall.'

They still looked startled but they couldn't deny it because there was the scarf. Stirling picked it up and gave it to me; and as he did so he said: 'What have you done to your hand?'

'Oh dear,' said the girl, 'it's bleeding.'

'I grazed it against a tree when I was trying to catch my scarf,' I stammered. Stirling was looking at me with amusement and I thought for a moment that he was going to tell them I had climbed a tree to look at them.

The girl appeared concerned. She had a sweet expression. 'Are you staying here?' asked the one named Lucie. 'I feel sure you don't live here or we should know you.'

'We're at the Falcon Inn,' I said.

'Nora,' cut in Stirling quickly, 'you are feeling faint.' He turned to the girl. 'Perhaps she should sit down for a moment.'

'Certainly,' said the girl. 'Certainly. Your hand should be

attended to. Lucie could bandage it for you, couldn't you, Lucie?'

'But of course,' said Lucie meekly.

'You should take her into the house and bathe it. Take her to Mrs Glee's room. She is certain to have water on the boil, and I do think it should be washed.'

'Come with me,' said Lucie. I wanted to protest because I was interested in the girl and would have preferred to stay and talk with her.

Stirling had sat down and was being offered a cup of tea.

I followed Lucie across the lawn towards the house. We went through a heavy iron studded door and were in a stone walled corridor. Facing us was a flight of stairs.

Lucie led the way up these stairs to a landing. 'The housekeeper's room is along here. This corridor leads to the servants' hall.'

We went up a spiral staircase to a landing on which there were several doors. Lucie knocked at one of them and we were told to enter. On a spirit stove was a kettle of hot water, and a middle-aged woman in a black bombazine dress with a white cap on her thick greying hair was sitting in an armchair dozing. I guessed this to be Mrs Glee and I was right. Lucie explained about the scarf and I showed my hand.

'It's nothing but a light graze,' said Mrs Glee.

'Miss Minta thinks it should be washed and dressed.'

Mrs Glee grunted. 'Miss Minta and her bandages! There's always something. Last week it was that bird. Couldn't fly so Miss Minta took charge. Then there was that dog which was caught in a trap.'

I didn't much care to be compared with a bird and a dog, so I said: 'Really there's no need.' But Mrs Glee ignored me and poured some water from the kettle into a basin. My hand was deftly washed and bandaged while

I told them we were staying at the Falcon Inn and shortly leaving for Australia. When this was done I thanked Mrs Glee and Lucie conducted me back to the lawn. I apologized as we went. I was afraid I was being rather a trouble, I said. It was no trouble, she informed me in such a way as to suggest in fact it was; but perhaps that was her manner.

'Miss Minta is very kindhearted,' I said.

'Very,' she agreed.

There were many questions I should have liked to ask but that would have been difficult even if she were communicative which she decidedly was not.

On the lawn Stirling was talking to Minta, and Lady Cardew was looking on languidly. I felt irritated by his complacent manner. It was due to me that we were here and he was getting the best of the adventure. I wondered what they had been talking about while I was away.

'You must have a cup of tea before you go,' said Minta, and as she poured the tea and brought it to me I was again struck by her grace – and kindness too. She really did seem concerned.

'Miss Cardew was telling me about the house,' said Stirling, 'It's the finest I ever saw.'

'And the most ancient,' laughed Minta. 'He tells me he has recently come from Australia and that he is taking you back with him because his father has become your guardian. Sugar?'

The egg-shell china cup was handed to me. I noticed her long white delicate fingers and the opal ring which she was wearing.

'How exciting it must be to be going to Australia,' she said.

'It must be exciting to live in a house like this,' I replied.

'Having lived all my life in it I think I have become

somewhat blasé. It would only be if we lost it that we should realize what it means to us.'

'But you will never lose it,' I replied. 'Who could possibly part with such a place?'

'Oh never, of course,' she answered lightly.

Lucie was busy at the table. Lady Cardew's eyes were fixed on me but she did not appear to see me; she had scarcely spoken and seemed half asleep. I wondered if she were ill; she did not seem very old, but she certainly behaved like an old woman.

I asked Minta about the house, telling her that the cab driver had pointed it out to me. Yes, she said, it was true that it had been built on the site of the old nunnery. In fact quite a lot of the original building remained.

'Some of the rooms really are like cells, aren't they, Lucie?'

Lucie agreed that they were.

'It's been in the family for years now and of course I've disappointed them because I'm a girl. There are often girls in this family. But we've been here . . . how long is it, Lucie? 1550? Yes that's right. Henry VIII dissolved the monasteries and Whiteladies was partially destroyed then. My ancestor did something to please him and was given the place to build on, which he did in due course. There were lots of the stones left, so they were used; and, as I said, a good deal of the place remained.'

'Mr Wakefield is here,' said Lucie. A man was coming across the lawn – the most exquisite man I had ever seen. His clothes were impeccably tailored and I discovered that his manners matched them.

Minta jumped up and ran towards him. He took her hand and kissed it. Charming! I thought. I knew Stirling would be amused. Then he went to Lady Cardew and did the same. He bowed to Lucie. Oh yes, Lucie was not quite one of the family.

Minta had turned to us. 'I'm afraid I don't know your

names. You see, Franklyn, a scarf blew over and it belongs to Miss . . .'

'Tamasin,' I said. 'Nora Tamasin.' He bowed beautifully. I added: 'And this is Mr Stirling Herrick.'

'From Australia,' added Minta.

'How interesting!' Mr Franklyn Wakefield's face expressed polite interest in my scarf and us and I liked him for it.

'You're just in time for a cup of tea,' said Minta.

I realized of course that there was no reason why we should stay and unless we took our departure immediately we should become ungracious intruders. Stirling however made no attempt to move. He had settled back in his chair and was watching the scene and in particular Minta with an intentness which could only be described as eager.

I said, rising: 'You have been most kind. We must go. It only remains to say thank you for being so good to strangers.'

I sensed Stirling's annoyance with me. He wanted to stay; he seemed to have no idea that we were intruding on their privacy, or if he had he did not care. But I was determined.

Minta smiled at Lucie who immediately rose to conduct us to the gates.

'I do apologize for intruding on your tea-party,' I said.

'It was quite a diversion,' replied Lucie. There was that in her manner which I found disconcerting. She was aloof, yet somehow vulnerable. She seemed over-anxious to maintain a dignity which was perhaps due to the fact that she was a poor relation.

'Miss Minta is charming,' I said.

'I'll endorse that,' added Stirling.

'She *is* a delightful person,' agreed Lucie.

'And I am grateful to you for bandaging my hand, Miss . . .'

'Maryan,' she supplied. 'Lucie Maryan.'

'A poor relation certainly,' I thought.

Stirling, who, I was to discover, snapped his fingers at the conventional rules of polite society, asked bluntly, 'Are you a relation of the Cardews?'

She hesitated and for a moment I thought she was going to reprove him for his inquisitiveness. Then she said: 'I am nurse-companion to Lady Cardew.'

And then we had reached the gate. 'I trust,' she said coldly, 'that the hand soon heals. Goodbye.'

When we had passed through the iron gates Lucie shut them firmly behind us. We walked in silence for a few moments then Stirling laughed.

'Quite an adventure,' I said.

'Well, you certainly wanted to know what was going on behind that wall.'

'And so it seems did you.'

'It's a pretty scarf. We should both be grateful to it. It was our ticket of entrance, you might say.'

'It's an odd household.'

'Odd! How do you mean . . . odd?'

'On the surface there are the mother and daughter and nurse-companion. Very ordinary probably. But I felt there was something different there. The mother was quiet. I believe she was half asleep most of the time.'

'Well, she's an invalid.'

We were both silent after that. I glanced sideways at him and I knew he shared my mood. We were both bemused in some strange way.

I said, 'Do you know, when I stepped through that gate I felt as though I had walked into a new world . . . something quite different from anything I had known before. I felt that something tremendously dramatic was happening and because it was all so quiet and in a way ordinary that made it rather sinister.'

Stirling laughed. He was definitely not the fanciful type.

It was no use trying to explain my feelings to him. Yet I did feel that I knew him better since this adventure in Whiteladies. I had forgotten that this time yesterday I was not aware of his existence. And for the first time since my father had died I felt excited – it was all the more intriguing because I was not quite sure why.

The next morning we left the Falcon Inn for London and the day after that we boarded the *Carron Star* at Tilbury.

My journey to the other side of the world had begun.

Chapter Two

I QUICKLY realized that life on the *Carron Star* was going to be a little spartan, even though we travelled first class. I shared a cabin with a young clergyman's daughter who was going to Melbourne to be married. She was both elated and apprehensive; her fiancé had left England two years before to make a home for her in the New World and now had a small property there. She was worried about her trunks of clothes and the linen she was taking out. 'One has to be prepared,' she told me. Fortunately she wanted to talk about herself so much that she did not ask questions about me, for which I was glad.

She told me that the fare was £50 and I felt a glow of satisfaction because my new guardian was paying so much to have me conveyed to him.

We were lucky, she explained, in the first class, because passengers in the other two classes must bring their own cutlery, drinking mugs, cups and saucers, besides a water bottle. Her fiancé had been most insistent that she travel first class. It was really a great adventure for a young girl to travel across the world by herself; but her aunt had seen her safely aboard and her fiancé would be waiting to greet her. She wanted me to know that she was a very cherished young lady with her trunks of clothes and fine linen.

She did ask if I were travelling alone, so I told her I was with my guardian. She opened her eyes very wide when she saw Stirling who, she commented, seemed somewhat young for the role of guardian; and I am sure she thought there was something very odd about me from that moment.

In the dining-room I sat with Stirling. At first most people thought we were brother and sister, and when it became known that I was his ward there was some raising of eyebrows, but the wonder of this soon passed. The weather was rough to begin with and that meant that many were confined to their cabins; and when they emerged the unconventionality of our position seemed to have been accepted by most.

During the gale Stirling and I sat on deck and he talked to me about Australia. Lynx was never long out of the conversation and I was more impatient to see him than I was to see the new country. Every day seemed to bring me closer to Stirling. I began to understand him. His manner could be brusque, but this did not mean that he was angry or indifferent; he prided himself on his frankness and if he was blunt with me he expected me to be the same with him. He despised artificiality in any form. I learned this through his attitude to our fellow passengers. I thought often of those people whom we had met at Whiteladies and it seemed to me that Stirling was the complete antithesis of Franklyn Wakefield as I was to Minta. It was strange that these people whom I had seen so briefly should have impressed themselves so much on my mind that I compared them with everyone I met.

Life at sea might have been monotonous to some passengers who longed for their journey's end; not so to me. I was interested in everything and most of all in Stirling. He undoubtedly chafed over the tediousness and was longing to be home. We breakfasted about nine and dined at twelve; and between that time Stirling and I would pace the decks for exercise while most people wrote their letters home so that they could be dispatched at the next port of call. But I had no one to write to – except a note to poor Mary. I often thought of her in the dreary attic, confined to life at Danesworth House and was sorry for her.

I remember sitting on deck with Stirling when most of the people were confined to their cabins because of the weather and feeling pleased because he admired me for being a good sailor. He was apt to be impatient with people's failings, I had learned. I wondered how I should match up to his expectations. I gathered that he spent a good deal of time on horseback. My father had taught me to ride when we were in the country, but I imagined that hacking through English country lanes might be different from galloping across the bush.

I mentioned this to Stirling and he hastened to reassure me.

'You'll be all right,' he told me. 'I'll find a horse for you. A gentleman of a horse at first, with as fine manners as that Mr Wakefield you were so taken with. And after that . . .'

'A manly horse,' I suggested. 'As manly as Stirling Herrick.'

We laughed a great deal together. We argued, because there were so many things about which we did not agree. Stirling was often at variance with our fellow passengers; he would allow himself to be drawn into discussions with them and during these never minced his words. He was not very popular with some of the pompous gentlemen, but I noticed that many of the women had a ready smile for him.

44

Later I realized how good this voyage was for me. It took me completely away from those wretched months when I had first waited anxiously for news of my father and then staggered under the terrible blow when it came.

The pattern of life on board was breakfast in the saloon, the long mornings, luncheon at twelve, the slow afternoons, dinner at four for which passengers put on their more elaborate clothes and during which the band played light music, and then strolling about the decks until tea at seven.

We went ashore at Gibraltar and spent a pleasant morning there. It was wonderful to ride in a carriage with Stirling and see the sights of the place: the shops, the apes, and the rock itself.

'Sometimes,' I said, 'I wish this trip could go on for ever.'

Stirling grimaced.

'Suppose we missed the ship,' I suggested. 'Suppose we built a ship of our own and went on sailing round the world wherever the fancy took us.'

'What crazy things you think of!' He was derisive. How different from my father who would have gone on with the wild, impossible story of how we built our ship and the exotic places we sailed to.

'I remember him,' he said. 'He would talk in the most fantastic way, pretending that what he knew was impossible would happen.'

'It was a lovely way to live.'

'It was crazy. What sense is there in pretending something will happen when you know it won't?'

I would not allow any criticism of my father.

'It made life gay and exciting,' I protested.

'It was false. I think it's a waste of time to pretend you believe in the impossible.'

'You are very matter-of-fact and . . .'

'Dull?'

I was silent and he urged: 'Come on. Tell the truth.'

'I like to think wonderful things can happen.'

'Even when you know they can't?'

'Who says they can't?'

'Like coming ashore for a few hours and building a ship and sailing off round the world without a navigator, a captain or a pilot, taking no account of harbour dues and navigation. You'll have to grow up, Nora, when you're in Australia.'

I was annoyed, seeing in this an attack on my father.

'Perhaps I shouldn't have come.'

'It's too early to comment on that.'

'If you're going to think I'm childish . . .'

'We certainly shall if you indulge in childish fantasy as –'

'As my father did. Did you think him childish?'

'We thought him not very practical. His end showed that, didn't it? If he had handed over the gold he would be alive today. What sense is there in deluding yourself into thinking that you can hold something and giving your life to prove you're wrong?'

I was hurt and angry and yet not able to discuss my father logically. I grew silent and was angry with Stirling for spoiling a perfect day. But this was typical of my relationship with him. He made no concessions to polite conversation; he stated what he believed and nothing would make him diverge from it. I knew that what he said was right but I could not bear that my father should be subjected to censure.

Although at times I disliked his overbearance, when he showed – as he often did – that he was taking care of me, I felt a warm, comfortable emotion.

The weather had grown warm and I loved the tropical evenings. After the seven o'clock meal we would sit on deck and talk. Those were the occasions to which I most looked forward, even more than the sunlit days when we would walk up and down the deck or lean over the rail and he would point out a frolicking porpoise or a flying fish.

One evening as we sat on deck looking out into the warm darkness of the tropical waters I said to Stirling: 'What if Lynx doesn't like me?'

'He'd still look after you. He's given his word.'

'He sounds difficult to please.'

Stirling nodded. This was true. Lynx might be all-powerful but he was not always benevolent.

'He sounds like one of the Roman gods whom people were always placating.'

Stirling grinned at the comparison. 'People do try to please him naturally,' he said.

'And if they don't?'

'He lets them know.'

'Sometimes I think I should have done better to stay at Danesworth House.'

'You'll have to learn to be truthful if you want to please Lynx.'

'I'm not sure that I want to. I should hate to be his meek little slave.'

'You wait and see. You'll want to please him. Everybody does.'

'You're brutally frank about *my* father. Why shouldn't I be about yours?'

'You should always say what's in your mind, of course.'

'Well, I think your Lynx sounds like a conceited, power-crazy megalomaniac.'

'Let's consider that. He has a high opinion of himself – he shares that with everyone else. He likes to be in command and there is no one like him. So, slightly modified, your description might not be completely inaccurate.'

'Tell me more about him.'

So he talked of his father as we sat there and I made many pictures in my mind of this powerful man who had so impressed my father that he had left me in his care.

'He was sent out of England as a prisoner thirty-five years ago,' said Stirling. 'It had its effect on him. He's going back one day . . . when he's ready.'

'When will he be ready?'

'He told me once that he will know when the time comes.'

'He does talk to you sometimes like an ordinary human being then?'

Stirling smiled. 'I believe you have made up your mind to dislike him. That is very unwise. Yes, he is human, very human.'

'And I've been thinking of him as a god!'

'He's like that too.'

'Half-god, half-man,' I mocked because I remembered how Stirling had talked of my father, and I knew that he compared the two of them; and as, in Stirling's opinion no one on earth could shine beside his father, mine suffered miserably in the comparison.

'Yes,' he went on, 'Lynx is human. He's a man . . . a real man, but much grander in every way than other men.'

'You tell me so much of your father. What of your mother? Does she subscribe to the general view of your father's greatness?'

'My mother is dead. She died when I was born.' His face had darkened almost imperceptibly with some emotion.

'I'm sorry. I know you have a sister because she was coming to meet me. Have you any other sisters and brothers?'

'There are only two of us. Adelaide, my sister, is eight years older than I am.'

I wondered about Adelaide. I asked questions, but a very colourless picture emerged. He only glowed when he talked of Lynx. I thought of my own mother who had 'gone away'; and I wondered about the sort of woman whom Lynx had married.

'What of your mother?' I asked. 'Did she go out as a prisoner, too?'

'No. My father was sent to work for hers. Imagine the Lynx being *sent* to work for anyone!'

'Well, he was a prisoner then, not the great Lynx he is today.' I reminded him.

'He was always a proud man. I suppose my grandfather realized that.'

'Your grandfather?'

'The man my father was sent to work for. Very soon my father had married his daughter – my mother.'

'That was clever of him,' I said ironically.

'It happened,' he replied laconically, unsure, I believed, whether to applaud his father's cleverness or deny his calculation.

'So he married out of bondage, one might say.'

'You have a sharp tongue, Nora.'

'I thought I was to speak my mind.'

'Certainly. But it's a pity you must believe the worst of people.'

'I was thinking how clever he was. He was sent as a servant to work out his term of imprisonment, so he made his master his father-in-law. I consider that clever and just the sort of thing I should expect from Lynx.'

'How can you expect anything of him when you don't know him?'

'I've spent quite a long time in your company and to do that is to know quite a bit about this wonderful man, for you talk of nothing else.'

'Very well, I'll not speak of him. You asked questions and I replied to them. That's all.'

'Of course I want to hear about this wonderful god-like creature. But tell me more about your mother.'

'How can I when I never knew her?'

'There must have been some stories.'

He frowned and was silent. There *were* stories, I decided, and he did not want to tell them. Why? Because I imagined they were not very flattering to Lynx.

'And did he never marry again?' I went on.

'He did not marry again.'

'All those years without a wife! I should have thought Lynx would have wanted a wife.'

'You should not judge him until you know him,' said Stirling rather sourly. Then he changed the subject quickly and talked about the country. It would be the end of winter when we arrived for I must not forget that winter in Australia was summer at home. The wattle would be in bloom and I should see the fine brave eucalypts – red stringybarks and grey ghost gums; and we should have to travel north from Melbourne through parts of the bush. I was not listening very intently. I kept thinking of Lynx's marrying and becoming his master's son-in-law. Perhaps, I thought, Fox would have been a better name for him. The more I heard of the perfections of this man the more I set my mind against him because I imagined that in every account of his prowess was some implied criticism of my father.

We sat gazing over the water while Stirling talked of my new home and at last I said: 'It's getting late. I must go in.'

Stirling conducted me to my cabin and said good-night. When I entered, my companion, who was already in her bunk, remarked that I seemed to find the company of Mr Herrick very intriguing.

'Naturally we have a great deal to talk about since he is taking me to his country which will be my new home.'

'Mrs Mullens was saying how *odd* it was for a young girl to have such a *young* guardian.'

'There is no law laid down that a guardian should be of a stipulated age. A guardian can be of any age. No one can prevent his being a guardian because he is not middle-aged, nor can people be prevented from gossiping. Nor again is there any law to prevent one listening to gossip – only that of good breeding, of course.'

That silenced her and I chuckled to myself. Stirling was right. I had a quick tongue. I must make of it a defensive weapon. Perhaps I should have an opportunity of trying it on Lynx. The thought amused me.

I should not let him command me, I assured myself, though he was my guardian and appointed as such by my own father. I would never be dominated by anyone as this man appeared to dominate people – even Stirling. I would ask no more questions about him. I would shut him out of my mind.

I fell asleep then, but my dreams were haunted by a tall man with the eyes of a lynx and the face of a fox.

We were three days out of Cape Town when we discovered Jemmy. We had had our usual meal at seven and gone out on to the deck to sit side by side while Stirling talked about his country. I was beginning to build up a clear picture. I saw the bush with its yellow wattle and enormous trees. Stirling was not one to offer glowing descriptions; his conversation was in fact inclined to be terse; but he did make me guess at the beauty of the jarrah tree blossom and the red flowering gum. I could image the red and yellow glory of the flowers they called kangaroo paws;

I could see the yellow swamp daisies and the many coloured orchids. He mentioned casually the gay rosellas; and I longed to see the green lorikeets and red-winged parrots. Each day I was learning a little more about the country which would soon be mine.

Suddenly we heard the sound of violent sneezing. We were startled, believing ourselves to be alone on deck.

'Who was that?' said Stirling, looking about him.

There was a paroxysm of coughing which could only have come from someone close by. It was clear that the sufferer was desperately attempting to stifle his cough. Stirling and I looked at each other in amazement for we could see no one.

We took a few steps along the deck suspended from which were the lifeboats and as we passed one of these the coughing started again.

'Who's there?' called Stirling.

There was no answer – but the cough had started again, and this time there was no doubt that it came from the suspended lifeboat.

Stirling was agile. It did not take him long to hoist himself up to the boat. I heard his exclamation.

'It's a boy,' he said.

I saw the boy's head – tousled and dirty; his frightened eyes were enormous in his white, scared face.

Stirling had him by the arm and lowered him on to the deck. In a second the three of us were standing there together.

'A . . . stowaway!' I cried.

'Don't you tell them,' whimpered the boy.

I could see that he was in a poor state of health when that terrible racking cough started again.

'Don't be frightened,' I said. 'It's all right now.'

I must have sounded convincing because as the cough subsided he looked at me trustingly.

52

'You've no right to be on the ship, have you?' I said gently. 'You stowed away.'

'Yes, miss.'

'How long have you been on?'

'Since London.'

Stirling cried: 'You young rogue! What do you think you're doing?'

The boy cowered towards me, and I was determined to protect him as much as I could. 'He's ill,' I said.

'Serve him right.'

'You're hungry, I daresay,' I said to the boy. 'And you have a bad cough. Why, you're shivering. It's time you came out of hiding.'

'No!' he cried fearfully, and looked about him so wildly that I was afraid he was contemplating jumping overboard. I was filled with a deep pity for him.

'You've run away from home,' I said.

'Of course he has,' said Stirling.

'I haven't got a home.'

'Your father . . .'

'No father. No mother,' he said; and my heart was deeply touched. After all, hadn't I known what it meant to be without a mother and father, without a home? The misery of Danesworth House came back to me – not so much the bleak attic, the shivering draughts and the stuffy heat, but the memory of what it felt like to be abandoned, alone and unwanted.

'What's your name?' I asked.

'Jemmy,' he said.

'Well, Jemmy,' I assured him, 'you are not to worry. I'm going to see that everything is right.'

Stirling had raised his eyebrows, but I went on: 'You'll have to confess what you've done, but I'll explain; and the first thing is to get some hot food and a bed. You haven't slept in a bed since you left London, have you?'

He shook his head.

'And you have had no proper food. Only that which you have managed to steal.'

He nodded.

'That's going to be changed. You can trust me, Jemmy.'

'I don't want to go back.'

'You're not going back.'

That satisfied him.

One of the officers came on deck just then and seeing us with the boy hurried towards us. We explained what had happened and he took charge of Jemmy. The look the child gave me as he was taken away haunted me.

'You certainly played the lady bountiful,' said Stirling. 'Making everything right for stowaways – even rewarding them for their sins.'

'I think you are rather hard-hearted.'

'At least I haven't made promises I can't fulfil.'

'What do they do to stowaways?'

'I don't know, but I feel sure they receive the punishment they richly deserve.'

'That poor child was ill and hungry.'

'Naturally. What did he expect? To be received on board as a passenger? He must have had some idea of what would happen when he stowed away.'

'He wouldn't have thought of that. He would have seen a big ship as an escape from an intolerable existence. He would have dreamed of sailing away into the sunshine, starting a new life.'

'Another of those dreamers, it seems.'

That angered me. He was referring, of course, to my father. I said firmly. 'I don't want that child to suffer. How will they punish him? They'll be harsh, I suppose.'

'He'll probably have to work on board and when we get

to Australia he'll be punished and sent back to England to be punished there.'

'It's cruel.'

'It's justice. Why should he evade it?'

'He's young and some people manage to evade punishment . . . by marrying their master's daughter, for instance.'

It was unfair, but he had criticized my father and I couldn't resist retaliating by attacking him. He merely laughed.

'People have to be clever to get the best out of life.'

'Some are helped,' I said. 'And if I can help that boy I will.'

'You should, shouldn't you? You've promised. Rashly, of course, but you have given your word.'

He was right. I was determined to do what I could for poor little Jemmy.

Everyone on board was talking about the stowaway. They had taken him to the sick bay and for days it was doubted whether he would survive the hardships he had suffered. He had spent a great deal of the time in the lifeboat, cleverly ascertaining when there was to be lifeboat drill and then hiding himself in one of the cupboards where spare life-jackets were stored. He had prowled about the ship at night looking for food and had found a little now and then. He had almost died of exposure and hunger. So at least for a time he was comfortable, well cared for and too sick to contemplate what trouble might be awaiting him when he was well enough to be judged.

I thought of him constantly, and was troubled to think of the punishment in store for him.

I spoke to Stirling as we sat on deck. 'I want to do something about that boy.'

'What?' he asked.

'I want to save him. He is very young. All he has done is run away. It must have been something terrible he ran from. I'm going to help him. I must.'

'How? Will you build a ship and make him your captain?'

'Be serious. You must help me.'

'I? This has nothing to do with me.'

'It has to do with me and I'm your sister . . . or rather your father is my guardian. Surely that makes some sort of relationship between us?'

'It doesn't mean I have to take part in your crazy schemes.'

'If his fare was paid, if you employed him as your servant, if you took him with us, I am sure your all-powerful father could find some employment for him. You'll help, of course.'

'I can't think why you should assume that for one moment.'

'I don't believe you're as hard-hearted as you would like me to believe.'

'I hope I'm a practical man.'

'Of course you are. That's why you'll help this boy.'

'Because *you* have made a rash promise you can't keep?'

'No. But because the boy will be grateful to you forever, and in your father's many concerns he must find it not always easy to discover good servants. The boy can be given work on your father's property, in his hotel, or in some place in the Lynx Empire. So you see it is to your benefit to rescue him from his present dilemma.'

He laughed so much that he could not speak. I was uneasy. There was a hardness about him which I am sure he had inherited from his father. I was very worried about my poor little stowaway for whom no one but myself seemed to have any sympathy.

'Well,' said my cabin companion, 'Mr Mullens says that this is an encouragement for people to hide themselves on ships. He said he never heard the like. We shall have half the riff-raff stowing away if they are going to be rewarded for doing so.'

'One can hardly say the poor boy has been rewarded,' I retorted, 'simply because he has been put to bed and nursed back to health. What did Mr Mullens expect? He would be invited to walk the plank? Or perhaps be clapped into irons? These are not the days of the press gang, you know.'

She tossed her head. I was very odd, in her opinion. I suppose she discussed me with the Mullenses.

'Mr Herrick has rescued him they say,' she smirked. 'So the boy is to become his servant.'

'Servant!' I cried.

'Doesn't he confide in you? *I* heard Mr Herrick is paying his fare, so all is well and our young rascal has been turned into an honest boy overnight.'

I smiled happily. I went to Stirling's cabin and knocked on the door. He was alone and I threw my arms about his neck and kissed him. Embarrassed, he took my hands and removed them but I was too excited to feel rebuffed.

'You've done it, Stirling,' I cried. 'You've done it.'

'What are you talking about?' he demanded. But he knew.

Then he tried to excuse himself. 'He's travelling third. It may be rough but it's all he deserves. The fare was only seventeen guineas but naturally they don't need that since he's been sleeping in the lifeboat and hasn't been fed. I've paid seven pounds for him and he'll have quarters in the third class until Melbourne.'

'And then you'll find work for him?'

'He can act as my servant until we find something for him to do.'

'Oh, Stirling, it's wonderful! You've got a heart after all. I'm glad.'

'Now don't you go endowing me with anything like that. You'll be bitterly disappointed.'

'I know,' I replied. 'You're hard-hearted. You wouldn't help anyone. But you think the boy will be useful. That's it, eh?'

'That's it,' he agreed.

'All right. Have it the way you want it. It's the result that counts. Poor little Jemmy! He'll be a happy boy tonight.'

I felt close to Stirling after that. I even liked his way of pretending that he had acted from practical rather than senti-mental reasons.

The rest of the journey was uneventful; and it was forty-five days after we had left Tilbury that we came to Melbourne.

It was late afternoon when we arrived and by the time we had disembarked, dusk was upon us.

I shall never forget standing there on the wharf with our bags around and Jemmy beside us in the ragged clothes which were all he had. This was my new home. I wondered what Jemmy was thinking. His dark eyes were enormous in his pale tragic young face. I reassured him and in comforting him, comforted myself.

A woman was coming towards us and I knew immedi-ately that she was Adelaide – the one who should have come to England to fetch me. Adelaide was plainly dressed in a cape and a hat without trimming, which was tied under her chin with a ribbon for the wind was high. I was a little disappointed; she had none of the unusual looks of Stirling and was hardly as I would have expected the Lynx's daughter to be. The fact was she looked like a rather plain, staid countrywoman. I knew immediately that I was wrong to be disappointed because what I saw in her face was undoubtedly kindness.

'Adelaide, here's Nora,' said Stirling.

She took my hand and kissed me coolly. 'Welcome to Melbourne, Nora,' she said. 'I hope you had a good journey.'

'Interesting,' commented Stirling. 'All things considered.'

'We're staying at the Lynx,' she said, 'and catching the Cobb coach tomorrow morning.'

'Goodo,' said Stirling.

'The Lynx?' I queried.

'Our father's hotel in Collins Street,' Adelaide explained. 'I expect you'd like to be getting along. Is all the baggage here?' Her eyes had come to rest on Jemmy.

'He's part of the baggage,' said Stirling. I frowned at him, fearing that Jemmy might be hurt to hear himself so described; but he was unaware of the slight. 'We picked him up on the ship,' went on Stirling. 'Nora thinks he should be given some work to do.'

'Have you written to our father about him?'

'No, I am leaving it to Nora to explain to him.'

Adelaide looked a little startled but I pretended to be not in the least disturbed at the prospect of explaining Jemmy to their formidable parent.

'I have a buggy waiting,' she said. 'We'll get all this stuff sent to the hotel.' She turned to me. 'We're some forty miles out of Melbourne, but Cobb's are good. You can rely on Cobb's. So we come in frequently. The men ride in but I like Cobb's. I hope you will settle down here.'

'I hope so too,' I said.

'She will if she makes up her mind to,' said Stirling. 'She's a very determined person.'

I walked off with Adelaide and Stirling – Jemmy following. I was only vaguely aware of the bustle all around me, and the carts drawn by horses or bullocks and loaded with wool hides and meat.

'It's a busy town,' said Adelaide. 'It's grown quickly in the last few years. Gold has made it rich.'

'Gold!' I said a little bitterly; and she must have known that I was thinking of my father. There was something very sympathetic about this woman.

'It's pleasant to have the town not too far away,' she said. 'I hope you won't find us too isolated. Have you ever lived in a big city?'

'I did for a time, but I have lived in the country, too; and I felt very isolated in the place where I was first a pupil, then a teacher.'

She nodded. 'We'll do our best to make you feel at home. Ah, here's the buggy. I'll tell John to see about the baggage.'

'Jemmy will help,' said Stirling. 'Let him be worth his salt. He can come along later with John and the baggage.'

So it was arranged and I rode beside Stirling and Adelaide – my new brother and sister – into the town of Melbourne, just as the lamplighters, riding on horseback, were lighting the street-lamps with their long torches. They sang as they worked – the old songs which I had heard so often at home. I remember particularly 'Early One Morning' and 'Strawberry Fair'; and I felt that although I had journeyed thousands of miles, I was not far from home.

The hotel was full of graziers who had come in from the outback to Melbourne in order to negotiate their wool. They talked loudly of prices and the state of the market; but I was more interested in another type – those men with bronzed faces and calloused hands and an avid look in their eyes. They were the diggers who had found a little gold, I imagined, and came in to spend it.

We ate dinner at six o'clock in the dining-room. I sat between Adelaide and Stirling, and it was Stirling who talked of these men and pointed out those who had struck lucky and those who hoped to.

I said, 'Perhaps it would have been better if gold had not been discovered here.'

'Many of the good citizens of Melbourne would agree with you,' conceded Stirling. 'People are leaving their workaday jobs to go and look for a fortune. Mind you, many of them come back disillusioned before long. They dream of the nuggets they are going to pick up and a few grains of gold dust is all they find.'

I shivered and thought of my father and wondered if he had ever come to this place and talked as these men were talking now.

'It's a life of hardship they lead at the diggings,' said Adelaide. 'They'd be much better off doing a useful job.'

'But some of them make their fortunes,' Stirling reminded her.

'Money is the root of all evil,' said Adelaide.

'The love of it,' Stirling corrected her. 'But don't we all love it?'

'Not it,' I put in. 'The things it can buy.'

'It's the same thing,' Stirling replied.

'Not necessarily. Some people might want it for the sake of others.'

Both he and Adelaide knew that I was thinking of my father and Adelaide hastily changed the subject. She told me once more that the homestead was some forty miles north of Melbourne. Their father had built it ten years before; he had designed it himself and it was a fine house – as houses in this part went. It was not exactly like an English mansion of course; but that would be absurd in such a place.

I asked what I should be expected to do there and Adelaide replied that I could help in the house. She supposed that in all the activities that went on I would be sure to find something which would appeal to me.

'Lynx doesn't like idle folk,' said Stirling.

'Don't call him by that ridiculous name,' reproved Adelaide. She turned to me. 'I'm sure you'll find plenty to do.'

She talked a little about the country until Stirling said: 'Let her find out for herself.'

Then Adelaide asked me questions about England and I told her of Danesworth House and how I had become a pupil teacher there.

'You must have been most unhappy there,' she said and seemed rather pleased about this. I understood. She felt I should fit more happily into my new life since the old had not been very good.

And so we talked until dinner was over; then I returned to my room and when I had been there a short time there was a knock on the door and Adelaide came in. She looked so anxious that I immediately asked her if anything was wrong.

'Oh no. I just thought we should have a little talk about everything. I'd like you to be prepared.' Then I knew that she was anxious on my behalf and that I had been right when I had thought her kind.

She sat down on the armchair and I took my place on the bed.

'This must be very strange to you.'

'Strange things have happened since my father died.'

'It is terrible to lose a father. I know what it is to lose a mother. I lost mine when I was eight years old. It's a long time ago, but it's something I shall never forget.'

'She died when Stirling was born. He told me.'

She nodded. 'Don't be afraid of my father,' she said.

'Why should I be?'

'Most people are.'

'Perhaps that is because they are dependent on him. I shall not feel that. If he wants to be rid of me I shall go away. I suppose it would be possible to find a post here – perhaps with a family who need a governess and are going to England. Perhaps . . .' I was making situations to fit my needs, Stirling would say – just as my father had.

'Please don't talk of leaving us just as you have come. You'll give it a fair trial, won't you?'

'Of course. I was only thinking of what I should do if your father decided he didn't want me here.'

'But he has promised to look after you and he will. Your father was insistent that he should.'

'My father seemed to fall under his spell.'

'They were drawn to each other from the start. Yet they were so different. Your father dreamed of what he would do; my father did it. In a short time they had become great friends; your father had come into the mine and managed it with an enthusiasm which we had never known before. My father used to say: "Now Tom Tamasin is here we'll strike rich. He believes it so earnestly that it will come to pass." And then he died bringing gold from the mine.'

'So they have found gold.'

'Not in any quantity. There is a lot of hard work; a lot of men to be employed; and the yield is hardly worth the effort and expense. It's strange. In everything else my father has prospered. The property which came through my mother is worth ten times what it was when he took it over. This hotel which was just a primitive inn is now flourishing. As Melbourne grows so does the hotel with it. But I believe he loses money on the mine. He won't give up, though. In his

63

way he is as obsessed by the desire to find gold as those men you saw downstairs tonight.'

'Why do men feel this urge for gold?'

She shrugged her shoulders. 'As we were saying tonight, it is the thought of being rich, fabulously rich.'

'And your father . . . is he not rich?'

'Not in the way he wishes to be. He started years ago to search for gold. He'll never give up the search until he makes a fortune.'

'I wonder people can't be content if they have enough to make them secure, and then enjoy living.'

'You have a wise head on your shoulders. But you would never get some men to see it your way.'

'I thought your father was a wise man. Stirling talks of him as though he is Socrates, Plato, Hercules and Julius Caesar all rolled into one.'

'Stirling has talked too much. My father is just an unusual human being. He is autocratic because he is the centre of our world – but it is only a little world. Stand up to him. He'll respect you for it. I understand you, I think. There is a little of your father in you, and you are proud and not going to bow to anyone's will. I think you will be well equipped for your new country. I hope you will get along with Jessica.'

'Jessica? Stirling did not mention Jessica. Who is she?'

'A cousin of my mother's. She was orphaned early and lived with my mother since their childhood. They were like sisters and when my mother died she was nearly demented. I had to comfort her and that helped me to get over my own grief. She can be rather difficult and she is a little strange. The fact is she never quite got over my mother's death. She takes sudden likes and dislikes to people.'

'And you think she will dislike me?'

'One never knows. But whatever she does, always remember that she may at any time act a little strangely.'

'Do you mean that she is mad?'

'Oh dear me no. A little unbalanced. She will be quite placid for days. Then she helps in the house and is very good in the kitchen. She cooks very well when she is in the mood. We had a very good cook and her husband was a handyman – very useful about the place. They had a little cottage in the grounds. Then they caught the gold fever. They just walked out. Heaven knows where they are now. Probably regretting it in some tent town, sleeping rough and thinking of their comfortable bed in the cottage.'

'Perhaps they found gold.'

'If they had we should have heard. No. They'll come creeping back but my father won't have them. He was very angry when they left. It was one of the reasons I couldn't come to England as was first planned.'

'Everyone there thought it was Miss Herrick who was coming for me.'

'And so it would have been, but my father couldn't be left to the mercy of Jessica . . . so I stayed behind and Stirling came alone. Don't imagine that we haven't servants. There are plenty of them but none of the calibre of the Lambs. Some of them are aboriginals. They don't live in the house and we can't rely on them. They're nomads by nature and suddenly they'll wander off. One thing – you will never be lonely. There are so many people involved in my father's affairs. There's Jacob Jagger who manages the property; William Gardner who is in charge of the mine; and Jack Bell who runs the hotel. You will probably meet him before we leave. They often come to see my father. Then there are people who are employed in these various places.'

'And your father governs them all.'

'He divides his attention between them, but it's the mine that claims most of his attention.'

And there we were back to gold. She seemed to realize this, for she was very sensitive.

'You're tired,' she said. 'I'll leave you now. We have to be up early in the morning.'

She came towards me as though to kiss me; then she seemed to change her mind. They were not, I had already learned, a demonstrative family. My feelings towards her were warm, and I believed she would be a great comfort to me in the new life.

Early next morning we boarded the coach, which seated nine passengers and was drawn by four horses. It appeared to be strong though light and well sprung, with a canopy over the top to afford some protection against the sun and weather. This was one of the well-known coaches of Cobb and Co. who had made travel so much easier over the unmade roads of the outback.

I sat between Adelaide and Stirling and we were very soon on our way. Jack Bell, to whom I had been introduced before we left, stood at the door of the hotel to wave goodbye. He was a tall thin man who had failed in his search for gold and was clearly relieved to find himself in his present position. He was slightly obsequious to Stirling and Adelaide and curious about me; but I had seen too many of his kind the previous night to be specially interested in him.

Besides, the city demanded all my attention. I was delighted with it now that I could see it in daylight. I liked the long straight streets and the little trams drawn by horses; I caught a glimpse of greenery as we passed a park and for a time rode along by the Yarra Yarra river. But soon we had left the town behind. The roads were rough but the scenery magnificent. Above us towered the great eucalypts reaching to the heavens, majestic and indifferent to those who walked below. Stirling talked to me enthusiastically of the country and it was easy to see that he loved it. He pointed out the red stringybarks, the ash and native beech; he directed my attention to the tall grey trunks of the ghostly-looking gums. There were some, he told me, who really believed that the souls of departed men and women occupied the trunks of those trees and turned them grey-white. Some of the aboriginals wouldn't pass a grove of ghost gums after dark. They believed that if they did they might disappear and that in the morning if anyone counted they would find another tree turned ghost. I was fascinated by those great trees which must have stood there for a hundred years or more – perhaps before Captain Cook sailed into Botany Bay or before the arrival of the First Fleet.

The wattle was in bloom and the haunting fragrance filled the air as its feather flowers swayed a little in the light breeze. Tree ferns were dwarfed by the giant eucalypts and the sun touched the smoke trees with its golden light. A flock of galahs had settled on a mound and they rose in a grey and pink cloud as the coach approached. Rosellas gave their whistling call as we passed; and the beauty of the scene moved me so deeply that I felt elated by it. I could not feel apprehensive of what lay before me; I could only enjoy the beautiful morning.

It was the proud boast of the Cobb Coaching Company that horses were changed every ten miles, which ensured the earliest possible arrival. But the roads were rough and clouds of dust enveloped us. I thought it was an adventurous drive but no one else seemed to share my opinion and it was taken for granted that there would be mishaps. Over hills and dales we went; over creeks with the water splashing the sides of the coach, over rocky and sandy surfaces, over deep potholes which more than once nearly overturned the coach. All the time our driver talked to the horses; he seemed to love them dearly for he used the most affectionate terms when addressing them, urging them to 'Pull on faster, Bess me darling!' and 'Steady, Buttercup, there's a lady!' He was cheerful and courageous and laughed heartily when, having rocked over a hole in the narrow path with a sizeable drop the other side, we found ourselves still going.

Stirling was watching me intently as though almost hoping for some sign of dismay which I was determined not to show; and I gave no indication that travelling over the unmade roads of Australia seemed to me very different from sitting in a first-class carriage compartment going from Canterbury to London.

There was an occasion when one of the horses reared and the coach turned into the scrub. Then we had to get out and all the men worked together to get the coach back on to the road. But I could see that this was accepted as a normal occurrence.

We were delayed by this and spent the night at an inn which was very primitive. Adelaide and I shared a room with another traveller and there was no intimate conversation that night.

In the morning there was some difficulty about the harness and we were late starting. However, our spirits rose as we came out into the beautiful country and once more I smelt the wattle and watched the flight of brilliantly plumaged birds.

We were coming nearer and nearer to what I thought of as Lynx Territory and it was here that I had my first glimpse of what was called a tent town. To me there was something horribly depressing about it. The beautiful trees had been cut down and in their place was a collection of tents made of canvas and calico. I saw the smouldering fires on which the inhabitants boiled their billycans and cooked their dampers. There were unkempt men and women, tanned to a dirty brown by sun and weather. I saw women, their hair tangled, helping with the panning or cradling, and turning the handles to bring up the buckets full of earth which might contain the precious gold; along the road were open-fronted shacks displaying flour, meat and the implements which would be needed by those concerned in the search for gold.

'Now you're seeing a typical canvas town,' commented Stirling. 'There are many hereabouts. Lynx supplies the shops with their goods. It's another trade of his.'

'So we are coming into the Lynx Empire.'

That amused Stirling. He liked to think of it as such.

The diggers' children had run out to watch the coach as we galloped past. Some tried to run after it. I watched them as they fell behind and my heart was filled with pity for the children of the obsessed.

I was relieved when they were out of sight and I could feast my eyes on the dignified trees and watch for sleepy koalas nibbling the leaves which were the only ones they cared for, and now and then cry out with pleasure as a crimson-breasted rosella fluttered overhead.

It was dusk when we arrived.

The driver had gone a mile or so out of his way to drop us at the house. After all, we belonged to the Lynx household, which meant we must have special treatment. And as we stood there in the road before the house the grey towers of which made it look like a miniature mansion, I had the strange feeling that I had been there before. It was ridiculous. How could I have been? And yet the feeling persisted.

Two servants came running out. We had been long

expected. One of them was dark-skinned; the other was named Jim.

'Take in all the baggage,' commanded Stirling. 'We'll sort it out later. This is Miss Nora who has come to live with us.'

'Here we are,' said Stirling. 'Home.'

I walked with them to the gates which were of wrought iron. Then I saw the name on them in white letters. It was 'Whiteladies'.

Chapter Three

WHITELADIES! The same name as that other house. How very strange! And stranger still that Stirling had not mentioned this. I turned to him and said: 'But that was the name of the house near Canterbury.'

'Oh?' He pretended to look puzzled but I did not believe that he had forgotten.

'You remember,' I prompted. 'We climbed trees to look over the wall. Don't pretend you've forgotten.'

'That place,' he said. 'Oh, yes.'

'But it's the same *name*!'

'Well, I daresay there have been other houses called by that name.'

'That one was so called because of the nuns. There were no nuns here.'

'I expect my father just liked the name.'

I thought it was rather mysterious. 'You might have mentioned the coincidence,' I said.

'Oh come, we're home. Don't waste time on unimportant details.'

Adelaide joined us. 'This way, Nora.'

We went under an arch and through a stone-flagged

passage into a cobbled courtyard. There was a door in a wall and over this hung a lantern. The place in the dim light of evening could have been built centuries ago. I knew it hadn't been, but whoever had built it had tried to make it seem so.

Adelaide pushed open the door and we went through a lobby into a large rectangular hall in which a refectory table stood. There were some straight-back carved chairs which were either antiques or very good imitation.

'It's like one of the old mansions at home,' I said.

Adelaide looked pleased. 'My father likes everything to look as English as possible,' she explained. 'We grow English flowers in the garden whenever possible. Do you like gardening, Nora? If so, you can help me. I have my own little flower garden and I grow all my father's favourites there – or try to.'

I said I hadn't done much gardening so I wasn't sure whether I should be a good gardener.

'You can try and see,' said Adelaide cheerfully.

There was a staircase leading from the hall and we mounted this and were in a gallery. There were several rooms leading from this and a corridor at each end. Adelaide led the way down one of these and we mounted another staircase at the top of which was a landing.

She opened the door and said: 'This is your room. I'm sure you'd like to wash. Your baggage will arrive soon. Dinner will be served in half an hour.'

She left me and I found a can of hot water so I washed my hands and face. I was combing my hair when there was a knock at the door and Adelaide looked in. She appeared to be somewhat harassed.

'My father is asking to see you.'

'Now?'

'Yes. He's in the library and he doesn't like waiting.'

I looked in the mirror. My eyes were brilliant. I was about to meet the man of whom I had heard so much. Already there was a defiant tilt to my head. I had made myself dislike him. If my father had never met him, I told myself illogically, he would be alive today.

My heart was beating faster. Suppose he disliked me? Suppose he decided to send me back? I felt afraid. I didn't want to go back. I had grown fond of Stirling. I could grow fond of Adelaide. They had made me feel already that I belonged; and it is better to belong to anyone than to no one at all. Yet a deep resentment burned in me towards that man who had governed their lives and was now preparing to govern mine.

'He will be getting impatient,' Adelaide warned me.

Let him! I thought defiantly. I would not allow him to dominate me. I would rather be sent back to England. It was only because Adelaide was anxious that I would hurry, so I put down my comb and followed her.

As soon as I set eyes on him I knew that they were right. He *was* different from other men. There had never been anyone quite like him. He stood by the fireplace in which a few logs burned, his back to it, his hands in the pockets of buckskin breeches. He wore highly polished riding boots, I noticed, and wondered why I should think of his clothes at such a time when it was his personality which dominated everything in the room. His entire being expressed Power. He was very tall – six feet four at least – his fair hair was very faintly touched with white at the temples and he had a golden Vandyke beard. I could not see his lips because they were hidden by his moustache but I guessed they were thin and could be cruel. His nose was aquiline and arrogant; but of course the most startling feature was those eyes. They were like those of a jungle animal – predatory, alert, proud, cruel, implying that he would have little mercy on any who offended him; yet there was laughter in them as though they mocked those who could not match up to him. They were a dazzling blue, and they were on me now though he did not greet me. He said over my head: 'So this is the girl.'

'Yes, Father,' said Adelaide.

'She has a look of her father, eh, Adelaide?'

'Yes, there is a resemblance.'

'Nora. Is that her name?'

I disliked being discussed as though I weren't there. My heart had started to thump uncomfortably because in spite of my determination not to be overawed, I was. I said in a voice which sounded both imperious and pert: '*I* can answer all questions concerning myself.' He raised his bushy golden eyebrows and the fierce blue fire was turned on me. I went on: 'I am indeed the girl and my name *is* Nora.'

For a second his expression changed. I thought he might be angry with what he considered my impertinence, but I was not sure.

'Well,' he said, 'it's been doubly confirmed so we can be sure of it. Do you think she'll like it here, Adelaide?'

I replied before Adelaide could speak: 'It's too early as yet to say.'

'She'd better like it because she has to stay.' He half closed his eyes and said: 'Send Jagger in and put dinner forward ten minutes. She'll be hungry. We don't want her to think we are going to starve her.'

This was dismissal. I turned, glad to escape. As we went out of the room we passed a man who was waiting to go into the library.

'This is Miss Nora Tamasin, Mr Jagger,' said Adelaide. 'Nora, Mr Jagger, who runs the property.'

Mr Jagger, was shortish and plump. I thought him most undistinguished; but perhaps that was because I had just left what I had sardonically christened 'the presence'. He had a very florid complexion and rather bold dark eyes; and I did not like the way they regarded me. But I scarcely noticed this; I was still burning with resentment against the Lynx. I realized that I had no idea what his library looked like; from the moment the door had opened I had seen only him.

Adelaide took me back to my room.

'I think you surprised him,' she said.

'And that didn't please him,' I added.

'I'm not sure. In any case, don't be late for dinner. You'll have to come as you are. There's not time to change. He said it was to be put forward ten minutes. I'll come and collect you so that you will be on time. He hates people to be late.'

As soon as she had left me I went to my looking-glass. My cheeks were scarlet and my eyes brilliant. He had had that effect on me. He had talked over me as though I did not exist and he had done it deliberately in order to disconcert me. Why had my father so admired him? Why had he given me into the care of a man like this? I was seventeen and it was therefore four years before I would be of age. And then what should I do? Become a pupil teacher? Oh, poor Miss Graeme with birds' nest hair and dreams of what might have been! But I would rather that than become a chattel of his. The term amused me and I began to laugh. I was actually excited – yes, I was! I was looking forward to seeing him again because I wanted to show him that although he might dominate the rest of his household, this should not be the case with me.

Almost immediately it seemed Adelaide was back to take me to dinner.

To my astonishment the table was laid in the big hall on the refectory table which I had noticed when we had entered.

It was laid for about twelve people. Adelaide was obviously relieved because her father had not yet arrived.

'We are a very big party,' I said.

'We are never sure how many there will be,' she told me. 'Sometimes the managers are here. The family, now that you are here, are five in number. Tonight Mr Jagger is here, and I believe William Gardner too. They often are. My father likes to discuss business affairs with them over the dinner table.'

Stirling came hurrying in – also relieved that his father had not yet put in an appearance. They were all apparently afraid of the man.

'So you have met,' he said. He wanted to hear me say how wonderful I thought his father was. 'You've spoken to him now.'

'Yes,' I admitted. 'Though he hasn't exactly spoken to me – rather *at* me. I replied on behalf of myself – if you can call that speaking to a person.'

'How did it go, Adelaide? Did he like her?'

'It was as Nora said; and it is early days yet.'

I could see that he thought the interview had not gone well and was disappointed and a little anxious. I liked his concern for me while I deplored his subservience to that man.

He came in then with his managers and I was angry with myself because I shared that awe which the others clearly felt. On one side of him was Jacob Jagger and on the other the man whom I discovered to be William Gardner. He looked round the room and nodded. Then he said: 'Where is Jessica? Not here yet. Well, we'll start without her.'

Stirling sat on his right hand. I thought there was some ritual significance in this. I, to my surprise, was placed on his left. Adelaide sat next to Stirling and there was an empty place beside me which I presumed was for the unpunctual Jessica. As the two men took their places farther down the table, servants came in and served the soup. It was hot and savoury but I was too excited to enjoy it.

The Lynx – I could not think of him by any other name – led the conversation. I had the impression that we were expected to speak only when spoken to. He talked to Stirling about the trip and asked what he thought of England. He listened with interest to his son's replies. Stirling was the only one present who did not appear to be afraid of him, but he implied a complete respect and behaved, I thought, as though he were in the presence of a deity.

'And what sort of sea trip, eh?' he asked.

'Rough at times. We had some rocky moments along the African coast. Some of the passengers did not care for it.'

'And what about Nora? How did she like it?'

He was still looking at Stirling, but I put in quickly: 'Tell your father, Stirling, that the rocking of the ship did not disturb me unduly.'

I fancied there was a glint of amusement in his eyes. 'So she was a good sailor, eh?'

'I would say she was.'

'Well, perhaps she'll settle in to our rough ways, then. Do you think she will?'

'Oh, I think so,' said Stirling, smiling at me.

'Can she ride? She'll need to here.'

'I have ridden at home,' I said, 'So I daresay I can here.'

He turned his gaze on me then. 'It's rough riding here,' he said, 'in more ways than one. You'll notice a difference.' He had a way of lifting one eyebrow which I fancied was meant to intimidate, but I felt a small triumph because I had made him stop this slighting way of talking over me. He had at last addressed a remark to me.

'I shall have to adjust myself to it,' I said.

'You are right; you will. You shouldn't give her a mount that's too frisky, Stirling.'

'Certainly I won't.'

'She's come out here to live in Australia, not to meet an untimely end.'

'You are unduly concerned,' I said. 'I am able to take care of myself.'

'Well, that's going to make everything a lot easier for us.'

He turned his attention then to the men and there was a great deal of animated conversation about the mine. William Gardner was mainly concerned with this; I listened to the answers and questions and was aware of Lynx's avid interest in everything connected with gold.

While this conversation was going on the door opened and a woman came in; she glided to the chair beside me where she sat down.

'We wondered what had happened to you, Jessica,' said Adelaide. 'This is Nora.'

'Welcome to Whiteladies.' Her voice was quiet yet rough; she was very thin and gave the impression that she had dressed hurriedly. The fichu of lace at her neck was grubby and I noticed that a button on her dress was hanging by a thread. Her grey hair was abundant but not well dressed. What struck me most was the strange lost expression in her eyes; which might have been those of a sleep-walker.

'Didn't you hear the gong?' asked Adelaide.

Jessica shook her head; she was still looking at me intently. I smiled at her – reassuringly, I hoped, for I felt she was in need of reassurance.

'I hope you'll find it not too difficult to settle in,' said Jessica.

'I don't think I shall.'

'Have you brought clothes from England? There's not much here.'

I said I had brought a little.

'Your bags are in your room,' she told me. 'They've just been taken up.'

Lynx, impatient of this trivial conversation, talked loudly of the mine and the property and the talk was dominated by the men. I had noticed the mildly indifferent and faintly contemptuous glance Lynx had given to Jessica. She was aware of it too and her response baffled me. I wasn't quite sure what it meant – fear, dread, awe, dislike – even hatred? Of one thing I was certain. No one in this house was indifferent to Lynx. Stirling was more animated than I had ever seen him before; his attitude was little short of idolatry; and there was a strong feeling between father and son. I could see that if the Lynx cared for anyone beyond himself that one was Stirling; and I fancied that he wanted to make his son another such as himself – a worthy heir to his empire. He listened to Stirling's views, applauding them now and then with a certain parental pride of which I should not have thought him capable, or demolishing them with a devastating attack which nevertheless held a flavour of indulgence. So he was capable of loving someone other than himself. His feelings towards his daughter were less strong. She was calm and intelligent – a good woman, and she was useful to him. So he showed a certain affectionate tolerance towards her. But these were his own children; to others he was the stem master; and towards me he had no feelings at all; I represented a duty to him.

But there was a flicker of interest in his eyes as he turned to me.

'About her mount, Stirling,' he said. 'I had thought Tansy for her, but perhaps that wouldn't be wise.'

'It's very good of you to concern yourself,' I replied.

The blue eyes were on me now. 'You'll have to go carefully at first. This isn't riding in Rotten Row, you know.'

'I have never ridden in Rotten Row, so I couldn't know how different this may be.'

'No, certainly not Tansy,' he went on. 'Blundell. You'll ride Blundell. Her mouth's been toughened by beginners. She'll do till you're used to the land around here. Stirling, you might take her out tomorrow. Show her the property. Not that she'll ride round that in a day, eh Jagger?'

Jagger laughed sycophantically. 'I'd say it was an impossibility, sir, even for you.'

'Distances are different here from where you come from. You think fifty miles is a long way, I don't doubt. You'll have to get used to the wide open spaces. And don't go off by yourself. You could get lost in the bush for days and that wouldn't be pleasant. We don't want to have to send out search parties. We're too busy for that.'

'I shall try not to inconvenience you in any way.'

He was smiling again. I was glad that he had dropped that irritating habit of talking at me.

'I think we shall find Nora very self-sufficient,' said Adelaide.

'That's what we have to be out here,' he replied. 'Self-sufficient. If you are, you'll get on. If not . . . then it's better to get out.'

'Nora will be all right,' said Stirling, smiling at me reassuringly.

The conversation turned to England, and I was waiting for Stirling to mention to his father that we had seen a house called Whiteladies; but he said nothing of this. He talked of London and his father asked many questions, so the conversation flowed easily. Then he asked me about Danesworth House and I found myself talking freely. One quality he had: he seemed to be deeply interested in many things. This surprised me; I should have thought that, seeing himself as the centre of his world, the affairs of others would have seemed trivial to him. He regarded us all as lesser than himself; he was the ruler of us all, the arbiter of our lives and fates – but I was to learn that he was acutely interested in every detail of our lives. Even during that meal I became aware of the many facets of the affection between Stirling and his father and the milder emotion he felt for his daughter. I was aware of the silent Jessica beside me who contributed little to the conversation yet made me aware of her, perhaps because I had heard that she was strange. And there was William Gardner with the fanatical gleam in his eyes when he talked of the mine where my father had worked with him. There was Jacob Jagger – and whenever I looked his way I met a bold glance of approval. Dominating that table, of course, was the man of whom I had heard so much and whose reputation I had already begun to feel was not exaggerated.

The next morning I awakened early and lay in bed thinking of the previous night until a maid – whose name I discovered to be Mary – brought in my hot water. Adelaide had told me that breakfast was between seven-thirty and nine and that I could go down at any time during that period. I rose from my bed and looked out of the window. I was looking out on a lawn, in the centre of which was a pond and in this pond was a statue; water-lilies floated there. I caught my breath in amazement. If I could have put a table there and set up a blue-and-white sunshade over it, this could be that other Whiteladies on the summer afternoon when I had seen it.

I am imagining this, I told myself. Lots of gardens have lawns and a pond with water-lilies. After all, hadn't Adelaide told me that her father was anxious to recreate an English atmosphere? What had startled me was the coincidence of the names being the same, and the odd thing really was Stirling's not mentioning it when we went to that other house.

I looked at my watch. I must not be late for breakfast. I thought of quiet Jessica's gliding into the dining-room and the displeasure of Lynx, and Jessica's indifference – or was it indifference? She had some strong feeling for Lynx. She seemed as though she hated him and was deliberately late to show her defiance. I could understand that defiance. Hadn't I felt a little of it myself?

I found my way down to the hall, which was not used for breakfast. It was evidently not the ceremonial occasion that dinner seemed to be. At dinner, I thought, *he* likes to place himself at the head of the table like some baron of old while his fiefs sit in order of precedence and his serfs wait on him. At least I was above the salt. The thought amused me and I was smiling as I went into the small dining-room to which I was directed by Mary the maid.

Adelaide was already there. She smiled a good morning and asked if I had slept well. She said Stirling had already breakfasted and would come along very soon to take me out and show me round.

I replied that I was looking forward to seeing the neighbourhood and that I was deeply interested in the house. I had seen a house near Canterbury which it resembled.

'That doesn't surprise me,' said Adelaide. 'My father designed this place. He built it ten years ago.'

'He is an architect then?'

'He is an artist, which may surprise you. When I say he designed the place, I mean that he supervised the architect and told him exactly what he wanted.'

'Your father seems remarkably endowed.'

'Unusually so. He saw houses like this when he lived in England and was determined to create a little bit of England here. He even had the gates brought from England. They are really old and were in fact taken from an English country house.'

'What a lot of trouble he went to!'

'He'll go to any amount of trouble to get what he wants.'

And here we were talking of him again. I changed the subject and asked about the garden. She was eager to show me and said that perhaps later in the day she would do so. I could probably give her advice as I was so recently from England.

Stirling came in, dressed in riding breeches and polished boots. He looked somewhat like his father – not quite so tall nor so commanding, and his greenish eyes lacked that hypnotic blue dazzle; but there could be no doubt that he was his father's son. I felt a sudden happiness to be with him. He made me feel secure here as he had on the ship; and although I put on a bold show and was determined that no one should think I was afraid of the man my father had appointed to be my guardian, the fact remained that I was. I found him completely unpredictable and I was not at all sure of the impression I had made on him.

'Are you ready?' Stirling wanted to know.

I said I must change into my riding habit as I had not known we were to start immediately.

As soon as I had finished breakfast I went to my room and put on the riding clothes I had bought before leaving England. I remembered how shocked poor Miss Graeme had been because I had chosen green and my black riding hat had a narrow matching green ribbon about it.

When I went down to the stables Stirling looked at me with approval.

'Very elegant,' he commented. 'But it's your skill with the horse that counts.'

I was delighted to see Jemmy in the stables, dressed in breeches and coat which were a little too large for him; but he looked very different from the shivering scrap we had found on board ship; and he had a very special smile for me, which was gratifying.

I don't know what possessed me that morning. I knew I was wrong; but there was something in the fresh morning air and the bright sunshine which made me reckless. They were saddling Blundell, the horse *he* had thought fit for me to ride.

'It's little more than a pony,' I said scornfully. 'I thought I was to have a horse. I stopped having riding lessons years ago.'

Stirling grinned and said: 'You'd better have a look at Tansy.'

So I looked at Tansy – a lovely chestnut mare; and I was determined to ride her if just to show him that I was not one of the minions who accepted his word as law.

'She's frisky,' said Stirling.

'She's a mare, not an old nag.'

'Are you sure you can manage her?'

'My father taught me to ride when we lived in the country, I know how to manage a horse.'

'The country's rough here. Wouldn't you rather feel your way?'

'I'm not going to ride Blundell. I'd rather not ride at all.'

So they saddled Tansy and we set off. She *was* frisky and I knew I was going to need all my skill to control her; but, as I said, on that day I was reckless. For the first time since my father had died I felt a great uplifting of my spirits. I had not forgotten him; I should never do that; but it was almost as though he were beside me, rejoicing because at last I was delivered into safe hands. But it was not my guardian who gave me comfort; it was Stirling, riding beside me, so much more at home here than he had been in England, who made me feel secure. I knew then that I loved Stirling, and although he did not dominate my thoughts as his father did, my relationship with him brought me a deep contentment which I felt sure I could not feel with any other person. Instinctively I was aware that the affection I had for him would grow stronger every day.

'Does the sun always shine here?' I asked.

'Always.'

'Really always?'

'Almost always.'

'You're boastful about your country.'

'Put it down to national pride. You'll feel it after a while.'

'Do you think I shall come to accept this as my home?'

'You will. I'm certain of it.'

'I'm not. Your father didn't, did he?'

'What do you mean?'

'Why should he have to build a house like that one we saw near Canterbury? Why should Adelaide have to make an English garden for him? He must be homesick . . . sometimes. Stirling, why didn't you tell me that this house had the same name as that other? It must have struck you forcefully.'

'It struck me, yes.'

'Then why didn't you *say*?'

'You'd never seen this. Then I thought it would be a nice surprise.'

'You think the most absurd things. Anyway, I'm glad. Going to that place seemed significant in some way. I don't think I shall ever forget it. Those people on the lawn, for instance. Minta! Wasn't she lovely? And Mamma . . .'

'Not forgetting the exquisite Mr Wakefield.'

'You mean *you* can't forget him.'

'Come now, you were the one who admired him. Such a perfect gentleman with his bows and hand-kissing.'

'Well, it *was* charming. And what of poor Lucie, the companion?'

'Poor Lucie! A pity she can't marry Mr Wakefield and live graciously ever after.'

'He is obviously for Minta.'

'I believe you envy her.'

'What nonsense!'

'I hope so. If you're going to settle in here it won't do to hanker after fancy gentlemen.'

'I'm going to be perfectly happy here, thank you, in spite of the obvious lack of well-mannered gentlemen.'

That pleased him. He really was concerned for me.

'What a heavenly morning!' I cried.

'Careful!' he warned as Tansy caught her foot in a hole and nearly threw me. His hand was stretched out to grasp my reins but we were all right, I assured him.

The grounds of the house were, in my English eyes, very extensive. There were flower and kitchen gardens where men were working and large orchards where there were orange and lemon trees, with figs to give their fruit in the appropriate seasons. I saw that we could live off the land.

We left the estate behind us and rode for miles over rough country; Stirling pointed out land on the horizon which was part of the property managed by Jacob Jagger.

'It is indeed a vast Empire,' I said. 'Your father is the monarch of all he surveys, and you are the crown prince. How does it feel to be heir to all this and your father's son?'

'It feels good,' he said, and I understood that.

We rode in silence for a while and then he said: 'I think you have made a good impression on him.'

I was pleased but shrugged my shoulders to feign indifference.

'*I* think he expected me to bow three times and walk out backwards.'

'He doesn't like subservience all the time.'

'Only some of the time?'

'Only from those he considers should show it.'

'He's a bit of a tyrant, a bit of a brigand – but I can understand your feelings for him a little more, now that I've seen him.'

'I knew you would. I knew you'd feel the same. I want you to, Nora.'

'It will depend on the way he treats me.'

That made him laugh. As we cantered over the ground and I felt the wind on my face I experienced again that feeling of happiness. He felt it too, I think, for he said: 'Nora, I'm going to make you love this country. I'll take you into the bush; we'll camp out. It's the only way if you want to see the country beyond where a coach can take you. I'll show you how to boil a billycan for tea and how to make dampers and johnny cakes on a camp fire.'

'It sounds good. I should like it, I'm sure.'

He was glowing with pleasure.

'What did your father say about Jemmy?'

'He said if he's prepared to work he can stay. If not, he'll be sent packing.'

'Did you tell him I persuaded you?'

'No. I let him think it was my idea.'

'Why? Because you thought it was rather weak of you to be persuaded by me?'

'I didn't know how he was going to feel about your making such a decision.'

'I suppose, had he known it was my idea, he might have said he wouldn't take in the boy.'

'He wouldn't have turned him away.'

'Well then, you wanted him to like me and you didn't want him to start off thinking I was domineering.'

'Perhaps. But I shall tell him later. It was just at first.'

'Stirling, you're nice to me.'

'Of course I am. My father's your guardian and I'm his deputy.'

We rode in silence for a mile or so. The eucalypts were thick about us; a startled kangaroo, baby in pouch, leaped across our path and then sat on her haunches looking at us with curiosity. For the first time I saw the beautiful lyre bird, his fantastic tail spread out in all its glory. We pulled up, for he was perched on a tree fern not far off. As we halted he began to imitate the cries of other birds as though giving a performance for our benefit. While we remained stationary I noticed how blackened were the trunks of some of the eucalypts, and I pointed this out to Stirling, who told me they had been so rendered by fire. Then he began to tell me about the terrible forest conflagrations which ravaged the country. I could have no conception of these until I saw one and he hoped I never would, though it seemed hardly likely that I would not if I stayed in Australia.

'Every living thing for miles around is in acute danger,' he told me. 'It is the most fearful tragic thing imaginable. There are dangers in this land, Nora, that you wouldn't dream of.'

'I have thought of the dangers. Remember, my father died here.'

'Robbery with violence can happen anywhere.'

'Where there is greed,' I added. 'And here there is gold, and gold means greed.'

He called my attention to an emu which was running at great speed along the path. I had never seen such a large bird; it was about five feet high.

'You're getting to know the land and its inhabitants,' said Stirling. 'First the family, then the wild life. Look at those trees. I reckon they're all of three hundred feet high.'

'They're magnificent. More beautiful than all the gold in the world.'

'They're not all that benevolent. I've known a falling branch impale a man. Imagine one falling three or two hundred feet. It happens now and then. We call those branches widow-makers out here.'

I looked up at the tall trees and shuddered.

' "In the midst of life we are in death," ' quoted Stirling half serious, half mocking.

I didn't want this morning spoilt by talk of death so I whipped up Tansy and galloped off. Stirling came up behind and passed me. Then it happened. I had been aware all the morning that I was managing Tansy only because she was permitting me to do so. I heard a strange mocking laugh not far off; perhaps Tansy heard it too. I don't quite know what happened but suddenly I was sailing over her head. I had the sense to release the reins when I saw I was falling and luck was with me on that day. I was tossed into a heap of bush, growing up three or four feet from the ground; it was thick and strong enough to hold me. I was scratched and shocked but I was alive. For some moments I was bewildered, staring up at the sky, trying to grasp the bracken which scratched my hands and was breaking under my weight. Then I heard again that mocking laughter and in my somewhat bemused state I half believed that Lynx was somewhere at hand where he could witness and enjoy my plight.

I heard Stirling calling me; and there he was, extricating me from the bush, an expression of great concern on his face.

He said: 'Can you stand?'

'Yes . . . but my ankle hurts.'

'Sit down,' he commanded, and I sat on the grass while he knelt beside me.

He gently pulled off my boot. My ankle was swollen.

'Sprained no doubt,' he said. 'What happened?'

'Where's Tansy?'

'I saw her making off. She'll go home. She knows the way. But what, for heaven's sake . . . ?'

'Someone laughed and then I was in the bush.'

'Laughed! Who?'

'I don't know. It was so close. I think it frightened Tansy and so she threw me.'

'We'd better get back,' he said. 'We'll have to see what damage is done. I'll take you on Weston.' He whistled and Weston came obediently. As he helped me to mount I heard the laughter again – one burst followed by another.

'There!'

'Those are birds. The old kookaburras. You'll have to get used to their laughter for you'll hear it often enough.'

So I was carried ignobly home to find that Tansy had already returned. I had been extremely fortunate to have emerged with nothing more than a few bruises and a sprained ankle, but I was sick with shame wondering what Lynx would say when he heard of my adventure.

Adelaide greeted us with relief.

'I heard that Tansy had come home and that you rode her this morning.' Her voice was faintly reproachful. Hadn't her father said I should ride Blundell?

'She was all right until she was startled,' I explained. 'I managed her all right until then.'

Adelaide was concerned, but I discovered that accidents here were not treated with the same anxiety as they would be at home, because here in the bush they were so frequent. Adelaide applied hot and cold compresses, telling me that she had studied first aid as it was often necessary since there could be a delay of two to three days before a doctor arrived. She made me drink a cup of hot sweet tea and said I must keep my weight off my ankle for the next day or so.

I felt stupid and ashamed of myself but I was relieved that the horse had come home. I lay on a couch in Adelaide's sitting-room. I should be quiet for a while, she said; and when I felt a little recovered from my shock I could read or perhaps do some sewing. There was always a great deal to be done at Whiteladies.

I lay by the open window and thought of how foolish I had been to have ridden a horse which was far too good for me. 'Pride goeth before a fall,' Miss Emily had said often enough; and for once I had to admit that she was right.

Then I heard *his* voice below my window.

'So she rode Tansy after all and came a cropper. Serve her right. At least she shows more spirit than sense.'

I fancied there was a faint note of approval in his voice and I exulted in it.

I lay there idly. What an end to my first day at Whiteladies – *Little* Whiteladies, as I had christened it, for there could only be one true Whiteladies.

Somewhere in the garden I heard the laughter of the kookaburras, mocking me, it seemed.

Adelaide would not allow me to put my foot to the ground for the next three days, so I spent the time in her sitting-room. Stirling carried me to my bedroom every night. Both Adelaide and Stirling were determined to look after me, and show me that they welcomed me as their young sister. I did some sewing for Adelaide. This consisted of making garments for the numerous people who worked in the house. There were several small cottages in the grounds where these people lived and I had already discovered that there were several children.

'My father likes them all to be treated as though they are part of the family,' she said; and she looked at me quickly to see what effect that remark had had on me. I didn't understand then but it gradually dawned on me that many of the children had been fathered by Lynx. Later it became a habit of mine to look for his features. I found them often. It was understandable. Lynx was virile in every sense. He was not the sort of man to lead the existence of a monk. He took these young women according to his whim and no one thought the worse of him for it. I never found those startling blue eyes anywhere else. Even Stirling – the legitimate heir – had not inherited those.

During those days Stirling called in often to see me. I told him I was ashamed of what had happened and hoped Tansy had suffered no harm.

'It's nothing,' he reassured me. 'It's better to be bold than scared out here.' And I was grateful to them for making light of my adventure. I was growing fond of Adelaide, whom I had already begun to regard as my kindly elder sister. She brought me trays with tea and scones served just as they were at home; and there was peach jam and passion fruit jelly which she had made herself.

Those days appeared strange after all that had gone before – so quiet and peaceful. I felt that I had come to a little oasis, but I knew that my stay there would be only temporary. Lynx did not come to see me. I realized that that would be expecting too much. Stirling's visits were mainly in the evenings. He was away most of the day at the mine, making up for lost time, he told me. I heard a lot of talk about the mine and longed to see it, and yet in a way I didn't want to. I felt it would bring back memories of my father too vividly.

Mary, the maid, helped me dress in the mornings; she would bring me a breakfast tray and after that my hot water. She was shy and seemed afraid of something. I tried to discover of what but was not successful. Then Stirling would insist on carrying me to Adelaide's sitting-room, which was unnecessary for I could easily hobble there. All the same, I must admit I liked this attention; I liked the feel of his strong arms supporting me. He carried me so effortlessly, but I told him that this accentuating of my disability only called attention to my folly.

It was on the third day after my accident and I was lying on the sofa in Adelaide's room stitching at a calico shirt, working diligently, feeling that this was one way of showing my penitence for being so foolish, when the door opened slightly and Jessica glided in. I felt a sudden shiver run down my back which could have been due to the wild look in her eyes and the noiseless manner in which she had entered the room.

'How are you?' she asked and drawing up a chair sat down near my couch. Imperceptibly I felt myself shrink away from her.

'I'm getting on very well, thanks,' I said. 'In fact I'm a bit of a fraud. I should really be walking about but Adelaide won't hear of it.'

'There are other frauds about.' She smiled. 'And not far away from here either.'

'Is that so?'

She nodded conspiratorially. 'Has *he* been in to see you?'

I knew to whom she referred but I feigned not to do so. 'Who?' I asked.

'Him. The master.'

'No. I didn't expect him.'

'He cares neither for God nor man,' she told me. 'You could have been killed on that horse and he wouldn't have cared.'

'He did warn me not to ride Tansy, so it was entirely my own fault.'

'All he'd care about would be the horse.'

'Well, it's a very fine horse.'

She turned those strangely wild eyes on me. They were brown and I could see the round staring pupils looking full at me.

'Valuable,' she whispered. 'He thinks of goods, property, gold. That's what he cares about.'

'So do many people.'

She came closer to me and I felt trapped on my couch.

'But he cares more than anyone else. He's quite ruthless, as we all find out when we get to know him. I found out. Maybella found out. My uncle found out. He came as nothing . . . nothing . . . a prisoner, a slave. Seven years transportation and in a year he was ruling us all.'

'He's a very unusual man.'

'Unusual!' She laughed and her laughter reminded me of that of the kookaburras which I insisted had startled my horse. 'There has never been a man like him. I hope there never is another. Beware of the Lynx. He hypnotizes people. My uncle, Maybella . . . and look what happened to Maybella. He killed her.'

'Maybella. She was . . . ?'

'He married her, didn't he? Why? Did he want Maybella? Did he care that much for her?' She snapped her fingers. 'And what happened to Maybella, eh? Do you know?'

'I don't,' I said, 'but I should like to.'

The door opened and Adelaide came in. She frowned at

Jessica. Then she said lightly: 'Oh, there you are, Jessie. Just in time for a cup of coffee. I was making some for myself and Nora.'

She was carrying a tray with a crochet-bordered cloth. The coffee smelt delicious, but I wanted to hear what Jessica had to tell me and I knew she would not go on while Adelaide was there.

Adelaide set down the tray and briskly poured out the coffee. 'Plenty of milk, Nora,' she said. 'That'll do you good. Here, Jessie. Just as you like it.'

Jessica's hands were trembling as she took the cup.

'I think that tomorrow you might walk about a bit, Nora,' went on Adelaide. 'Not too far, of course. In the garden perhaps. Don't go wandering out into the bush yet, will you?'

Jessica had fallen into silence and when she left us Adelaide said, 'Did she talk wildly? She does now and then and I'm afraid this is one of her bad days. It doesn't do to encourage her or to take too much notice of what she says.'

All the same I wanted to hear Jessica's version of what happened to Maybella.

In a week my ankle had completely recovered and I felt as though I had been much longer than that time at Little Whiteladies. I was so anxious to make up for the Tansy incident that I helped Adelaide as much as I could. I began to learn to cook; I did a little gardening; I gleaned a little knowledge of the herbs she was so fond of growing; I sewed; and I became like a daughter of the house. Adelaide and Stirling were pleased with me. I began to know the servants and this was when I realized how useful I could be, for the aboriginals were notorious for going 'walk-about' as they called it; and they were constantly disappearing. Even their fear of

Lynx didn't prevent them; or perhaps it was one of the reasons for it. And whenever a white servant could not be found, it was always presumed that he or she had gone off to the diggings.

'I wish they'd never found gold in Victoria,' said Adelaide.

It was not long before I was riding again. One could not get along in this country without a horse, so it was no use letting one little mishap deter me. On Stirling's advice I had a strawberry roan named incongruously Queen Anne; she was neither the old hack Blundell was nor was she of the calibre of Tansy.

'When you're used to the country,' said Stirling, 'we'll find a better mount for you. In the meantime be a wise girl and stick to the good old Queen.'

So I did and I knew he was right, for I felt perfectly confident to control my Queen in any circumstances.

When I first saw the mine I looked at it in dismay. We had ridden to it through magnificent country and there it was replacing all that beauty with its ugliness. There was the poppet head supporting the wheels over which the steel ropes passed as the cages were hauled to the surface; the noise was deafening and even while I stood there an explosion rent the air.

'We're using this new substance which Alfred Nobel has invented,' Stirling told me. 'It's called dynamite and it saves endless work because it breaks up the rock and enables us to get at the gold. There are two hundred men working here.'

'Are they content to find gold for your father?'

'They are glad to work here. Most of them have been digging for years. They've known hardship and think it's good to work for a steady wage. They know that those who found fortunes with the simple cradles are few and far between. The chances are too great; the hazards too many.

96

This is a safe job. They eat every day; all they have to do is work for the master.'

He pointed out the stampers, which were a new kind of machine to pound the ore and so extricate the gold from the quartz rock. It was all noise and activity. About the mine were rows of tents in which the miners and their families lived; some even had cottages consisting of two rooms, one back one front; these were the fortunate ones.

I said: 'And your father owns this mine?'

'You have a share in it. Your father put in what money he had. There are other shareholders too, but my father owns the bulk of the shares, so he is the one with the controlling interest.'

'It's nice to know that I am not entirely a pauper. Perhaps I'm even rich.'

'The mine runs at a loss.'

'Then why all this . . . for a loss?'

'Hope is the answer. It goes with gold. There is more hope in this country than there ever was gold.'

'And even your father is affected by this mad gold hunger.'

'Even he. He came from England. He knew people there, rich people, who lived as he said "graciously". They did not concern themselves with money because they had so much that they never gave a thought to it. He told me once that that was how he wanted to live, that was how he was *going* to live one day.'

'But he is secure . . . even rich. He commands you all. What more does he want?'

'He wants to bring about the realization of a dream. He wants first to find gold . . . such gold as has never before been found. From then he will go on with his plans.'

'What plans?'

'Oh, he has plans. But the first step is his golden fortune.

You see how we live. We do not stint ourselves – a large house, many servants, interests in several places. It is costly living thus; and the mine eats up money. You've seen all these workers; they have to be paid. Machinery is expensive. The mine costs a great deal to run. My father wants an easy fortune in gold. Then he might go to England.'

'He could go back now.'

'Not as he wants to go. He would like to go back like a lord.'

I laughed derisively. 'Does he plan to have a title too?'

'Perhaps.'

'So meanwhile he builds a little Whiteladies and has an English garden and throws all his money into a gold mine that doesn't pay.'

'Not at the moment, but later it will. My father will strike gold in a big way. Have no doubt of that. He has always found what he wanted.'

'How long has he been here? Thirty-five years, is it? And all that time he has wanted to go back and never has!'

'He only wants to go back in certain circumstances.'

'He, it seems, suffers as acutely as everyone else from this lust for gold. You talk of him as though he is some sort of god, but he is a worshipper in his turn. He worships gold.'

As we talked an old man passed us. At least, at first I thought he was an old man, until I saw that it was disease which made him seem so. A sudden paroxysm of coughing shook him and he stood doubled up with pain until it was over.

'Poor man,' I said, 'he should be in bed. He should have a doctor.'

I was about to speak to him when Stirling laid a hand on my arm. 'He's one of hundreds,' he said. 'He has the miners' complaint – phthisis. It's caused by dust and grime in the

98

mines; it affects the lungs and in the end kills the victim. There is nothing to be done about it.'

'Nothing!' I cried. 'You mean men go down into the mine and it is known that they can contract this terrible disease?'

'It's a hazard,' said Stirling lightly. 'They know it and they accept it.'

'And when they get it? What then?'

'What then? They die in time. It's a killer.'

I was angry, thinking of that man, their master, who, in his lust for gold, sent those men down into the mine to work for him.

'It's wicked,' I said. 'It should be stopped.'

Stirling laughed at me. 'The trouble with you, Nora, is that you're soft. Life is not. Especially out here. That man has a job. He's fed his family . . . if he has any. He came out here looking for gold and failed to find it, as thousands have. So he finds work in the gold mines. It's dangerous work, but there's danger everywhere in life. Even in cosy England there's sudden death. Don't take life so seriously.'

'I take death very seriously. Unnecessary death.' Then I thought of my father who had died for gold just as this man was dying; and I hated gold more fiercely than I ever had before. I saw them loading the dray which would take the gold to the Melbourne bank, and I thought of his setting out on his journey and giving his life to save the gold.

From that moment I personified Gold. I saw it as a cruel woman, greedy, rapacious, sly, capricious. The Gold Goddess – a kind of Circe, a Lorelei, who now and then rewarded those who served her in order to lure more victims from their homes, their families and all that was serene and secure in life that she might destroy them.

'I want to see the spot where my father was shot,' I said.

'Why don't you forget all that?'

'Forget that my father was murdered!'

'There is no good in remembering.'

'Would you forget if *your* father had been killed?'

He flinched. I knew he could not contemplate a world that did not contain the mighty Lynx.

'I loved my father dearly,' I said. 'There was no one like him in the world. And here, in this country, he was wantonly killed by someone who didn't even know him. And you ask me to forget that!'

'Come on, Nora. Let's get away from here.'

He turned and walked his horse to the road. I followed.

'Now,' I said, 'take me to the spot where my father was shot, and after I've seen it I won't speak to you again about him if you don't want me to.'

We rode for some three miles and there he stopped. It was a beautiful spot – quiet and peaceful; and as we stood contemplating that perfect peace, the silence was broken by the notes of a bell bird.

'The dray came along the road from the mine,' said Stirling. 'It was just about here. He was not killed at once, you know. We brought him back to Whiteladies and there he wrote the letter which was sent to you – the last he ever wrote. He had already talked to my father about you. That was how it happened.'

I looked about me at the grove of eucalypts in which the assassin might have hidden. Beyond them was a hill – a small mountain perhaps, down which a stream trickled into the creek below.

It was one of the most beautiful places I had ever seen.

'And here he met his death,' I said bitterly, 'he who was in love with life, who had made such plans and had so many dreams. It need never have happened. He died . . . for gold. I *hate* gold.'

'Come away, Nora,' said Stirling. 'He died and you've lost him, but you have us now. Nora, you have me.'

I turned and looked at him; he brought his horse closer to mine and taking my hand pressed it briefly.

'I'll make it up to you, Nora,' he said earnestly. 'You'll see.'

All that day and the next I kept thinking of my father and that poor man who was dying of phthisis; and when I was weeding in Adelaide's garden I suddenly looked up and saw Lynx standing there watching me.

'How long have you been there?' I demanded.

Up went an eyebrow. 'I don't answer questions when they are put so peremptorily.'

'I don't like being watched when I'm unaware of it.'

'I don't like people who are impolite.'

'Nor do I,' I retorted, standing up. The thought of that poor man dying of his lung complaint made me angry and I didn't care whether or not I offended Lynx.

He decided not to be offended. 'I'm glad to see you working,' he said. 'I don't like idleness in this house.'

'If you expect me to work you should say so. Perhaps you would like me to work down in your gold mine.'

He pretended to consider this. 'In what capacity, do you think?'

I decided not to answer that and said: 'I understand that I own some shares in the company.'

'Your father had a few . . . a very few. They are not worth much.'

'Like the mine itself, perhaps.'

'You are an expert on mining?'

'I know nothing of it, and don't want to. I would rather not be connected with such a thing.'

He said: 'I think it is time you and I had a talk. There are certain things we should know about each other.'

'I am eager to know of what concerns me.'

'Come to the library after dinner tonight.'

He left me and I turned to Adelaide's herb garden; the strong smell of sage was in the air. I thought: Tonight I will be bold. I will tell him what I think of this mine in which young men become old men before their time and ruin their lungs.

He did not appear at dinner that night, and I wondered whether when I went to his library he would be there. He was. He was sitting at table sipping a glass of what I presumed to be port wine. I guessed he had eaten dinner alone in this room, which I understood he did on some occasions.

'Ah,' he said. 'Come in, Miss Nora. Sit there opposite me where I can see you.' I sat down. The light in the room was dim. Only two of the several oil lamps had been lighted.

'You will have a glass of port wine.'

I declined because he made it sound more like a statement than an invitation.

He lifted the decanter and poured himself another glassful. I noticed his hands then for the first time; the fingers were long and slender and on the little finger of the right hand was a ring with a carved jade stone. There was an elegance about his smallest gesture and I could imagine his living graciously in an old English country mansion.

'You wanted to know about your position here,' he said. 'You are my ward. I am your guardian. This was arranged by your father before his untimely end. He knew the hazards of this country and he often talked, in this room, of his fears and anxieties; and I gave him my promise that in the event of his death before you reached the age of twenty-one, I would take you into my care.'

'He must have had some premonition that he was going to die.'

He shook his head. 'Your father was a man who dreamed

wild dreams. He was enthusiastic about them but in his heart he knew they would never come true. Deep in his mind he admitted to himself that he would never make his fortune; but it was only when he considered you that he made practical plans. You can count that as a measure of his affection for you. For you he stepped outside himself and admitted the truth as he knew it to be. So he made this bargain with me and before he died he drew up a document appointing me as your guardian. I agreed to his request – so here we are.'

'Why did he choose you?'

Again that tilt of the eyebrow. 'You say that as though you think me unworthy of his trust?'

'He knew you such a short time.'

'He knew me well enough. We knew each other. Therefore, you have to accept me. You have no alternative.'

'I daresay I could earn my living.'

'In the mine . . . as you suggested? It is not easy for a young woman to earn a living unless it is as a housemaid or something such, which I do assure you would be a very poor one.'

'I have these shares in the mine.'

'They don't amount to much. They wouldn't keep you for long.'

'I would rather not have any money which belonged to me supporting a gold mine.'

'The shares can be sold. They won't realize very much. The mine is known to be a not very profitable concern.'

'Why continue with it?'

'Hope. We always hope.'

'And meanwhile people die while you continue to hope?'

'You are thinking of your father. That is a fate which many people have met in this country. These bushrangers are everywhere. We could all encounter them.'

'I am thinking of a poor man I saw the other day. He was suffering from a lung complaint.'

'Oh . . . phthisis.'

'You speak as though it were about as important as a headache.'

'It's a mining hazard.'

'Like death from bushrangers?'

'Are you suggesting that I close the mine because a man is suffering from phthisis?'

'Yes.'

He laughed. 'You are a reformer, and like most reformers you understand little of what you hope to reform. If I closed my mine what would happen to all my workers? They would be starved to death in a week or so.'

'I want nothing to do with this mine.'

'Your shares shall be sold and the money banked for you. I warn you it will not be much more than a hundred pounds. And if we struck gold . . .'

'I don't want anything to do with gold mining.'

He sighed and looked at me over his port, his eyes glistening. 'You are not very wise. There is a saying at home: 'Your heart rules your head.' You think with your emotions. That can get you into difficult situations and is not much help at extricating you.'

'You would be different. You think with your head.'

'That's what heads are for.'

'And hearts?'

'To control the circulation of the blood.'

I laughed and so did he.

'Is there anything else you wish to know?' he asked.

'Yes. What am I expected to do here?'

'Do? You will help Adelaide perhaps, as a younger sister would. This is your home now. You must treat it as such.'

I looked round the room seeing it for the first time.

Books lined one wall, there was an open fireplace in which logs were burning; several pictures hung on the walls and it was exactly as one would expect an English library to be. On a highly polished oak table was a chess set. The pieces were laid out as though someone were about to play, and an exclamation escaped me because I knew that set well. It was beautiful; the pieces were made of white and brownish ivory, and there were brilliants in the crowns of the kings and queens; the squares on the board were of white and deep pink marble. I had played on it with my father.

'That is my father's,' I accused.

'He left it here with me.'

'It would belong to me now.'

'He left it to me.'

I had stood up and went over to look at it closely. I held the white ivory queen in my hand and was reminded so vividly of my father that I wanted to cry.

Lynx stood beside me. 'Your name is on it,' he said, pointing to one of the squares.

'We wrote our names on it when we won for the first time. That's my grandfather. The chess set has been in the family for years.'

'Three generations,' he said. 'And the outsider.' He pointed to his own name written boldly in one of the centre squares.

'So you beat my father.'

'Now and then. And you did, too.'

'He was a fine player. I believe that when I won he allowed me to.'

'When you play with me I shall not allow you to win. I play for myself and you will play for yourself.'

'You are suggesting that we play chess together?'

'Why not? I enjoy the game.'

'On my father's board,' I went on.

'It has become mine. You forgot. And why not play on it? It is a joy to touch such beautiful pieces.'

'I always understood it would be mine.'

'Let me strike a bargain with you. On the day you beat me it shall be yours.'

'Should I be asked to play for what should be mine by right?'

'It is suggested that you play to regain it.'

'Very well. When do we play?'

'Why not now? Would you care to?'

'Yes,' I said. 'I will play now for *my* chess board and men.'

'There is no time like the present. And that is another saying from home.'

We sat down opposite each other. Clearly I could see the golden eyebrows, the white slender hands with the jade ring. Stirling's hands were slightly spatulate and I found myself continually comparing the two men. He reminded me of Stirling, yet the son was like a pale reflection of the father. I hated to admit that I had thought such a thing because it was disloyal to Stirling. Stirling is kind, I thought. This man is cruel. I understand Stirling but who could ever be sure what was behind that glittering blue barrier. He had noticed that I was looking at his hands and held them out for me to see more clearly.

'You see the carving on this ring. It's the head of a lynx. That is what I am called. This ring is my seal. It was given me years ago by my father-in-law.'

'It's a very fine piece of jade.'

'And a fine carving. Suitable, don't you think?'

I nodded and reached for the white king's pawn.

I quickly realized that I was no match for him, but I played with such concentration that again and again I foiled

106

his efforts to checkmate me. It was a defensive game for me and it was three-quarters of an hour before he had cornered me – a climax, I sensed, he had expected to achieve in ten minutes.

'Checkmate,' he said quietly and firmly; and I saw that there was no way out.

'But it was a good game, wasn't it?' he went on. 'We must play again some time.'

'If you think me worthy,' I replied. 'I am sure you could find an opponent more in your class.'

'I like playing with you. And don't forget you have to win that set. Don't forget, also, that I am not like your father. I shall give no concessions. When you win you will know that the victory was genuine.'

I was very excited when I left him and I could not sleep for a long time that night; when I did I dreamed that all the pieces on the board came to life and the victorious king had the eyes of the Lynx.

It was October and spring was with us. The garden was beginning to look lovely. I discovered that Stirling had brought over several plants with him and we already had scarlet geraniums and purple lobelias growing on the lawn. I was wishing that I had some definite duties. I went in Adelaide's wake helping where I could, but I felt I was very inadequate. I wanted some task which was my entire responsibility. Adelaide assured me that the help I gave in the house was invaluable, but I couldn't help feeling that she said this out of kindness.

One day I was in the summer-house where I had often sat while my ankle was strengthening, sitting for a moment because my back ached after weeding, when Jessica seemed to appear from nowhere. What a disconcerting habit this was when people moved so noiselessly and you were suddenly aware of them standing there.

'Why, Jessica!' I cried.

'I saw you coming from the library,' she said. 'You had been with him a long time.'

I felt annoyed to be so spied on. 'Does that matter?' I asked coldly.

'He's taken to you and you're flattered, aren't you? He takes to people and then . . . he's finished with them. He doesn't think of anything, you know, but what use they are to him.'

'Why do you hate him?' I asked.

To my surprise she flushed scarlet and looked as if she were going to burst into tears. 'Hate him? Yes, I do. No . . . I don't know. Everybody's afraid of him.'

'I'm not,' I said uncertainly.

'Are you sure? He's different from other people. You should have seen him when he first came to Rosella Creek.'

'Where's that?'

'It's the property. It's called Herrick's now – after him – but at one time it was Rosella Creek. Uncle Harley ran it then and we had good times. It wasn't so big in those days and there was always something to worry about. That time when the fires encircled us. We just escaped then by the skin of our teeth, Uncle Harley said. Then there was the blight and the floods and the land erosion. But we got through and Maybella would have married well. There was a man who used to come in from Melbourne. His father had a store there and he was comfortably off. He would have spoken for Maybella.'

I had a feeling that I was prying into something I was not meant to know, that Adelaide would have wished me to make some excuse to evade Jessica but the temptation was too strong for me. I wanted to know the strange story of

Stirling's father, thoughts of whom were beginning to dominate my life.

So I said: 'Tell me about it.'

She smiled at me slyly. 'You want to know, don't you? You're interested in everything about him. That's what happens to people. It happened to Maybella. She was in a kind of daze from the moment he came. I remember the day he came.'

She paused again and a soft dreamy expression came into her eyes. Her lips softened and she was smiling. I did not prompt her this time. I waited; and then she began to speak quietly but intensely as though she were unaware of me and was recalling the scene for her own pleasure.

'Uncle Harley went to Sydney for the ship that was coming in. He was going to choose a couple of men because we needed help on the station. He said, "I'll bring back two strong rogues. We'll have to be careful of these convicts but we'll get work out of them. What we need is two strong men." He rode out with his saddle bags and provisions for the journey; he was going to pick up a couple of horses for the convicts and they'd be back in two weeks, he reckoned, that's if they weren't held up by floods and weather. He was three weeks gone because there'd been rain and some of the creeks were flooded. Maybella and I were in the kitchen baking in readiness for his return. He came in and kissed first Maybella and then me. He said: "I've got two fellows, Maybell." That was what he called her. "One of them . . . well, you'll see for yourself." And we did. We were standing at the kitchen window when we first saw him. The size of him amazed us. "What a big man," said Maybella. "Did *he* come off the ship, then?" Uncle Harley nodded. "Seven years. Just think of that, my girl. Wrongly accused, he says." "Don't they all," said Maybella; and we laughed. But he was different. Those eyes of his burned right through you. You couldn't treat him as a convict nor even as a servant. Uncle Harley felt it, too. He sort of quailed before him. He hadn't been there a week before he was talking to him like an equal. Oh, he was clever. He could do twice the work of an ordinary man and he was soon telling Uncle Harley how the place could be improved. It was odd, because Uncle Harley, who had always thought he knew best about everything, used to listen to him.'

She paused and looked at me. 'You wouldn't believe what a man could do in such a little time.'

'I could,' I told her.

'Three weeks after his arrival he was taking meals with us. There was something they had to discuss, Uncle Harley would say. His manners were different from those of the other men – different from Uncle Harley's. When he sat at the table with us he made us feel awkward, as though he were the host and we the servants. He talked a lot to Uncle Harley. He'd take a piece of paper and make a sketch of this or that bit of the property. He'd tell Uncle how he could erect some sort of woolshed which would be raised from the ground so that the wool could be kept dry. He said our wool press was out of date and that we should have another. Uncle Harley used to listen to him fascinated and say: "Yes, Herrick," in a sort of hushed reverence as though he were the master and Uncle the servant. Shearing came and we had never been so successful. He made everyone come in and work at it – the gardeners, the servants, anyone with a pair of hands was set to work. By this time he had become a sort of overseer. They were all afraid of him. Uncle Harley said: "Nothing escapes you. You've got the eyes of a lynx." Then they called him Lynx and the aborigines thought he was some sort of white man's god. They would work when he was there but when he was absent they would sit with their hands in their laps doing nothing. I remember how he made us laugh when he drew a picture of himself and it was so lifelike that you would think he was looking out of the paper. He coloured the eyes – the same blue as his own and he pinned the picture up in the woolshed and said: "Even when I'm not here I'm watching you." They were afraid then; they'd look at the picture and think it really was Lynx on the wall. That was the sort of man he was. So it was small wonder . . .'

She stopped again and shook her head as though she wanted to linger over the memory. I waited eagerly for her to continue.

'Maybella was bewitched. The storekeeper's son was nothing to her. Her eyes would light up when Lynx was around and she grew quite pretty. She wasn't really pretty . . . rather plain, in fact. I was prettier than she was – but I was only the master's niece. She would inherit the property because there was no son. There'd be nothing for me. I'd been given a home; that was all. "Don't worry," Maybella used to say. "There'll always be a home here for you, Jessie." And she meant it. She had a kind heart, Maybella had.'

'So she fell in love with him?'

'The place wasn't the same. It had already started to improve. Uncle Harley thought the world of him. "Hi, Lynx," he used to say. "Now this fellow Jim, or Tom – whoever it was – do you think we can trust him to take these bales to Melbourne?" It was always "we". So you see the way things were going. Maybella talked of nothing but him. She was mad about him. I don't think there was anything she wouldn't have done for him – and so it proved. When she was going to have the child she was afraid of telling her father. He was very religious and she thought he might turn her out. I knew there could only be one who was the father and I was horrified. I said, "A convict, Maybella!" And she held up her head and cried: "I don't care. He was wrongly accused and

I'm proud. I don't care about anything but that I'm going to have his child." She told her father so, and that was the most astonishing thing of all, because all he said was: "There's only one thing to be done. There'll have to be a wedding." So less than a year since he had come over as a convict to Rosella he had married Maybella. Then Adelaide was born and soon after that he was the master and everyone knew it.'

She turned to me her eyes blazing with an emotion I could not quite understand. 'If I had been Uncle Harley's daughter *I* should have been the one.'

'Perhaps he loved Maybella.'

She laughed. 'Loved Maybella! He despised Maybella. He showed that clearly. Poor Maybella, she went on adoring him until he killed her.'

'Killed her?'

'As sure as if he'd taken a gun and fired it at her. He was disappointed in Adelaide. He wanted a son. He wanted a son who would look exactly like himself. Poor Maybella nearly died having Adelaide. I thought at the time that it was all the worry beforehand, but it was the same with the others. She wasn't meant to bear children, and she was terrified. She had suffered so much with Adelaide. He called her Adelaide after Adelaide the town. "A tribute to his new country," he said. Perhaps he thought he had done rather well in it. Uncle Harley doted on Adelaide. He would have spoilt her but Maybella didn't take much notice of the child; all her thoughts were for *him*. He had bewitched her all right. He knew it and he seemed to despise her for it.'

'You said he killed her.'

'So he did. Year after year there was a miscarriage. Oh, she was frightened. She was almost an invalid. But he wanted a son. He had taken over the management of the place – he, a convict. Seven years he had to serve and he served them as the master. Uncle Harley was like Maybella; they were afraid of him; they never did anything without consulting him; and he despised them both. He killed Maybella with her constant pregnancies. We all knew that she was not strong enough to endure them. Uncle Harley died six years after he had gone off to Sydney to bring back the servants. I remember his death-bed. We were there, Maybella, little Adelaide, myself and *him*. Uncle Harley believed in him until the end. "Rosella's yours, Maybella," he said, "yours and Lynx's. He'll look after you and it. I leave you in good hands, daughter. And there'll always be a home for you here, Jessie." Then he died, believing that he had set everything in order. He didn't know that within a year Maybella would be buried beside him.'

'But you said he killed her,' I insisted.

'She died when Stirling was born. I hated him. I said to him: "You'll kill her!" And he looked at me with those contemptuous eyes of his as though he considered me a fool. I loved Maybella. We were like sisters. When she died part of me died. I've heard people say that before. It's a cliché, isn't it? But it can be true, you know. And it was true for me. He killed Maybella because every year he forced her to try to bear the son he wanted, though she was more or less an invalid after Adelaide's birth. But he was cruel and hard. He got his son, though. He got Stirling. And that was what finally killed Maybella. She would have been here today but for his determination to get a son.'

I was silent and she added: 'He always gets what he wants. You'll see.'

I thought of his dream of a golden fortune which he had never found and I said: 'No one gets all they want.'

'He'll ride over everyone to get what *he* wants. He'll have it, in the end.'

'You hate him and yet . . .'

'I hate him for what he did to Maybella.'

'And yet . . .'

She turned on me fiercely. 'Why do you say that?'

'I feel that you don't hate him all the time.'

She drew away from me as though she were afraid of me. Then she rose abruptly and left me.

November had come and it was sheep-shearing time. This was the climax of the year's work. There was a great deal of activity and Stirling and his father were at the property every day. I went over with Adelaide to help with the meals. In the big stone-floored kitchen we worked hard, cooking for the men employed there and the extra hands who had been called in to help at this time. Often in the evenings sundowners would appear at the property and ask to stay the night in return for the help they would give next day. We were never sure how many we should have to cater for.

I found it all of great interest and different from the life we lived at Little Whiteladies.

One day when I was mixing dough and was alone in the kitchen Jacob Jagger came in. He leaned against the table watching me.

'You make a pretty picture, Miss Nora,' he said, his warm little eyes seeming to take in every part of me.

'Thank you,' I replied. 'I hope my bread will be as appreciated as the picture you mention.'

'I like a ready tongue,' he said.

'*I* like the kitchen to myself when I'm working.'

'Pert,' he said, 'very pert. I like that, too.'

'Well, Mr Jagger,' I retorted, 'all I can say is that you are easily pleased.'

'As a rule I'm not all that easy to please where females are concerned.'

'That's unfortunate for you, considering the dearth of them in this part of the world. Now if you would kindly stand aside, I should be grateful. I have to get to the oven.'

He stood aside but would not go. I felt myself flushing as I opened the oven and took out the bread.

'My!' he said. 'That looks good. Almost as good as its maker. I'd like to see you in this kitchen more often, Miss Nora. If you'd like to see round the property at any time when there are not so many people around, you just ask me.'

'I should probably ask Mr Stirling,' I said, gazing intently at the brown loaves just from the oven. 'Well, good day, Mr Jagger,' I went on pointedly. 'I am sure Mr Herrick will be expecting you at the shearing.'

I had implied that I might even mention the fact to Mr Herrick that he was chatting in the kitchen when I did not wish him to be there; and one mention of Lynx was enough to make him consider his action.

He bowed ironically and left.

When the shearing was over everyone seemed to remember that Christmas would soon be upon us.

'We celebrate it here,' explained Adelaide, 'in very much the same manner as it is celebrated at home. My father likes it to be so.'

She would make Christmas puddings and mincemeat although she would not be able to get all the ingredients which were available in England. They would kill some of the best of the fowls and although it would be high summer everything must be as much like England as possible. I was amused that Adelaide who had never seen England should refer to it as 'home', and that she should know so much about our customs. Even so, she was constantly asking me how this and that was done; and I knew this was to please her father.

She and I took the Cobb's coach into Melbourne and shopped there. That was quite an adventure because we stopped at The Lynx Hotel for two nights and one of the evenings we were taken to the Theatre Royal by Jack Bell, presumably on the instructions of Lynx. We took great pleasure in the shops and I spent some of the money which had been banked for me when my shares in the mine had been sold. I felt quite rich and bought presents – and for myself some strong boots and material to make dresses.

It was about a week after our return when I noticed that Mary, the maid who looked after me, was in distress. When she brought my hot water one morning, she tripped over the rug and went sprawling on the floor, spilling the water.

When it was cleared up, I said to her, 'Something's wrong, isn't it, Mary?'

'Why, Miss Nora,' she said flushing painfully, 'whatever do you mean?'

'You seem distraught. You're constantly dropping things. Come and sit down and tell me what the trouble is.'

At this she did as I bid, and sitting down burst into floods of tears.

Then the story came out. She was going to have a baby and didn't know what to do about it.

'Well,' I said, 'that's bad, but it's not the end of the world. Perhaps you can get married.'

That brought more tears. It wasn't possible, it seemed. She murmured something about going away to bear her shame.

'It's this man's shame as well,' I said firmly. 'He can bear some of it, too.'

There was nothing to be done, she told me. She only hoped she would not be turned away.

'That shan't happen,' I said fiercely, as though I were the mistress of the house and all decisions rested with me. I added that the first thing we must do was tell Adelaide.

Adelaide sighed when I told her.

'It happens far too often,' she said. 'But here we are, away from a town and these people are young and hot-blooded. They don't think of consequences. Who is the man?'

'She won't say.'

I was not surprised when Mary at length revealed that the man was Jacob Jagger.

'Will he marry her?' I asked Adelaide.

'I shouldn't think so for a moment.'

'If your father insists, he will.'

'I don't think he would insist.'

'I should have thought he might very well.'

'You don't know him yet, Nora.'

It seemed I didn't, for he did not take a very serious view of the matter. Mary could have her child in the house and it would be brought up there. As for Jagger, naturally he didn't want to marry a girl like Mary. He managed the property well and it wasn't easy to get men; he had to amuse himself now and then. That was Lynx's view.

I overheard some of the servants discussing it afterwards.

'Master was very mild over the affair,' said one.

'Couldn't be ought else, considering . . .' was the answer.

I knew that meant his own conduct was not exemplary and I wondered why my father had sent me to live in such a household.

Mary was immensely relieved and almost happy. I asked her whether she would have liked to marry the father of her child.

'God forbid, Miss Nora,' she said.

'But you must have liked him . . . once.'

'I never did. He frightened the life out of me.'

'But . . .'

'You're wondering why I did, Miss. Well, he sort of cornered me, and I didn't have much say, come to think of it.'

I said, 'He couldn't have *forced* you!'

'Well, I reckon that's about it,' she replied.

I felt very uneasy.

Chapter Four

I T seemed strange to wake up to a hot and sunny Christmas morning. A few days before, Stirling and I had ridden out into the bush and come back with a kind of mistletoe which was a parasite on the gum trees. It wasn't quite like our mistletoe at home, but it served. We hung some over the door and some in the middle of the room. When we had finished Stirling kissed me beneath it.

'May it be the first of many Christmases in Australia,' he said.

'What if your father struck gold?' I demanded. 'Then we should all be transported, lock, stock and barrel, to England.'

He didn't answer that and I knew he didn't want to think of leaving.

We had dinner in the middle of the day and I spent most of the morning in the kitchen with Adelaide. We cooked the chickens while the plum pudding steamed away in a saucepan; the heat was great. I went outside to get a breath of fresh air, but it was as hot outside as in the kitchen. I stood for a moment looking at the flowering gums and reminding myself that this time last year I was at

Danesworth House growing more and more anxious because I had not heard from my father. A great deal had happened in a short time.

Adelaide came out and said, 'The passion fruit is ready for picking. Should I pick now?' She answered herself. 'No. It would spoil the illusion and wouldn't be a bit like Christmas at home.'

It was a big party for Christmas. Lynx sat at the head of the table and I retained my seat on his left hand, Stirling opposite as we had sat since the first night. Several men from the property and the mine were there. Jack Bell was busy at the hotel so he did not join us. I had avoided looking at Jacob Jagger since the Mary incident. If he had been in love with her and she with him I should have felt differently. I kept thinking of Mary's description of being 'cornered'. I knew that he constantly looked my way, that he was always endeavouring to make me speak or smile at him. This I refused to do. The man disgusted me. One day I would speak to Stirling about him. Across the table my eyes met those of Stirling, and he smiled at me with such pleasure that I glowed with happiness.

It was a pleasant meal. Lynx was in a benevolent mood; it was clear that he enjoyed presiding over his table, which might have been in an English country house. Mary brought in the Christmas pudding and brandy was poured over it before it was set alight. It tasted good.

We were drowsing over our port when there was a commotion in the kitchen followed by the sound of raised voices and someone crying: 'Let me see him. Or let me see Miss Adelaide.'

Adelaide had turned white; she rose and went out. In a short time she returned. Lynx said: 'What is it?'

'It's the Lambs,' replied Adelaide. 'They've come back.'

'What for?' demanded Lynx.

'They want to come back into the house.'

'They want to come back! I thought they went after gold,'

'They did . . . but they're back.'

'Without the fortune they were going to make?'

'They're in a pitiable state,' said Adelaide.

'I won't have them back,' retorted Lynx coldly.

I tried to catch his eye but he was not looking at me.

'Perhaps . . .' began Adelaide.

'Tell them to go. I don't take people back into this house once they have run away.'

Adelaide turned. I rose in my chair. 'They might be hungry,' I said.

Lynx's steely gaze was on me. 'They went to make a fortune. It's no business of mine if they failed. When they left this house they left it for ever.'

Adelaide went out and I sat down dumbly. The joy of Christmas had gone for me.

When Stirling and I rode out next day I was still thinking of the Lambs.

'It was so cruel,' I said. 'And on Christmas Day.'

Stirling could never bear any criticism of his father. 'The day makes no difference.'

'No,' I agreed. 'It would have been cruel on any day, but on Christmas Day it is worse because it makes nonsense of all Christmas means.'

'We can't allow people to run off when they want to and then come back and expect us to kill the fatted calf.'

'Perhaps not, but they could have been given some food and help.'

'It wouldn't surprise me if Adelaide did.'

'But he wouldn't help them. He's a very hard man.'

'He knows what he's doing. He has to show these people that they can't walk off to look for gold one day and come back the next when they've failed to find it.'

Stirling's jaw was obstinately set. I realized in that moment that I was jealous of his love for his father. It would always be Lynx who came first with him.

We argued the point during our ride and we finally quarrelled when I said he hadn't a mind of his own and readily accepted everything Papa told him. He retorted that I was a self-opinionated schoolmarm who thought that because I had once taught little girls of five I could teach my elders . . . yes, and betters.

I galloped on ahead of him, hurt and angry, because I was beginning to build up a picture of being with Stirling for ever, marrying him and having Lynx for a father-in-law. I was not sure whether I wanted the latter or not. I wished that there were no Lynx and that Stirling's father had been an ordinary sort of man. And then I thought: No, I wouldn't like that. I could not imagine the place without Lynx. My growing relationship with him excited me. I was exultant because he was not indifferent to me. I wanted him to be interested in me, to listen to me, to respect me and to grow fond of me. I wanted to be important to him. But I wanted to be more important to Stirling than anyone else in the world and while Lynx existed I felt that never would be.

The next day Stirling behaved as though there had been no quarrel between us. He was treating me as though I were his sister. I did not want this but I felt happily secure because our relationship was one which would strengthen as it grew and I was certain that in due course I would be as necessary to him as he was to me.

The Lambs were never mentioned again. I liked to think that Adelaide had helped them and I felt sure she had. Mary was happy again and growing noticeably larger. I saw Jemmy often in the stables; he had developed an assurance which must always have been not far from the surface. I often heard him whistling at his work and I felt so happy because we had been able to help him. Therefore I was surprised when one day in early February Jemmy was reported missing.

It was the same story. He had confided in one of the stable boys that he was going off to find gold.

When Lynx heard, he laughed. 'That's another of them,' he said. 'Don't take him back when he's had enough of the goldfields.'

He asked me that night to have a game of chess with him after dinner. We did not play immediately, though, and I believed that he wanted to taunt me about Jemmy, for Stirling had since told him how eager I had been to help the boy when we had found him on the ship.

'It doesn't do to play the ministering angel, Nora,' he said. 'Come, you are going to drink a glass of port with me.' He filled the glasses. 'You see how your Jemmy has turned out.'

'Surely you can understand the desire to find gold?'

'I understand it. I have experienced it.'

'Then why are you so hard on others?'

'I'm not concerned with others – only with myself.'

'You condemn these people because they go off to look for gold.'

'You are mistaken. All I say is that I will not have them back when they fail. I will not have my servants walking off when the whim takes them. They are free to walk off, it's true, but not to come back.'

'The Lambs . . .'

'Ah, you hated me then, didn't you?'

'I thought you were very hard and on Christmas Day too!'

'My dear, sentimental Nora, the day has nothing to do with it.'

'So Stirling said.'

'You have thrashed the matter out with him?'

'I have discussed it with him.'

'And attacked me furiously.'

'Yes, but he defended you.'

He smiled. Then he said, 'Nora, life *is* hard, you know, and it is no use being soft in a hard world. You are too sentimental, too emotional. You will be hurt one day.'

'Are you sentimental? Are you emotional? No! But you have been hurt . . . so hurt that you have never forgotten it.'

He raised those bushy eyebrows and regarded me. Then he held out his hands so that his long shirt cuffs were pulled back and I saw the scars on his wrists. 'Manacles,' he said. 'Fetters and chains. The marks are still there.'

'They have no meaning now. You are no longer fettered. You are in command. You rule the lives of all those around you.'

'But the scars remain.'

'In your heart as well as on your wrists.'

He was silent for a moment and his eyes narrowed as he went on, 'You are right, Nora. What happened to me is something which will never be forgotten. Only when a certain action has been taken can the score be settled.'

His eyes blazed and I knew that he was thinking of revenge.

'How long ago did it happen?' I asked.

'It is thirty-five years since I came out here . . . in chains.'

'And you still talk of settling the score!'

'I shall go on thinking of it until the settlement is made.'

'It is a long time to harbour resentment.'

'For such an injury?'

'Times have changed since those days. People are perhaps less cruel. Could it be the times which were to blame?'

'I do not see it that way. But for one man I should never have been obliged to endure those months of degradation and humiliation.'

'But you are here now. You have everything a man could wish for. You are a king in your world. You have a son and daughter, and most people go in fear and trembling of you. Isn't that what you want?'

He looked at me and smiled slowly. 'You are a bold girl, Nora. You don't care in the least that you offend me with your criticism.'

'Men like you hate criticism, I know. All the more reason why some should not be afraid to give it.'

'And you have chosen yourself for that role?'

'I am determined to show you that I am not afraid of you.'

'Suppose I asked you to leave my house?'

'Then I should pack my bag and depart.'

'Where to?'

'I am not without some qualifications. Remember I taught at Danesworth House. I could be a teacher or governess in some family.'

'A sad life for a proud woman.'

'Better than being where she is not wanted.'

His blue eyes were fixed steadily on me. 'And do you think you are not wanted here?'

'I am not sure.'

'The truth, please.'

'I think you have made a promise to my father and that you are a man who likes to keep his promise if . . .'

'Pray go on.'

'If keeping it does not inconvenience you too much.'

'Well, Nora, let me tell you that having you in this house does not inconvenience me one little bit. If there was any sign of this I should cease to think of your existence. You have been truthful with me, so I will be truthful with you. I will say that I did not altogether dislike the addition to my family. I wanted sons, but daughters are very well, and can be useful.'

'Then I am of use?'

'I am not displeased with my family. Come, let us have a game. You still have to win the set, you know.'

We played. I was aware of his growing interest in me. And was elated by it.

Stirling was right. One could not live under his roof and not be affected by him.

The hot summer weather was with us. I would work in the kitchen or in the garden in the mornings and in the afternoons try to find a shady spot under a wattle tree and lie and read, although the flies – and I had never seen so many before – were a pest. It was more comfortable to sit in Adelaide's cool sitting-room and sew with her or read aloud to her as she sewed, which she very much enjoyed. She liked Jane Austen and the Brontës; she was as passionately interested in the English scene as her father was. Sometimes Jessica would creep in and sit and listen while I read. I must confess that I always felt a little uneasy at such times. She would sit very quietly, her hands folded in her lap, and I had the impression that she wanted to be alone with me so that she could talk to me about those days when Lynx had first come to Australia and settled into the place which was then called Rosella Creek.

So passed that summer and when the weather showed signs of becoming a little cooler Adelaide suggested that we take another trip to Melbourne. There were several things she wanted; it was easy to get them brought to the house because one of her father's businesses supplied goods to the small shops and traders on the goldfields; but as Adelaide said, it was a luxury to choose for oneself from a large selection. We could put up at The Lynx and this time, as I was accustomed to the country and was now a very creditable horsewoman, we might ride and I could try camping out, which was often more convenient than waiting on the Cobb coaches. Stirling could accompany us and there should be another man of the party. Someone would certainly have business in Melbourne and wish to join us.

During the summer evenings I had played chess with Lynx several times. He invariably displayed a rather sardonic amusement because he knew how desperately I wanted to beat him. It had become rather an obsession with me and it was typical of our relationship. I had always wanted to show him that I was not in awe of him; perhaps the fact that I continually stressed this showed that I was.

But those evenings in the library with the rose-quartz lamp beside us throwing its rosy glow over the chessmen had become part of my life. I found a certain content in sitting there, watching those long artistic hands with the green jade signet ring. I would grow tense with excitement when I could see him checkmated in a few moves, but he was always ready with some devastating counter move-ment which turned my attack into defence. I would look up and find those magnetic eyes on me, full of mocking laughter, brilliant with pleasure because he always enjoyed showing me that however I tried to outwit him, he would always win in the end.

'Not this time, Nora,' he would say. 'What a pity. They

are such unusual pieces. Look at this castle. So delicately formed. And when you win, you will still play with me, won't you? I should not like the games to cease just because the set has changed hands.'

I began to learn more and more of him; in fact there were times when he seemed to lift that invincible barrier which he had erected round himself. When it was there he was the Lynx, proud, invulnerable, all powerful. But it could be lifted and in some way I had found a means of doing it. It had begun when he had shown me the fetters on his wrists; and then there was the time when he showed me his pictures.

I was a little early going to the library for our game because my watch was ten minutes fast. I knocked but there was no answer so I went in. He was not there, but a curtain on one side of the room had been drawn back to show a door, and this stood ajar. I had not known that there was a door there.

I stood for a while in the room. I had never seen it when he was not there and it was surprising how his absence changed it. It was now an ordinary room – pleasantly furnished, it was true, with its thick rugs and heavy velvet curtains, strong oak chairs and the books lining the wall. A library which one would find in any English country house! On the oak table stood the chess set in readiness for our game.

I crossed the room and looked through the open door. He was there but he did not see me immediately. On a table before him were several canvases and I remembered then what Jessica had told me about the picture of himself which he had set up to make the aborigines afraid of him.

He glanced up and saw me.

'Why, Nora,' he said, 'is it time?'

'I am a little early. My watch is fast.'

He hesitated – something I had rarely seen him do before. Then he said: 'Come in.'

So I went in. On an easel stood a canvas and on a chair lay a paint-scattered jacket.

'This is my sanctum,' he told me.

'Have I intruded?'

'On the contrary, you are here on my invitation.'

'You are a painter.'

'Is that a question?'

'No. I know it.'

'Are you surprised? You did not expect me to have such talents? Perhaps you consider I have no talent. Judge for yourself.'

He linked his arm through mine; it was the first time there had been any demonstration of affection.

'These pictures on the walls are my work,' he said.

'Then you *are* an artist.'

'You are *not* a connoisseur – that much is evident.'

'But these pictures . . .'

'Lack form, technique, or whatever you like to call it. They are not really very good.'

I had paused before a portrait of a woman. I thought I had seen the face before.

'Well, you like that?'

'Yes. It's soft and gentle and the expression is . . . good.'

'What were you going to say before good?'

'I don't know. Perhaps that she looked helpless, clinging, entirely feminine.'

He nodded and drew me to the next picture. 'Self-portrait.'

There he was. It was a good likeness and I guessed he was an easy subject. The mane of fair hair, the beard, the pride in the expression, and the animal quality – all these would be easy to capture in a facile way. Some of the arrogant power of the man was missing, but that was inevitable.

Then he took me to the table and showed me the canvases there. I saw it. The house. The real Whiteladies. The one Stirling and I had seen when we climbed the oak trees.

I gave an exclamation. 'That's it,' I said.

'You went there with Stirling,' he replied. 'He told me how your scarf blew over the wall and you both went in.'

'I suppose he tells you everything.'

'Whoever tells everything? But I know a great deal of what is in Stirling's mind. After all, he is my son.'

'And you love him as you never loved anyone else.'

'That's not entirely true. I am capable of affection. I don't give it freely, but that may mean that when I do I have the more to give.'

'How could you paint that house when you have never seen it?'

'Who said I have never seen it? I have lived in that house, Nora. I know it well.'

'You lived there! It was yours! So that is why you have built one to look exactly like it.'

'What conclusions you jump to. I lived there, it is true; but I did not say that it was mine. I worked there for a year in the humble position of drawing-master to the young lady of the house.'

'And Stirling happened to discover it . . .'

'You are wrong again. Stirling went there because he knew the house was there. I told him to go.'

'So that was why I had to meet him in Canterbury. Miss Emily Grainger said it was a little odd.'

'It was at my request that he went there.'

'You wanted to know if it had changed since you were last there. Houses don't change much. It's the people living in them . . .'

'Ah, there you have it. I wanted him to see not so much the house but the people living in it.'

'Because you knew them long ago. He did not say so. He didn't even tell them his name. I don't think they asked. It was all a little odd and unconventional.'

'He would not have told them his name. That might have been unwise.'

'There was some quarrel with this family?'

He laughed bitterly, harshly. Then he said. 'I was hardly in a position to quarrel with them. I was, as I said, the young lady's drawing-master. They were rich then. I don't think they are so happily placed now. Times change. The old man was a gambler . . . and not a clever one. I believe he lost a great deal of money after my departure.'

'A fact which appears to give you some satisfaction, I gather.'

'You gather correctly. Would you not dislike someone who condemned you to exile from your own country, to seven years' servitude in a penal settlement.'

'So it was the owner of Whiteladies!'

'Sir Henry Dorian, no less.'

'For what reasons?'

'Robbery.'

'And you were guiltless.'

'Completely so.'

'And could you not prove your innocence?'

'If I had had justice, yes. But he and his friends saw that I had not. I was in his house unlawfully, he said. I *was* in his house and not at his request, but the object of my visit was not to steal.' He smiled at me. 'You have an enquiring mind, Nora,' he added lightly.

'I admit it. I want to hear more. I remember the place so clearly. I felt when I was there it was important to me in some way. I had no idea at that time that it was connected with my new guardian.'

He shrugged his shoulders. 'A wonderful old place. How

I should like to own such a house!' His eyes gleamed with covetousness. 'I have built this place – a poor imitation. No! I want the stones which were used hundreds of years before. There is only one Whiteladies and it is not this one.'

'You have a very comfortable house of the same name.'

'It's a fake, Nora. I hate fakes.'

'It serves well.'

'It serves as a substitute until . . .' He stopped. Then he laughed and added, 'You wheedle, Nora. You lure confidences from me. And the fact that I allow you to, shows you that I already think of you as my daughter. Now isn't that strange? I am not a sentimental man to drool over a daughter – yet I allow you to tempt me to talk.'

'It is always good to talk. I am your ward. I have seen this house and the people there. There was the girl, Minta her name was, and there was Mamma.'

'Tell me about her. Stirling could not describe her. Women are better at that sort of thing than men.'

'Why, Mamma would be the one to whom you taught drawing!'

He nodded.

'She was old . . . well, perhaps not old, but she seemed so.'

'To you she seemed old – as I do.'

'No, not you. One would not think of age in connection with you. But she seemed fretful and concerned about her health. The girl was charming. And there was someone called Lucie.'

'Fretful,' he said and laughed lightly. He indicated the canvas he had already shown me. 'Was she like this? I drew from memory.'

Then I knew of whom the picture reminded me. It was the girl Minta, of course.

'It is a little like the girl,' I said. 'But she is not so help-less-looking. No, the woman in the chair was not like that. Perhaps she might have been years ago.'

'Thirty-five years ago when she was seventeen. She was beautiful then, but she was not very good at drawing. I was going to marry her.'

I was beginning to understand. She was the daughter of the house in which he occupied a minor position. I thought of Jessica's account of his arrival at Rosella Creek.

'So you went to the house to be her drawing-master and you decided to marry her. You admired the house and you would like to have been master of it.'

'I did admire the house and I should have enjoyed owning it, but in those days I was nineteen years old and senti-mental. I was even romantic. You may find that hard to believe, but it was so. I fell in love with Arabella and she with me. I was egotistical. You smile. You are thinking, Yes, I can believe that! It was true. I believed myself to be as good as any man and I could not conceive that her father, Sir Henry Dorian, would not welcome me as a son-in-law. I was the drawing-master, it was true. I had nothing but my talents; but on the other hand I could have managed his estate as it had never been managed before. If he had not been such a fool the family might not now be reduced to . . . well, scarcely penury – but it must be trying to have to consider every shilling when you have a position to uphold and have been accustomed to luxury.'

'Tell me what happened.'

'He was outraged by my suggestions. His daughter to marry her drawing-master! No. He had some neighbouring fop in mind for her. Someone of the right family. Very different from the drawing-master. Bella and I decided to elope. There was a maid in the house in whom she confided. Silly Bella! The maid turned traitor. I had been dismissed from the house so I came back one night for her. She had been locked in her room; so I took a ladder from one of the potting-sheds and setting it against the wall climbed into her room. She gave me her jewels and I slipped them into my pockets. At that moment Sir Henry with four of his menservants burst into the room. There, Nora, I have told you the story.'

'But surely she explained to them.'

'She tried to. She wept. She entreated her father to listen. They said she was shocked and did not know what she was saying, that I had threatened her and she was afraid. They were determined to be rid of me. They knew that if I had stayed in England I should in time have persuaded her to come to me. So what an excellent opportunity this was to get me out of the country, to arrange it so that I could not come back.' He lifted his hand and the lynx eyes in the ring glittered.

'It is a terrible story,' I said.

'You would be sure of that if you could picture the filthy prison, the convict ship. I was chained, Nora.' He held out his wrists again. 'The chains made sores; the sores festered. I was battened down in the hold for months on end with all the scum of England. Robbers, prostitutes, murderers . . . all going to Australia. Cargo for the settlers, cheap labour at the best. I remember the day we arrived in Sydney and how we came up on deck; the brilliance of the sunshine, that blue sea around us, and the birds. Yes, what I remember most vividly were the brightly plumaged birds – red-winged parrots, rainbow lorikeets, yellow-crested cockatoos and pink and grey galahs. They swooped and chattered above that sea and the thing that struck me was that they were free. Have you ever felt envious of a bird, Nora? I was then . . . and then I despised myself and started thinking of revenge. One day I would take it, and that made me want to live.'

'Soon after you arrived in Australia you were married.'

'Yes. I married the mother of Adelaide and Stirling.'

'She was the daughter of the man into whose hands you had fallen.'

'Why, you know a great deal of my history. I knew you were inquisitive.'

'It interests me. You quickly forgot your devotion to Arabella.'

'I never forgot my devotion to Arabella. That is one thing you can't accuse me of – fickleness.'

'But you married.'

'Maybella. She was a Bella too.'

'Don't tell me you married her because of her name.'

'No. She could have been Mary, Jane, Grace, Nora . . . any name you can think of. What's in a name?'

'But at least you could call her Bella.'

'Which I did.'

'And did she remind you of that other Bella?'

'Never.' He sounded contemptuous.

'Poor Maybella!' I said.

'It was I admit a marriage of convenience.'

'Convenience for you – perhaps inconvenience for her.'

'She was eager for it.'

'Did she ever regret it?'

'Jessica has been talking to you, I gather. Poor Jessica! She was very jealous of Maybella.'

'She gave me the impression that she was devoted to her.'

'She was that, too. People's motives are so mixed. Yes, certainly she was devoted to Maybella. She nursed her through her many illnesses.'

I forbore to mention that I knew what those illnesses were.

'She wanted to be in Maybella's place,' he added.

'She wished she were the daughter of the house so that she could have been the one to bring you out of bondage.'

'How discerning you are! And how we talk! All that is over and done with.'

'But you said it was not. You said you would never forget.'

'I shan't forget,' he said vehemently and I saw the ring glitter as he clenched his hands. 'But it is past now. Come, let us have our game.'

He drew me into the library and we sat facing each other over the board as we had so many times before.

He was absent-minded that night and I almost beat him. He rallied in time. He did not want me to win – whether it was because he did not want to give up the chess set or because he hated to be beaten by a woman, I was not quite sure. Both probably.

But that night of confidences had drawn us closer together. He might have become a little wary of me and felt that he had betrayed too much – but we were closer for all that.

After that we planned our visit to Melbourne. Stirling, Adelaide and myself were to be accompanied by one of the men from the property; we could do the forty miles or so into the town, taking about three days which would mean camping out for two nights.

'Just a little trip for Nora to try,' was Stirling's description of the jaunt.

We would not take more than we needed, pointed out Adelaide, because it all had to be carried. We had sent on ahead clothes and things we should need for our stay at The Lynx in Melbourne so that they would be waiting for us when we arrived. Then we could be elegantly and fashionably clad; we could do our shopping and have our purchases sent to Whiteladies; then we would journey back, camping on the way.

We were taking a few spare horses and a couple of pack horses; and we should carry a little in our saddle bags. There was a tent which could be used for Adelaide and myself. Stirling and the man who was to accompany us would sleep under the stars. It all sounded exciting and I was looking forward to it.

It was only an hour or so before we were due to start that I discovered that the man who was to accompany us was Jacob Jagger.

'That man!' I protested to Adelaide.

'He has to go into Melbourne on business and he said he would like to take this opportunity.'

'I shouldn't have thought he could have been spared from the property.'

'Really, Nora! What do you know of the property?'

'Well,' I floundered, 'he's supposed to be the manager of it and . . .'

'Even so, he doesn't have to remain there all and every day.'

'I don't like him, Adelaide.'

'Oh, I daresay he's no worse than anyone else.'

'It was that affair of Mary.'

'It happens now and then.'

'But she said that he . . . forced her.'

'Girls tell these tales. We didn't hear anything about the forcing until she was going to have the baby.'

'She seemed to me as though she were absolutely terrified.'

'Of course she was when she knew she was found out. It's always the same story. And you mustn't judge people by the standards you've been used to in England. People out here are . . . isolated. These things happen. My father understands this. He is never hard on these cases. Mary is receiving every consideration, so stop being sorry for her, and don't be hard on Jacob.'

I didn't care what she said. I didn't like the man.

When he arrived he grinned at me.

'I'm happy to be making this trip,' he told me; and I lowered my head coldly and looked away. I was glad Stirling was with us.

Riding along in the early morning, revelling in the aspects of the bush, listening to the birds, now and then catching sight of some wild animal or bright plumage, I refused to be depressed by the presence of Jacob Jagger and my thoughts turned to Stirling.

They were pleasant thoughts. There he rode beside me, now and then turning to smile at me or point out some feature of the countryside which he thought I might have missed. I was contemplating the difference he had made in my life and how important he had become in it. There were times when it seemed that Lynx was more often in my thoughts than his son was, for I thought a great deal of Lynx. I accepted him as the dominant figure on the scene. Stirling reminded me of him in many ways. He was a gentler, kinder version of his father. But one could not help being impressed by Lynx, admiring him, even feeling for him this absurd sort of devotion – which I called idolatry in Stirling – but for Stirling I had a warmer, more human feeling. I could not imagine the house – my little Whiteladies – without Lynx. Even to think of his not being there affected me deeply; and the excitement of the days was intensified by seeing him at the head of the table at dinner, or best of all playing chess with him trying to beat him or, as he said, to wheedle confidences from him. I thought more often of Lynx perhaps than I did of Stirling, but I had no doubt of my feelings for Stirling – I loved him. And I was not sure how to describe my feelings for Lynx. I believed that one day Stirling would ask me to marry him and when he did I would say 'yes' without hesitation. I believed that Lynx would give us his blessing (for I was sure this would be what he wanted) and that we should be happy ever after. We would be prosperous here – although we would give up the mine. I would urge Stirling to do this. Then my thoughts grew blank because I was thinking as though Lynx were dead. Lynx . . . dead! That seemed impossible. No one – not even Stirling – had that immense vitality, the reflection of which revitalized one. No, I would persuade *Lynx* and Stirling to abandon the mine. I could not bear to think of men dying of phthisis, nor the look on Lynx's face when he talked of gold.

We rode south and as the day wore on we found a spot where we would pitch our tent. It was near a creek so that we had water, which Stirling went to get while Jacob Jagger made a fire. Adelaide said she would show me how to make dampers and we would soon have tea. There was boiled bacon in the saddle bags and some mutton too.

What an exhilarating experience it would have been but for the fact of Jacob Jagger's presence. I had to admit that he was very skilful in making a fire. He insisted on explaining how to make the wood kindle and how important it was to choose the right spot.

'It's easy to start a forest fire,' he added, 'and that, Miss Nora, is something I hope you'll never see.'

'The last one was terrible,' put in Adelaide. 'I really thought it was going to be the end of the property.'

'So did we all,' agreed Jacob Jagger, his plump face more sober than I had ever seen it. 'There were hours when we were actually ringed by fire. I was waiting for the gums near the house to explode and that would have been the end.'

It was difficult for me to imagine the horror of a forest fire. I suppose nobody can until they have seen one. Now this friendly little fire which Jagger had made was cooking our dampers and boiling our water for tea.

It was so pleasant lying there, on rugs which Adelaide and I had spread out on the turf, propped up by our saddles.

'What do you think of camping, Nora?' Stirling was asking me.

'I think it's fun.'

He threw himself down beside me, his elbow resting on the ground, his arm propping up his head.

'I knew you'd enjoy it.' His eyes were warm with approval. 'I knew you wouldn't be one of those helpless females who scream at the sight of a spider.'

'Surely we didn't have to come camping for you to discover that?'

'No. I always knew it.' He was smiling at me in a way which delighted me. He was fond of me; there was a bond of understanding between us. I knew that he looked upon me as his protégée. He liked people to admire me, applaud me; that was why he had been so anxious that I make a good impression on his father. It showed that he loved me.

This was indeed my home. I should spend the rest of my days here. Little Whiteladies was the setting for my future happiness. Lynx would be the master, always, but benign, indulgent and pretending that he was not. He would accept me as his daughter and love me as such; I believed he was very close to doing so already. And there would be children – my home would not be complete without them. Lynx would love them and be proud of them and love me the more for giving him grandchildren.

It was easy to dream out there in the bush. Perhaps Stirling was dreaming too and there was a similarity in our thoughts.

When it was dark we sat round the fire talking desultorily and even Jacob Jagger seemed likeable. Adelaide told us of other journeys she had made and how on one occasion she had been lost in the bush. She had gone off to get water and had lost her way back to the camp.

'It's so easy,' she said. 'The contours of the land change so subtly that you don't realize they've changed. You take what you believe to be the right track – so many tracks look alike – and then you find you have wandered off in the wrong direction. It's a terrible experience to be lost in the bush.'

'I remember the occasion,' said Stirling. 'We all went off in different directions to look for you. We found you only half a mile away. You'd been going round in circles.'

Adelaide shivered. 'I shall never forget it. Let it be a warning to you, Nora.'

'Oh, we'll take care of Miss Nora,' said Jacob Jagger.

'No fear of that,' added Stirling. 'Still, Nora, take warning. Don't go wandering off on your own.'

I promised not to and we talked some more; then Stirling and Adelaide sang songs which they had sung together as children. They were songs from England. 'Those were the ones our father liked to hear,' said Adelaide. They were 'Cherry Ripe', 'Strawberry Fair', and 'On a Friday Morn When We Set Sail' – all the ballads that English children had been singing for years.

Adelaide and I went into our tent and the fresh air and long ride had made me so tired that I was soon asleep.

I was awakened by the kookaburras laughing overhead. Adelaide and I slipped on our dresses and went down to the creek to wash. She brought back water which she boiled in some quart-sized pots and with this made tea which we drank from tin mugs. Tea had rarely tasted so good before.

We left early after breakfasting from dampers and cold

bacon; there was passion fruit jelly, too, which Adelaide had had the foresight to slip into her saddle bag.

How I enjoyed that morning ride through the bush! But there was one incident which spoiled the pleasure of the trip. We stopped at midday and I was putting the water to boil for tea on the fire which Jacob Jagger had made when I was aware of him, standing very close.

'You've certainly taken to the bush, Miss Nora,' he said.

I replied without looking round, 'I find it very interesting.'

'It's a great life,' he said. Then he knelt beside me and the awareness of him made me stand up immediately. I looked over my shoulder. There was no sign of Adelaide or Stirling.

'Where are they?' I asked.

He laughed. 'Not far off. No need to be scared.'

'Scared?' I retorted coldly, annoyed because that was exactly what I was, to find myself alone with him. 'Of what?'

'Of me?' he suggested.

'I can see no reason for that.'

He gave an exaggerated sigh of relief.

'I'm glad. There's no need to be. I'm very fond of you, Miss Nora.'

'I'm glad, too, that I need not be scared, as you put it. Your feelings for me don't really concern me either way.'

'Well, we could change that.'

'I think I am the best judge of my feelings.'

Oh, where were Adelaide and Stirling? Why didn't they appear so that there might be an end to this conversation which he was forcing upon me. Well, not really forcing. I supposed I could walk away, but I did not want him to know how abhorrent I found him, for that would be to some extent betraying my fear.

'You are a very haughty young lady. I could change that, too.'

'Since when have you believed that you have the power to mould *my* character?'

'Ever since I saw you. In fact, Miss Nora, I have not ceased to think of you since that moment.'

'How strange!'

'It's not strange at all. You're a very remarkable young lady. The most remarkable I ever saw. I have never felt so interested in a young lady before.'

'What of Mary?' I suggested; and I felt the colour burning in my cheeks.

'Now you wouldn't be jealous of a servant girl!'

'Jealous! You must be mad.' I walked away but he was beside me, walking close. He laid a hand on my arm.

I blazed at him. 'Mr Jagger, kindly remove your hand. If you ever dare pester me again I shall speak to Mr Herrick . . . I mean . . . Lynx!'

That name could strike fear into people. Jagger flinched and drew back immediately; and to my immense relief I heard Stirling's voice.

'Nora, is tea ready yet?

That evening we reached Melbourne. In the excitement of shopping I forgot Jagger. I bought some green silk material from which I planned to make a dress. I saw myself wearing it in the evenings when I played chess with Lynx. Adelaide would help me; she was adept with the needle and she loved having beautiful materials to work with.

She said to me as the material was being measured, 'It's nice to make lovely things. You'll look pretty in that, Nora.' She pressed my arm and said quietly: 'I'm glad you're here with us. I can't imagine what it would be like without you now.'

After four days we left and made the journey back. It

was uneventful. I could kindle a fire, make dampers and boil tea in billycans. I had experienced life in the bush.

'You're one of us,' Stirling told me with approval.

I sat at the chess table; the long fingers caressed the ivory queen with her crown of gold and brilliants and he said: 'So you enjoyed your trip?'

'It was wonderful.'

'You liked sleeping rough?'

'Well, for a few nights it was interesting.'

'I like my comforts. I am a sensual man. I'm like a cat. I like to sleep in a warm bed, take a bath frequently, change my linen every day. It's hardly possible to do these things in camp. But you liked it.'

'Perhaps I prefer my comforts too, but it was interesting to see the bush and to get some idea of how people have lived out there.'

'I imagine you are something of a pioneer, Nora. So you found your trip perfect in every way.'

'Well . . .' A vision of Jagger rose before me. I don't know why it was that I had such fear of that man. Perhaps it was due to what had happened to Mary and the look in her eyes when she said she had been forced. Adelaide might not believe Mary, but I did.

'Oh . . . a fly in the ointment?'

How insistent he was! I could hide nothing from him.

'Adelaide and Stirling are good at everything,' I said quickly. 'They taught me how to make fires and dampers and so on . . . and how to live in the bush.'

'Jagger was with you, wasn't he?'

I felt the slow flush creep into my cheeks.

'Oh yes, he was there.'

'He's the best manager we've had,' he said. 'It's not easy

to get them. Most men would rather go after gold. So it's not easy to keep them, and once they've gone they don't come back. I see to that. Yes, Jagger is a good man with the property.'

Then the game started. I was quickly beaten on that occasion. I never had a chance to get into the attack.

'You're not playing well tonight, Nora,' he said. 'Your thoughts are far away. In the bush perhaps.'

In a few weeks' time Adelaide and I between us had made the green dress; we had also made up the more serviceable materials. Autumn was with us and we were preparing for winter. Logs were being brought into the wood house and Adelaide was stocking up with provisions. We were some-times cut off by floods, she explained; and there might even be snow. Her father did not like to be short of anything so it was her task to make sure that the house was well provided for. She had made jars of passion fruit jelly, peach jam and orange marmalade.

After the heat of the summer I found the days delightful for riding and when Adelaide or Stirling could not accom-pany me I went alone. I never forgot Adelaide's warning about being lost in the bush – one of the worst fates which could befall anyone – so I was always careful to watch for landmarks. I had my set rides and rarely diverged from them. Only by promising that I would either ride to Kerry's Creek, Martha's Mound or Dog Hill could I be given permission to go, and I believe they were always rather uneasy when I was alone while at the same time they did not wish to restrict me. Characteristically they had agreed that I should not be coddled; and I was now a fair horse-woman and could be trusted to manage a horse.

On this morning I decided to ride out to Kerry's Creek –

my favourite spot. Here the creek ran between a grove of ghost gums and when the wattle was in bloom it was one of the loveliest spots in the neighbourhood. I liked to tether my horse to one of the gums and sit watching the water. A man named Kerry had come there twenty years before and found a little gold along the creek; he had spent ten years trying to find more and had gone away disappointed. Hence its name. But now it was free of the seekers after gold for Kerry had proved it to be barren of that much coveted metal. Perhaps that was why it appealed to me.

I sat there on this lovely late April morning looking into the water and thinking of everything that had happened over the last months and how happy I was to have escaped from Danesworth House. Over there now the buds would be appearing on the trees and bushes; the aubrietia and arabis would be in flower; and Mary would be thinking that the cold nights were over and that for a brief spell before the heat of the summer she would be comfortable in her attic bedroom. Poor Miss Graeme would be reminded that spring was here again and another year had passed and she was a year nearer the time when Miss Emily would have no further use for her services.

How sad! Poor Miss Graeme! Poor Mademoiselle, getting less and less able to control her class. And here was I – escaped, as free as those lovely galahs flying overhead. Then I thought of Lynx's coming up from the hold of the convicts' ship and envying the birds.

Dear Stirling! Dear Lynx! I loved them both, and, in a lesser way, Adelaide. In a short while they had become my family and made up in some measure for the loss of my beloved father. I could be happy again. I *was* happy.

I heard a movement somewhere not far distant. How sound carries in the bush! Now I distinctly heard the galloping of horses' hoofs. I stood up and shaded my eyes.

I could see no one; so I sat down again and returned to my pleasant ruminating.

Yes, I was happy here. I believed that I was going to marry Stirling. I was young yet, being only eighteen. Perhaps on my nineteenth birthday he would ask me. I pictured us in the library receiving Lynx's congratulations. He would draw me into his arms and kiss me. 'Truly my daughter now,' he would say; and I would feel that happy glow within me. I, who had once been abandoned by my mother and had lost my father, would now be joyfully claimed by the Lynx as his daughter. These were dreams – but one has to be happy to dream pleasant dreams.

There were footsteps behind me. 'Good day, Miss Nora.'

I felt suddenly cold with dread for it was Jacob Jagger who stood behind me. He was almost upon me as I sprang to my feet and faced him. I was immediately aware of the silence all about me – the loneliness of the bush. In a flash I thought of the other occasion when he had stood close to me – but then Stirling and Adelaide were not far off.

'You!' I heard myself stutter.

'You don't look very pleased to see me. And to think I've come here specially to see you!'

'How did you know—'

'I make it my business to know what you're about, Miss Nora. I saw you come this way and I said to myself, "Oh, it's Kerry's Creek this morning."'

'But why should you follow me?'

'You'll know in good time. Don't let's rush this.'

'I don't like your manner, Mr Jagger.'

'I haven't liked yours for a long time.'

'Then there can be no point in our continuing this conversation.' I turned away, but he had caught my arm and a feeling of terror came to me because I was immediately aware of his strength.

'I have to disagree again, Miss Nora.' He brought his fat, leering face close to mine. 'And this time,' he went on, 'I call the tune.'

'You have forgotten that I may report this when I return.'

'You are not going to return just yet.'

'I fail to understand.'

'You are not as calm as you pretend to be, and I think you do understand a great deal.'

'You are being very offensive, Mr Jagger. I don't like you. I never have. Now please stand aside. I am ready to go back. Goodbye.'

He laughed most unpleasantly. I couldn't hide the fact that I was terrified. A picture of Mary flashed into my mind. Had it happened so with her?

'You are not going yet, Miss Nora. I've something to say to you. I haven't got a wife. I wouldn't mind having one . . . if she were you.'

'You're talking nonsense.'

'You call an honourable proposal of marriage nonsense?'

'Yes, when it comes from you. So now stand aside. If you attempt to detain me any longer you will regret it.'

He was still laughing at me; there was a tinge of purple in his face now; his mouth was ugly.

'So *you* manage affairs now at Whiteladies, do you? By God, Miss Nora, it's time someone taught you a lesson.'

'I learn my own lessons, thank you.'

'Well, this morning you're going to learn another. I've set my heart on you and nothing on earth is going to stop me having my way.'

I wrenched myself away from him and started to run to the tree where my horse was tethered. I hadn't a chance. He was beside me; then he stood in front of me barring my way.

'Will you leave me, Mr Jagger?' I panted.

'No, Miss Nora, I will not.'

'Then . . .'

He waited, mocking, his face working with a terrifying passion which I recognized as lust. This was what I had feared since I had first met him. He was a man who could not restrain his desires; he had no doubt found it easy to impose his will on some of the poor serving girls; and Lynx had made it easy for him. But he should realize that I was not as one of those, and that if he dared touch me he would have to answer to Lynx . . . and Stirling.

I tried to push past him but he caught me. His thick horrible lips were on my face. I caught at his hair and pulled it; but I was no match for him. I fought desperately; I kicked him and he gave a yell of pain, and for a moment I was free, running wildly towards my horse, but he was upon me. I fell and he fell with me. I called loudly: 'Lynx! Stirling! Oh, help me.'

I heard two kookaburras laughing as though at my plight. My breath was coming in great sobs; he was angry, hating me, I sensed, but his hatred did not lessen his desire, rather did it increase it.

He muttered that I was a she-devil. I wanted to shout back at him, to tell him I loathed him, that he would have to kill me before I gave in – but I needed my breath for the fight.

I was no weakling but he was a strong man. I heard myself praying: 'Oh God, help me. Oh, Lynx . . . Lynx . . .'

Then I heard a voice, *his* voice, and for a second I thought I had imagined it.

The voice said distinctly: 'Jagger! Get up, Jagger.'

I was lying on the ground, panting, my riding jacket torn, my hair hanging about my face. I pushed it aside with a trembling hand and I saw him, more magnificent than he had ever seemed before, seated on a big white horse. His eyes were like blue ice.

He commanded: 'Stand there, Jagger.'

Jagger obeyed as if in a trance. Then I saw Lynx raise his hand and I heard a deafening report.

Jagger was lying on the ground and there was blood.

Time appeared to stop. It seemed a very long time, but it could only have been for a few seconds that I lay there where Jagger had thrown me and Lynx remained still on his horse, the smoking pistol in his hand, calm, all-powerful.

'Don't look, Nora,' he said. 'Get up. Get on your horse.'

I obeyed him as Jagger had done. I felt weak and could scarcely breathe, but I went to my horse and mounted. Lynx was beside me and quietly we rode back to Whiteladies.

Adelaide looked after me. I was so shocked that I just lay in my bed and said nothing. She brought me brandy and eggs in milk. I turned away and she insisted, 'My father said you were to have these.' So I took them and felt better.

She gave me something to drink that evening and I did not wake until morning. Then I felt different. I had slept without dreams which I did not think I should ever do again, for I believed that that scene with all its terror and its blood was imprinted on my mind for ever. I kept going over it: the moment when I had turned and seen Jagger and had known I was at his mercy alone in the bush; the mounting horror; and that other moment when Lynx had come as though in answer to my call; I could never forget the sight of him on the white horse and the cold way in which he raised his gun and fired.

'There was blood,' I kept saying to myself. 'On the bushes . . . on the ground . . . blood everywhere. Lynx has killed Jagger.' No, I assured myself, he has only wounded him. Even he would not dare kill a man. That would make him a murderer.

But I knew in my heart that Lynx had killed Jagger and it was because of what he had attempted to do to me.

There was a hush over the house. A coffin had been made for Jagger. It was taken into the biggest of the sheds which had been built to store the bales of wool.

Every man in the Lynx Empire – the property, the house, the mine – was summoned to the shed. It was a strange, quiet day, a day of mourning, and yet more than that. It was as though some solemn ritual was about to take place.

Adelaide would say nothing. Stirling came and held me in his arms. 'You're all right, Nora,' he said. 'Don't ever worry again. Don't ever think of it. You're safe now.'

Adelaide came to my room. 'Nora, my father wants you to go to the wool shed. Don't be afraid. You'll feel better. I'm going with you and so is Stirling.'

'I'm not afraid.'

'My father says you are not to be afraid again. He says we should have taken better care of you.'

'You were always warning me that I might get lost in the bush.'

'But I should have thought of this.'

'There was Mary,' I reminded her. 'But you did not believe her.'

'Oh, Nora. My poor Nora. But it is over and it will never happen again. My father is determined on that.'

I shall never forget the scene in the wool shed. This was my first introduction to the law of the land. Justice had been done to Jagger. That was the verdict. Any man finding his daughter in the position I was in had every right to kill her would-be ravisher.

The coffin stood on trestles at one end of the barn; at either end of it burned two candles. Lynx was standing beside it and the candle light caught the blue fire of his eyes.

When he saw me he held out his hand and I went and stood beside him. Adelaide and Stirling remained at the door. The shed was full of men – some of whom I knew, others whom I had never seen.

Lynx took my hand and looking at the coffin said: 'In this box lies what is left of Jacob Jagger. This is my daughter. If any man here lays a hand on her he will receive the same punishment as Jacob Jagger. It will be well for every man among you to remember this. I am, as you will know, a man who keeps his word.'

Then still keeping my hand in his he walked out of the shed with me; and Adelaide and Stirling fell in behind us.

Chapter Five

NOTHING could be quite the same afterwards. I had become subdued. I seemed to have grown up suddenly. People looked at me a little furtively – the men of the estate as though they were afraid of me. I suppose every time they saw me they thought of Jacob Jagger.

Stirling managed the property until a new manager could be found in James Madder, who soon learned of the fate of his predecessor and scarcely looked my way. Adelaide tried to make everything normal by behaving as though nothing had happened; but you cannot be involved in sudden death and pretend it is an everyday occurrence.

For some days I had no desire to ride again. I stayed near Adelaide; there was something safe about her. She understood my feelings and was constantly inviting me to help in some task or other. Together we produced new curtains for some of the rooms; we made up materials for ourselves and altered old dresses. There was always some project afoot. Then, of course, there was the garden.

Sometimes I would wake in the night calling for help. I could not always remember the dreams, but they were concerned with that nightmare day.

'Stirling,' I said to him one day when we rode together, 'you never speak of that day. Isn't it better to talk of it?'

'Isn't it best to forget?'

'Do you think that it is something one can ever forget?'

'You have to try. In time it will fade. You'll see.'

'It was like something one dreams of, too bad for reality.'

'I should have been there. I should have guessed. Jagger was a swine. I should have known. Did you have any idea?'

'I was always afraid of him.'

'You didn't say so.'

'I didn't think it was important until that moment when I was alone.'

'Don't speak of it.'

'But we *are* speaking of it. And then your father came. He was there on his white horse and suddenly . . . there was blood. I thought . . .'

'There, I told you not to speak of it. Listen, Nora, it's over. My father was there. He came in time, and that is the end of Jagger. He can never attempt to harm you again.'

'He was killed. Your father *killed* a man because of me.'

'It was the right thing to do. It was the only thing to do.'

'He could have dismissed him. He could have sent him away. Why didn't he do that?'

'My father did what was right. Life is different out here, Nora. Not long ago in England a man could be hanged for stealing a sheep. Out here any man has a right to kill another who attacks his womenfolk.'

'But it was murder.'

'It was justice.'

'But does no one question it?'

'There has been an enquiry. My father would not let you go because he thought it would be too upsetting for you. He would not have you questioned, he said. He told what had happened; he had killed Jagger, he said, and he would do the same to any man who acted as Jagger did towards his daughters. Jagger was notorious. It was well known what kind of man he was. The women of the community would have been in danger if my father's action was not accepted as the right one, and the verdict was that justice had been administered. And that is the truth. You must stop thinking about it.'

They wanted me to live as I had before; to ride when I wished, to stop thinking of that terrible day.

My relationship with Lynx had undergone a subtle change. Even he was ill at ease. I went to him to play my usual game of chess but it was some weeks before I could bring myself to talk of the matter.

I said to him then: 'What brought you to Kerry's Creek on that day.'

He frowned in concentration. 'I'm not entirely sure. I seemed to sense that something was wrong. Do you remember when we talked of that trip you made to Melbourne when you camped on the way? We mentioned Jagger and something in your manner told me that you were afraid of the man. I guessed for what reason . . . knowing Jagger. That morning I felt uneasy because I saw him riding in the direction of Kerry's Creek. I wondered where he was going and I asked at the stables which direction you had taken that morning. No one was sure but they said that it would either be Martha's Mound, Dog Hill or Kerry's Creek. I decided to ride out after Jagger. That was how it happened.'

'What good fortune for me! And it cost Jagger his life.'

Lynx's eyes glittered. 'You don't think I would have let him live.'

'He forced Mary,' I said. 'She told me so.'

He shrugged his shoulders.

'You can be indifferent to that?' I said.

'That is beside the point. Do you think I could ever be indifferent to anything that happened to you?'

There was silence in the library broken only by the ticking of the clock. It was a beautiful French clock which he had had sent out from London.

He said abruptly: 'Let us have our game of chess.'

So we played the strangest game we had ever played. Hitherto he had always beaten me, but that night I turned the tables. I took his queen and a strange feeling of triumph ran through me as I seized her.

'There,' he said rather mockingly, 'now you have me . . . provided you play with care.'

So we played on and an hour passed and every time I was ready to make the winning move he baulked me.

But finally I had him cornered.

'Checkmate!' I cried.

He sat back, his elbows on the table surveying the board as if in dismay, and I knew suddenly that he had allowed me to win, just as my father had.

'You let it happen,' I accused.

'Do you think I would?' he asked.

I looked into those extraordinary eyes and did not know the answer.

Yes, indeed our relationship had changed.

Jessica came into Adelaide's sitting-room where I was sewing. She sat down, looking at me.

'Did you come to hear the book?' I asked. 'Adelaide is busy today so I am not reading.'

'Then we can talk,' said Jessica. 'You affect him deeply,' she went on.

I knew to whom she referred, of course, but I pretended not to.

'He changes when you're there. I've never seen him like that with anyone else . . . except perhaps Stirling.'

'Stirling is his son,' I reminded her. 'And he looks upon me as his daughter'

'Not for Adelaide,' she said with a look of triumph. 'She is his daughter. But he was never like that with Adelaide. He killed a man for you.'

I shivered. 'People don't talk of it.'

'Things are still there even if you don't talk of them.'

'Plants stay green through constant watering,' I said. 'So do memories. If they are pleasant, that's good; if not, it's folly.'

'You're clever with your talk,' she said. 'It may be that. I wonder whether she was clever.'

'Who?'

'That woman in England. Poor Maybella wasn't clever. I was cleverer than she was. If I had been the daughter instead of the niece, I should have been the one. I daresay I would've had sons. I wasn't such a weakling as Maybella. He preferred me.' A cunning look came into her eyes. 'He wasn't faithful to her, you know. There were others besides me.'

Then I understood her feelings for Lynx. He had been her lover. She had loved him and now she hated him; and she had allowed this double-edged emotion to govern her life. She had loved Maybella and been deeply jealous of her; she had alternately loved and hated Maybella's husband. Life had suddenly become very complicated. The present was deeply overshadowed by the past. What had happened in Whiteladies all those years ago haunted the present just as what had happened later at Rosella did.

'Be careful,' warned Jessica. 'It's not good to come too near to him. He's unlucky for women.'

'He's my guardian. He has taken good care of me. Why should I be afraid?'

'Poor Maybella! She was the most unhappy woman I knew. He despised her; he ignored her; if he had quarrelled with her it would have been better for her. But to be nothing to him, nothing but the means of getting a son. That wounded her; if she had not died in childbed, she would've died of a broken heart. I wouldn't die of that. I wasn't so weak. I just let my hatred grow and loved to plague him. For he is plagued by my presence here. I see it in his eyes when he looks at me. He would like me out of the way, but he can't send me away, can he? "Jessie shall always have a home." My uncle said it; Maybella said it. He couldn't flout the dead, could he? But he's a man who would flout the devil. He pretends he doesn't care that I'm here, that it makes no difference one way or the other. I'm just nothing . . . nothing in his eyes. But I think he'd like to see the back of me.'

'Whatever took place years ago is best forgotten when no good can be done by remembering.'

She narrowed her eyes and gazed intently at me. 'He didn't kill Jagger for attempted rape. He didn't care about Mary, did he? But this was you. He's killed a man for *you*. That's why I say Beware.'

I put down my sewing. 'Jessica,' I said, 'it is good for you to be concerned for me, but I can look after myself, you know.'

'You couldn't, could you, at Kerry's Creek? So he came to look after you and he killed a man for you.'

I wanted to get away. She was bringing up the memory of that day in all its horror; and superimposed on it was a picture of Lynx arriving at Rosella Creek, with festering sores on his wrists where the manacles had cut into him, and bitter hatred in his heart and a determination that he would one day take his revenge. So he took the short cut to freedom. He married Maybella and Jessica was angry because she had felt that magnetic power and had been his mistress for a time; and had she been the daughter of the house instead of the owner's niece, she would have been Lynx's wife instead of Maybella.

I understood Jessica's bitterness as I never had before. Yes, my experiences had made me grow up.

The winter came and the grazing lands were under water. This was an anxious time for the property, but James Madder proved to be a skilful manager. With the help of Stirling, who was spending more and more time on the property, he worked so hard in these difficult circumstances that the damage proved to be less than had been feared. The winds were bitingly cold and we had snow; it was hard to believe that at Christmas time the heat had been almost unendurable.

There was an explosion in the mine and several men were hurt. Stirling and his father rode over and spent two weeks there. The mine was of greater concern to Lynx than the property. I wondered what disaster would strike next.

I was very sad one morning when the body of a boy was brought in. He had been found by some of the men who worked on the property. Evidently lost in the bush, he had died of exposure and starvation. It was a further blow to discover that the boy was Jemmy, the stowaway. He must have been trying to find the road back to us, though what his reception would have been had he arrived, he must have known. Perhaps he believed that I would have intervened to plead for him and that I should have succeeded again as I had on the ship.

'He was lost in the bush, poor boy,' said Adelaide. 'It can so easily happen, as I told you. One takes the wrong path without knowing and goes on and on through country which looks exactly the same as that a hundred miles back.'

'Poor Jemmy, if only he'd stayed here.'

'If only they would all stay here, but this lust for gold is the irresistible temptation.'

We buried poor Jemmy; and I wondered what he had run away from in London that had been so terrible. Poor Jemmy, who had come to Australia to be buried in the bush.

Lynx talked to me of the boy and there was a return of the old mockery.

'Your efforts were of no avail,' he said.

'How that boy suffered in his short life!'

'He brought on his own suffering. He could have stayed here and lived. But he chose to go after gold . . . and he died.'

'He's not the first one,' I said bitterly.

'Save your sympathy. He was a runner, that boy. He would never have settled anywhere; and if he had ever found gold he would have squandered his fortune and then been in dire straits again.'

'How can you know?'

'I know men and women – and that is Jemmy. So don't grieve for him. You did your best. You brought him here. He left us of his own free will. He chose the way he would go. No one is to blame but himself.'

'Some people have hard decisions to make.'

'We all do. Let's forget him. Come, let us play on your board with your beautiful pieces.'

'I believe you regret letting me win them from you.'

'I do . . . deeply.'

'I don't believe they were ever yours.'

'Then I did right to let you have them back.' He laughed ruefully. 'What matters it, Nora, that they are yours or mine? We still play with them. They are here in this house and this house is your home.' He had brought the board and set it between us. He stood for a moment looking across at me. 'I hope, Nora, that it will always be.'

It was indeed true. Our relationship had changed. There was a new gentleness in his manner.

The winter was over and September had come. I spent a good deal of time out of doors, often in the garden. The bush was lovely in springtime when the wild flowers were in bloom; and I had taken to going out riding alone again. I felt safer than I ever had before. At least that terrible affair had done that for me. Everyone for miles round had heard of it and they knew what would happen to any man who dared molest me. They would have to answer to Lynx.

It was a bright and beautiful morning when I rode out. The crows were cawing overhead and the inevitable kookaburras were laughing at the scene; the lovely galahs and rosellas flew back and forth and I feasted my eyes on the wild flowers – reds and blues, pinks and mauves. In a week or so they would be magnificent – so pleasant to the eye after the winter scene, and even in summer there were few blossoms except those of the flowering gums.

I was glad to be here and alive; I had learned to enjoy again the solitude of my rides. During them I could think of the two men who were rarely out of my thoughts. I did not understand my feelings entirely. I loved Stirling, but I was not sure whether I was in love with him. My feelings for Lynx were difficult to define. I admired him; I was to some extent in awe of him. I enjoyed as much as anything else in the world to cross swords with him; I loved to see his eyes flash with appreciation when I said something which amused him.

I said aloud: 'I'm happy.'

And I was. What had gone before did not matter. The

future lay bright before me; I only had to move towards it – and it contained both Stirling and Lynx.

I was in a strange mood that morning. I had always avoided the spot where my father had been killed; but I had a sudden desire to go there. I was not going to brood on the past; I would ignore the shadows it cast. I would accept the fact that life was different here, it was cheaper and death could come suddenly, more suddenly than at home. Men lost their way in the bush and died, or they were shot for disobeying the moral code laid down by the people. This was the nature of things and one did not brood.

My father had died. I had lost the one I had loved beyond all others . . . then. But now my life had changed and there was another . . . others, perhaps I should say. I had a father to replace the one I had lost; he was entirely different and I was not sure of my feelings for him, but that he was important to me there was no doubt. And there was Stirling – my dearest Stirling – named after one of the rivers of this country, a tribute to Australia from one of its unwilling sons because here he had found a way of life which was tolerable for a man of his spirit. I did not believe he could live in quite the same way in England. I remembered an occasion when I had mentioned this to him and he had replied: 'Some men can, Nora. It depends. A man can rule his village if he is its squire. He lives in a big house; he controls the lives of all those around him; that is how it was with Sir Henry Dorian.'

I had replied that it was a sad thing when people could not be content with their lot. They might have a great deal but they hankered after what they fancied they had missed. Did he think he could have more power, or whatever it was he craved, in his English village than here in his Lynx Empire?

He had laughed at me; he knew what he wanted; he had fashioned a dream, I told him, and if he ever realized it it might well be that the reality was different from the dream.

How we talked and how reluctant I always was to leave him!

I had come to the clearing – that spot where my father had been shot. The sheer beauty of it was breathtaking. It looked different from when I had last seen it; the multi-coloured wild flowers had transformed it; the ghost gums rose high, majestic and imperious, indifferent to what happened so far below them. Here was the path along which the dray would have come. The bushrangers would have been hiding in the grove of wattles. I must not think of it, or if I did I must remember that it was in the past, and mourning could do no good, and that because it had happened I had a new father. And I had Stirling to love and cherish me – perhaps for ever.

I was thirsty and wondered whether the water in the creek was drinkable. I dismounted, tied up Queen Anne and walked over to the creek. The water was silvery in the sunlight as it trickled down from the high plateau. There were deep gullies on the side of the hills; here and there I saw the granite rock, the slate and what looked like quartz.

I cupped my hands and caught the water as it tumbled down the side of the plateau. It was not drinkable, I decided; it was muddy and as it trickled through my fingers it left a sediment.

I stared. I could not believe it. The sediment was like yellow dust.

I had begun to tremble. I looked up at the plateau. I stared at the trickling water. I held out my hands again and caught it as it fell. There was the same yellow sediment.

Could it be? I had heard such talk of it. Was this possible? Gold! Could it fall into one's hands when one was not searching for it?

I looked up again at the plateau. The sides were steep; the water trickling over could be conveying the message.

'There is gold up here.' But if that was so, why had no one discovered it? The answer to that was: Because someone has to for the first time.

I remembered stories of how shepherds minding their sheep had come across gold in the fields, and a humble shepherd had become a rich man. It had happened more than once.

I stood uncertainly. Then I heard the kookaburras laughing.

It was ironical, if this should be true, that I who hated gold should be the one to find it.

But wait, I cautioned myself. Had I found it? Had I become touched by that madness which gold seemed to bring? I was trembling with excitement. Perhaps it was not gold at all. What did I know of it? It was just some sort of dust which had been coloured by the rocks above me.

I thought of my father's pursuing the back-aching work of cradling and panning for months, the hardships he must have suffered before throwing in his lot with Lynx. I pictured his searching wildly for the precious metal. Could it be possible that I, without thinking, had meant to drink from a stream and had found instead of water, gold!

Then I was certain, for on the bank of the creek lay a small shining piece of metal about the size of a nutmeg. I bent down and picked it up. It was yellow gold.

I don't know how long I stood looking at the nugget. The impulse came to me to throw it away, to ride back and say nothing of what I had found. Something told me that if I took it back it would lead to disaster. I imagined the excitement there would be in the house. Surely if I had discovered it so easily there must be a great deal very near at hand. It had killed my father; it had done something to Lynx. I thought of the Lambs who had gone in search of it, and poor Jemmy. I thought of men dying of phthisis. All for gold.

I looked up at the tall ghost gums as though asking them to decide for me. Their leaves moved slightly in the breeze, aloof, indifferent to the fortunes of men. They had stood there perhaps for hundreds of years. They would have seen the convicts come, the gold rush start; and the days before it had all happened when the country was peopled only by the dark men.

There was no answer up there.

Could I find gold and not tell? How could I face Lynx in the library and keep the secret?

I put the nugget into my pocket and rode back to Little Whiteladies.

I went straight to the library. Lynx was there alone. He stood up when he saw me. 'Nora,' he cried. 'What's happened?'

I did not speak. I merely drew the nugget from my pocket and held it out to him in the palm of my hand.

He took it gingerly; he stared at it; I saw the quick colour flame into his face. His eyes were like blue flames. He was on fire with excitement.

'By God,' he exclaimed. 'Where did you get this?'

'At the creek where my father was shot. I held out my hands to get a drink of water from the stream coming from the plateau. It left a deposit in my hands, a yellow dust. I wasn't sure what it was. Then I stooped and found this.'

'You found it! Lying there on the bank of the creek!' He stared at the nugget which he had taken from my hand. 'It'll weigh all of twelve ounces. And you found this dust and this . . . Then it's there somewhere. It's there in quantities . . .' He laughed. 'And Nora found it. My girl, Nora!' He drew me to him and gave me a hug which was almost suffocating. I thought though: He is embracing gold, not me.

He released me; he was still laughing.

'I can't help it,' he said. 'All those years, all that toil and sweat, all that hope. And Nora goes out, thinks she would like a drink of water, and it falls into her hands!'

'It may be nothing much.'

'Nothing much! With the dust coming down in the water so that all you have to do is catch it. And the nugget lying there on the bank! And you say that may be nothing! You don't know gold country.' He was sober suddenly . . . 'Not a word to anybody . . . nobody at all. We're going out there at once. We'll take Stirling. And no one is to know where we're going. Nobody must guess what's there until I've made it mine.'

I caught his excitement. Gold! And I had found it. I knew how men felt when they had their lucky strike. I was triumphant, exultant, excited as I had never been before – because I had found gold. Then I realized that this sensation did not come from merely finding gold; it was because I had found gold for Lynx.

The weeks slid by in a feverish tension which was all the more intense because the news must be kept secret. No one knew about the find but myself, Stirling and Lynx. No one must know. We lived in terror that anyone should find what I had found.

Lynx and Stirling had examined the terrain and were absolutely certain that it would give the richest yield ever found in Australia. On the top of the plateau, which was difficult to scale – and it must be for this reason that the gold field had never been discovered – was a fortune. It had been there, so close, for all these years. That was what amazed them. They regarded me as though I were some genius to have discovered it.

I myself was elated. *I* had brought them this luck. I had made all this possible. I was to be the maker of their fortunes.

I felt proud of myself and refused to listen to the inward warning which demanded to know what good had ever come from gold.

I was caught up in the excitement. I had forgotten all the unhappy events of the past. It was only the urgent need to keep our secret which made me able to hide my exhilaration.

There were conferences in the library in the evenings when I was supposed to be playing chess with Lynx. Stirling would come in to join us. Lynx was buying the land and it was not just the ground which held the plateau that he was negotiating for. That would have been to arouse suspicion. He wanted to extend his property, he said; he was thinking of getting more sheep. It was some time before he acquired the land but he and Stirling had already scaled the plateau and found what lay at its summit. There was no doubt that it was gold. They had already discovered rich alluvial deposits as they had expected from the gold dust which was carried down by the stream; but Lynx was certain that the real wealth lay beneath the surface.

'There'll be lodes of gold at various levels,' he explained. 'We'll take the shafts down as deep as need be.'

Stirling was impatient to get to work. So were we all. But for the time, until the golden plateau was Lynx's own, there must be secrecy.

There came the day when he called Stirling and me to the library. He solemnly opened a bottle of champagne and filled three glasses.

He said: 'The land is mine. We have our fortune. We are going to be rich as few people have ever been.'

He handed a glass, first to me then to Stirling before he took the other.

'First,' he said, 'to Nora, the founder of our fortunes.'

'It was sheer luck,' I insisted. 'I shouldn't have known what to do about it without you.'

'You did the right thing. You came straight to me.' His eyes were shining with love and approval; and I thought I had never been so happy in my life.

'Now,' he said, 'to us. The triumphant Triumvirate.'

Then we drank.

I said: 'Are you sure? After all, as yet you have not sunk your shafts.'

Lynx laughed. 'Nora, even now we have found a nugget which weighs two thousand ounces. I'll guarantee it is worth ten thousand pounds. And we have not yet begun. There's gold up there, gold to make any miner's dream come true. Don't fret. We're rich. After all these years you've led us to what we've been looking for.'

We put down our glasses. I held out my hands. Lynx took one, Stirling the other.

'This is what I wanted more than anything,' I said.

Lynx laughed at me. 'So you felt the gold fever, too, Nora.'

'No, not gold fever. I just want to give you both what you most want.'

Then Lynx held me in his arms again and said softly in a strangely tender voice: 'Nora, my girl Nora.' Then he let me go and handed me as it were to Stirling. Stirling's arms were round me and I clung to him.

'I believe I'm crying,' I said. 'People who don't cry when they're hurt will cry for happiness.'

Now the activity had started. Everyone was talking about the find. Lynx had struck gold – real gold. They had always known he would one day. It was just his luck. The ground yielded its alluvial gold – a fortune in itself. But Lynx was not stopping there. He was sinking deep shafts and he was going to get the gold which he knew lay in the quartz reefs below the ground. He closed the old worthless mine, all workers were transferred to the new one and more were engaged. The scene of my father's murder had changed completely. The birds had deserted the place; the sound of gunpowder explosions had frightened them away; steps had been cut in the earth to enable men to mount the plateau; drays were constantly passing along the road taking the gold to the bank in Melbourne. The place had been renamed. It was: Nora's Hill.

I saw less of Lynx and Stirling. They were always at the mine. A place had been built there so that they could sleep in some sort of comfort when they did not come home. The fortune was being accumulated. I was constantly hearing of nuggets that had been found. I remember the excitement when one over two feet long was discovered. It was mentioned in the Melbourne papers and reckoned to be worth twenty thousand pounds.

There was a kind of breathlessness everywhere, but for me the excitement had worn off. I was not as happy as I had been in the first flush of discovery.

A stranger came to the house and was closeted a long time with Lynx. Adelaide told me that he was her father's lawyer and that he was going to England on Lynx's business.

It was said that Lynx was now a millionaire. This was probably true, but he wasn't satisfied. I wondered if he ever would be.

Once I said to him: 'You are very rich now.'

He admitted it. 'You too, my dear. Don't forget you have your share in our good fortune. Didn't I say it was a triumvirate?'

'How rich?'

'Do you want figures?'

'No. They would mean little to me. But I believe it is rich enough.'

'What do you mean by that?'

'That now you might give up this feverish activity and leave others to work for you.'

'Other people never work for you as you work for yourself.'

'Does it matter? You have enough.'

'I'm going to get all the gold out of that mine, Nora.'

'You are insatiable . . . for gold.'

His eyes gleamed. 'No,' he said. 'I shall know when I have enough. I need to be very rich.'

'And then?'

'And then I shall do what I have always planned to do. I have waited a long time, but now I see the fulfilment in sight.'

He said no more then, but he alarmed me a little because there was a hardening of his lips and I knew that the thought of revenge was in his mind.

Revenge on the man who had had him sent away over thirty-five years ago! Did people harbour feelings of revenge for so long? A man like Lynx did, I knew. It worried me because I knew that there was no happiness to be found in revenge.

The months went by and Christmas had come once more. We had the usual celebrations in the English style: the hot meal in the burning heat of the day; the plum pudding steeped in brandy; the mock mistletoe. I remembered the last Christmas when the Lambs had come and been turned away. I wondered what had happened to them now and remembering the relentlessness of Lynx on that occasion I was apprehensive.

At the beginning of January, the lawyer came to the house and spent a long time with Lynx and Stirling. I was not admitted to these councils, but I noticed that afterwards there was a triumph in Lynx's eyes; and I guessed it had something to do with his dreams of revenge.

One evening he asked me to play a game of chess with him and when I went to him, the door to his studio was open and he called to me to come in.

'Come here, Nora,' he said; and when I went to him he put his hands over my eyes; then he turned me round until I was facing the wall. Then he took his hands away and said: 'Look!'

It was a portrait of me in my riding habit, my top hat slightly to one side, my eyes wide and the colour in my cheeks.

'All my own work,' he said.

'When did you do it?'

'Is that your first question? I show you a portrait of yourself and all you say is "when?"'

'But I did not sit for it.'

'Did you think that was necessary? I know every contour of your face, every fleeting expression.'

'But you have been so busy.'

'I have still had time to think of you. Tell me, do you like it?'

'Isn't it rather flattering?'

'It's as I see you.'

'I'm glad I look like that to you. I don't to myself.'

'That's how you are when you look at me.'

'But why is it hanging there?'

'It's a good place for it . . . the best in the room.'

'But the other picture was there.'

He nodded and I saw it then, with its face to the wall.

'But when you sat at your table you could look straight at it.'

'Now I look straight at this.'

'Is that what you want?'

'My dear Nora, you are not showing your usual good sense. Should I put it there if I didn't?'

I went close and examined it. It did flatter me. Had I ever looked so vital? Were my eyes so large and bright? Did I have that rosy flush? 'It's as I see you,' he had said.

'So now you will look at my picture instead,' I commented.

'Yes.'

'And Arabella . . .'

'She is dead.'

'I see. That's why you have hung me up there. When did you learn that she was dead?'

'Morfell – he's the lawyer who has been to England on business for me – went to Whiteladies. He came back with this news.'

'I see.'

'Do you, Nora?' he said; I believed he was on the verge of confidences, but he changed his mind and suggested we play our game of chess.

<hr/>

The heat was intense – far greater than last summer. The grass was dried up and there was anxiety about the sheep at the station; some of the workers died of the heat; but at Nora's Hill the gold yield continued to be spectacular.

I had seen so little of Stirling since the discovery that when I came face to face with him on the stairs one day I complained of this to him.

'We're busy at the mine, Nora.'

'You always are,' I retorted. 'Sometimes I wish I hadn't found it for you.'

He laughed. 'Where are you going now?'

'To sit in the summer-house.'

'I'll join you in five minutes.'

It was pleasant to be with him, I told him when he came.

'It's a mutual pleasure,' he answered.

'I wish there need not be this mad rush for more and more gold.'

'The mine has to be kept going.'

'Couldn't you sell out now that you have your fortune?'

'I think that's what my father will probably do, in due course.'

'Do you think he ever would? The more he gets the more he wants.'

Stirling rose at once in defence of his father, as I expected him to. I wouldn't have had it otherwise.

'He will know when the moment comes to stop. He's making us all rich, Nora.'

'Yet what have these riches brought us? Things are the same – except that I see less of you.'

'And that's a hardship?'

'The greatest hardship.'

He looked at me with a happy smile. I thought: He loves me. Why does he not say so? Now is the time. They have their gold; they can stop thinking of it. Let us give our minds to more important things.

'It's too much to hope,' I said, 'that you would share this feeling.'

'I told you when you came out here that you would receive frankness and be expected to give it. You know very well it's not too much to hope for.'

'Then I'm gratified. Only I must say you don't make much effort.'

'I'm constantly making efforts which are foiled.'

'Well, don't let's waste the little time we have for talking together in discussing lost causes. How rich is your father now and how rich does he want to be?'

'He has plans. He wants to see them fulfilled. That's how he looks at it.'

'He confides in you.'

'He always has.'

'And you know more than anyone what is in his mind.'

'I think I do. I believe he is going to England.'

'Going to England!' I had a picture of him on the lawns of Whiteladies. 'And we shall stay here?'

'I don't know what his plans are for us.'

'His plans? Should we make our own?'

He was staring ahead of him, a puzzled expression in his eyes. I thought: Lynx has said something to him. There is something I don't know.

I wanted him to tell me that our future was together. I wanted him to ask me to marry him at once. It was important. I had a feeling that there was a danger in delay. I loved Stirling. I wanted the future to be as I had so often imagined it. I knew exactly what I wanted – and I wanted it now. *Now!* I thought. We should go to Lynx and tell him. I would say it. 'Stirling and I are going to be married. I am going to belong here for the rest of my life.' And the three of us would go to his study and drink a glass of champagne as we had on that other occasion; and I would make them realize that this was a far more worthy object of celebration than that other. My happiness would be shared with Lynx as well as with Stirling. I would say to him: 'The three of us belong together.' I would make him give up his ideas of crazy revenge. So even when I was thinking of marriage with Stirling, it was Lynx who was uppermost in my mind.

Stirling was smiling at me and I was sure that he loved me. 'Now,' I wanted to say. 'Now is the time.'

But be said nothing. I knew that he wanted to tell me that he loved me but that something was restraining him.

And that moment passed.

It was a week later before I was alone with Lynx. The heat was more intense than ever. Even Adelaide felt it and rested in the afternoons. We longed for the nights but when they came they were so hot that it was impossible to sleep.

We had played our game and sat over the chess board on which my defeated king was held by a knight, a bishop and an aggravating little pawn.

I said: 'There is something afoot.'

'How would you like to go to England?' asked Lynx.

'Alone?'

'Certainly no: We should all go – you, myself and Stirling.'

'And Adelaide?'

'She would stay behind to hold the fort here – unless she wished to go, of course.'

'She is allowed free will?'

He laughed at me. 'The asperity of your tone tells me that you do not altogether relish the idea of visiting your native land.'

'For what purpose?'

'To complete a little business.'

'Revenge?'

'You could call it that.'

'You are very rich now.'

'Rich enough to do everything I have ever dreamed of . . . apart from one thing.'

'And what puts that out of your reach?'

'Time. Death.'

'Not even you are a match for such adversaries.'

'Not even I,' he admitted.

'Are you in the mood for confidences?'

'Are you in the mood to receive them?'

'Always . . . from you.'

He laughed with pleasure. 'My dear Nora, my *dearest* Nora, you have done a great deal for me.'

'I know. I discovered gold for you.'

'And perhaps more important . . . I hope more important . . . my youth.'

'That's a little enigmatic.'

'Perhaps one day you will understand.'

'One day? Why not this day?'

He was silent, raising one eyebrow in the familiar gesture
which used to intimidate.

'We'll see,' he said. He leaned back in his chair and
regarded me seriously. 'You know my lawyer has been to
England where he has completed certain business deals for
me. There has been a little buying, a little selling of certain
shares. But I'll not bore you with the details. This has put
me into a position with regard to certain people which gives
me a great deal of gratification.'

I said quickly: 'Does it concern Whiteladies?'

'You're a clever girl, Nora. Do you know that the only
way in which I was able to live through that most terrible
period of my life was by dreaming of myself at
Whiteladies . . . not a humble drawing-master but the owner.
I saw myself sitting at that table in the hall. You should see
that hall, Nora. It's grand. It's noble. The ceiling is carved
with the arms of the family; the family motto is engraved
there. *Service to Queen and Country*. Elizabeth was the
Queen referred to and the decorations are Tudor roses in
honour, of course, of the royal house which gave the family
its home after turning the pious white ladies out into the
countryside to starve or beg. The walls are panelled; the
great fireplace is of stone and there are seats carved out of
that stone on either side of it. There are suits of armour
there in which the men of the family lived up to their motto.
There is a dais at one end and a table on it. Kings and
queens have dined at that table. *I* wanted to dine at that
table. I made a vow, Nora. I was going to be master of

Whiteladies. I was going to take my revenge on the man who ruined my life. I knew there was one thing he cared for beyond all else . . . more than his wife or his daughter. Whiteladies! So I said: One day I will take it from him. I will marry his daughter and sit at that table where kings and queens have sat. I will look over that hall and say: "Whiteladies is mine."'

'But he's dead now. So is his daughter. And she was married, you told me. She married the fop whom you so despised.'

'I believed I would wipe away the difficulties.'

'But death and time defeated you, as you say. So what now?'

'I have sworn that Whiteladies shall be mine.'

'And you are going to England to take it.'

He smiled at me. 'You think I can't do it.'

'I can't see how you can if the owners won't let it go.'

'You will, Nora.'

'You are wrong. I know you are wrong. I know that revenge brings no happiness to anyone. You have your home here. You have people who admire you and care for you. Why can't you be content?'

His burning gaze was fixed on me. 'Does that include you, Nora?'

I answered him at once. 'You know it does.'

He leaned forward. 'Why, Nora, I could almost settle for that.'

'If you are wise, you will,' I said. 'You will drop this stupid notion of revenge. It was all very well when it was useful to get you through that unhappy period. Now it is of no use whatsoever and it is folly to continue with it.'

'You dare to scold me, Nora.'

'Yes, I do.'

'No one else does.'

'Then you should be thankful that there is at least one person in your life who is not afraid of you.'

'I am thankful for that.'

'Then why do you not rest here in your contentment?'

'Nora, all these years I have waited. I made a place for myself in this country. I was secure; I had my son; we worked together. I was a man of substance but I had made this solemn vow to myself. If you think I would give up the theme of my life you do not know me.'

'I know you well and I think that you are wrong. We grow up; we change. Because when we are young we set up goals, that does not mean we must continue to follow them when we have learned more wisdom.'

'But Whiteladies is a beautiful house, Nora. Wouldn't you like to live in such a house?'

I hesitated. 'I like this house.'

'You know this is an imitation – a poor copy. Come, admit it.'

'I do admit that the original Whiteladies is a fine old house.'

'And you would enjoy calling such a place your home?'

'Yes, if it were mine by right.'

'And wouldn't it be, if you had bought and paid for it?'

'I suppose so. But the family who had lived in it for generations would never sell it.'

'They might be forced to. We are only just beginning, Nora. My plans are in their infancy. They could not begin until I had made a vast fortune. Now, thanks to you, that is exactly what I have done. Did I tell you the whole story, Nora? Arabella married the man her father chose for her – a weakling, he was. His name was Hilary Cardew – *Sir* Hilary Cardew he would be when his father died. He could trace his family back to the Conqueror – even farther than the Dorians. He had a certain amount of money. The

Cardews' place was some ten miles from Whiteladies. The families had always been friends and young Hilary was meant for Arabella right from the start.'

'And when you went away she married him.'

'I didn't hear of this until years later, not until I was able to send someone over to find out.'

'Why didn't you go yourself?'

'I had vowed to myself that I would not set foot in England until I did so as a millionaire. Besides, I had married Maybella. I had a son and daughter of my own.'

'You might have been satisfied with that.'

'I am a man who always demands the ultimate satisfaction.'

'But doesn't one always have to compromise in life?'

'I don't.'

'But that is exactly what you have had to do.'

'Only with the idea of waiting for complete satisfaction. I always believed that if I had the money I needed I should get what I wanted. I wanted Whiteladies . . . and Arabella at that time.'

'But she had a husband and you had a wife.'

'My wife died with Stirling's birth. I thought I would go back and find Arabella unable to maintain the estate. In fact, had I had the money, that was something I might have arranged. Did I tell you that Sir Henry was a man who did not believe in other people's wasting their time? I gave Arabella a drawing lesson each day, but it was only a matter of two hours at the most. A resident drawing-master was an expense; therefore I acted also as Sir Henry's secretary. I had a flair for business and was soon managing his investments. So I knew exactly how he was placed. He had extravagant tastes; he was a connoisseur of wines; he drank rather to excess; he gambled. His financial status had become a little shaky even while I was there. That was why he wanted the Cardew marriage – to bolster up the family fortunes. But Sir James Cardew was another such as himself. I used to hear them discussing their business affairs. I wrote letters from my employer to Sir James and to his London brokers. I knew a good deal about the financial affairs of both families.'

'And you have found this of use.'

'Recently, yes.'

'Recently?'

'My man in London has been working for me. I have invested a great deal of money in London. I have become richer through this . . . and certain people have become poorer.'

I caught my breath. 'You mean that you have deliberately arranged this?'

He spread his hands. 'Let us say that it has happened. It may be that in order to maintain a certain standard of living it will be necessary for certain people to sell their property.'

'Lynx!' I cried, and indeed he looked like that creature now, the hatred glinting in his eyes, revealing the memory of the humiliation of years. 'You have deliberately impoverished these people?'

'You don't understand these matters, Nora. Never mind.'

'I believe that whatever you do they will never sell the house.'

'If they can't afford to keep it up they will be forced to.'

'I wouldn't,' I declared, 'if I were in their place. I'd think of something to keep it. I'd take paying guests; I'd work myself – particularly if I knew that someone was deliberately trying to take it from me.'

'You would, Nora. But other people are not you. You'll see.'

'They'll never sell. I just know it. I've been there. I've seen that girl.'

'There are more ways of selling than by making a cash bargain and handing over the property.'

'What ways?'

'You will see. One thing I know, Nora. I am going to see my son master of Whiteladies. My grandchildren are going to play on those lawns. They are going to be brought up in gracious surroundings. That is my plan and I am going to see that in this I am not disappointed.'

'And Stirling . . . he wants this?'

'My son knows what's in my mind. It has always been so. He more than anyone knows what I have suffered. I have seen him weep with anger when he looked at the scars on my wrists. I have seen him clench his fists and vow that the score must be settled. And when Whiteladies is mine, I shall be content. I shall be able to tell myself that everything that led to this was worthwhile.'

I was silent for a moment and he said my name softly. I looked up into his face and his gaze grew gentle. 'I want you to understand this,' he said. 'You belong to us now. We will strengthen that bond. You will grow even closer as the years pass. I had never thought that I could take anyone to my heart as I have taken you.'

'I know,' I told him. 'But I know too that you are wrong. This is revenge. You want to hurt people because long ago *you* were hurt. There is no happiness in revenge. I am certain your attitude is wrong. It can only bring unhappiness.'

'Wait until you see those gardens – those lawns with the grass like green velvet, well tended for hundreds of years. The fountains play over the statue of Hermes and water-lilies float on the water. The walled pond garden is a replica of the one at Hampton Court. On sunny days in that garden there is perfect peace. The peacocks strut over the lawns. I never saw such beauty, Nora.'

'But you will have to take this away from the people to whom it rightly belongs.'

'The people who took from me my freedom! The people

who reduced me to animal status, who all but killed me with their brutality.'

'But you escaped. You married Maybella and escaped.'

'Maybella was a fool.'

'So you used her to escape.'

'It was necessary.'

'You have not been a happy man,' I said. 'You have used people to get what you want. You have spent your life in search of revenge. It should have been spent in search of happiness.'

'You preach, Nora.'

'I say what I feel.'

He laughed suddenly, his eyebrow rising with that odd little quirk.

'Oh, Nora, what should I do without you?'

'I don't know and I suggest you don't put it to the test. Give up your plans. Stay here. Forget about your golden fortune, your cruel plans. Forget revenge and enjoy happiness.'

'I shall be happy. Never fear. And I shall get what I want. I want to talk to you, Nora . . . about the future.'

'Then promise me that future will be here.'

He shook his head. 'Whiteladies,' he said.

'It's wrong. I know it's wrong.'

'I shall have to convince you that it is absolutely right.'

'You wanted to talk to me about the future.'

'You are in too analytical a mood tonight. Tomorrow perhaps.'

We left it at that, but I was uneasy. I kept thinking of the lawn at Whiteladies and the girl and the older woman named Lucie. So the mother in the chair had been Lynx's Arabella and she was now dead. I wondered what had happened to the man she had married and if he were still alive. Then I thought of that awful moment in Kerry's Creek when Lynx's voice had thundered behind me. 'Stand up, Jagger!' And Jagger stood up to be shot dead.

Lynx never hesitated and death meant little to him. He could kill a man and not be haunted by what he had done. I thought of his marrying the poor ineffectual Maybella and insisting on her giving him a son. Was I beginning to understand Lynx? He gave his love to few but for those to whom he gave it he would kill. To be hated by Lynx would be terrifying; and to be loved by him could perhaps be too.

He loved Stirling. He loved me. He was going to have his way and we were all going to bow to his wishes. Every one of us . . . myself, Stirling and the people at Whiteladies. No, not all of us.

I won't be dominated, I told myself, even by Lynx.

The next day there was consternation throughout the district. The bush fires which were burning some thirty miles away were coming in our direction. When I awoke the acrid smell was everywhere and there was no escaping from it. From my window I could see the glow in the sky.

Adelaide was worried. 'It will be on our land,' she said. 'I do hope we're not going to lose anyone. Some of the shepherds' huts are out that way.'

'They'll manage to get away surely. They must be aware of its coming nearer to them.'

'You have no idea what a forest fire can be like, Nora. The trees explode because of the oil in them, and fresh fires break out all round.'

'Aren't precautions taken?'

She smiled again ruefully. 'All I can say is that you have no idea what it's like. I hope you never do.'

The atmosphere of the house had changed. Everyone was

solemn; the servants went about their work not speaking, and when they did it was to talk of the fires.

'They can be seen from Melbourne,' one of them said. 'They say this is one of the worst outbreaks for years.'

'Can't wonder at it – the weather we've been having. Did you hear the thunder last night? The lightning must have struck a grove of gums. That could've started it.'

The wind was fierce – high and hot coming from the north. Rumbles of angry thunder rolled across the sky. I went out into the garden. I couldn't bear the atmosphere indoors; yet outside it seemed worse. The glare in the sky had grown more angry and the hot wind carried on it that unmistakable smell.

The place seemed deserted. I wondered where everyone was. Lynx, I supposed, was at the mine. I doubted whether he would have any fears about that. I presumed the fire could pass over it without disturbing the lodes below although it would ruin the machinery and everything at ground level.

I went indoors and to the top of the house. I looked out. I could see dark clouds of smoke in the distance. I came down again and as I passed Jessica's door she called to me. She was lying on her bed, a cold compress on her forehead.

'That horrid smell!' she said. 'It gives me a headache. It reminds me of once at Rosella. We were ringed by fire. That was before *he* came. Uncle was terrified. He thought we should lose everything. Maybella wanted to run away but Uncle wouldn't let her. He said, Better stay where we were. Maybe we'd run into danger. That's how it is with these fires. You never know where they're going to spring up . . . and in a matter of seconds you're in a ring of fire.'

I didn't want to listen to her, so I left her. I went past Lynx's room knowing he was not there. I felt again the great desire to get out of doors, to ride as far as I could from that smoke cloud on the horizon, to get the smell of smoke and fire out of my nostrils.

I went down to the stables and saddled Queen Anne.

She seemed uneasy as though aware of the danger. I talked to her soothingly. 'We'll go for a ride out into the open air . . . where it's fresh and clean and we can escape from this horrid smell.'

I rode for a mile or so but I could still smell the smoke. I pulled up and looked behind me. If anything the smoke seemed nearer.

I urged the Queen to a gallop and off we went. I forgot the fire and thought about the things Lynx had said to me on the previous night in his study and I wondered whether his plans would ever come to anything.

Stirling and I would marry – in England perhaps. I remembered the old Norman church with its grey stone walls and the graveyard with its crazy-looking tombstones, some of which were propped up against the wall, presumably because no one knew exactly where they belonged. Lynx would give me away in my white wedding-dress and Stirling and I would come down the aisle together while Lynx looked on with pride and gratification. The gates with their white ornamentations would be flung open and our carriage would go through, along the drive to the mansion.

And what of Minta? Poor Minta, she would be living in one of the cottages. Perhaps she would serve teas to the local people with little home-made cakes and scones with jam or honey. Lucie would help her.

How absurdly my mind ran on. I was like my father. I did not believe that Minta and her father – if he was still alive – would ever allow the house to be sold, no matter with what prizes the richest of golden millionaires tempted them.

I pulled up and looked over my shoulder. The smoke was

thick now. I couldn't understand it. I was riding away and yet I seemed to be coming nearer.

I realized that I had been foolish to leave the house. But I was not lost. I knew the direction which I had taken. Yet I could not understand why I seemed to be coming nearer to the smoke. The bush was deceptive. So much of it looked alike. But I had been to this spot before and I knew where I was.

Then suddenly I heard an echo. 'Cooee. Nora.'

I called back. It was Stirling.

I curved my hands about my mouth and shouted. 'Stirling . . . here.'

I saw him then. He came galloping towards me. He was white with anger.

'Nora . . . you fool!' he shouted.

'What do you mean?' I retorted sharply.

'Don't you know better than to come out like this? My God, you could be caught. Don't you understand what's happening? Haven't you learned anything?'

'I know there's a fire somewhere.'

'A fire somewhere! Do you know that miles of bushland are ablaze. And you ride blithely out. Come on.'

He turned his horse and meekly I followed.

'You were mad,' he threw over his shoulder.

'I rode away from it. Is that madness?'

'How do you know where it will be next? In seconds you can be surrounded.'

'I should have remembered the warnings. Well, I know now.'

'You don't. You don't understand a thing about it. Can't you imagine? No. You have to risk your life before you understand. If they hadn't seen you leave the stables I wouldn't have known which direction you'd taken.'

'Am I always to be watched?' I remembered with horror

that other occasion when I had been seen riding out and followed. I went on irritably: 'Oh, do stop nagging, Stirling. I rode out. That's that. Here I am. All's well and I'll promise not to do it again.'

His mouth was sternly set and he looked remarkably like his father. We rode on in silence for some miles, then I said: 'Stirling, I didn't know you could be so sullen. I'm learning. I must say if there's one thing I dislike—'

I stopped because it was clear that he wasn't listening. I had begun to cough and wherever I turned I saw clouds of smoke.

He pulled up suddenly.

'Which way?' I asked.

'I wish I knew.'

'Well, aren't we going home?'

'I don't know. It looks as though we may be cut off.'

'Cut off by . . .'

'By fire, you idiot!'

'How dare you talk to me like that!'

'Oh God,' he groaned. 'Listen, Nora. We're in danger. We're surrounded. Can't you see that? I just don't know which road to take. Any could be disaster.'

I thought he was exaggerating to teach me a lesson until there was a loud explosion close to us and a grove of gum trees suddenly burst into flame.

'Come on,' said Stirling, and we galloped in the opposite direction. But it was not long before he pulled up again. We were approaching a heavy pall of smoke.

'We're cut off,' said Stirling tersely.

I stood there looking at him fearfully. I felt the smoke in my eyes and nostrils. I was frightened, yet comforted by Stirling's presence. I had a childish notion that if he were there everything would turn out right.

'I wonder,' he was saying to himself. 'There may be time. Come on. Keep close to me. It's worth a try.'

We galloped towards the smoke and suddenly he turned off the bush track and we rode into the bushes.

I heard him mutter: 'It's a chance. The only one. We'll try it.'

A creek containing a very little water lay ahead of us. He dismounted, tore off his coat and asked for mine. I gave it to him. 'We'll have to leave the horses,' he said. 'There's nothing we can do for them. It's just possible they'll find their way.'

'Oh no, Stirling . . .'

'Do as I say. There's just a faint chance of saving ourselves.'

He soaked our coats in the creek and ran to where a grey rock protruded above the creek. In front of this was a small aperture. Stirling thrust the wet coats into my hands and kneeling frantically began to dig out the dirt with his hands. It was loose and soon he had made a hole. He signed me to crawl through it and by this time I knew I must obey unquestioningly.

To my surprise I was in a cave about the size of a small room. Almost immediately Stirling was beside me. He stuffed the wet coats into the aperture. We were in complete darkness.

'Nora.' His voice sounded hoarse with tension.

'I'm here, Stirling.'

Groping he found me and held me against him.

'Better lie down,' he said.

Lying there, we were silent for a second or so, then he said: 'Nora, we'll be lucky if we come out of here alive.'

I was silent, thinking: It's my fault. I was careless. What a lot I have to learn about this country where sudden death seems constantly to be lying in wait for the foolish and unwary.

'Oh Nora,' he said, 'to think you came out here . . . to my country . . . for this.'

'It was my fault, Stirling.'

'No.' His voice was tender. 'It could happen anywhere. Who knows what's happening at the house even now. The fire was getting closer.'

'But Lynx will know . . .' And then I thought of the house being surrounded by fire; I pictured its coming close, so fierce, so all-consuming that not even Lynx could hold it off. The thought of Lynx in danger made me forget that which threatened us. But I told myself he would know what to do. No harm could come to him. I realized then that I had learned to think of him as Stirling did: he was godlike, immortal.

Stirling was whispering: 'I remembered this cave. An aboriginal family lived here. They came to work for my father, and the boy who was my age used to bring me here. It's got to save us, Nora. It's our only chance.'

I knew he was trying to comfort me. Outside, the fire was encircling us; soon the ground above us would be ablaze. How could we possibly survive?

In the darkness he seemed to read my thoughts.

'There is a chance,' he said. 'A slight one; but a chance.'

For the first time in my life I was close to death. I felt lightheaded, as though I were dreaming. Stirling and I would lie forever underground and this would be our grave, though no one would know it. I reached for his hand; it was as though it were on fire. Everything seemed on fire for the heat was becoming unbearable.

His lips were close to my ear. 'The fire will be right above us presently,' he said.

'Soon, Stirling,' I answered. 'Very soon.'

We could hear the roar and crackle, the sudden explosion; and the acrid smell was creeping into the cave.

'If we can keep the smoke out,' said Stirling and paused. 'If not . . .' He didn't go on. There was no need to. I understood. Our chances of survival were very small.

'Stirling,' I said, 'I'm not sorry I came out here.'

He did not answer. We had moved away from each other because the heat was so great but we kept our fingers entwined. There was comfort for me in this; I wondered if he felt it too.

'Nora.' His voice seemed to come to me from a long way off. 'We loved you, Nora. It was different when you came.'

I was loved as I had been when my father was alive. But what did it matter now? He used the past tense as though we were already dead. It can't be long now, I thought. I couldn't die . . . not now that I had found my home and people to love me. I felt angry with fate which had made me suffer and then when I could be happy again to say: This is the end. Now your life is over.

'No,' I said, but so quietly that he did not hear me.

There was nothing we could do but lie still waiting. I had never known there could be heat like this. I was gasping for my breath.

'It's all right, Nora.' I heard a voice – or at least I believed I did. 'Nora, my love, we'll be all right. Lynx would never forgive us if we died.'

It's true, I thought. We have to live . . . for Lynx.

I can't describe the ever-increasing heat. I believe I must have been only half-conscious because there were times during that fearful period when I was not sure where I was. I lay perfectly still, having no strength to move, for in that terrific heat all energy had left me. There was only one thing to do: to lie and wait either for death to come or for life to deliver us.

But all through this terrifying experience I was aware of Stirling close to me; and I knew that he loved me. I was certain that if only I could escape from death the future of which I had dreamed would be mine.

I think I was in a sort of trance, dreaming of a future in

which we were all there – the three of us, because I had learned now, if I had not known it before, that Lynx must always have a place in my life – on the lawns of a beautiful old house. My children – mine and Stirling's – were there with their grandfather: a new Lynx, a man who had come to terms with life, who had thrown aside a dream of revenge for one of contentment.

'Nora! Nora!' Stirling's face was close to mine. There was a little light in the cave. The first thing I noticed was the smoke. I started to cough.

'Oh God, Nora, I thought you were dead.'

'What's happened?' I asked.

'The wind's changed. There's a light drizzle falling. The fires will be damped down and they'll stop spreading. We're going to get out of here.' He pulled me to my feet and I staggered, falling against him.

He laughed with relief because I was alive, I knew; he held me against him briefly but with an inexpressible tenderness.

'We're going to get out of here,' he repeated.

My limbs were stiff; I could scarcely move. The temperature in the cave must have been about a hundred and forty degrees, although it was much cooler than it had been.

'You follow me,' he said; and I watched him crawl through the hole. Soon he had dragged me out to stand beside him. It was like walking into an oven; then I held up my face and let the light drizzle fall on it.

A fearful sight met our eyes. The remains of trees were black and smouldering. There was a quietness everywhere and it occurred to me that one subconsciously heard the birds and insects of the bush without being aware of them. Several trees were still burning.

I turned to Stirling who was scarcely recognizable. His face was black; so were his clothes. I knew I presented a similar spectacle.

He put his arms about me and held me close to him. We just stood there, too emotional to speak.

Then I said: 'We're alive, Stirling. We have a future after all.'

He released me and took my hands, looking searchingly into my face. I saw the joy rather than the grime of smoke and dirt, and for a few seconds I was happy.

He said: 'I wonder what's been happening at home.' A terrible fear had taken possession of us both, for although we had just been assuring ourselves that we had a future, neither of us could be happy if it did not contain one other.

'We must get back quickly,' I said. 'We must find out.'

The countryside was devastated and it was difficult to know which scarred and mutilated road to take. I should have been lost without Stirling. He had known this country all his life but even he was bewildered. We were both driven by an urgent desire to know what had happened at Little Whiteladies. Stirling loved me; I was sure of that. I believed that our future lay together; but if we had lost Lynx should we ever be happy again?

I don't know how we made that journey. We were weak from shock; we must have been at least six hours in the cave. Our limbs were cramped, our throats parched; we struggled on and there was only one thought in our minds: Lynx.

Night fell and Stirling said we must rest awhile; we lay down but our minds could not rest.

'How far?' I whispered.

'It can't be more than six or seven miles.'

'Stirling, why don't we go?'

'We must rest for a while.'

'I'd rather go.'

'So would I, but you'd collapse before we got there.'

'Oh Stirling,' I cried. 'You do take care of me.'

'Always, Nora,' he answered.

'For ever,' I murmured; but even then I was thinking of Lynx.

❦

I slept at last and felt it was a measure of Stirling's love for me that he let me sleep. I was apologetic when I awoke. It seemed so wrong to sleep when we did not know what had happened to Lynx.

We trudged on. We did not speak of Lynx but each knew that the other thought of him exclusively, and that our failure to mention him was deliberate.

Never shall I forget the last hour of that walk, and finally discovering the land untouched by fire. There stood the house, impregnable, as though defying destruction to come near.

Stirling gave a shout when we saw it. He started to run pulling me with him.

'Home!' he cried. 'We're home.'

Adelaide came running out of the house. She was crying with relief. She took us into her arms and would not let us go. I noticed, as one does on such occasions, how the smoke and grime blackened her gown.

'The master must be told!' she cried. 'Jenny! Mary! They are here. They are home.'

We stumbled into the house.

'*He* . . . is safe,' said Stirling.

'But nearly demented,' replied Adelaide. 'He has been searching for you. He has called in everyone.'

'Look after Nora,' said Stirling.

'He's safe?' I murmured. 'He's truly safe?'

They had put me to bed by the time he came. Only when I was between the cool sheets did I realize how exhausted I was. I lay luxuriating in my bed, having drunk the broth which Adelaide had brought. 'Not too much at first,' she had said. And I lay there thinking of the heat and terror of the dark cave, and Stirling's saying that he would look after me for ever. Lynx was safe. There would be the three of us.

I knew that he was in the house. One sensed his presence. I knew too that he would come to me first . . . even before he went to Stirling. Oh no, surely not. Stirling was his beloved son. I was only the adopted daughter.

He was at the door, his eyes shining with the greatest joy I ever saw in any eyes. Why was everything he did so much more intense than what others did?

'Nora,' he said. 'My Nora.'

Then he came to the bedside and held me in his arms. He put his face close to mine. 'My girl Nora,' he kept saying. I said: 'I'm back Lynx. Dear, dearest Lynx, we're back together.'

For a few moments he did not speak. He just held me.

Then he said: 'I thought I'd lost you. I was mad with fury. But you're back. My girl Nora.'

'I was terrified of what might be happening to you.'

He laughed loud and confident. As if anything could happen to him!

'All the time,' I told him, 'we thought of you, we talked of you.'

He laughed again and all he said was: 'My girl Nora!'

Later he went to see Stirling.

Chapter Six

WE recovered quickly from the shock of our experience. I think the fact that we came back to the house and found it untouched and the family safe made us so happy that we threw off the ill effects of our terrifying adventure with the greatest possible speed.

The damage had been tremendous. The property had suffered most; many sheep had been lost and two of the shepherds had died in their cottages. The mine had escaped.

Adelaide insisted that I stay in bed for two days. I was cosseted and fed with special invalid's food which she said was necessary. Stirling refused to be treated like an invalid; but I enjoyed it.

Jessica came to see me. She sat by my bed looking intently at me. 'I've never seen him so affected as he was,' she said. 'He sent parties out looking for you, risking their lives.'

I smiled happily. I just wanted to lie and think about the future.

When I was up he asked me to come to his library after dinner.

'A game of chess,' I said, remembering that during those hours of semi-consciousness in the cave I had imagined myself in his study, the chessmen between us.

He did not join us for dinner and when I went up he was waiting for me. He looked excited and yet restrained; and different from when I had seen him last.

'You are a little pale, Nora,' he said. 'But you'll recover in a few days' time. You're young and healthy and resilient.'

He poured out two glasses of port wine and brought them over to me. I noticed the eyes of the lynx on his finger glitter as he handed me one.

'To us, Nora. Your safe delivery to me. What should I have done if you had not come back?'

'We have Stirling to thank. Stirling is wonderful.'

'Stirling is wonderful,' he repeated.

I started to talk about the cave, although he had heard it all before. I had suddenly become nervous and felt the need to go on talking.

'My dear,' he said, 'you are back, and you have made me the happiest of men when I should have been the most wretched.'

My hands had started to tremble which, I told myself, was due to the recent shock. But it was not that. A sudden idea had come to me but I would not accept it.

He took my glass from me. 'You're not afraid, Nora. It's not like you to be afraid.'

'Of what should I be afraid?' I demanded.

'There speaks my girl Nora. You have nothing to fear ever . . . because I shall be here to look after you.'

'That's a comforting thought,' I said, with a touch of my old lightness.

'Then be comforted, my dearest. I believe you know what has been in my mind for some time. You have been aware of the change you have wrought in me.'

'I!'

'You have brought my youth back to me. After all, I am not an old man. Do I appear old to you?'

'To me you have always appeared to be immortal. Even before I knew you Stirling spoke of you as though you were Zeus.'

He smiled, but he did not wish to discuss Stirling.

'You are old for your years, my dear,' he said. 'You are no foolish child. Nor were you ever. You had to fend for yourself and I'm glad of it. I never thought this would happen to me. Yes indeed, you have given me back my youth, Nora.'

'How?'

'By being yourself. By coming here among us and showing me that my life lies before me . . . not behind me.'

'I'm glad of that. So you have dropped this stupid notion of revenge.'

He laughed again. He was laughing a good deal tonight.

'You bully me, Nora. You always did. You must go on doing so when we are married. I like it, my darling.'

'When I am married to –' In that second I had told myself I had not heard him correctly. He meant when Stirling and I were married; but in my heart I knew that he was not thinking of Stirling.

'To me,' he said. 'You don't think I'd let you go to anyone else?' There was a fierceness in his eyes which both frightened and delighted me. As ever in his presence I was unsure of my feelings for him.

He gripped me by the shoulders and drew me towards him. 'Never again, my love, will you wander off into a forest fire. I have you back, and I'll keep you with me for as long as we both shall live.'

'Lynx!' I stammered and he gripped me more tightly.

'That ridiculous name!' he said.

'But I always think of you as Lynx,' I said foolishly, as though that mattered when there was so much of importance to think and talk about.

'A predatory animal,' he said. 'It fits. Oh God, Nora, I thought I'd die when you didn't come back. I was fit to throw myself into that raging furnace, and it was only the certain knowledge within me that you'd come back that restrained me. I need you, Nora, as I have never needed anyone. I see that now. What's wrong, my dear?'

'Marriage,' I said. 'I hadn't thought of marriage.'

'What else?'

'You talked of being my father.'

'That was in the beginning. But it changed, didn't it? I'll be everything to you, Nora. You'll lack nothing.'

'I'm bewildered.'

'Not you, Nora. You knew it, really. I was aware of it. You knew it and were glad.'

'But . . .'

'There are no buts. I have planned it all.'

'Without consulting me?'

He laughed. 'A touch of the old Nora. Yes, without consulting you in so many words, but it was clear to us both, wasn't it? When we sat there playing our chess, when I let you win the set. You didn't think you could have done that if I hadn't allowed you to, do you?'

I said slowly: 'And Jagger?'

His eyes narrowed. His emotions frightened and yet in some strange way thrilled me. There was a violent hatred on his face.

'Jagger!' he cried. 'Yes, by God, Jagger!'

'You killed him. You killed a man.'

'My love, he had to die. I could never have looked at him again without wanting to murder him. I would have killed him with my own hands some time. At least I let him die quickly.'

'Oh, Lynx,' I said weakly, 'you frighten me.'

'I frighten *you*! When I love you! And I've never loved anyone as I love you. Arabella! What a fantasy! It was my pride that suffered there. I wanted Whiteladies. I wanted to live in that house with my wife and children. And I'm going to, Nora.'

'You go too fast,' I said.

'My imperious Nora!' he retorted with a smile. 'Would you have me go slowly? We are going to Whiteladies, you and I; and you shall sit at the table on the dais where kings and queens have sat; and the nursery at the top of the house where poor simple Arabella learned her ABC will be for our children.'

'I have not yet said that I agree.'

'My darling, you will not be allowed to do anything else.'

'If I refuse.'

'You won't.'

'What does . . . Stirling say? Have you told him?'

'He knows something of my plans.'

'He knows that you are asking me to marry you?'

'He knows. Adelaide knows. They have guessed at my feelings for you for some time past.'

'And Stirling . . . he thinks it is a good idea?'

'Of course. He realizes the strength of my feelings for you.'

'And that means that he will wish it too.'

'He has been a good son. He has always been eager for my happiness.'

'I see.'

'So it is only for my imperious Nora to say that she loves me, which I know she does.'

'You are adopting that irritating habit of speaking of me as though I'm not here as you did when you tried to demoralize me on my arrival.'

He laughed delightedly. 'Cruel of me. And foolish really because it never succeeded for a moment, did it? We'll announce to the family that the ceremony is to take place. You know I'm not a man for wasting time.'

'I will not be hurried into anything. I like to make my own decisions.'

'So you shall, for I see that you are as eager for this ceremony to take place as I am.'

'You take too much for granted. I was not prepared for this, I do assure you. I thought of you as my father . . .'

'I will make a better husband than a father, you see.'

I held him off. I said: 'I want time . . . *time*. I shall say nothing until I have thought about this.'

'Tonight I am going to announce to them our imminent marriage.'

'Not yet,' I protested and then wondered why I had put it that way, as though it would come in due course. Marry Lynx! It was a bewildering and exciting project. What had my feelings for him been – something beyond that of an adopted daughter towards a father – and yet there was Stirling.

Stirling! He knew of this and accepted it. I would live under this roof with Stirling and I should be married to Lynx. It was an incongruous situation, but it was what Lynx had been planning.

I turned away but he was at the door before me, barring my way. His eyes were brilliant with a passion which alarmed me as I had been alarmed when I stood face to face with Jagger; and yet at the same time I had no desire to run away from him.

He took my chin in his hands and lifted my face to his. 'You are afraid,' he said, 'afraid of what you have not yet experienced. You have discoveries to make, Nora. We'll make them together. You have nothing to fear, my darling.'

His face was close to me, those gleaming jungle eyes alight with a passion of which I could only guess.

I held him off. 'No,' I said. 'Not yet. I must go away. I must think. I *insist*. If you announced anything I should deny it. I will not be forced.'

He dropped his hands.

'You are afraid of me. Oh God, Nora, is that true?'

'Why will you harp on fear? It is not fear. I object to being told whom I shall marry and when the ceremony will take place before I have been consulted. If this marriage took place it would have to be understood that I am not a puppet to be moved this way and that, nor should I be expected to bow down and worship my husband as though he were one of the gods stepped down from Olympus.'

'Oh Nora, you delight me. So my darling wants time to think. She wants to make her own decisions. My only wish is to give her everything in the world she asks for. This is a small thing compared with the gifts I shall shower on her.'

'The first thing I ask is that you stop that ridiculous habit. It infuriates me.'

We were laughing again – back for a moment to the old relationship.

'Now,' I said, 'I will leave you. I will go to my room and when I have decided I will tell you.'

He dropped the hands which had imprisoned me. As I turned he caught me and I felt his lips on my neck. I wanted both to stay and to escape; and as ever, I did not understand my feelings.

I went to my room and closed the door. I stood against it pressing my cool palms to my burning cheeks.

You knew it, I accused myself, and you refused to see it. You had made up your mind that you would marry Stirling. It had all seemed so right and natural. But I love Stirling, I protested.

Yes, you love Stirling. *And* Lynx.

I could think of no one but Lynx. He filled my mind as he seemed to dominate every room in which he stood. He was exciting; he was magnificent; he was more than human.

I tried to be calm. Marry Lynx! Be with him day and night! I was so inexperienced of life. I had so much to learn of men and marriage; and Lynx would be my instructor. I was aghast at the thought and yet completely obsessed by it. I love *Stirling*, I kept telling myself. It was always Stirling, ever since we stood on the deck of the *Carron Star* together. Yes, but at that time I had not met Lynx.

Yet having met Lynx my feelings towards Stirling had not changed. I remembered that terrible night when we had lain in the cave together and had known that we might never come out alive; and when we had emerged and had known that after all we had a future, it had been like an unspoken declaration of love.

Yet even in the cave Lynx had been constantly in my thoughts – in both our thoughts.

If I married Lynx I should be Stirling's stepmother. Stepmother to the man I had thought of marrying! It was incongruous. Suppose I talked to Stirling? Suppose he told me he loved me? We should have to go away. We could not marry and live under the same roof as Lynx, now that he had declared his passionate need of me.

But when I thought of life without Lynx I was filled with dismay. It would be flat and dull. With Stirling? Yes, perhaps even with him. But Lynx would never allow us to go away. That thought comforted me. I remembered vividly the sight of him on his white horse, the gun in his hands. A murderer! He said he would do the same to any man who laid hands on me. And Stirling?

I was caught up in the whirlwind of my own emotion. I did not know what I should do.

I must see Stirling.

I spent a sleepless night and was up early. I saw Stirling at breakfast and told him I must speak to him soon and alone.

We took our horses and rode out into the bush.

Before we had covered a mile, I said to him: 'Stirling, your father has asked me to marry him.'

'Yes,' he said, his face impassive.

'It surprised me.'

'Did it?'

'He talked to *you* about it?'

'It came out in his plans for going to England.'

So Stirling had indeed known about it for some time. Before the fire. Then I had misunderstood everything. To him I was only a sister. I had made this mistake of believing that our relationship went deeper than that. I had misunderstood everything – Stirling as much as Lynx.

'I see,' I said blankly.

There was silence. His face betrayed nothing. I felt disappointed, deflated. How stupid I had been!

'If I married your father I should be your stepmother,' I said with a foolish little laugh.

'Well?'

'That seems very odd.'

'Why?'

'You're older than I am.'

'It wouldn't be the first time someone had a young stepmother.'

'Stirling, what do you think of it?'

'My father would be happier than he has ever been in his life. And you know how fond of you we have grown. You're already one of us. This will . . .'

I waited breathlessly for him to continue. He shrugged his shoulders.

'It will bring you closer than ever,' he finished.

Again I felt that maze of bewilderment. What did I want? Stirling to break down, to tell me that he could not endure to see me married to another man – even his own father? Did I want him to plan our escape?

I did not know. I think part of me clung to the old dream of myself and Stirling going through the years together, our children climbing on to their grandfather's knee, venerating him, adoring him, as we all did. It was the old conventional dream. But how could Lynx play the background figure in any story?

I started to gallop and immediately heard Stirling's horse thudding behind me. He doesn't care, I thought. He's glad because it's what his father wants. Stirling has no will of his own; his only will is that of his father. He had been fond of me, yes – but as his sister.

So now I knew what I should do. Stirling had made the decision for me. But was that true? Should I ever have been able to tell Lynx that I could not marry him because I loved his son?

I love them both, I thought in desperation. How strange it should be that with the younger man I envisaged the peaceful and conventional life, and with the other – old enough to be my father – the adventure.

When we arrived back at the house Lynx must have seen us for one of the servants came down at once to say that he wished to see me in the library.

It was like a command, I thought with a faint but indulgent exasperation. But while his arrogance irked me I wanted it.

I deliberately delayed and he was impatient.

'How long you took,' he complained.

'I stopped to comb my hair and wash my hands before entering the royal presence.'

'Didn't you know that I expect immediate obedience?'

'I knew you expected it, but things don't always happen as one expects.'

He laughed as he did so readily now. In fact I seemed constantly to amuse him. But perhaps it was the laughter of triumph for he knew that I was going to succumb to his wishes. I think I had known it right from the start . . . in spite of Stirling.

'You are more self-assured this morning than you were last night.'

'I was a little taken by surprise then.'

'And now you have had an opportunity to consider . . .'

'My good fortune?'

'*Our* good fortune,' he amended. 'But you need not go on. I know your answer.'

'You were so sure of it from the beginning that you didn't really think it necessary to ask me.'

'I know what is best for you.'

'Do you also know what is best for yourself?'

'You are best for me and I for you. It's as simple as that. You had a good ride with Stirling?' He looked at me steadily. 'He is delighted. My family knows that my marriage with you is what I desire more than anything in the world. Therefore they are happy that it should take place.'

I held out my hands to him and he grasped them eagerly. 'I am a member of that family,' I said, 'so I suppose I must fall into line.'

I saw the triumph in his eyes as I was caught up in his embrace.

'I shall disappoint you,' I said.

'Impossible.'

'You will find me too young and stupid.'

'I shall find you as I always have – enchanting.'

'You will be impatient with me.'

'And you will be imperious with me.'

'I think it is somehow incongruous.'

'Nonsense. You love me.'

'Is it *lèse-majesté* to love the gods of Olympus as one would an ordinary mortal? Shouldn't one adore merely.'

'That will do for a start,' he said.

There was a ceremonial dinner that evening and every place at the table was filled. I sat beside him. He was benign; his eyes shone rather than glinted. I had never seen him look as he did then and I was elated because I was responsible for it.

He laughed a great deal; he was tolerant with everyone; and at the end of the meal he made the announcement. He and I were shortly to be married – very shortly, he added. This was a great occasion and everyone was to drink the health of his bride-to-be. They stood and lifted their glasses. There were men at the table who had been present at that scene in the wool shed after the shooting of Jacob Jagger. There was Adelaide looking flushed and delighted because at last her father was happy; there was Jessica, her lips pursed, a gloomy Cassandra; and there was Stirling, his face betraying nothing of that which I half hoped to see.

I thought about them as I lay in bed that night – and particularly did I think of Stirling. I tried to look back on everything that had happened between us and ask myself how I could have misconstrued his feelings for me. If he had given me some sign that he loved me . . . but what should I have done? Somehow I knew that I could never have refused Lynx. He would not have allowed it. Nor did I wish him to. He loved me a thousand times more than Stirling ever could. He was capable of deeper, more searing emotions. I should be honoured to have won the love of a man like Lynx. My life would be frightening sometimes perhaps, but exciting.

I could not sleep, and as I lay in the darkness trying to visualize the future, I heard a movement outside my room. My heart started to flutter uncomfortably as the door moved silently open. I thought for a moment: It's the ghost of dead Maybella come to warn me.

I might have known that it would be Jessica. Indeed, she looked like a ghost, with her nightcap tied over her hair which was in steel curlers, her long white flannel nightdress flowing about her and the candle in her hand.

She had come to warn me, I knew.

'Are you asleep?' she asked.

'No. You'll catch cold wandering about the house like that.'

She shook her head. 'I wanted to speak to you.'

'Sit down and wrap the quilt about you.'

She shook her head. She preferred to stand by the bed holding the candle high. It made her look more like a prophetess of doom than she could have done sitting down.

'So it's come to this. You're going to be his wife,' she said. 'There'll be nothing but disaster.'

'Why should there be?'

'I know it. Maybella came to me in a dream last night. She said: "Stop it, Jessie. Save that poor young girl."'

'So Maybella had pre-knowledge of the announcement?'

'The dead know these things. Particularly when they don't rest.'

'Doesn't Maybella?'

Jessica shook her head. 'She comes back to haunt him. After all, he murdered her.'

'I don't think you should say that. She died having her son.'

'It killed her and he knew it would.'

I sighed. 'It's your way of looking at things. I daresay she wanted a son too.'

'And what do you think is going to happen to you?'

'I shall do my best to be a good wife and mistress of the house.'

'He thinks of no one but himself.'

'It's a common enough human failing.'

'Clever talk! It makes him laugh. Maybella had none of that. Then there was that woman in England.'

'You should go back to bed,' I said gently. 'You really are going to catch cold if you don't.'

'Maybella wants me to warn you. He's cruel and selfish. He's lustful and he'll not be faithful to you. He never has been to any woman, so do you think he will be to you?'

'There's always a time to begin.'

'You're making fun of me.'

'I'm not, Jessica. But I don't think you understand. All that has happened is in the past. He and I are going to start a new life together. I will do everything in my power to make it a success and so will he.'

'He'll use you as he uses everyone. What of Stirling, eh?'

'What of Stirling?' I asked.

'Well, there was a time when we thought it would be you two . . . it would have been natural and it was what he wanted.'

'What who wanted?'

'Stirling, of course. We all said it. A match between you two young ones . . . that's what we all wanted . . . that's what we all expected. And what happens? You take his fancy, so he says: "No, Stirling, you stand aside for me and if you don't, well, I'll shoot you as I shot that man Jagger".'

'How dare you say such a thing of him!'

'It's what Maybella thinks. He's told Stirling: "Hands off.

I want the girl." So Stirling says: "Yes, Papa," as he has been brought up to do. It's always been the same. He must have his way and the devil take the rest.'

I said: 'I'm tired, Jessica. Nothing you can say will alter my plans. I have promised to marry him and I will keep my promise. We all change. He has changed. He is not the same man who came to Rosella.'

'He *is* the same man. I don't forget. He stood there in the yard and the marks were on his wrists – and nothing was the same afterwards. He comes into your life. He takes you up and when he's finished with you, you are thrown aside. He hasn't altered. It happened to Maybella. It will happen to you.'

'I don't intend to be thrown aside.'

'Nor did she. She thought he was wonderful at first. So will you. He can play the lover all right . . . even when it's all pretence as it was with Maybella. She used to go about in a dream during those first months. She used to say to me: "Ah, Jessie, if only I could explain to you!" I knew . . . even then.'

'It's over, Jessica. There's no point in recalling it.'

'But I want you to know. Maybella wants you to know. Well, I've done my duty.' She came close to the bed; the candle tipped and I thought she would set light to the bedclothes. 'Run away,' she said. 'Run away while there's still time. Run away with Stirling.'

'You're mad,' I said angrily.

She shook her head. Then she said sadly: 'In some ways perhaps, but it's his fault. I see this as clear as daylight. You could persuade Stirling. Try. He'd go. I'm sure of it. *Don't* let that man win every time. Go away, the two of you.' She gave a hollow chuckle. 'Wouldn't I like to see his face when he was told you'd gone!'

'Your candle grease is dripping on the quilt.'

She straightened the candle and held it under her face. In the dim light it looked like a skull. I thought: So would Maybella have looked if she had indeed come back from the dead to warn me.

'I've done my duty,' she said. 'If you won't listen, that's your look-out.'

'Go back to bed now, Jessica,' I answered. 'And do be careful with that candle.'

She went to the door and looked back at me.

'It's you that should be careful,' she said.

'Thank you for coming,' I replied, for I was sorry for her, she who had loved Lynx – she had betrayed that much to me – she who had no doubt yearned for a return of that old relationship which she believed she had once shared with him.

'I've done what Maybella wanted,' she muttered. 'I can do no more.'

Then she left me to lie there, thinking of what she had said, and wondering afresh about the strange man with whom I was committed to spend the rest of my life, and to ask myself what the future held. And there at the back of my mind was Stirling, who loved me perhaps but who loved Lynx better.

And I?

The terrible indecision had come back. I love them both, I thought. My life would be incomplete without either of them. But they had made the decision for me. If Stirling had indeed ever thought of asking me to marry him, he was now handing me over to his father who was waiting with urgent hands and the predatory gleam in his eyes.

Adelaide made my wedding-dress. It was white silk with many frills and flounces and trimmed with rows of lace.

'It will be useful, too, when you go to England,' she said.

To England! I thought. We shall not go to England. I am going to persuade him to stay here, to drop that ridiculous notion of taking Whiteladies away from those pleasant people whom Stirling and I had glimpsed so fleetingly.

'For there,' went on Adelaide, 'you will live in the grand manner. Just think, you will dress for dinner every evening. You will wear velvet. I think green would become you most, Nora. You will sit at one end of the table, and my father, at the other, will be very proud of you.'

'I would rather be here.'

'But there you will live in a befitting style.'

'This style suits me.'

'You forget that your husband will be one of the richest men in England.'

'Who wants to remember that? If one has security that is enough.'

'Not for him, Nora, and his will will be yours when you are married.'

'I don't take that view of marriage. It's a partnership. I shall not change my personality because I'm married.'

'A husband naturally moulds his wife's way of thinking.'

'I shall want to come to my own conclusions.'

Adelaide's indulgent smile irritated me so I burst out: 'I don't think he expects me to change. He became interested in me in the first place because I refused to treat him as though he were some sort of oracle, as the rest of you did.'

Adelaide did not reply but I could see that she clung to her views.

She and I made a trip to Melbourne. How very respectfully I was treated at The Lynx!

I grimaced and said to Adelaide: 'I am the elect. It makes me feel holy in a way.'

We shopped lavishly and bought silks and velvets which Adelaide would make up for me. I bought a sable muff and a sable-trimmed mulberry-coloured velvet cloak.

'Don't buy too much here,' advised Adelaide. 'You'll find everything so much more fashionable in England.'

I didn't stress the fact that I was going to make a stand against going back to England.

We arrived back at Little Whiteladies with the goods we had bought.

'I've been in a torment of anxiety,' said Lynx. 'I'll not let you go away without me again.' I was gratified and exultant because I meant so much to him.

Adelaide busied herself at once in her sewing-room. I spent a great deal of time with her – not that I cared much for sewing but at times I wanted to shut myself away from both Stirling and Lynx, so that I might contemplate this step I was taking. There in the sewing-room where the conversation was only desultory and concerned the width of a sleeve or the best way to cut a skirt, I could think of the future and try to come to some decision before I made the final step.

It was nonsense, of course. As if I could draw back! As if I wanted to! But I wished I could understand myself. If it had not been for Stirling . . . I might as well say: If it had not been for Lynx . . .

No, I told myself a hundred times a day: It is Lynx. It is the strong man I need. And yet I could not get Stirling out of my thoughts.

The time was passing rapidly and I often felt that I wanted to ride out alone into the bush and that there by some miracle I should find the answer which would set my fears at rest. But Lynx had given orders that I was not to ride out alone.

I discovered this one morning when I went to the stables and asked the groom to saddle my horse. He told me then that they had all been warned that I should never go riding alone. I was insistent and the groom was alarmed. I was thinking to myself: No, Lynx. I won't be put into a cage. And you will have to know this.

I saddled the horse myself and rode out. I had not gone very far when I heard a horse galloping behind me and I saw the white horse on which he had ridden that day when he had shot Jacob Jagger.

I dug in my spurs but I could not outdistance him. He was soon beside me, his eyes gleaming with excitement. He looked like a satyr, I thought.

'Nora!' he roared.

I pulled up level with him and said: 'Why the excitement?'

'I gave orders that you were not to go riding alone.'

'And if I want to?'

'You won't because you know it is against my wishes.'

'And you won't tell your grooms to do their feeble best to stop me because you know that would be against mine.'

'You know why I don't want you to go out riding alone.'

'Because you think I'm incompetent and fit only for . . . what was that horse's name, Blundell?'

'I suffer torments of fear when you are out of my sight. I visualize all sorts of dangers which you might meet in the bush. It is for this reason that I don't want you to go out alone.'

'Do you mean that for the rest of my life I must always be accompanied wherever I go like some young girl with her duenna?'

'It will be different when we leave here. So it is only for a short while.'

'You know,' I said slowly, 'that I don't want to leave here.'

'That's because you don't realize how much more gracious living can be.'

'I have seen the grand house of which you are thinking.' I turned to him. 'You say you love me.'

'With all my heart.'

'Then you will want to please me.'

'It shall be the object of my life.'

'Then we shall stay here and I shall spend the rest of my days riding with the chosen duenna of the moment whenever I sally forth. But perhaps in due course you will consider that I have grown a little less stupid . . . or perhaps you will not care so much if I did run into some of those dangers you visualize.'

'What nonsense are you talking?'

'It is by no means nonsense. Husbands grow tired of wives. It's not an unusual state of affairs.'

'We shall not be as other husbands and wives.'

'I wonder what it will be like . . . married to a god!'

'You will discover . . . most joyfully.'

He had moved his horse very close to mine. Some galahs were imitating the songs of others. In the distance a brown kangaroo loped over the dry grass. I was very much aware of the sounds and smells of the bush since I had emerged from the cave into the blackened silence.

I said: 'I have grown fond of this country.'

'You will love England more.'

'I want to stay here.'

'It will make no difference to you where we are for we shall be together.'

'Then if it makes no difference why need we go?'

'We have to go. One day you will understand. I will make you see it as I do. Then you will see how inevitable it was. When you are there, where I am going to take you,

214

you will thank me for it, for the rest of your life. Yes, you will.'

'I know what you are thinking. It is that house. It can't be yours. It doesn't belong to you. Your desire to live there is unworthy of you.'

'You have too high an opinion of me, Nora.'

'But you insist on everyone's sharing that high opinion.'

'You're trying to make a saint of me. I'd never be that.'

'Lynx,' I began, 'dear Lynx . . .'

He smiled and said: 'When you speak to me like that I want to lay the earth at your feet.'

'Then, dear Lynx, just give me this. Give me all your plans for revenge and I'll destroy them and it will be as though they never existed.'

'But they do exist, Nora.'

'They can be destroyed.'

'It's too late. They are too strong. They are part of me.'

'You said you loved me.'

'Do you doubt it?'

'If one loves, one wants to give the loved one what he or she most desires.'

'That is why you, who love me, will not ask the impossible. Listen, my love. We are going to England – you, I and Stirling. In time Adelaide will join us. I came to this country unwillingly.'

'It has been good to you.'

He conceded this. 'Yes,' he agreed. 'I served my sentence here. I have my reward . . . gold and Nora.'

'In that order of precedence?'

'You are more important to me than all the gold in Australia.'

'I am glad to hear you confirm this because I was by no means sure. But there is one thing which is more important to you than either of these two contestants for your affections. That is revenge.'

All he would say was: 'One day you will understand.'

As we rode back together he made me promise not to ride out alone again. I reminded him that I had done it often in the past. He then recalled the occasion when I had been thrown from my horse; then there was the affair of Jacob Jagger and the fire.

My riding had improved, I pointed out. I would not take a mount that I couldn't manage. No man would dare molest me now and if there was a fire in the neighbourhood I would be aware of it and certainly would not venture out. What other dangers were there?

'I'm afraid of losing you,' he said. 'That you have come to me is like a miracle. Everything I ever wanted in life is mine, or about to become mine. I don't trust life. I can't help experiencing this fear that just as I am about to grasp complete contentment it may be snatched from me.'

'*You* have such thoughts! You surprise me.'

'I'm serious.'

'Well, I'll make this concession. I won't ride out alone until after the wedding. Then you will have to begin persuading me again.'

'It's a bargain,' he said; and we rode home indulging in that lighthearted banter which seemed to amuse him and which no one had dared exchange with me before.

My wedding-day was almost upon us, and preparations were going on apace. The smell of pies and pastries permeated the house. Adelaide made an enormous wedding-cake of six tiers. But I could not rid myself of the idea that something tremendous was about to happen to prevent the wedding's taking place. There would be some impediment. How absurd! As if anything could prevent happening that on which Lynx had set his heart. Is this a premonition? I asked myself.

Stirling avoided me although I had gone out of my way to seek his company. If only he would say something; that he was as pleased as Adelaide at my approaching marriage hurt me deeply. And yet was he?

We were to be married in the little church about a quarter of a mile from the house; the ceremonial reception would follow in the house itself. In the wardrobe in my room hung my wedding-dress. Adelaide had put it there the previous day; she had only just finished it. It was a work of art, I told her. I was to wear a veil and orange blossom which we had bought in Melbourne.

On the night before my marriage my doubts and fears returned a hundredfold. I suppose, I reassured myself, many brides feel like this on their wedding eves. I kept thinking of Jessica's grim warning. Would he change towards me as he had towards Arabella and Maybella? He had compared his love for me with that he had felt for Arabella as a forest fire compared with a candle flame. A forest fire – an unfortunate comparison! And how absurd to brood on Jessica's grim warnings. She was half mad anyway.

I pictured his eyes tomorrow when he saw me and I wanted to put on my wedding-dress to reassure myself that I looked beautiful. I slipped it on marvelling at the work which had gone into it. What a devoted daughter Adelaide was! And now I should be her stepmother – stepmother to Adelaide and Stirling!

I put the veil over my face and adjusted the orange blossom. The effect was delightful. 'All brides are beautiful,' I said aloud.

'Yes,' I answered myself, 'but you really are, dressed like this.'

'It's only the dress and the veil. It hides your face just enough. Will he think you are beautiful?'

'He already does.'

'As beautiful as Arabella . . . Maybella . . . and the others?'

'What nonsense! They are dead and you are young. You are here and you are not just a desirable young woman. You are more to him than anyone has ever been. You gave him back his youth. He said so. And you gave him gold.'

I started, my cheeks burning. I did wish Jessica would stop that unpleasant habit of creeping about the place and suddenly appearing without warning.

'Jessica,' I said reproachfully, 'I didn't hear you knock.'

'It's because you were talking to yourself. Maybella used to talk to herself. You look just like her with the veil hiding your features. It could be Maybella standing there, more than thirty years ago.'

'I'm sure fashions have changed since then.'

'The veil was different. She didn't have orange blossom. There was just white satin ruching. It was a lovely veil and she looked so beautiful. I've never seen anyone so happy as Maybella was on her wedding morning. But then she didn't know what was waiting for her.'

I tried to be practical. 'Now you're here, Jessica, you can unhook me.'

I took off the veil and orange blossom and laid them in their box. Then I turned my back to her while she fumbled with hooks and eyes.

'It's unlucky to try your dress on the night before your wedding.'

'What nonsense!'

'Maybella tried hers on the night before . . . just as you did. There she was parading in it. "Do I look beautiful, Jessie?" she asked. "I must. He'll expect it."'

'Old wives' tales shouldn't affect us. Now I must get to bed. I have a busy day before me tomorrow. Good night, Jessica.'

She shook her head in resignation. 'Good night.'

I undressed and got into bed but in a short time she was back again.

'I've brought you some hot milk. It will make you sleep.'

'That's kind of you, Jessica.'

She set it down on the table by my bed, and stood there waiting.

'Don't wait,' I said. 'I'll have it in a moment. Good night and thank you.'

She glided out. I had an impulse to lock the door. Then I laughed at myself. Why be afraid of simple Jessica? I took a sip of the milk. I didn't really want it but she would be hurt if I didn't drink it.

I thought of Lynx and all those years ago when he had made love to both of them – Maybella because she was his master's daughter and Jessica presumably because he had wanted to. That was all over. He was changed. He was not the same man who had come into the yard with the marks of manacles on his wrists. But he had never forgotten that nor forgiven it. Oh Lynx, I thought, you are as vulnerable as the rest of us; and I told myself that he needed me to look after him. He, too, had lessons to learn from life; and one was that revenge was futile – a destroyer of peace, and peace was at the very foundations of happiness.

Wise Nora, I commented and smiled to myself. And dear Lynx, to whom on the morrow I should make my vows. It was what I wanted – to be with him, to cherish him, for better for worse, for richer for poorer, in sickness and in health until death did us part. At last I understood. I was the luckiest of women. Lynx loved me. Lynx himself, beloved and feared above all other men, Lynx loved *me*.

Now I understood Jessica's hatred; it was due to the fact that she had loved him and lost him. She may have been little or nothing to him but he had been everything to her; and she had seen him marry her cousin, and had lived under the same roof for years. No wonder she had grown a little mad. How mad?

I looked at the milk and a terrible suspicion came to me. On impulse I picked it up and, going to the window, threw it out. Then I laughed at myself.

'Wedding eve dramatics!' I said aloud. 'You imagine that a poor little woman might try to poison you, to take revenge on the man she once loved – perhaps still does – because she cannot bear to see him marry.'

I opened the cupboard door and looked at my dress. Then I opened the box and fingered the veil.

After tomorrow, I thought, all doubts will be gone. We shall be together . . . until death do us part.

I was asleep almost immediately.

I must have dreamed that the ghost of Maybella came to me and stood by my bed. She took the veil and orange blossom from my head – for in the dream I was wearing it – and put there instead a veil with white satin ruching.

Then I heard a voice. It was Jessica's. 'You are ready now, Maybella. But remember it is only for a little while.'

I woke up and was clammy with sweat. In the first few seconds of waking I thought Maybella had indeed returned from the grave to warn me, for there before me was the wedding veil with white satin ruching; and it was a moment or two before I saw that it was draped over the figurine on my dressing table.

I got out of bed and went over to it.

It was the veil of which Jessica had talked. She must have brought it down after I was asleep. I looked at my bedside table. Yes, the glass which had contained the milk had gone.

I took up the veil and looked at it. There was an odour of mothballs surrounding it. I supposed Jessica had treasured it all the intervening years since Maybella had taken the vows which I was about to take tomorrow . . . no, it would be today.

What an old ghoul she was!

I laughed, draped the veil back over the figurine and went back to bed. I slept deeply until Adelaide came in to wake me, bringing with her a cup of tea.

And that day I was married to Lynx.

Everything faded into insignificance but my life with Lynx. I had started on a voyage of discovery and had found new heights and depths of emotion which I had not known existed. Lynx had drawn me away from everyday existence. I was living on another plane.

I said to him: 'You have carried me with you up to Mount Olympus. I feel like a goddess now.'

He loved me, he said, and no one before had ever been loved as I was.

I could believe it. There was no room for anything in my life but the magical presence of Lynx. We rode together; we took meals alone in the library; we even played chess once or twice but he never allowed me to win.

I was gay and lighthearted, and so was he. He was a different man from the one I had first seen in this house; there seemed to be a glow about him – but perhaps that was because I was looking at him through the eyes of love. Once I awoke in the night after a bad dream and for a few moments thought I had lost him. I cried out in fear. And there he was bending over me, his arms about me.

'I thought you'd gone,' I said. 'I thought I'd lost you.'

I heard his laughter in the darkness, exultant, triumphant. I, who had been reluctant to marry him, was now in a cold sweat of terror for a few moments because I had dreamed I had lost him.

The house seemed different. I loved it. I wanted to live in it for ever and make it my home. Adelaide would have made no objections. I could make any changes, have anything I wished, providing it did not clash with Lynx's desires.

'I will refurnish the drawing-room,' I said. 'I would like yellow curtains – but not too bright a yellow.'

'I know,' said Adelaide, 'the colour of gold.'

'Not gold,' I cried. 'The colour of sunshine.'

I wouldn't think about the future. The present offered everything I wanted. *Now* was the important time – not yesterday, not tomorrow.

'Although,' went on Adelaide, 'since you are going away, will you want to refurnish?'

'I don't want to go away, Adelaide.'

'It will be exciting for you.'

'Stirling won't want to leave everything here.'

'Stirling will want to do as his father wishes.' She was looking at me and gently implying: And so must you.

I thought about it: to leave for England with Lynx and Stirling, to leave this wonderful world which I had just discovered to start on a voyage of discovery. White-ladies . . . that girl on the lawn . . . the older woman. My husband could be a little fanatical with his plotting and planning. I would make him see reason, I promised myself again; but not yet. I was not going to spoil this honey-moon period with the clash of opinions which must inevitably occur.

I said nothing to Lynx of leaving the country. We laughed; we bantered; we were serious; we made love in many moods – light-hearted, tender, abandoned and passionate. I would not have believed there could be so many moods.

I was happy, saying: This is *now*. There has never been

such a perfect time. Nothing must spoil it. I must cling to it, make it last for ever.

But nothing lasts for ever.

How tiresome people could be! It seemed that Jessica was deliberately trying to spoil my pleasure in life. When I passed her open door one day she called me into her room and I could not refuse to go although I should have loved to.

She was sitting in front of her mirror trying on my wedding veil.

'Where did you get it?' I asked.

'Ah, you didn't miss it, did you? I just wanted to try it on.'

She looked incongruous with her wild eyes and pale skeleton-like face; and she seemed to read my thoughts for she said: 'I look like the bride in "The Mistletoe Bough". You know the story. She hid in a trunk and was locked in. They found her years later.'

'What a gruesome story!'

'I used to sing that song.'

I thought: Trust you!

'Perhaps it was as well for the bride that she was locked in the trunk.'

'What a thing to say!'

'Slow suffocation, I suppose. But she would soon be overcome by the lack of air. It wouldn't take long. Better than a lifetime of suffering. I can't tell you how Maybella suffered with her miscarriages.'

I turned away. I did not want to think of my husband's first marriage. I knew it had been a marriage of convenience for him. I made excuses for him – a proud man, a captive, wrongly accused; marriage was his only means of escape. I was glad that it had been such a marriage. I wanted no one else to have shared this passion which swept me along as though I were caught in a whirlwind.

Jessica took off the orange blossom and veil and underneath was the one with the satin ruching. She had been wearing the two.

I said accusingly: 'You put that in my room the night before my wedding.'

'Yes, I knew you'd like to have it.'

I thought: She prowls about my room on her own admission. I felt angry with her for prying; and then her helplessness struck me as pitiable and my anger subsided.

She was folding the veils carefully.

'I shall keep them both,' she said. 'I have a lovely sandalwood box. There's plenty of room in it.' She looked at me obliquely. What was she implying? That one day there would be three veils in the box?

But I refused to be affected by a foolish woman whose mind was clearly not well balanced.

I left her and went into the library. Lynx was there, his eyes agleam with pleasure at the sight of me.

Lynx and I went to Melbourne in style. We drove in the special carriage he had had made for himself and we changed horses every ten miles at the coaching inns. He drove part of the way himself, and then how we sped along!

We lived in the grand suite in his hotel, and I was alone some part of the day when he was doing business. I was surprised that he did not take me with him but I realized later that it was because this business concerned his leaving Australia, and knowing my feelings about this, he did not wish to spoil our holiday.

We dined in our private suite and I was so happy that I refused to listen to the voice within which told me that there was another reason for this visit than simple pleasure.

But holiday it was. In the mornings we drove into the nearby country, out to Richmond and beyond along the Yarra Yarra, almost out to the Dandenong country. We went to concerts and to the theatre. Lynx was, of course, well known in Melbourne and there were many invitations, most of which he declined; but he did give an evening's entertainment at the hotel and the big dining-room was turned into a banqueting hall. There was supper and a concert to follow when a new pianist, who was much admired in Europe, was making his debut in Australia.

Wearing a white satin dress, my only ornament a diamond brooch and a ring with one enormous diamond, I stood beside him and received our guests. I was proud because I could see the great respect he inspired was not with his family only.

We were congratulated. I knew that eyebrows were raised because I was so much younger than he was. I wanted to explain to them that age was of no importance, particularly where Lynx was concerned. Lynx was ageless; I felt convinced then that he would live for ever – long after I was dead.

I sat listening to the pianist. Those haunting Chopin melodies would always remind me of this evening. There was something sad and wistful about them; I felt that they implied the transience of joy and happiness, the inevitable disillusion. How absurd! It was due to Jessica with her veils and boxes that I should have such thoughts.

Now he had gone into the Military Polonaise. That was stirring and lively and my spirits were lifted.

I heard two women whispering together.

'Lavish! No expense spared.'

'Expense! This is nothing. He's many times a millionaire.'

'What luck! Trust him to get it. And so much.'

'Now he's got this young girl *and* his fortune.'

I shouldn't listen. I wished I hadn't such acute ears. I was sure I heard someone say: 'Do you think it will last?' And I shivered because it seemed as though Jessica was beside me, folding her veils neatly into a box in which there was plenty of room for more.

I was not in the least shy of these people. Since my marriage I had changed. I had become a woman of the world; I was desired; I was loved by a man who could not enter a room without every eye being turned on him. I could say to myself: 'And he chose me!' And that made me hold my head higher. In my white satin gown I felt perfectly groomed and at ease. Perhaps I looked more than my nineteen years, but that was unimportant since I was the wife of Lynx. I was constantly catching his eye and we exchanged looks of understanding. I wanted him to be proud of me.

I mingled with the guests. We talked of Melbourne and how it had grown since I had arrived in Australia. I discussed the new buildings, the shops and the theatre.

'I hope you will come into Melbourne more often, Mrs Herrick,' said one woman. 'There is plenty of time before next February.'

I was not quite sure what she meant and I repeated: 'February?'

'Isn't that when you are leaving us? Your husband was saying that he thought it would be better to arrive in England during the warm weather.'

'Oh yes,' I said, 'of course.'

'And how excited you must be! I hope you will come back some day. But England was quite recently your home, wasn't it? So it will not be new to you.'

I was not listening. So he had arranged the date of leaving and he had not told me. I felt angry because once more as in the days before our marriage he had shown me that although he would indulge me in unimportant matters of our life, the big issues would be decided by him.

He said: 'What a success you were! I was proud of you. You looked very different from the school teacher who arrived in our midst two years ago.'

I was silently standing before the long mirror and he came and put his arms about me, looking over my head at our reflection.

'I hear you have made arrangements for us to leave for England,' I said stonily.

'Oh, that's it! Did one of those fools tell you? It must have been the Adams woman. Really, Adams should not discuss his client's business with his wife.'

'The fact remains that you have made these arrangements.'

'I like to get everything in hand.'

'That's in five or six months' time, then.'

'I thought you would like to arrive in good weather.'

'That,' I retorted, 'was extremely considerate of you.'

'My darling knows I always consider her comforts.'

I stared at his reflection in the mirror. 'Since we are falling into this irritating habit of discussing her as though she is not present, she will say that she would like her wishes to be considered as assiduously as her comforts.'

'It is my pleasure to give in to those wishes whenever possible.'

'Which means when they don't inconvenience you at all.'

'It's this ridiculous matter of leaving the country. I'm surprised at you, Nora. This town – which I admit is growing and will doubtless be a very fine place in due course – can't be compared with home.'

'I want to stay here,' I said. I turned to him pleadingly. 'Please, I know that it is best for us to stay here.'

'How can you know such things? You talk as though you're a prophetess.'

'I know why you're going to England.'

'I am taking my family there because there they can live in a manner suited to their . . .'

'Fortune,' I said. 'Which was founded by me.'

'My clever Nora! I'll never forget that day you came in and held out the nugget to me. You looked scared as though you had behaved in some reprehensible manner.'

'I wish . . .' I began. But it wasn't true that I wished I hadn't found gold. I was glad now even, as I ever was, that I had been the one to make the miraculous discovery.

He had become tender suddenly as though my discovery of gold gave me the privilege of being stupid about other matters. 'Nora, leave everything to me.'

'I daresay it would please you to have a stupid wife who said, "Yes, yes, you are wonderful. You are always right. Do just as you wish and I will go on saying how right and clever you are."'

He burst out laughing. Then he shook his head at me. 'It's no use, Nora. We're going.'

'And when we get there we are going to acquire Whiteladies by evil hook or wicked crook.'

'How beautifully you express it.'

'So you are determined. Oh, Lynx, why do you want that house? Let's get another house nearby if you like that part of the country. Or we could build our own.'

His face had hardened. He was like the man I had met when I first came. There was a certain coldness in his manner towards me which frightened me and which wounded me more than I had thought possible.

'This is something you don't understand,' he said. 'We

are going to England, and when we get there I shall decide what we are going to do.'

'You mean I have no say in it?'

I turned away and walked to the window. I was fighting the impulse to give way, to say: 'I will do as you wish. I only want you to go on loving me.' But that would be false to myself. He had loved me for myself in the beginning. I had not been afraid of him then; I would not be now.

'I mean,' he said, 'that you will be sensible as you usually are and realize that you know nothing of this matter and be happy to leave it to me.'

I turned to him and ran into his arms. 'Then tell me,' I said. 'Tell me everything.'

There was a sofa in the room; he sat down and drew me to him. I lay against him while he began to talk of those long ago days. I had heard it before but I don't think I ever fully realized before the depth of degradation he had plumbed nor how deeply the bitterness had entered his soul. He was going to own that house; the wound festered still; this was the only balm which could heal it.

'Need it be?' I asked. 'It's changed, hasn't it? You have me now.'

'I have you,' he agreed, 'and when I have Whiteladies I shall be completely content.'

'Am I not enough?'

'You give me all I hoped for in human relationships. You are my precious jewel. But I need a setting for you and only one will satisfy me.'

'I would be quite happy in a different setting.'

'But I would not.'

'Because I do not believe this is the right setting for me.'

'How can you know?'

I lifted my head and looked at him fiercely. 'I do know. I am certain of it. Revenge is an evil thing. It hurts people.

229

There is no happiness to be gained by hurting others. Oh, Lynx, you have given me so much. You have changed me. You have taught me how to grow up and I love you with all my heart. I ask this one thing of you. Give up this wild plan.'

'It's the only thing you could ask which I can't give you.'

'But, Lynx, we are together. We have our lives. A house is only bricks and mortar.'

'It can be a symbol.'

'You are rich. You could buy a great house . . . a stately home of your own. There must be some for sale in England.'

'You say you do not wish to go to England.'

'Should I care where we were if we were together?'

'My dearest girl,' he said tenderly.

And because of his softened mood, I went on: 'It is revenge and hatred that I am afraid of. There is no happiness through them. If you acquired this house you would never be happy there.'

'Nonsense!' he said sharply.

'How could you be, knowing you had turned out the rightful owners.'

'For precisely that reason. And they would no longer be the rightful owners. I should. Don't let's speak of it any more. You will see for yourself when you are there.'

'I don't believe in shelving a subject and pretending it doesn't exist just because it is unpleasant.'

He yawned. My common sense told me to drop the subject, to accept what he had planned and perhaps later do my best to heal this terrible wound which he had kept open all these years. But some persistence drove me on.

'There is something petty about it,' I insisted.

'Petty!' he cried. 'What nonsense are you talking?'

'It's like visiting the sins of the fathers on the children.'

'My God, Nora, you've become like some ranting missionary.'

'I only know that it is not only wrong to nurse a griev-ance, it's also folly.'

'And you call seven years' degrading captivity a grievance?'

'It doesn't matter what suffering there was . . .'

'Certainly not to those who didn't have to endure it.'

'I didn't mean it that way.'

'Do you know what you do mean? Listen, Nora. I'm losing my patience.'

'And I'm in danger of losing mine.'

He laughed, not in the pleasant happy way to which I had become accustomed, but disagreeably. His face hard-ened and his eyes glinted; he squared his shoulders and looked invincible.

'Perhaps,' he said, 'it is time you and I came to an under-standing. You have to realize that I am master in my own house.'

'Does that mean that I am not to speak unless spoken to?'

'I shall always be glad for you to speak when you have something sensible to say. But you must understand without delay that I expect obedience from my wife.'

This was not like the lover I had known. This was the arrogant man of whom I had been aware and resented when I first came to Australia. No, I thought. I shall not be the meek wife he wants. I shall be myself and if I have an opinion I am not going to deny it simply because he doesn't share it. He might have his desires for revenge with which he was not going to allow me to interfere – well, I had my integrity, my determination to preserve myself as an individual, and much as I loved him, much as my being called out for a return to the old tenderness, I was not going to pay the price he was asking for it.

I said: 'If you imagine you will get a meek yes from me to everything you say you have made a mistake. In fact I am beginning to think that our marriage may have been a mistake.'

'You are in a frivolous mood tonight,' he said lightly. 'Your success with the ladies and gentlemen of Melbourne has gone to your head.'

'I am completely serious and this has nothing to do with the ladies and gentlemen of Melbourne. It is a matter between us two. I will not agree with all your views. I cannot regard you as my lord and master whose word must be law and whose opinion is always right because he is a man and I am a woman.'

'Did I ever ask you to be such an insipid fool?'

'It seems you are telling me that is what you expect.'

'Which shows how illogical you are. You know I like to hear your opinions, but I will not have you dictating to me on matters of major importance. I've had enough of this. Let's go to bed.'

But I stood my ground firmly. I knew that we could not dismiss the matter as simply as that. It would be a continual irritation between us. I could see it building up to a great barrier.

'I must discuss this with you.'

'I have said I have nothing to discuss.'

'So you plan to go to England, to acquire Whiteladies and not talk it over with me.'

'If you are going to be sensible . . .'

'That's what I am trying to be. I know this is wrong.'

'Stop talking rubbish.' He caught my arm. 'You look so pretty tonight. The dress is most becoming.'

He started to unhook it but I swung away from him.

'No,' I said. 'I will not be treated in this way.'

I ran into the dressing-room. He was startled and I had locked the door before he reached it. There were tears in my eyes. At least I had prevented his seeing them. I had a feeling that he would despise tears.

It's changed, I thought. The honeymoon is over. My relationship with him was not what I had thought it to be.

I sat down on the small bed and thought about Stirling. Did he really love me? Yes! I answered myself. Remember when we lay in the cave. But his father had said: 'Stand aside. I want her.' So Stirling stood aside. And now Lynx was saying to me: 'You will do as I say. You will take your share in my grand plan for revenge.' And although my brain said: 'It is wrong and no good can come of it,' my heart was crying out: 'What does it matter? You will be with him and he will go on loving you. But if you defy him . . .'

And there was a vision of Jessica holding the sandalwood box in her hands. 'Plenty of room . . .'

Oh yes, the honeymoon was over.

I had spent a sleepless night. I had lain on that uncomfortable bed, having removed my satin dress, hoping that he would knock at the door and beg me to come out. But he did not. It was I who unlocked the door next morning.

He was sitting in a chair reading when I went in. I was in my petticoat, carrying my satin dress.

'Ah,' he said, 'the woman of principles.' His mood had changed. He was no longer angry and the tenderness had come back in spite of the words. 'I trust, madam,' he went on, 'that you had a comfortable night.'

'Hardly that,' I retorted, catching his mood.

'Remorse?'

'A very hard mattress.'

'And you prefer a feather bed.'

'In certain circumstances.'

He laughed. 'My poor child! What a brute I am! I should have insisted that you leave your hard mattress, but you were so full of determination to defend the rights of women and freedom of decision – so what could I do?'

'Nothing. You knew I was determined at all costs.'

'Now you wish to bathe and dress. While you are doing so I will order breakfast to be sent up to us. Are you agreeable to this or would you like to put forward your suggestions?'

'I am perfectly agreeable.'

I was happy. It was not the end. I had been foolish. I must be less blatant. I must persuade him gently, subtly.

We sat at the table which had been wheeled in. I poured out coffee while he served bacon and devilled kidneys from the chafing dishes. There was a cosy intimacy about the scene which made me happy.

'Now,' he said, 'we'll discuss this matter in a civilized manner. We have a difference of opinion. I say that we are going to England and our children will play on the lawns of Whiteladies. My grandchildren will be there with my son and daughter, for Stirling will marry and Adelaide will join us in due course. Whiteladies is not yet in my possession. It may be a little difficult to arrange, but I always enjoyed surmounting difficulties. Now you, Nora, have your own puritan ideas. To settle old scores seems pagan to you. "An eye for an eye," say I. You say. "Turn the other cheek." But this is my affair. I have to fight for Whiteladies and I shall have an opponent in my own family – my wife. It's a situation which appeals to me.'

'So you are going to England.'

'*We* are going to England.'

'And you are going to acquire this house.'

'By wicked crook or evil hook, remember. And if you are going to stop me – well, Nora, that gives an added fillip to the affair. You are going to show me why I should not acquire Whiteladies. I am going to show you why I should.'

'So you are not going to put from you a wife who does not mildly agree that you are always right?'

'Of what use would such a creature be to me? All things considered, I am reasonably satisfied with my Nora. She can be obstinate at times; she can be arrogant; but what maddens me most is this piety of hers, that missionary spirit . . .'

'And what maddens me,' I said, 'is my husband's irritating habit of talking in my presence as though I am absent.'

'Then we both madden each other, which is as it should be.'

'And you have decided graciously to pardon a wife who doesn't think her husband omnipotent and omniscient?'

'I have come to the conclusion that I love the girl and that means I'll endure a great deal. In fact I am looking forward to some sturdy battles with Nora preaching turn the other cheek; and all the time I shall be showing her how happy she can be in her English mansion.'

'I shall never agree with you.'

'I know,' he said. 'Well, we'll start our journey back today. We have our preparations to make.'

'Preparations . . .'

'For England and the battle between us.'

We left Melbourne that day. There was a compromise between us. I would plunge into my preparations; we were leaving for England in March of the following year, it had been decided – Stirling, Lynx and myself, plus the servants we should need. I would make no objections to these preparations. My task was to persuade Lynx to abandon his plan for taking Whiteladies when the time came.

He never told me what his plans were. I believe he told Stirling. I felt a little shut out; but I stifled that resentment. I was determined that we were not going to take Whiteladies from its owners. Not that I saw how we could. These were not medieval times when castles were taken by force. I would persuade Lynx to buy the house that I wanted. I visualized it – grand and gracious. It would have to satisfy him. But whenever I pictured it it always took the form of Whiteladies.

We were approaching the end of summer and the winds were both cool and fierce. I would hear them whistling across the bush; they rattled our windows and buffeted the house as though they were trying to tear up its foundations.

When I rode out, usually with Lynx, sometimes with Adelaide, never with Stirling whom I now rarely saw, I would shudder at the damage which the fires had done, although many of the trees were not entirely dead and in due course would recover.

Lynx and I had returned to our old relationship, though perhaps we bantered more than we had just after our wedding. He liked to argue with me and enjoyed my having a different point of view. This delighted me. I ceased to fret over his obsession with revenge, for I was certain that I could turn him from it.

We had by no means shelved the matter. We often talked of Whiteladies – but he never explained to me how he hoped to wrest it from its owners.

How suddenly violent life could be in this country! Death was never far away.

That bright sunny morning I was riding out with him to the mine. We were not alone. Stirling was with us, also two or three of the men from the mine. Lynx had recently sold out most of his share and was keeping only a small interest.

'It's the time to sell,' he had explained. 'We've had most

of the gilt off the gingerbread though there's still a considerable amount in those quartz reefs. It'll be worked for some years yet.'

He was getting rid of most of his interests in Australia because he was determined never to come back. Adelaide would stay behind for a few months and then would sell up the house and join us. It was all settled.

The sun was warm on that morning but the wind was piercingly fresh and of almost gale force. Lynx rode on ahead of our little party with the men from the mine. Stirling and I were some short distance behind. It was the first time I had been alone with Stirling since my marriage – if one could call this being alone.

'Are you happy about going to England, Stirling?' I asked.

He said he was, and I felt angry with him. He had no will but his father's.

'You are happy about leaving all this?' I persisted.

'And you?'

'At least I have been here a comparatively short time. It is home to you.'

'It'll be all right in England.'

We had come to that spot where Jacob Jagger had lost his life. There seemed to be something eerie about it now. The ghost gums rose high and imperiously indifferent; some of the trees were blackened. So the fire had scorched this spot too. Perhaps, I thought, that is how places become haunted. A man died there . . . suddenly his life was brought to an end in a moment of passion. Could his spirit remain for ever, seeking revenge?

Stirling was glancing at me. Was he, too, thinking of Jagger?

'So the fire got as far as this,' I said; and my words were carried on the wind as it whistled past me.

Then it happened. The great branch fell from the top of

the tallest eucalypt. There was a sudden cry as it swooped like an arrow from the sky.

Then I saw Lynx; he had fallen from his horse and was lying on the ground.

I heard someone cry: 'My God, it's a widow-maker.'

They carried him home on an improvised stretcher. How tall he looked – taller in death even than in life! He had died as one of the gods of old might have died – from a falling branch which had descended with such force that it had driven itself through his heart, impaling and pinning him to the ground. And it had happened there, not far from that spot where he had deliberately shot Jacob Jagger.

The widow-maker had caught him as it had caught lesser men before him.

I could not believe it. I went to the library. I touched the chessmen; I took his ring with the lynx engraved on it and I stared at it until it seemed as though it were his eyes which looked at me in place of those glittering stones.

Lynx . . . dead! But he was immortal. I was stunned. I felt as though I myself were dead.

Stirling came to see me and it was then that I was able to shed my pent-up tears. He held me in his arms and we were as close as we had been in the cave when the fire had raged above us.

'We must go to England,' he said. 'It was what he would wish.'

I shuddered and replied: 'He would not wish us to go, Stirling. What good could that do? *He* wanted to go, but that is impossible now. It's over.'

But Stirling shook his head and said: 'He wished us to go. We shall leave as we should have done had he been here.'

I thought then that Lynx was living on to govern our lives. Subconsciously I had always believed that death could not touch him. Perhaps that was so.

Minta

Chapter One

$\mathcal{T}$ONIGHT as I sat in my room looking down on the lawn
I decided that I would write down what had happened.
To do so would be to keep the memory of the days with me
for ever. One forgets so quickly; impressions become hazy;
one's mind distorts, colouring events to make them as one
would like them to have been, highlighting what one wants
to preserve, pushing away what one would rather not
remember. So I would keep a sort of journal and write down
everything truthfully and unvarnished just as it took place.

What prompted me to do this was that afternoon's adventure, the day Stirling came. It was ridiculous really. He had
come briefly into my life and there was no reason why he
should appear again. It was absurd to feel this urge to write
down what had happened. It was an ordinary enough incident. I knew his name was Stirling and the girl's was Nora
because they had addressed each other so – perhaps only
once, but my mind had been receptive. I was more than
usually alert, so I remembered every detail.

Her scarf had blown over the wall and they came to
retrieve it. I had a notion that the incident was contrived.
A foolish thought really. Why should it have been?

I was on the lawn with Lucie and it was one of Mamma's more fretful days. Poor Mamma, she would never be happy, I knew. She was looking back into a past which could not have been so wonderful as she made it out to be. It seemed that she had missed great happiness. One day she would tell me about it. She had promised to do so.

Lucie and I sat on the lawn. Lucie was working at her tapestry; she was making covers for one of the chairs in the dining-room. My father had dropped his cigar ash on the seat of one of these and burned a hole in the tapestry, which had been worked in 1701. How like Lucie to decide that she would copy the Jacobean design and provide a cover which would be indistinguishable from the rest. In her quiet way Lucie was clever and I was so glad that she was with us. Life would have been very dull without her. She could do most things; she could help my father with his work; she would read the latest novel or from the magazines and newspapers to Mamma; and she was a companion for me. I was marvelling at the similarity of her work to the existing chair seats.

'It's almost exact,' I cried.

'Almost!' she replied in dismay. 'That won't do. It has to be exact in every detail.'

'I'm sure we shall all be satisfied with something slightly less,' I comforted. 'Who is going to peer into it for discrepancies?'

'Some people might . . . in the future.' Lucie's eyes grew dreamy. 'I want people a hundred years hence to look at that chair and say, "Which was the one which was done towards the end of the nineteenth century?"'

'But why?'

Lucie was a little impatient. 'You don't deserve to belong to this house, Minta,' she scolded. 'Think what it means. You can trace your family back to the Tudors' day and beyond. You have this wonderful heritage . . . Whiteladies! And you don't seem to appreciate it.'

'Of course I love Whiteladies, Lucie, and I'd hate to live anywhere else, but it's only a house after all.'

'Only a house!' She raised her eyes to the top of the chestnut tree. 'Whiteladies! Five hundred years ago nuns lived their sheltered lives here. Sometimes I imagine I hear the bells calling them to compline, and at night I fancy I hear their voices as they say their prayers in their cells and the swish of their white robes as they mount the stone staircases.'

I laughed at her. 'Why, Lucie, you care more for the place than any of us.'

'You've just taken it for granted,' she cried vehemently and her mouth was grim. I knew she was thinking of that little house in a grimy town in the Black Country. She had told me about it, and when I thought of that I could understand her love for Whiteladies; and I was so glad that she was with us. In fact she had made me appreciate the home which had been in my family for hundreds of years.

It was I who had brought Lucie into the house. She had taught English literature and history at the boarding-school to which I had been sent, and she had taken rather special care of me during my first months there. She had helped to alleviate the inevitable homesickness; she taught me to adjust myself and be self-reliant; all this she had done in her unobtrusive manner. During my second term we had been told to write an essay on an old house we had visited and naturally I chose Whiteladies. She was interested and asked me where I had seen this house. 'I live in it,' I answered; and after that she often questioned me about it. When the summer holidays came and the rest of us were so excited about going home, I noticed how sad she was and I asked her where she was spending the vacation. She had no family, she told me.

She expected she would try to get a post with some old lady. Perhaps she would travel with her: When I said impulsively: 'You should come to Whiteladies!' her delight was touching.

So she came and that was the beginning. In those days the tiresome subject of money was never mentioned. The house was large; there were many unoccupied rooms and we had plenty of servants. Often we had a house full, so Lucie Maryan was just one more. But there was a difference. She made herself so useful. Mamma liked her voice and she did not tire easily; she could listen to Mamma's accounts of her ailments with real sympathy, for she knew a great deal about illnesses and could entertain Mamma with accounts of people who had suffered in various ways. Even my father became interested in her. He was writing a biography of a famous ancestor who had distinguished himself under Marlborough at Oudenarde, Blenheim and Malplaquet. In his study were letters and papers which had been found in a trunk in one of the turrets. He used to say, 'It's a lifetime's work. I often wonder if I shall live long enough to complete it.' I suspected that he dozed most of the afternoon and evening when he was supposed to be working.

On that first visit I remember Lucie's walking with Papa under the trees in the grounds, discussing those battles and Marlborough's relationship with his wife and Queen Anne. My father was delighted with her knowledge and before the end of the visit he had accepted her help in sorting out some of the letters and papers.

That was the beginning. After that it became a matter of course that Lucie should spend her holidays with us. She was so interested in Whiteladies itself that she urged my father to write a study of the house. This appealed to him and he declared that as soon as he had finished with General Sir Harry Dorian he would begin his researches on the history of Whiteladies.

Lucie was passionately fascinated by his work; and I was amused that Papa and Lucie should be so much more interested in the house than Mamma and myself, when my father had merely married into it and Lucie was not connected with it at all.

When I left school my mother suggested that Lucie join us. We knew what her circumstances were; she was alone in the world, forced to earn her own living; and life at school was not easy. There was so much she could do at Whiteladies.

So Lucie was paid a salary and became a member of our household; we were all fond of her and she was so useful that we could not imagine what we should do without her. She had no specific duties – she was my father's secretary, my mother's nurse and my companion; moreover she was the friend of us all.

I was seventeen on that day when Stirling and Nora came; Lucie was twenty-seven.

One of the servants had brought Mamma's chair into the garden and Lucie put down her work and went over to it. We had chosen a pleasant spot near the Hermes pond under a tree for shade. Mamma could walk quite easily but she liked her invalid's chair and used it frequently. I sat idly watching Lucie wheel Mamma across the lawn, wondering whether it was one of her peevish days. One could often tell by the expression on her face. Oh dear, I thought, I do hope not. It's such a lovely day.

'Do make sure we're not in the sun,' said Mamma. 'It gives me such a headache.'

'This is a very shady spot, Mamma,' I told her.

'The light is so bright today.' Yes, it was one of her bad days.

'I will place your chair so that the light is not on your face, Lady Cardew,' said Lucie.

'Thank you, Lucie.'

Lucie brought the chair to a standstill and Jeffs, the butler, appeared with Jane, the parlourmaid, who carried the tray on which was bread and butter, scones with jam and honey, and fruit cake.

Lucie busied herself with making Mamma comfortable and I sat at the table waiting for one of the servants to bring out the tray with the silver teapot and spirit lamp. When it came I poured out the tea, which Mamma said was too strong. Lucie immediately watered it and Mamma sat sipping in silence. I understood. Her thoughts were in the past.

I glanced at the house. The window on the first floor which belonged to my father's study was open a little. There he would be sitting at his desk, papers spread out round him, dozing I could be certain. He never liked to be disturbed when working; secretly I suspected he was afraid someone would catch him sleeping. Dear Papa, he was never cross with anyone. He was the most easy-going man in the world; he was even patient with Mamma, and it must have required a great deal of forbearance to be constantly reminded that she regretted her marriage.

'Lucie,' she was saying now, 'I want an extra cushion for my back.'

'Yes, Lady Cardew. I think I'll go indoors for one of the larger ones. In any case I'm always afraid the garden ones may be a little damp.'

Mamma nodded and as Lucie went off she murmured: 'She's such a good creature.'

I didn't like Lucie's being referred to as a 'creature'. I was so fond of her. I watched her walking across the grass – rather tall, very straight-backed, her dark hair smoothed down on either side and made into a knot at the nape of her neck. She wore dark colours – mulberry today – and they became her rather olive skin; she had a natural elegance so that not very expensive clothes looked quite modish on her.

'She's a good friend to us all,' I said with slight reproof. I was the only one who occasionally reproved Mamma. My father, hating any sort of fuss, was invariably gentle and placating. I have known him take endless trouble to avoid the smallest unpleasantness. And Lucie, because after all she was employed – a fact which my father and I always strove to make her forget – was quick to respond to my mother's whims, for she was proud and determined that her job should be no sinecure.

'Good heavens, Lucie,' I often said, 'you needn't fear that. You are guide, comforter and friend to us and all for the price of a housekeeper!'

Lucie's reply to that was: 'I shall always be grateful for being allowed to come here. I hope you will never regret taking me in.'

Mamma was saying that the wind was cold and the sun too hot and that the headache she had awakened with had grown worse throughout the day. Lucie came back with the cushion and settled it behind Mamma, who thanked her languidly.

Then they were coming across the lawn. They looked a little defiant as indeed they might, being uninvited and un-announced. He was tall and dark; she was dark, too – not exactly pretty but there was a vitality about her which was obvious as soon as one saw her, and that was very attrac-tive.

'Good afternoon,' said Stirling, 'we have come to get my ward's scarf.'

It seemed an odd announcement. It struck me as strange that he should be her guardian. I thought she was about my age and he perhaps Lucie's. Then I noticed the green scarf lying on the grass. She said something about its blowing from her neck and sailing over the wall.

'By all means . . .' I began. Mamma was looking on in

astonishment; Lucie was unruffled. Then I noticed that the girl's hand was bleeding and I asked if she were hurt. She had grazed it, she told me. It was nothing. Lucie said it should be dressed and she would take her to Mrs Glee's room where they could bandage it.

There was some protest but eventually Lucie took the girl to Mrs Glee and I was left alone with Stirling and Mamma.

I asked if they would like tea and he declared his pleasure. He was greatly interested in the house. He was different from any men I knew, but then I knew so few. I was, I suppose, comparing him with Franklyn Wakefield. There could not have been two men less like. I asked him where he lived and was astonished when he said Australia.

'Australia,' said Mamma, leaning forward a little in her chair. 'That's a long way off.'

'Twelve thousand miles or thereabouts.'

There was something very breezy and likeable about him and the intrusion had lifted the afternoon out of its customary monotony.

'Have you come here to stay?' I asked.

'No, I shall be sailing away the day after tomorrow.'

'So soon!' I felt a ridiculous dismay.

'My ward and I leave on the *Carron Star*,' he said. 'I came over to escort her back. Her father has died and we are adopting her.'

'That's very . . . exciting,' I said foolishly.

'Do you think so?' His smile was ironic and I flushed. I feared he was thinking me rather stupid. He was no doubt comparing me with his ward who looked so lively and intelligent.

Mamma asked him about Australia. What was it like? Where did he live? She knew someone who had gone there years ago.

That was interesting, said Stirling. What was the name of the settler she had known?

'I . . . er can't remember,' said Mamma.

'Well, it's a big place.'

'I often wonder . . .' began Mamma and then stopped.

He said he lived about forty miles north of Melbourne. Was it to Melbourne her friend had gone?

'I couldn't say,' said Mamma. 'I never heard.'

'Was it long ago?' he persisted. There was an odd quirk about his mouth as though he were very interested and perhaps a little amused about Mamma's friend.

'I find it hard to remember,' said Mamma. Then she added quickly: 'It would be such a long time ago. Thirty years . . . or more.'

'You never kept in touch with your friend?'

'I'm afraid not.'

'What a pity! I might have been able to take him . . . or her . . . news of you.'

'Oh, it was long, long ago,' said Mamma, a little flushed and quite excited. I had never known her like this. Our unexpected visitors seemed to have affected us both strangely.

I gave him tea and noticed his strong brown fingers on the Crown Derby. He smiled as he took the cup from me; there were wrinkles round his eyes, caused I supposed by the hot sun. I asked him questions about Australia and I was very interested in the property his people owned. There was a hotel, too, in Melbourne, and a gold mine.

'What exciting lives you must lead!' I said.

He admitted it; and for the first time I felt restive. It hadn't occurred to me before how uneventful life was at Whiteladies. Lucie was constantly implying that I should be grateful; he had the opposite effect on me. But it seemed that he, too, was fascinated by Whiteladies. He asked a great many questions about it and we were on this subject when the girl came back with Lucie. Her hand had been bandaged. I poured out tea for her and we continued to talk of the house.

Then Franklyn arrived. There was something very charming about Franklyn. He was so calm. I had known him all my life and never had I seen him ruffled. On the rare occasions when it was necessary for him to reprimand anyone or assert himself in some way, one felt he brought a judicial attitude to the matter and that it was done from a sense of the rightness of things rather than in anger. Some people might have called Franklyn dull. He was far from that.

The contrast between him and Stirling was marked. Stirling might have appeared clumsy if he had been a different kind of man; but Stirling was completely unaware of any disadvantage. He clearly was not impressed by the immaculate cut of Franklyn's suit – if he noticed it at all.

It was difficult to make introductions, so I explained to Franklyn that the scarf had blown over the wall and that they had come to retrieve it.

Then Nora rose and said they must be going and thanked us for our kindness. Stirling was a little put out, and I was pleased because he obviously would have liked to stay; but there was nothing I could do to detain them and Lucie went with them to the gates.

That was all. A trivial incident in a way and yet I could not get them out of my mind; and because I wanted to remember it exactly as it happened, I started this journal.

We sat on the lawn until half past five; then my father came down. His hair was ruffled, his face slightly flushed. I thought: He's had a good sleep.

'How did the work go, Sir Hilary?' asked Lucie.

He smiled at her. When he smiled his face lit up and it

was as though a light had been turned on behind his eyes. He loved talking about his work.

'It was hard going today,' he said. 'But I tell myself I'm at a difficult stage.'

Mamma looked impatient and Franklyn said quickly: 'There are, I believe, always these difficult stages. If the work went too smoothly there might be a danger of its being facile.'

Trust Franklyn to say the right thing! He sat back in the garden chair looking immaculate, bland and tolerant of us all. I knew that Mamma and my father had decided that Franklyn would make a very good son-in-law. We would join up Wakefield Park and Whiteladies. It would be very convenient, for the two houses were moderately close and the grounds met. Franklyn's people were not exactly rich but, as it was said, comfortable; and in any case we were not rich either. I believe that something had happened to our finances during the last two years, for whenever money was mentioned Papa would assume a studied vagueness which meant that this was a subject he did not wish to hear of because it bothered him.

However, it would be very convenient if Franklyn and I married. I had even come to regard this as an inevitability. I wondered whether Franklyn did too. He always treated me with a delightful courtesy; but then he extended this to everyone. I had seen the village postmistress flush with pleasure when he exchanged a few words with her. He was tall – all the Wakefields had been tall – and he managed his father's estate with tact and efficiency, being a very good landlord to all the tenants. But behind Franklyn's easy-going charm there was an aloofness. His eyes were slaty grey rather than blue; there was a lack of warmth in them; and one felt that if he was never angry, he was never really delighted either. He was equable; and therefore, though a comforting person to be with, hardly an exciting one. Everything about him was conventional: his immaculate dress; his courteous manners; his well-ordered life.

These facts had not occurred to me before. It was because of those two people who had invaded my afternoon that I had begun this assessment. Well, they had gone. I never expected to see them again.

'Exactly,' Papa was saying. 'I always tell myself that I must accept this hard task for the sake of posterity.'

'I am sure,' added Franklyn, 'that you will complete it to the satisfaction of the present generation and those to come.'

My father was pleased, particularly when Lucie added earnestly: 'I am sure you will, too, Sir Hilary.'

Then Lucie and Franklyn began to talk with Papa, and Mamma yawned and said her headache was coming on again, so Lucie took her to her room where she would lie down before dinner.

'Franklyn, you'll dine with us?' said my father; and Franklyn graciously accepted.

Mamma did not appear for dinner. She sent for Lizzie, her maid, to rub eau-de-Cologne on her forehead. Dr Hunter had been invited to dine with us but he would first spend half an hour or so with Mamma discussing her symptoms before joining us.

Dr Hunter had come to us only two years ago and seemed young to have the responsibility of our lives and deaths, but perhaps that was because we compared him with old Dr Hedgling whose practice he had taken over. Dr Hunter was in his early thirties; he was a bachelor and had a house-keeper who was supposed to look after his material comforts. He was, I fancied, over anxious for our good opinion, while being aware that we considered him a trifle inexperienced. He was an amusing young man and Mamma liked him, which was an important point.

Dinner was quite lively. The young doctor had an amusing way of describing a situation and Franklyn could cap his stories often in a coolly witty manner. I was rather glad that Mamma had decided to have dinner sent up on a tray, for with her constant repetitions of her symptoms she could be a little tiresome and she most certainly would indulge in the recital of them if the doctor were present.

I think my father was pleased, too. He was always different when she was absent; it was almost as though he revelled in his freedom.

The doctor was talking of one or two of his patients, how old Betty Ellery who was bedridden refused to see what she called 'a bit of a boy'. 'While confessing to my youth,' said the doctor, 'I had to insist that my person was intact, and that I was whole and certainly not a bit of myself.'

'Poor Betty!' I said. 'She's been in bed since I was a little girl. I remember going to her with blankets every Christmas, plus a chicken and plum pudding. When the carriage pulled up at her door and we alighted, she would cry out: "Come in, madam, and you're almost as welcome as the gifts you've brought." I used to sit solemnly in the chair beside her bed and listen to the stories she told of when Grandpapa Dorian was alive and Mamma used to go visiting with her Mamma.'

'The old customs remain,' said Franklyn.

'And a good thing, too, don't you agree, Franklyn?' asked my father.

Franklyn said that in some cases it was good to cling to the old customs; in others better to discard them. And so the conversation continued.

After dinner Lucie and the doctor sat talking earnestly while I chatted with Franklyn. I asked him what he thought of the people who had come that afternoon.

'The young lady of the scarf, you mean.'

'Both of them. They seemed unusual.'

'Did they?' Franklyn clearly did not think so and I could see that he had almost forgotten them. I felt faintly annoyed with him and turned to Lucie and the doctor. The doctor was talking about his housekeeper, Mrs Devlin, whom he suspected of drinking more than sobriety demanded.

'I hope,' said Lucie, 'that you lock up your spirits.'

'My dear Miss Maryan, if I did I should lose the lady.'

'Would she be such a loss?'

'You clearly have no idea of the trials of a bachelor's existence when he is at the mercy of a couple of maids. Why, I should starve and my house would resemble a pigsty without the supervision of my Mrs Devlin. I have to forgive her her love of strong drink for the sake of the comfort she brings into my life.'

I smiled at Franklyn. I wondered whether he was thinking the same as I was. Dear Lucie! She must be nearly thirty and if she were ever going to marry she should do it soon; and what a good doctor's wife she would make! I could picture her dealing with the patients, helping him along. It was an ideal situation, although we should lose her, and what should we do without her? But we must not, of course, be selfish. This was Lucie's chance; and if she married the doctor, she would be living close to me for the rest of her life.

I turned to Franklyn. I was about to whisper that I thought it would be wonderful if Lucie and Dr Hunter made a match; but one did not say things like that to Franklyn. He would think it bad taste to whisper of such a matter – or even talk of it openly – when it concerned only the two people involved. Oh dear, how tiresome he could be! And what a lot of fun he was missing in life!

I contrived it so that we talked in one group and Dr Hunter told us some amusing stories of his life in hospital before he came to the district; and he was very entertaining.

But he and Wakefield left soon after ten and we retired for the night.

When I went in to say good-night to my mother she was wide awake. There was a change in her.

She said: 'Sit down, Minta, and talk to me for a while. I shall never sleep tonight.'

'Why is that?' I asked.

'You know, Minta,' she said reproachfully, 'that I never sleep well.'

I thought then that we were going to have an account of her sufferings, but this was not so. She went on quickly: 'I feel I must talk to you. There is so much I have never told you. I hope, my child, that your life will be happier than mine.'

When I thought of her life with an indulgent husband, a beautiful home, servants to attend to every whim, and freedom to do everything she wanted – or almost – I could not agree that she was in need of commiseration. But, as always with Mamma, I made a pretence of listening. I'm afraid that my attention often wandered and I would murmur a sympathetic 'yes' or 'no' or 'how terrible' without really knowing what it was all about.

Then my attention was caught and held because she said: 'It was those people coming this afternoon that brought it all back. The man came from Australia. That was where *he* went all those years ago.'

'Who, Mamma?'

'Charles. I wish you could have known Charles. There was no one quite like him ever.'

'And who was he?'

'How could you say who Charles was? He came here as a drawing-master, my drawing-master. But he was more than that. I remember the day he arrived. I was in the school-room then. I was sixteen – younger than you are now. He was a few years older. He came in looking bold and arrogant – not in the least like a drawing-master and said: "Are you Miss Dorian? I've come to teach you." And he taught me so much, Minta, so very much.'

'Mamma,' I said, 'what made those people remind you of him?'

'Because they came from Australia and that was where he went – where they sent him. And that young man reminded me of him in a way. There was an air about him. Do you know what I mean? He didn't care what people thought of him. He knew he was as good – no, better – than anyone. Do you know what I mean?'

'Yes, I do.'

'It was cruel,' she went on. 'I hated your grandfather after that. Charles was innocent. As if he cared about my jewels! He wanted *me* . . . not what I could bring him. I'm sure of that, Minta.'

She had changed. The peevish invalid had disappeared. She even looked beautiful as she must have been years ago. I knew there was something significant about that visit this afternoon and I was enormously interested. 'Tell me about it,' I begged.

'Oh, my dear Minta, it seems like yesterday. I wish I could describe Charles to you.'

'You were in love with him, I suppose.'

'Yes,' she said. 'And I have been all my life.'

I felt this was disloyal to my father and I protested. 'Isn't that because he went out of your life when he was young and handsome and you've always seen him like that? If you could see him now you might have a terrible shock.'

'If I could see him now . . .' Her eyes were dreamy. 'That young man reminded me so much . . . it brought it all back. Those days when we were in the schoolroom; and then he said we must work out of doors. We would sit under the

chestnut tree . . . where we were sitting this afternoon and
he would sketch the flowers or a bird and I would have to
copy it. Then we went for walks together, studying wild life
and trying to put it on paper. He used to talk about
Whiteladies as Lucie does. It's strange how people are
impressed by the house. He never tired of talking of it. And
then we were in love and going to be married; and of course
your grandfather would not allow it.'

'You were only about seventeen, Mamma. Perhaps you
were carried away.'

'There are some things one can be sure of however young.
I was sure of this. Once having known Charles, I was certain
that no one else would ever mean to me what he did. He
said we must not tell your grandfather, that he would forbid
our marriage and something dreadful would happen, for
your grandfather was a very powerful man. But he discovered what was going on. Someone must have told him, and
Charles was dismissed. We planned to elope. My father was
afraid of Charles for he knew he was no ordinary young
man. I was guarded all the time but the notes were smug-
gled in and we made our arrangements. He climbed to my
room on the night we were going away together. I gave him
my jewellery to put in his pockets and keep for me while
we climbed down.' Her lips began to tremble. 'We were
betrayed. The jewellery was found on him and he was transported for seven years. Your grandfather was a hard man
and my heart was broken.'

'Poor Mamma, what a sad story! But would you have
been happy with him?'

'If you had ever known him you would understand. I
could be happy with no one else. He thought that if we
married, my father would forgive us in time. I was after all
his only daughter. Our children would be his grandchildren.
Charles used to say: "Our children will play on the lawns

of Whiteladies, never fear." But they sent him away and I never saw him again. I shall never, never forget.'

I understood then the reason for all those peevish years. She believed life had cheated her. Her love for this man she had chosen had turned into discontent with the husband who had been chosen for her. I should have been more tolerant towards her. I should try to be now.

'And at the back of my mind,' she went on, in an unusually revelatory manner, 'I always thought there was something I should have done. I was my father's only child. I could have threatened to run away, to kill myself – anything. I believe now that if I had, something would have been done. But I was afraid of your grandfather and I let them take him away without protest and five years later I married your father because that was what my father wished.'

'Well, Mamma,' I reminded her, 'Papa is a very good man. And this drawing-master might not have been all you imagined him to be.'

'Life with him might not always have been easy, but it would have been wonderfully worth while. As it is . . .'

'You have a great deal to be thankful for, Mamma,' I reminded her again; and she smiled at me rather wanly.

'I was a little reconciled when you were born, Minta. But that was a long time after our marriage. I thought we should never have a child. Perhaps if you had arrived earlier . . . and then of course your birth had such an effect on my health.'

She was her wan self again recalling the terrible period of gestation, the fearful ordeal of my arrival. I had heard it before and was not eager to do so again.

'And because those people came this afternoon you were reminded of the past,' I said quickly.

'I wish I knew what happened to him, Minta. To be sent away as a convict. That proud man!'

'I daresay he was ingenious enough to find a niche for himself.'

She smiled. 'That was a thought I consoled myself with.'

There was a knock on the door and Lizzie came in. Lizzie was about a year or so older than my mother. She had been nurse to me and before that my mother's maid. She treated me still as though I were a baby and was more familiar with my mother than any of the servants were. She had thick grey hair which was a riot of curls about her head; it was her only beauty but striking enough even now to make people look twice at her.

'You're keeping your mother from her sleep, Miss Minta,' she said. 'I thought she was tired out.'

'We've been talking,' I said.

Lizzie clicked her tongue. 'I know.' She turned to my mother. 'Shall I settle you for the night?'

My mother nodded so I kissed her good night and went out.

As I shut the door I heard her say eagerly and with the rare excited note in her voice: 'When I saw that young man this afternoon, it took me back years. You remember how he used to sit on the lawn with his sketching pad . . .'

I went to my room. Lizzie would have been here at the time, I thought. She would have seen it all.

Poor Mamma! How dreadful to live one's life in discontent, constantly dreaming of what might have been.

I found it difficult to sleep. The afternoon visitors had affected me as they had my mother.

The memory of that visit stayed with me for days afterwards. I should have liked to discuss it with Lucie but I felt that what my mother had told me had been in confidence. There was a painting of her which had been done about two years after the abortive elopement and she certainly appeared very beautiful. I looked at it differently now and saw the haunting sadness in her eyes. I thought of Grandfather Dorian, whom I vaguely remembered as a great power in the house, whose gruff commands used to send shivers of alarm down my young spine. I could imagine how stern he would have been with his own daughter. He approved of Papa as a husband, of course. Papa had been a titled gentleman of some means and highly suitable; he would have been gentle and submissive and have agreed to take up residence at Whiteladies. He had had a house nearby and an estate in Somerset which had come into his family's possession in 1749 when they had sprung into prominence through their loyalty to the Hanoverian cause. After that they had begun to build their fortune. We used to visit Somerset sometimes twice a year, but Papa had sold the estate two years ago as he had his other house. It was expensive to run them and we needed the money, he said. I wondered how poor Mamma had felt when she knew she was to be married. But she must have known she had lost her Charles for ever. I wondered, too, whether she had made any pretence of loving Papa.

I was in the garden picking flowers for the vases when Dr Hunter came out of the house. I called to him and he stood smiling at me.

'You have just been to see Mamma?' I asked. He said that he had, and I went on; 'I'd like to talk to you about her. Don't let her see us, though. She may look out from the window. She would immediately imagine that we were discussing some terrible new disease she had contracted.'

'Why not show me the roses?' he suggested.

'A good idea, but better still, come into the pond garden. We'll be really out of sight there.'

The pond garden was surrounded by a pleasant alley

which, in summer, made a luxuriantly green arch. I loved
the pond garden; it seemed shut away from the rest of the
house. I was sure that Mamma and her artist lover had sat
there by the water making their plans, feeling shut away
from the world. The flowers used to be much more colourful
when I was a child. We had more people working in the
garden then, and gardeners would change overnight the
spring tints for the rich shades of summer. I remember particularly vivid blue delphiniums and the heavy scent of pinks
and carnations – and later the bronze and purples of chrysanthemums and the unmistakable odour of the dying year. But
now, because it was late summer, the flowers were plentiful.
There was a white statue in the pond and waxen-petalled
lilies floated on the water. This garden had been copied,
Papa told me, two hundred years ago from that one in
Hampton Court where it was said Henry VIII had walked
with Anne Bolcyn.

'How ill is my mother?' I asked the doctor.

'Her illness is within herself,' he answered.

'You mean imaginary?'

'Well, she does have her headaches. She does suffer from
lassitude and vague pains.'

'You mean there is nothing really wrong with her.'

'Nothing organically wrong.'

'So her illness is in her mind and she could be better
tomorrow if she wanted to.'

'It's not as simple as that. This is a genuine state of sickness.'

'Something happened recently. Some people came and
reminded her of the past. She seemed almost young again.'

He nodded. 'She needs an interest in life. She needs to
think of something other than herself, past excitements and
present boredoms. That's all.'

'What can she be interested in, I wonder?'

'Perhaps when you marry and have grandchildren she will be so enchanted with them that she will find a new interest in life. Interest! That's what she wants.'

'I have no intention of marrying for a long time. Is she to wait for a cure until then?'

He laughed. 'We will do our best. She'll continue with her pills and medicines and find some relief from them.'

'But if she is not physically ill does she need medicine?'

'They are placebos. They help her because she believes in them. I'm sure that is how we have to treat her.'

'What a difficult task – to attempt to cure someone of something that doesn't exist!'

'But you are mistaken. This illness does exist. It is real. This is what I used to attempt to argue out with my predecessor. He believed that an illness was only an illness if it gave an outward and visible sign of being one. Don't worry, Miss Minta. We have your mother's case well in hand. Miss Maryan is very helpful, isn't she?'

'Lucie is wonderful.'

'Yes,' said the doctor, smiling in such a way that he betrayed his feelings for Lucie.

'Have you explained this to her . . . my mother's condition, I mean?'

'She is fully aware of it. In fact she guessed it. We were speaking of it only the other day when she came over for your mother's medicine.'

'The placebo?' I said.

'Yes, the placebo.'

'And how is Mrs Devlin these days?'

'As usual. She was a little florid of complexion with a slight pinkness at the tip of the nose when I returned home from visiting yesterday.'

'One day she may take a little too much.'

'One day! I suspect it happens most evenings. Well, we

should count our blessings, we are told; and apart from one failing she is a treasure. Until I can make other arrangements I must not be too critical.'

'Oh,' I said, 'you are thinking of making other arrangements?'

'Nothing definite . . . as yet.' He looked a little embarrassed and I realized I had been too inquisitive. But I was sure he was referring to Lucie.

We went back to the house and I stood talking to him while he got into his barouche and drove away.

I went to Lucie's room. It was always so neat and tidy; she handled the furniture as though it were sacred, which amused me. This was the room which she had been given on her first visit to Whiteladies and she loved it. Its ceiling was lofty and the family coat of arms was engraved on it; the hanging-chandelier was small but beautifully cut; it jingled slightly like temple bells; there was a large window with a window seat padded in mulberry velvet and mulberry-coloured rugs on the floor. The bed had a canopy. It really was charming, I suppose, but we had several similar rooms in Whiteladies and it hadn't struck me that there was anything special about this one until I noticed Lucie's loving care of it.

'I've just been talking to the doctor, Lucie,' I said.

She was sitting at the dressing-table and, looking down, she began moving the toilet articles there. I sat down on the chair with the carved back and the rail on which one could put one's feet. I studied her. She was by no means flamboyantly attractive; it was only that innate elegance which lifted her from the ordinary. Her face was too pale, her features too insignificant for beauty.

'He seems a little . . . unsettled in his domestic arrangements.'

'It's that housekeeper of his.'

'We ought to persuade him to get another. You never know what she might do. She might get to his drug cabinet and help herself to something poisonous.'

'She's not interested in drugs. It's the wine cellar she cares about.'

'But in a mood of drunken exuberance . . .'

'Hers are stupors, I believe.'

'But a doctor's housekeeper should be abstemious.'

'Everyone should be abstemious,' said Lucie gravely.

'I *do* like Dr Hunter,' I commented. 'I'd like to see him with a wife to help him along. Don't you think that's what he needs?'

'Most professional men need a wife to help them along,' replied Lucie noncommittally.

I laughed. 'There's a lot of the schoolmistress about you still, Lucie,' I said. 'Sometimes I could imagine you in class. Talking of marrying, if you ever decide to, I hope you won't go too far away from us.'

But Lucie was not to be drawn.

It was a sunny afternoon. The house seemed quiet. My mother was resting; my father was, too, I suspected, although he was in his study. Lucie had driven the dog-cart over to the doctor's to collect my mother's medicine; so I brought my embroidery out on to the lawn and sat under the oak tree, thinking as I often did of that day when the scarf had blown over the wall.

Franklyn called. He came over the lawn as he had on that other day and settled into the chair beside me.

'So you're all alone,' he said.

I told him where everyone was.

He made one or two comments about the estate and some

of the tenant farmers; this was one of his favourite subjects. He made it his business to know the details of their family life and I had heard that his tenants had nothing to fear from their landlord. He liked to talk to me about these affairs – perhaps because he shared the general view that one day they would be my affairs too, for the wife of a landlord like Franklyn would have her duties to the estate. Franklyn was such a good man, but so predictable. One knew without asking what his views would be on almost any subject one could think of.

I felt a mischievous desire to shock him, so I talked of the matter which was uppermost in my mind – that of Lucie and her relationship with Dr Hunter.

'Lucie has gone over to Dr Hunter's to get Mamma's medicine,' I said. 'She enjoys riding over. I daresay she contemplates with pleasure the day when she will be mistress of the house.'

'So they are engaged to be married?' asked Franklyn.

'Nothing has been said, but . . .'

'Then how can you be sure?'

'But isn't it obvious?'

'You mean that there is an attachment? I should say there is the possibility of an engagement, but how can one be sure until it is an actuality?'

Dear Franklyn! He talked like a chairman addressing a board meeting. That was how his mind worked – precise, completely logical. He had a set of conventions and he would adhere to them rigidly.

'But, Franklyn, it will be absolutely ideal.'

'Superficially considered, yes. But one cannot really say that a marriage is ideal until there has been at least a year's trial.'

'Still, I think we should be delighted if Dr Hunter were to ask Lucie's hand in marriage and she were to accept him.

I should like to see Lucie happily settled. After all, Dr Hunter is so eligible and there is no one else in the district who is suitable to be Lucie's husband, so it will have to be Dr Hunter. She would have a calming influence on disturbed patients who arrive at the surgery, and she could probably learn to mix medicines. She is very clever.'

'I am sure you are right and it would be an admirable arrangement. There is something I have wanted to say to you for a long time, Araminta.'

He used my full name when he was being solemn so I knew that an important matter was about to be discussed. Is he going to propose? I asked myself. This talk of Lucie's marriage has put ours into his head. I was wrong. Franklyn would never propose marriage on the spur of the moment. If and when he came to ask me, he would come with the appropriate ceremony, having asked Papa's permission first.

'Yes, Franklyn,' I said, with a faint note of alarm in my voice, for I could not rid myself of the thought that he was working towards a proposal which I should be expected to accept – and I didn't want to.

His next words brought relief. 'I have tried to talk to your father but he is not anxious to hear. I could not, of course, talk to your mother. I think that there may well be cause for anxiety concerning your family's financial affairs.'

'You mean we are short of money?'

He hesitated. Then he said: 'I am convinced that your father's affairs are in an uneasy condition. I believe that it is a matter which should not be ignored.'

'Franklyn, will you tell me exactly what you mean?'

'I am a land-owner,' he said, 'not a financier. But one does not have to be that to understand what is going on in the markets. Your father and my father have been friends for years. They had the same man of business, similar investments. The bulk of my possessions are in land, but this is not the case with your father. He has Whiteladies and I am afraid little else. He sold the Somerset property some years ago and the money raised was invested – not wisely, I fear. Your father is not exactly a man of business.'

'Do you mean that we have become poor, Franklyn?'

'Hardly that. But I think you should curb any extravagance in the household. I am warning you because your parents don't seem to understand the necessity not to spend beyond their income. Forgive my candid talk, but I am a little worried. I should not like to see Whiteladies fall into disrepair.'

I felt depressed. So my father was worried about money, or at least he ought to be. He wouldn't be, of course. He would forget what was unpleasant; as for Mamma, she would be completely vague if I broached the subject to her. And Franklyn? What was the motive behind his warning? If he married me he would come to live at Whiteladies as Papa had come. If the house could not be passed down through the male line it would have to be through the female. Mamma had inherited; so would I. The family name might have to change but the blood link was there. So now Franklyn was thinking of Whiteladies; he was concerned because Papa's indigence might make it impossible for him to keep up the house until he, Franklyn, took over.

I remember that when I had told Papa that there was worm in the beams of one of the turret chambers, he had shrugged it aside, and I knew that the matter should have been dealt with. There were several floorboards which were in urgent need of repair and had been neglected for months. My father shut his eyes to these things and now I was picturing ourselves living on at Whiteladies with the place gradually becoming uninhabitable. I could imagine my father shut up in his room refusing to listen while the house slowly crumbled away.

I said: 'What can I do about this?'

'Try to bring in a little economy. If you get a chance talk to your father. Things are not what they were twenty years ago. Taxation has increased; the cost of living has followed; it is a changing world, and we have to adjust ourselves to it.'

'I doubt that I can do very much. If Papa won't listen to you, he won't to me.'

'If you tell him you are a little anxious . . .'

'But he won't *do* anything. He just shuts himself into his study and dozes over his manuscript.'

There! I had said it. I had let out the secret of Papa's work. But perhaps it was not really a secret and Franklyn knew as well as I did. What I had done was mention what politeness and convention ruled as unmentionable.

'I'll speak to Lucie,' I said. 'I daresay she would know how to institute economies far better than I.'

'That's an excellent idea,' agreed Franklyn.

Then having done his duty, which I was sure he always would, he changed the subject and we talked of village affairs until I heard Lucie coming back with the dog-cart.

After that night when she had confided in me, Mamma grew more peevish than ever. She spent a great deal of time in her room; trays were sent up at meal-times and I knew that she did justice to the food because I saw Lizzie bringing them away empty several times.

Lizzie was in her confidence and sometimes when I visited her last thing at night, she would seem almost eager to be rid of me and before I was out of the room she would start talking to Lizzie. 'You remember that day when Mr Herrick and I were in the garden . . .' or 'There was that occasion when Papa asked him to join us for dinner. We were a man short and he was so distinguished . . .' I imagined she bored poor Lizzie with her reminiscences of the past. But perhaps Lizzie could be more understanding than I since she had seen this superior gentleman who had been transported ignobly to Australia.

Poor Papa! She was so impatient with him. She seemed to have taken a great dislike to him; she was irritable and scarcely took the trouble to answer him civilly. So we were all glad when she decided to stay in her room for meals. It was a situation which I found both distressing and embarrassing. I wished that these people had never come. Once again I was grateful for Lucie's presence for she seemed to know exactly what to do. When Mamma had been very slighting to my father, Lucie would make some comment about his work and he would forget the insult for the compliment. It was such a pity because if ever a man knew how to be happy, that man was my father, with his talent for shrugging aside what was unpleasant. He kept away from my mother as much as possible and Lucie went more frequently to his study, so I daresay the book really was making progress.

Lucie was so devoted to us that our family affairs were hers and while she tried to give my father importance she also sympathized with my mother. I think that, next to Lizzie, she was confided in more than any of us. But it was becoming a somewhat uneasy household.

One day, having been to Dr Hunter's to get my mother's medicine, Lucie came back looking flushed and disturbed. She took the medicine to my mother's room and when she came out I called her into mine.

'Come in and have a chat,' I said. 'Mamma has been in a terrible mood today.'

Lucie frowned. 'I know. I wish those people hadn't come.'

'It seems so odd. People call like that, strangers, and things change.'

'It had begun before really,' said Lucie. 'But these people reminded your mother of the past.'

'How I wish she could see this superior being now. I daresay he is old and grey and no longer looks so handsome. Poor Papa, I'm sorry for him.'

'Yes,' said Lucie. 'It's so easy to make him happy and such a pity that he can't be.' Then she blurted out: 'Minta, Dr Hunter has asked me to marry him.'

'Oh, Lucie, congratulations.'

'Thanks, but I haven't decided.'

'But, Lucie, it would be an ideal marriage.'

'How can you know?'

I laughed. 'You sound just like Franklyn. I think you will make a wonderful doctor's wife. He'll be able to get rid of that drunken Devlin and you will look after him perfectly. I do hope he realizes how lucky he is.'

'But I told you I haven't decided yet.'

'You will.'

'You sound as though you'll be glad to be rid of me.'

'How can you say that when you know that one of the reasons why I'm so pleased is that it will keep you near us.'

'But I shan't be at Whiteladies.'

'I believe it's the house you like, Lucie, better than us. It was the same with . . .' No, I was going to forget that insignificant incident. But he *had* been abnormally interested in the house. I could understand it, in a way, because he had lived all his life in Australia and Whiteladies must have been one of the first ancient mansions he had ever seen. But Lucie was as obsessed as he was.

'Well,' I finished, 'you won't be far away.'

'He's very ambitious. I doubt that he will settle to be a country doctor all his life. He plans to go to London to specialize and set up his plate in Harley or Wimpole Street.'

'I hadn't thought of that. Even so, you will make a

272

wonderful doctor's wife, Lucie, and since he is so ambitious you are just the wife for him. I hate the thought of your going, but London is not so far. We could meet often.'

'You make it all sound so simple.'

'Well, I daresay it will be, and in any case he may decide to spend the rest of his life here. What would he specialize in?'

'He's interested in cases like your mother's.'

'You mean people who are not really ill to begin with but imagine themselves into illness.'

'Diseases of the mind,' said Lucie.

'I shall be desolate if you go, but at the same time I think you should.'

'My dear Minta, you have to let me manage my own affairs, you know. I haven't decided yet.'

I was surprised, realizing there was a great deal about Lucie that I didn't understand. I had imagined her to be calm and precise, choosing the sensible way; but perhaps after all she was romantic. It was clear that she was not passionately in love with Dr Hunter; but she must realize what a wonderful chance it would be for her to marry him.

It was a misty November day; there was not a breath of wind and everything was depressingly damp. There were countless spiders' webs draped over the bushes, glistening with tiny globules of moisture and everything seemed unusually silent. The mist penetrated the house. It was like a vague presence.

All the morning Lucie had been working about the house; it was wonderful the way she superintended everything. The servants did not mind, except perhaps Mrs Glee who vaguely suspected that she was taking over some of her duties. Lucie would go down to the kitchen and order the meals after having submitted suggestions to Mamma through Lizzie. Mamma never looked at them but Lucie insisted on their being shown to her. Lucie was a wonderful housekeeper and should have been running a house of her own.

I spent most of the morning in the flower-room. There was not much left in the garden besides chrysanthemums, asters, dahlias and Michaelmas daisies. As I arranged them I was thinking how dull life was here, doing the same things almost at the same time every day. I sniffed the subtle autumnal smell these flowers have and I saw myself through the years ahead arranging the flowers – primroses, daffodils, and the spring sunshine-coloured flowers down to the holly and mistletoe of December – always here in the flower-room which had once been a nun's cell with its stone floor and small high window in the wall with the three bars across it. And I longed for life to change. Afterwards I remembered the fervour of my longing and thought how strange it was that on that day life should change so drastically.

Looking into the starry faces of the daisies, I saw his face, the green eyes, the arrogant features. It was absurd to go on remembering a stranger whom I had met by chance and very likely would never see again.

One of the maids came in to carry the flowers away and put them in the places I had chosen. It was an hour before luncheon would be served; normally I should have taken a walk round the garden but it was such a damp and dismal morning. So I stayed in my room and my thoughts went back and back again to the incident of the girl with the scarf, and I thought of Mamma who in this house had been loved and had loved, and consequently must have been quite unlike the woman she was today. I wondered if I should grow old and peevish, looking back resentfully because life had passed me by.

Dr Hunter called and was with Mamma for half an hour.

Before he left he asked to see me and said he would like to have a little talk with Papa as well; so we went up to Papa's study and he and the doctor drank a glass of sherry while Dr Hunter talked to us of Mamma.

'You must realize,' said Dr Hunter, 'that there is no reason at all why Lady Cardew should not lead a reasonably normal life. She is breathless, yes – because she is out of condition. She stays in her room nursing a non-existent heart trouble. I am of the opinion that we have all been pandering to her whims, and I think we should now try different tactics.'

As I was listening I was visualizing him in tastefully furnished rooms in Harley Street treating rich patients and going home to Lucie, who would entertain brilliant doctors and learn enough of her husband's profession to join intelligently in the very learned conversation. It pleased me to think of her as the school teacher she had been before I had discovered her. I wondered why she did not give Dr Hunter his answer.

'We will try a little experiment,' he said. 'Not so much sympathy, please.'

Dr Hunter went on to expound his theories. He was going to start a new line of healing. He grew very animated talking of the experiments he intended to make. I was sure we should lose him to Harley Street very soon – and Lucie too to some extent if she married him. If! But of course she would.

'Just a little gentle reproof,' he went on. 'Don't be too harsh at first.'

Papa asked him to stay to luncheon but he was too busy. He finished his sherry and left us.

Mamma came down to luncheon in one of her more difficult moods. 'This weather brings on all my pains,' she grumbled. 'The damp seeps into my bones. You can't imagine the pain.'

Papa, eager to put into practice the doctor's suggestions

replied: 'We don't need to employ our imaginations, my dear, because you have described it in such detail so often.'

Mamma was completely taken aback. That my usually tolerant and easy-going father should criticize her in such an unsympathetic manner was a great shock to her.

'So I am a nuisance, am I?' she demanded.

'My dear, you misconstrue.'

'It was what you implied. Oh, I know I am ill, and to those of you who have the great gift of good health, that makes me dull and useless. How unkind you are! If only you knew how I suffer! I could almost wish that you were afflicted with one hundredth part of the pain that I feel – then you might have some understanding. But no, I wouldn't wish that for anyone. What has my life been but one long bed of pain. Ever since you were born, Minta, I have suffered.'

'I'm sorry, Mamma, that I am responsible.'

'Now you are jeering at me. I never thought you would do that openly although I have long known that I was a burden and a nuisance to you. Oh, if only my life had been different. If only I had had the good fortune . . .'

It was an old theme. My father had half risen in his chair, his face pink, his usually mild eyes clouded with distress. I knew that there must have been vague references over the years to what might have been if she had had the good fortune to marry the man of her choice instead of him.

My sympathies were entirely with him and I said: 'Why, Mamma, you have had a very happy life with the best husband in the world.'

She silenced me, looking wildly about the room and staring beyond my father as though she saw something of which we were not aware. I know she was thinking of that man and it was almost as though he were in the room, he who had been taken away and shipped abroad as a thief, as though he were taunting her with what might have been if she had been bolder and insisted on marrying him.

'The best husband in the world!' she cried mockingly. 'What has he done to make him that? He sits in his study working . . . working, he says! *Sleeping* his life away! His book, his famous book! That is like him. He is nothing, nothing. And I might have had a very different life.'

Lucie said: 'Lady Cardew, Dr Hunter told me that you must not get over-excited. Will you allow me to take you to your room?'

The thought of herself as an invalid soothed her. She turned almost gratefully to Lucie who led her from the room.

Papa and I looked after her. I felt so sorry for him; he looked completely bewildered.

'I don't think Dr Hunter's treatment worked,' I said. 'Never mind, Papa. We did our best.'

It was an uneasy day. Several of the servants must have heard my mother's outburst. My father seemed to have shrunk a little; there was something shame-faced about him. We had all suspected that he dozed at his desk and that most of the work had been done by Lucie; but it had never been said to his face before – and now that it had been, the fact had a significance it had never had before.

My mother spent the day in her room declaring that she did not want to see anybody. I saw Lizzie, who told me she had slept for some part of the afternoon having worn herself out crying.

'She'll be better tomorrow, Miss Minta,' comforted Lizzie.

I talked it over with Lucie, who was very distressed.

'It's quite clear that criticism doesn't help Mamma,' I said.

'Your father is too gentle by nature. Perhaps he should have continued as he began.'

'He is too kind to take up a new role. It's like changing his character.'

It was natural that Lucie would not admit that Dr Hunter's diagnosis was wrong. She repeated Lizzie's words: 'She'll be better tomorrow.'

Before I retired that night I went up to my mother's room, but hesitated before entering. As I stood at the door I heard my mother's voice: 'You're wicked! Oh, how I wish I could go back all those years. I'd know what to do because you're wicked . . . wicked.'

I pictured my father's mild bewildered eyes and I decided that I would not go into that room. So I went to my own and lay awake for a long time thinking of the sadness of my parents' lives and all the lost years when they might have been happy.

Neither of them was to blame. I wished that I had been able to go in and tell them this, to implore them to forget the past and start afresh from now.

How I wished that I *had* gone in that night! I never saw my mother alive again.

Next morning when Lizzie went in to awaken her she found her dead.

Chapter Two

*L*IZZIE said afterwards that she had a strange premonition; she was waiting for the bell to ring for the early morning tea and when it didn't come she went in.

'She was lying there,' said Lizzie, 'and there was something different about her. And when I went close . . . oh, my God!'

Lizzie had been hysterical and incoherent but she did run for Lucie and Lucie came to me. I awoke with a start to find them both standing by my bed.

Lucie said: 'Minta, you have to prepare yourself for a shock.'

I scrambled up and stared at them.

'It's your mother,' said Lucie. 'Something dreadful . . .'

'Is she . . . dead?'

Lucie nodded slowly. She was unlike herself – her eyes were wide, her pupils seemed dilated and her mouth quivered; I felt she was fighting hard to control herself. Lizzie started to sob.

'After all these years . . . It's not true. There's a mistake. She's fainted, that's what it is.'

'I have sent for Dr Hunter,' said Lucie.

'And my father?' I asked.

'I haven't sent word to him yet. I thought we'd wait until the doctor came. There's nothing he can do.'

'But he should know.'

'I went into her room,' murmured Lizzie. 'You see, she hadn't rung . . .' Then she covered her face with her hands and continued to sob.

I snatched up my dressing-gown and said: 'I'll go to her.'

Lucie shook her head. 'Don't,' she said.

'But I must. I don't believe she's dead. Only yesterday Dr Hunter was saying . . .'

I had moved past Lucie to the door; she was beside me and walked with me to my mother's room.

'Don't, Minta,' whispered Lucie. 'Wait . . . wait until the doctor's been.'

She held my hand tightly and drew me gently along the corridor to her room.

By the time Dr Hunter arrived my father was up. Lucie had talked to him as she had talked to me, soothing us, really taking matters in hand. My father was quite willing for her to do this; so was I.

It was Lucie who went with the doctor into my mother's room.

'Take your father to the library and stay there till we come,' she said. 'Look after your father. This is a terrible shock for him.'

It seemed a long time before the doctor and Lucie came to us. It was in fact fifteen minutes.

Dr Hunter was shaken; a good deal of his jaunty assurance had deserted him. No wonder! Since yesterday he had said my mother's ailments were more or less imaginary, and now she was dead.

'So it's true?' my father said blankly.

'She died of heart failure during the night,' said Dr Hunter.

'So she had a bad heart after all, Doctor?'

'No.' He spoke defiantly. 'It could happen to any of us at any time. There was nothing organically wrong with her heart. Of course the invalid life she led was not conducive to good health. This was a case of the heart's suddenly failing to function.'

'Poor Mamma!' I said.

I was sorry for Dr Hunter. He seemed so distressed; he kept his eyes on my father's face as though he expected sympathy. Sympathy for what? Making a wrong diagnosis? Suspecting his patient was a malingerer and treating her as such when she was seriously ill?

Lucie's eyes were fixed on him but he avoided looking at her. Once or twice he turned his gaze on me and then hastily back to my father.

'This is a great shock,' I said. 'Yesterday she was her normal self . . .'

'It happens like this now and then,' said the doctor.

'Minta and her father are very upset, naturally,' said Lucie. 'If they'll allow me I'll make the necessary arrangements.'

My father looked at her with gratitude and the doctor said: 'That would be very satisfactory, I think.'

Lucie signed to him and they went out together, leaving me with my father in the library. He raised his eyes to my face and I could not help being aware that it was shock not grief I saw there. Nor could I fail to notice his relief.

Later we went to see Mamma; she was lying in bed, her eyes closed; the frills of her white nightdress were up to her chin. She looked more peaceful in death than she ever had in life.

Something strange had happened to the house. It was no longer the same. Mamma lay in the churchyard where our family had been buried for the last five hundred years. The family vault had been ceremoniously opened; and we had gone through the mournful burial service. The shutters had been opened, the blinds drawn up. Lizzie had been ill for a week or so after the funeral and had emerged among us, gaunt and subdued.

Lucie had changed too; there was a certain aloofness about her. My father was different; it was as though a burden had been removed from his shoulders, and although he had tried to, he could not altogether hide his relief.

But perhaps the most changed of us all was Dr Hunter. Before my mother's death he had been a sociable young man; ambitious in the extreme, he had been the friend of local families as well as their doctor. He had endeavoured to make people forget his youth by his excessive confidence; he had clearly been eager to climb to the top of his profession. The change in him was subtle, but nevertheless marked – certainly to me.

I thought I understood. My mother had been ill. The pains she had complained of had been real; he had seen her, though, as a fractious, discontented woman – which she was – and had allowed his assessment of her character to cloud his judgment. It seemed clear to me that he had made a faulty diagnosis and that this had so upset his confidence in himself that it was having a marked effect on him. It would throw doubt on his advanced theories on which he was basing his career. I was sorry for him.

He called rarely at the house. None of us needed him professionally until I called him in to see Lizzie because I became worried about her. This was a week or so after the funeral and then I had a conversation with him.

'You're not looking well yourself, Doctor,' I said.

'Are you saying "Physician, heal thyself"?'

'I believe you are worrying about my mother's death.'

I was immediately sorry that I had introduced the subject so abruptly, for a nervous twitch started in his cheek, and his head jerked sharply like a puppet's.

'No, no,' he said quickly. 'It is not such an unusual case as you appear to think. It can happen to completely healthy people. A clot of blood to the brain or heart and death can be the result. There is in some cases no warning. And your mother was scarcely a healthy woman, although there was nothing organically wrong. I have read of many such cases. I have encountered several when I was in hospital. No, no. It was not so very unusual.'

He was talking too fast and too persuasively. If what he said was true, why should he blame himself? It was unfortunate that the very day before she died he had told me that she had imagined her illness and we must ignore it.

'All the same,' I said, 'you seem to reproach yourself.'

'Not in the least. It is something one cannot foresee.'

'I'm so glad I'm mistaken. We know that you took the utmost care of my mother.'

He seemed a little reconciled, but I was sure he was avoiding us for he never called socially at Whiteladies.

My father shut himself in his study for long periods. Lucie told me that he was a great deal more upset than he appeared to be, and the fact that for the first time he had spoken to his wife unsympathetically, filled him with remorse.

'I am trying to get him working really hard on the book,' said Lucie. 'I think it best for him.'

Lucie was wonderful during that time. She asked if Lizzie might be her personal maid. 'Not,' she said deprecatingly, 'that I need one, nor in my position should have one. I think, though, that for a time it would do Lizzie good. She has had a terrible shock.'

I said she must do as she liked for I was sure she knew best.

'Dear Minta,' she said, '*you* are the mistress of Whiteladies now.'

It was a thought which hadn't occurred to me before.

Franklyn was with us constantly from the day of my mother's death. He helped my father in all the ways which Lucie couldn't. I often wondered what we should have done at that time without Lucie or Franklyn.

He rode over to Whiteladies every day and I could be sure of seeing him some time. We talked about my mother and how unhappy she had been and I said how sad it was that she had gone through life never enjoying it, apart from one little episode when her magnificent drawing-master had come to the house and she had fallen in love with him. I rather enjoyed talking about such things with Franklyn because his prosaic views and his terse way of expressing them amused me.

'I suppose,' I said, 'that it's better to have had one exciting experience in your life than go along at a smooth and comfortable level all the time . . . even though you do spend the rest of your life repining.'

'That seems to me a very unreasonable deduction,' said Franklyn.

'You would say that! I am sure your life will be comfortable and easy for ever and ever, unruffled by any incident, disturbing or ecstatic.'

'Another unreasonable deduction.'

'But you would never make any mistakes; therefore the element of excitement is removed.'

'Why do you think it is only interesting to make mistakes?'

'If you know how everything is going to work out . . .'

'But nobody knows how everything is going to work out. You are being quite illogical, Minta.'

And I laughed for the first time since my mother had died.

I tried to explain to him the change in the household. 'It's as though the ghost of Mamma cannot rest.'

'That's pure imagination on your part.'

'Indeed it's not. Everybody has changed. Haven't you noticed it? But of course you haven't. You never notice things like that.'

'I appear to be completely unobservant to you?'

'Only psychologically. For all practical purposes your powers of observation would be very keen.'

'How kind of you to say so.'

'Sarcasm does not become you, Franklyn. Nor is it natural to you. You are much too kind. But there *is* a change in the household. My father is relieved . . .'

'Minta!'

'Now you are shocked. But the truth should not shock anyone.'

'I think you should be more restrained in your conversation.'

'I am only talking to you, Franklyn. There is no one else in the world to whom I would say this. And how can we blame him? I know one is not supposed to speak ill of the dead and therefore you never would. But Mamma was beastly to him, so it is only natural that he should feel relieved. Lizzie goes round looking lost and yet she and Mamma were always quarrelling and Lizzie was always on the point of being dismissed or leaving voluntarily.'

'That is not unusual in attachments such as theirs, and it is quite natural that she should be "lost", as you say. She has been deprived of a mistress.'

'But poor Dr Hunter is worse than any of them. I am

285

sure he blames himself. He seems to avoid calling at the house.'

'It is natural that he should since the invalid is no longer there.'

'And Lucie has changed.'

'I'm sorry to hear that. She appears to be the most sensible member of the household.'

'She seems shut in, aloof, not so easy to talk to. I suppose she's worried about Dr Hunter. I wonder she didn't announce their engagement when it happened.'

'Why?'

'Well, as Dr Hunter is depressed and thinks he made the wrong diagnosis . . .'

'Who said he did?'

'Well, I think he did.'

'You should not say such a thing, even to me. It's slander when discussing a professional man.'

'But, Franklyn, you are not a court of law.'

'You must not be frivolous, Minta. You must stop this romanticising, this attempt to build up a dramatic situation.'

'It's because you're such a close friend that I can say anything to you. Besides, I like to shock you. But I wanted to tell you something. Yesterday Lucie came to me and suggested we get rid of Mrs Glee. She's not really needed, she says. Lucie can do all that she does, for now that Mamma is dead Lucie is relieved of a lot of her duties.'

'It seems a reasonable and logical suggestion. I have tried to tell you many times that you are living beyond your means. Mrs Glee is the most expensive of your retainers. Yes, it's an excellent idea.'

'You would see the practical side of it. The point is, if Lucie is going to take on Mrs Glee's duties and run Whiteladies, what of her marriage to Dr Hunter?'

'There was nothing arranged.'

'He had asked her. She was considering. It was just before Mamma's death. Poor Dr Hunter!'

'Has it occurred to you that his depression may be due to the fact that his proposal has not been accepted?'

'I still think it has something to do with Mamma's death.'

'Minta, it's time you grew up. I wish you would. That would be desirable in many ways.'

I guessed then that he was thinking that when I showed more maturity he would ask me to marry him; and into my mind there flashed a picture of that scene on the lawn with Stirling lolling, somewhat ungracefully, in the chair, talking about Australia and Whiteladies.

And I thought: No, I'll not grow up yet. My immaturity is a kind of protection.

A few mornings later a rather disturbing incident occurred. I was in the flower-room splitting the stalks of some bronze-coloured chrysanthemums when Mrs Glee burst in.

'I'd like a word with you, Miss Minta,' she said.

Her face was red and her little eyes like pieces of black jet. She didn't have to tell me she was angry.

'Certainly, Mrs Glee. Come into the library.'

'There's no need for that. I'll tell you here and now. I've had orders to go and I'd like to know why, because these orders have come from a certain quarter and I've yet to learn that I take orders from that direction.'

'From Miss Maryan?' I said. 'As a matter of fact, Mrs Glee, we have become much poorer in the last few years and we have to cut our expenses in some ways.'

'And I'm chosen as the victim, eh?'

'Not a victim, Mrs Glee. It's simply a matter of necessity.'

'Now, miss,' she said, 'I've nothing against you. You're innocent of all this. A blind man could see that. But if people ought to leave this house – and I'd be the first to admit it mightn't be a bad thing if they did – there's some you could do better without than me.'

'It's very sad to have to do without anyone, and only a matter of finance.'

'You've had the words put into your mouth, Miss Minta. There's some funny things going on in this house. I could tell you . . .'

'What things?'

Mrs Glee pressed her lips together with an air of martyrdom. 'Things it's not my place to mention. You're the mistress of the house now your poor mother's gone, and it's not for you to take a step back and let others help themselves to what's yours by rights.'

'I shan't do that, Mrs Glee.'

'You might be forced into it. I don't like the way things are going in this house and it's not all that sorry I'll be to pack my bags and be off. But I'm sorry for *you*, Miss Minta.'

'How kind of you. I'm sure I don't deserve your sympathy.'

It was evidently the right line for her anger calmed considerably; she was changing rapidly from virago to prophet of doom.

She took a step closer to me and said: 'Your poor Mamma going off like that, and that Lizzie. What of her, eh? If anyone should go, she should. The way she talked to that poor dead soul. Shouting and screaming they were, the night before. I heard your poor mother say that Lizzie was to go. It was her last wish, you might say. And now Lizzie's to be kept on and I'm told to go. I, who never had a cross word with the dear dead lady. You see, Miss Minta, it's a funny state of affairs, wouldn't you say?'

'Hardly funny,' I said. 'Lizzie was very fond of my mother and my mother of her. Their quarrels meant nothing.'

'The last one did. But it's not so much Lizzie. She's nothing. It's Other People.'

'Which people?'

'Well, Miss Minta, have you ever thought you might soon be having a new Mamma?'

'No.'

'You see!' She folded her arms across her ample chest. 'I'm telling you, Miss Minta. It's not that I care for myself. I've had enough of service anyway. I'm going to my cousin once removed down Dover way. Very comfortably off she is and her rheumatics are crippling her. She wants someone to look after her, be a companion to her, and she'll leave me the cottage and a little bit to keep me going. So I'm not concerned for myself. But I says: There's that innocent young lady. And there's some funny things going on in Whiteladies. And that's why I'm warning you.'

'I'm so pleased, Mrs Glee, about your cousin.'

'You're a sweet young lady. Miss Minta, and I've often said so. But I'll repeat this: There's something peculiar going on and you should know of it. There's someone who wants to run this household. There's someone who has the trap set and there's innocent people who will walk right into it. And I'm to go. Why? Because I see a bit further than my nose.'

I sighed and picking up the pot carried it out of the flower-room. I looked over my shoulder and said: 'I'm sure your cousin will be pleased to have you, Mrs Glee.'

She stood shaking her head prophetically and I went through into the library. I put the pot down as soon as I comfortably could because my hands were shaking. I was quite upset, and relieved too, when, a few days later, declaring that she would not stay a minute longer than was necessary where she was not wanted, Mrs Glee accepted a month's wages and departed.

Her absence made no difference to the running of the house. Lucie was busy, but then she always had been. My mother had never been interested in household affairs, and Mrs Glee had been mainly occupied in keeping the maids in order and preserving a certain dignity in the servants' quarters. Lucie did this and much more besides. The maids were glad to be rid of the formidable Mrs Glee and readily accepted Lucie in her place. I saw less of Lucie, but my father saw more of her.

I was always waiting for Lucie to confide in me about Dr Hunter, but she didn't. She was in my father's study for an hour in the morning and again after tea.

'I'm urging him to get on seriously with the book,' she told me. 'It's the best thing for him. It keeps his mind off the tragedy.'

Lizzie took her tea in the morning just as she had taken Mamma's, and Lucie kept her busy doing her room and Papa's, and all sorts of sewing for the household at which Lizzie was very good.

Two months passed in this way. Christmas came and went. We celebrated it very quietly. Franklyn and his parents came to dine with us on Christmas Day and they stayed to supper. We played a quiet game of whist – Papa and Lady Wakefield, Franklyn and I; and Lucie was there sitting quietly by the fire chatting with Sir Everard and at appropriate times making sure that the servants brought in refreshments and performed those duties necessary to our comforts.

I recalled the Christmas before when we had dined in the great hall under bunches of holly and mistletoe, and how one of the most merry members of the party had been Dr Hunter. Mamma had been at one end of the table enjoying talking to the doctor of her ailments. Lucie, of course, had been present, unobtrusive and competent. I remember she had worn a dress the colour of mauve orchids and how elegant she had looked in spite of the fact that she had made the dress herself. Now Lizzie made clothes on Lucie's instructions – Lucie designing, Lizzie stitching. It was an excellent combination.

After the guests had gone and everyone had retired for the night I slipped on my dressing-gown and went along to Lucie's room.

'Do you mind?' I said. 'I couldn't sleep.'

She offered me the chair with the mulberry cushions and she sat on the bed.

'I kept thinking of last Christmas,' I said.

'Poor Minta, you miss your mother.'

I frowned. I didn't want to be hypocritical. I had loved Mamma, but she had made life uncomfortable from time to time and I couldn't forget that last scene in the dining-room and the look of abject misery I had seen on my father's face.

I said quickly: 'What about you and Dr Hunter, Lucie? You were considering marrying him.'

'Who said I was? Do you want me to go?'

'How can you ask such a thing! We should be lost without you. But I think poor Dr Hunter is in greater need of comfort and as you love him . . .'

'You jump to conclusions, Minta. I'm fond of the doctor. I'm fond of you all here, and when your mother died I seemed to be needed.'

'But you mustn't make such a sacrifice.'

'It's willingly made . . . if such it is.'

'But I'm so sorry for the doctor. I think he's very unhappy and you could help him. He feels he didn't do the right thing . . . for Mamma.'

'How can you be sure of that?'

'It's obvious. He thought she was pretending and it turned out she wasn't. Perhaps if he had believed she was really ill

291

he would have treated her case differently. Perhaps that was what she needed.'

'But you are accusing him of incompetence!'

'I'm not. I know he's competent. But people make mistakes.'

'Doctors can't afford to. For heaven's sake, don't talk of this to anyone.'

'I wouldn't to anyone but you . . . and Franklyn, who doesn't count.'

'Not to anyone,' she said fervently. 'Promise me.'

I thought: She does love him then? I promised readily.

'And forget it, Minta,' she went on. 'Put it right out of your mind. It's . . . unhealthy. Your mother died of a stroke. It could happen to anybody. I have heard of people, healthy people, being struck down suddenly, and your mother had impaired her constitution by her invalidism.'

'I know, Lucie, I know.'

'Your mother is dead and buried. We must try to go on from there.'

I nodded.

'Don't forget,' she added gently, 'that I am here to help and comfort you. Wasn't it always like that, from the time of our schooldays?'

I agreed that it was. 'But you shouldn't make sacrifices, Lucie. We can look after ourselves. And you wouldn't be far away at the doctor's house.'

Lucie shook her head. 'I don't think I shall ever be at the doctor's house,' she said. 'I believe my place is here . . . in Whiteladies.'

'I repeat, Lucie, you must not sacrifice yourself.'

'Martyrs are tiresome people,' she said with a smile. 'I have no intention of being one. This is where I want to be, Minta. This is where I want to stay.'

I should have seen it coming but it was a shock when it did.

It was May – six months after my mother's death – a lovely day, almost summer, with the birds singing their delighted chorus and the buds sprouting everywhere, the chestnuts in blossom and the orchard a mass of pink and white and in the air was that unmistakable feeling that life is wonderful and happiness is just round the corner. This is the miracle of the English spring.

I had been for a ride after luncheon as far out as the Wakefield estates and had come in thinking how pleasant a cup of tea would be. It wanted another quarter of an hour to four o'clock, so I went and sat under the chestnut tree.

And there Lucie joined me. I watched her walking across the lawn. She was very different from the school teacher she had been when I first met her. There had been an air of defiance about her then. Now she walked with a springy step and the new gown which Lizzie had made to her instructions became her well. She was what the French call *une jolie laide*. Taken feature by feature she was decidedly plain, but there was an unusual charm in the complete picture which almost amounted to beauty.

'I want to talk to you rather specially,' she said.

'Come and sit down, Lucie.'

She did. I looked at her profile – the too long nose, the jutting chin.

'I have something very important to say to you and I am unsure how you will take it.'

'You look sure that I am going to like it.'

'I wish I were.'

'Why do you keep me in suspense? Tell me quickly. I'm impatient to hear.'

She took a deep breath and said: 'Minta, I am going to marry your father.'

'Lucie!'

'There! You are shocked.'

'But . . . Lucie!'

'Does it seem so incongruous?'

'Well, it's so unexpected.'

'We have been fond of each other for a long time.'

'But he's years older than you, Lucie.'

'You are finding excuses to oppose us.'

'I'm not. It's true that you are half his age.'

'What of it? I'm serious for my years. Don't you agree?'

'But you and the doctor . . .'

'You imagined a great deal about that affair.'

'But he did ask you to marry him.'

'And I didn't accept him.'

'And now you and Papa . . .'

'Does it worry you that I shall be your stepmother?'

'Of course not. And how could I not want you to be a member of the family? You are in any case. It's just that . . .'

'It seems unsuitable?'

'It's just that it hadn't occurred to me.' I thought then: This is what Mrs Glee was referring to. So it must have been obvious to others if not to me.

She went on: 'We have grown very close during the last months when I have tried to comfort him. He reproached himself a little – unnecessarily, I have constantly to assure him. I think we shall be very happy, Minta. But I feel I want your approval. I couldn't be happy without it.'

'But what I say is of no importance, surely?'

'It's of the utmost importance to me. Oh Minta, please say you will welcome me as your stepmother.'

For my answer I stood up and put my arms about her.

'Dearest Lucie,' I said, 'it's a wonderful thing for Papa and for me. I was thinking of you.'

She stroked my hair. 'You are so romantic. You decided that the doctor was for me and you built up a pretty picture of my launching him to success. Well, it's not to be. What appears to be romantic does not always bring happiness. I am happy now, Minta. I want to be here. You and your father are my dear ones. This is my home. Go to your father now. Tell him I have told you the news and impress on him how happy it has made you.'

So Lucie and I went to Papa and I told him that it was wonderful news; and he was happy as I had never seen him before.

'We shall have to wait for the full year to pass,' said Lucie, 'or people will talk.'

'Let them talk,' said my father.

But Lucie thought it best to wait; and already he was relying on her judgment.

She was right, of course; and they waited.

It was a misty November day, very much like the one when Mamma had died that Lucie became Lady Cardew, my stepmother.

How different was our household now! The servants knew they must obey Lucie. She never lost her temper; she was always gracious. I doubt Whiteladies had ever had a more respected chatelaine.

She loved the house and the house seemed to respond to her love. I have seen her stand on the lawn looking at it with a sort of wonder, as though she couldn't really believe that she was the mistress of it.

I used to tease her about it. 'I believe you are the re-incarnation of a nun. You knew this place was your home from the moment you set eyes on it.'

'Minta's romantic nonsense,' she said teasingly.

Very little was done about my father's book. She had so much to occupy her now, and since he was not continually told what an unsatisfactory husband he was he did not feel the need to justify himself. He took an interest in the gardens and the house. Lucie quickly discovered that repairs were necessary.

It was soon after that that I saw her really shaken out of her usual calm. She told me about it because it was not easy to discuss such matters with Papa.

'Your father's financial affairs are in a wretched state,' she said. 'Those lawyers of his are no good whatsoever. He has lost a great deal of money on the stock exchange lately and has been misguided enough to jeopardize the house by borrowing money on it.'

'Franklyn hinted at this some time ago.'

'You didn't tell me.'

'I didn't think you'd be interested.'

'Not interested in Whiteladies!'

'Well, now you are of course. What does it mean, Lucie?'

'I'm not sure. I must find out. Whiteladies must not be in danger.'

'I think that now you're in command we shall be all right.'

She was pleased with that remark, but a little impatient. We were reckless. We didn't deserve Whiteladies because we had jeopardized it.

She would sit in Papa's study with a pile of bills and papers before her.

'We must cut down here,' she would say. 'We could economize there. We must make Whiteladies safe now and for the future.'

My father admired her greatly. He had a childish belief that now Lucie was mistress of Whiteladies everything would be all right. I shared that view. There had always been a quality about Lucie that inspired confidence.

I told her often how glad I was that she was now definitely a member of the family. I had only wanted her to marry the doctor, I pointed out, so that she could stay near us.

She was pleased. 'Stepmother is not an ugly word in this house,' she commented.

'Darling Lucie, it was a lucky day for us when you came to Whiteladies,' I told her; I knew my father told her the same.

Neither of us could openly say this, but Whiteladies was a happier and more peaceful place since my mother had died.

Then Lucie surprised us again. She told me first. I thought she had been a little subdued for a few weeks, and one day when I was sitting in my favourite spot in the pond garden, she came out there to me.

'I have something to tell you,' she said, 'and I want you to be the first to know. Even your father doesn't know yet.'

I turned to her, not understanding the ecstatic expression in her smoky eyes.

'I hope you'll be pleased, but I'm not sure.'

'Please tell me . . . quickly.'

She laughed in a rather embarrassed way. 'I'm going to have a baby.'

'Lucie! When?'

'A long time yet . . . in seven months' time, I should say.'

'It's . . . wonderful.'

'You think so?'

'Don't you?'

She gripped her hands together. 'It's what I've always longed for.'

I threw my arms about her neck.

'Oh, Lucie, how happy I am! Just imagine – a baby in the house! It'll be lovely. I wonder whether it will be a girl or a boy. Which do you want?'

'I don't know. A boy, I suppose. Most people like the first born to be a boy.'

'So you anticipate having a family!'

'I didn't say that. But I'm so excited. But I wanted to be absolutely sure before telling your father.'

'Let's tell him now. No, you should tell him on your own. You wouldn't want an intruder at a time like this.'

'You are the sweetest stepdaughter anyone ever had.'

She left me sitting here, watching a dragonfly hover over the pond and settle momentarily on the statue.

This, I thought, will compensate Lucie for everything. That horrid little house in the Midlands, all the hardships of her youth. What a happy day for Lucie!

My father was bewildered at first, then delighted. I am sure he had never thought he would have other children. But Lucie, it seemed, could provide everything. There was no talk in the house now of anything but the coming baby. Lucie softened considerably; as her body grew more shapeless and she lost her elegance she gained a new beauty. She loved to sit with me and talk about the baby. She planned the layette and Lizzie sewed it. Those were the lovely peaceful months of waiting.

We tried to coddle Lucie but she wouldn't let us. Her baby was going to be strong and healthy, she said. He wasn't going to have an invalid for a mother. I noticed she referred to the baby as 'he', which showed that she wanted a boy, although I guessed that when the child came she wouldn't care what its sex was.

Dr Hunter was calling frequently at Whiteladies now. He told me that there was nothing to worry about whatsoever. Lucie was strong and healthy; she would produce a lusty child.

It was Franklyn who pointed out to me what a difference the birth of a child might make to me personally.

'If the child is a boy,' he said, 'he will be your father's

heir, for when your mother married him her property passed into his possession. Has this occurred to you?'

'I hadn't thought of it.'

'What an impractical girl you are! Whiteladies would go to your father's son. You would have no claim to it unless some moral duty made him leave it to you.'

'Whiteladies would always be my home, Franklyn. What would it matter if it belonged to my stepbrother . . . or would he be half-brother?'

Franklyn said it could make a great deal of difference to me and implied that I was most unworldly.

I laughed at him, but he was very serious.

Such pleasant days they were. During summer afternoons on the lawn and winter evenings by the fire, we eagerly awaited the birth of Lucie's child. My father seemed younger; he was so proud of Lucie and could scarcely bear her out of his sight.

And then in November – the same month in which my mother had died but two years later – the child was born.

It was a girl and was christened Druscilla.

I think Lucie was a little disappointed that she had not borne a son and so was my father, but the delight at finding themselves parents of a charming little girl soon dispersed that.

Druscilla quickly became the most important person in the household; we all vied for her favours; we were all delighted when she chose to crow at us.

I often marvelled at the way in which everything had changed since my mother had died.

That was the state of affairs when Stirling and Nora came back to England.

Nora

Chapter One

I WAS going to England and it was much against my
will. I had argued persistently with Stirling.

'What good will it do?' I kept asking; and he set his lips
stubbornly together and said: 'I'm going. It was his wish.'

'It was different when he was alive,' I insisted. 'I never
agreed with his ideas but they had some meaning then.'

It was no use trying to reason with Stirling; and in a way
I was glad of this controversy because it took our minds
from the terrible searing sorrow which we were both experiencing. When I was arguing with Stirling I was not
thinking of Lynx lying on the brown earth, of their carrying
his body home on the improvised stretcher; and I had to
stop myself thinking of that. I knew it was the same with
Stirling. There was something else we both knew. There was
no comfort for either of us but in each other.

We should have turned to Adelaide. Her sound good sense
would have served us well. She said she would not leave
home; she was going to stay and keep things going for when
we came back.

I wanted to stay, yet I wanted to go. I wanted to get
right away from the house I had called Little Whiteladies.

There were too many memories there; and yet I took a fierce and morbid delight in remembering every interview with Lynx, every game of chess we had played. But perhaps what decided me was that Stirling was going, and I had to be with Stirling. My relationship with Stirling was something I could not quite understand. I saw it as through a misted glass. How often in the past had I thought of marrying Stirling and yet when Lynx had married me that had seemed inevitable; and Stirling had made no protest. I believed that he felt towards me as I did towards him; but for the mighty personality of Lynx we should have married and been content. So now I had to be with Stirling. He and I could only have lived through those desolate weeks which followed the death of Lynx because of the knowledge that it was a desolation shared, and we belonged together.

'I am going to England,' he said firmly. 'He would want me to.'

So I knew I must go too.

Jessica came gliding into my bedroom one late afternoon when I was busy with preparations.

'So you're going,' she said. 'I knew you would. You kept saying you'd stay but I knew you'd go.'

I didn't answer and she sat on the bed watching me.

'So he's gone,' she went on. 'He died, just like any other mortal being. Who would have thought it could have happened to him? But has he gone, Nora? He'd break free of death, wouldn't he, just as he broke free of captivity? Out he came on the convict ship, like all the others, a prisoner. Then within a few weeks he breaks the fetters. Could he break the fetters of death?'

'What do you mean, Jessica?'

'Will he come back? Do you think he'll come back, Nora?'

'He's dead,' I said.

'You were lucky. You lost him before you knew him.'

'I knew him well,' I retorted. 'I was closer to him than anyone.'

She narrowed her eyes. 'You didn't get to know the bad man in him. He was bad, Nora. Bad! You'd have found out in time just as the others did. All bad men see themselves as greater than other people. They see the rest of us as counters to be moved about to please them. You were a counter, Nora – a pretty counter, a favourite one . . . for the time being. He cherished you, but you were a counter all the same.'

I said: 'Look here, Jessica, I have a lot to do. Don't think you can change my feelings towards him. I knew him as you never could.'

'I'll leave you with your pleasant dreams. Nobody can prove them false now, can they? But he'll come back. He'll find some way to cheat death as he cheated others. He's not gone. You can sense him here now. He's watching us now, Nora. He's laughing at me, because I'm trying to make you see the truth.'

'I wish you were right,' I said vehemently. 'I wish he would come back.'

'Don't say that!' she cried fearfully, looking over her shoulder. 'If you wish too fiercely he might come.'

'Then I'll wish it with all my heart.'

'He wouldn't come back as you knew him. He's no longer flesh and blood. But he'll come back . . . just the same.'

I turned away from her and, shaking her head sadly, she went out. I buried my face in the clothes which I had laid out on the bed and I kept seeing hundreds of pictures of him: Lynx the master, a law unto himself; a man different from all others. And lifting my face I said: 'Lynx, are you there? Come back. I want to talk to you. I want to tell you

305

that I hate your plans for revenge now as I always did. Come back, Lynx.'

But there was no sign – no sound in the quiet room.

Adelaide drove with us to Melbourne and we stayed a night at The Lynx; the next day she came aboard to say goodbye to us. I am sure Stirling was as thankful as I was for precise Adelaide, who kissed us affectionately and repeated that she would keep the home going until we returned. So calm, so prosaic, I wondered then whether she was like her mother for she bore no resemblance to Lynx. As our ship slipped away she stood on the quay waving to us. There were no tears. She might have been seeing us off for a trip to Sydney.

I remembered sailing from England on the *Carron Star*. How different I was from that girl! Since then I had known Lynx. The inexperienced young girl had become a rich widow – outwardly poised, a woman of the world.

Stirling stood beside me as he had on that other occasion; and I felt comforted.

Turning, I smiled at him and I knew he felt the same.

We went first to the Falcon Inn. How strange it was to sit in that lounge where I had first met Stirling and pour the tea, which had been brought to us, and hand him the plate of scones. He was aware of it too. I knew by the way he smiled at me.

'It seems years ago,' he said; and indeed it did. So much had happened. We ourselves had changed.

We had talked a great deal in the ship coming over. He was going to buy Whiteladies because, he said, the owners would be willing to sell. They would, in fact, have no alternative. He would offer a big price for it – a price such as they could not possibly get elsewhere. What did it matter? He was the golden millionaire.

'You can't be certain they'll sell,' I insisted.

'They've *got* to sell, Nora,' was his answer. 'They're bankrupt.'

I knew who had helped to make them so and I was ashamed. The triumvirate, he had called us when I had discovered the mine. I wished I were not part of this.

There were things they could do, I pointed out. They could take paying guests, for instance.

'They wouldn't know how!' Stirling laughed and in that moment he was amazingly like Lynx.

My feelings were in a turmoil. I set myself against them. I felt there was something in what Jessica had said. Lynx was still with us. And I didn't want those people to sell the house. I was on their side.

Stirling's eyes looked like pieces of green glass glinting through his sun-made wrinkles. He was so like Lynx that my spirits rose and I was almost happy. Whatever I said, he would acquire Whiteladies. It would be as Lynx wanted it. The Herrick children would play on the lawns and in time be the proud owners; and those children would be mine and Stirling's. I could almost hear Lynx's voice: 'That's my girl Nora.' And I thought of the lawn on which I had once sat uneasily and the house with its grey towers – ancient and imposing – and I understood the desire to possess it.

'The first thing to do is to let it be known that we are looking for a house,' said Stirling. 'We have taken a fancy to the district and want to settle here for a while. We are particularly interested in antiquity and have a great fancy for a house such as Whiteladies. I have already mentioned this to the innkeeper.'

'You lose no time,' I said.

'Did you expect me to? I had quite a conversation with the fellow. He remembered our staying here before, or so he said. He tells me that Lady Cardew died and that Sir Hilary married the companion or whatever she was.'

'Her name was Lucie, I believe.'

He nodded at me, smiling.

'I thought she was very humble,' I went on. 'Not quite one of the family. That will be changed now, I daresay.'

'You're very interested in them, Nora.'

'Aren't you?'

'Considering we have come across the world to buy their house, I certainly am.'

'You are too sure,' I told him. 'How can you know what price will be asked?'

He looked at me in astonishment. What did it matter? He was the golden millionaire. But sometimes a price is not asked in gold.

That very day we paid a visit to the local house agent, and learned that a temporary refuge could be found which seemed the ideal place while we were looking round. By a stroke of great good luck the Wakefields were letting the Mercer's House – a pleasant place and ideal for our purpose while we searched. Only, he warned us, there was no house in the neighbourhood to be compared with Whiteladies except perhaps Wakefield Park itself – and even that was no Whiteladies. We said we were very interested in renting the Mercer's House and made an appointment to see it the next day.

The house agent drove us over in his brougham where Mr Franklyn Wakefield was waiting to receive us. I remembered him at once and a glance at Stirling showed that he did too.

He bowed to me first, then to Stirling. His manners seemed very formal but his smile was friendly.

'I hope you will like the Mercer's House,' he said, 'though you may find it a little old-fashioned. I have heard it called inconvenient.'

'I'm sure it won't be,' I told him, secretly amused because the agent's reports had been so glowing while it seemed that its owner was doing his best to denigrate it. 'In fact we are enchanted by it . . . from the outside, aren't we, Stirling?'

Stirling said characteristically that it was in fact the *inside* of the house with which we must concern ourselves if we were going to live in it.

'Therefore,' said Mr Wakefield, 'I am sure you will wish to inspect it thoroughly.'

'We shall,' said Stirling, rather grimly, I thought; and I remembered that he had taken a dislike to Franklyn Wakefield from the first moment he had seen him.

I said quickly: 'You understand we should only be taking the house temporarily?'

'I was cognizant of the fact,' said Mr Wakefield with a smile. 'But I daresay that however short the time you will wish for the maximum of comfort.'

I looked at the house with its elegant architecture – Queen Anne, I guessed. Over the walls hung festoons of Virginia creeper and I imagined what a glorious sight it would be in the autumn. There were two lawns in front of the house – one on either side of the path – trim and well kept. I felt the need to make up for Stirling's boorishness by being as charming as possible to Mr Wakefield.

'If the inside is half as delightful as the outside I shall be enchanted,' I said. He looked pleased and I went on. 'Am I right in thinking it is Queen Anne or early Georgian?'

'It was built in 1717 by an ancestor of mine and has been in the family ever since. We've used it as a sort of Dower House for members of the family. At this time there is no one who could occupy it. That is why we thought it advisable to seek a tenant.'

'Houses need to be lived in,' I said. 'They're a little sad when empty.'

Stirling gave an explosive laugh. 'Really, Nora! You're giving bricks and mortar credit for feelings they don't possess.'

'I think Mrs . . .'

'Herrick,' I supplied.

'I think Mrs Herrick has a good point,' said Mr Wakefield. 'Houses soon become unfit for human habitation if they remain unoccupied too long.'

'Well, we'd better look round,' said Stirling.

The house was elegantly furnished. I exclaimed with pleasure at the carved ceiling in the hall. 'That,' explained Mr Wakefield, 'is the mercer's coat of arms you see engraved on the ceiling. You will see it in many of the rooms.'

'Of course, it's the Mercer's House, isn't it?'

We went into the drawing-room with its french windows opening on to a lawn.

'We should need at least two gardeners,' said Stirling as though determined to find fault with the place. 'Would they be easy to get?'

'There is no problem about that,' Mr Wakefield assured him. 'The gardens are taken care of by our own gardeners at the Park. The cost of this has been included in the details the agent will have given you.'

'We are not concerned with the price,' said Stirling and I felt myself blush at what seemed to be his ostentation.

'Nor, I might add, are we,' went on Mr Wakefield. He smiled directly at me. 'The important point is to find the right tenant. I am sure, Mrs Herrick, that you and your husband would like to be alone to look over the house.'

I said quickly: 'We are not husband and wife. I am a widow and Mr Herrick's stepmother.'

If he was surprised he didn't show it. Mr Wakefield's manners were impeccable. He would have been brought up to believe that to show his feelings was the gravest social error. He, of course, added tact to his many social graces, and it was true that I wanted to be free to discuss the house with Stirling.

'If you would let us take our time . . .'

'But certainly, and if you would care to call at the Park when you have finished . . . that is, if you are interested . . . I should be delighted to see you there. I could send a carriage for you, or if you cared for the walk it is just across the park – about half a mile.'

I said we would walk and he left us.

As the door shut on him Stirling threw himself on to a sofa and began to laugh.

'If you would care to inspect this domicile, madam, and then take a short peregrination across the park . . .'

'Shut up, Stirling, he wasn't as prim as that.'

'Our landlord! My God!'

'It's not the landlord with which we have to concern ourselves but with the house.'

'We should have to see him sometimes, I suppose. He'd call . . . or perhaps his wife would. Do you imagine he has a wife? I wonder what she's like. She will alight from her carriage and leave three cards. Is that the correct number? And we should be invited to call and be bored to death.'

'How do you know we should be bored? How do you know he has a wife?'

'Of course we'd be bored and of course he has a wife. Mr Wakefield's life would run according to a pattern and you can be sure that pattern includes a wife.'

'I wonder what Wakefield Park is like.'

'Great old ancestral mansion.'

'Like Whiteladies.'

'There is no place in the world like Whiteladies.'

'Well, are we going to take this house?'

'Let's stay at the inn. If we're his tenants that might involve social obligations.'

'Which I am sure you would have no hesitation in ignoring.'

'You are right for once, Nora.'

'For once! What do you mean? I'm going to look all over this house, and I can tell you this: I like it. I've a great desire to know who the Mercer was and what connection a mere tradesman could possibly have with the elegant Mr Wakefield.'

We inspected the dining-room and descended to the enormous stone-flagged kitchen. I liked it. I liked the large pantries, the stillroom, the buttery and the laundry. It was a fascinating house.

'It's too big,' said Stirling.

'Too big for a millionaire!' I demanded ironically. 'You practically told him you were.'

'I felt you were on his side.'

'What nonsense! As if it were a matter of taking sides. Let's go up the staircase.'

There were three floors and some twelve rooms. The rooms were big and airy; I loved the long windows which reached to the floor.

'We're going to take it, Stirling,' I said; and he did not contradict. He was really as fascinated with the house as I was; and being tenants of the Wakefields, we could almost certainly meet the owners of Whiteladies. I was not sure what plans Stirling had and how quickly he hoped to acquire the place, but I guessed it would take a long time, and it would certainly be more satisfactory having the Mercer's House than an inn as our temporary home while we waited.

'Well?' he asked, when we had been through the house.

'We're going to tell Mr Wakefield that we're taking it.'

We walked across the park and to the house which was called Wakefield Park. It was a big house – early Victorian, I judged, with its heavy ornate architecture. It looked strong and solid. On the front lawn was a pond in which a fountain played. White stone steps led to a terrace on which were seats. The flowers grew neatly, even primly. 'It's just the sort of house he would have,' I commented.

'You can be sure everything is in its proper place,' added Stirling. Then he mimicked: 'It is fitting that each and every appurtenance of this house is lodged in the place assigned to it.'

'I don't believe you like him.'

'Do you?'

'I like the Mercer's House. That's good enough.'

Along one wall of the house was a vinery. I could see the vine trained along the glass to catch the sun. There were pots of exotic-looking flowers in there too.

'You must admit,' I said, 'that there is something imposing about his house.'

We mounted the steps of the terrace to the porch, on one side of which hung a bell. When pulled this gave a hollow clanging and almost immediately a manservant appeared.

'You would be Mr and Mrs Herrick,' he said. 'Mr Wakefield is in the library with Sir Everard and her ladyship. I'm requested to conduct you there.'

I threw Stirling a glance as much to say: 'You see how well ordered everything is.' 'What did you expect from Mr Wakefield?' he flashed back.

The hall was enormous and somewhat oppressive. The heads of two stags adorned the wall on either side of that of a tiger. There were various portraits which we had no time then to study. A staircase with elaborately carved banisters curved upwards. We mounted this in the wake of the butler.

'Mr and Mrs Herrick!' he announced after knocking and opening a door.

Mr Wakefield was there with a youngish man and an elderly man and woman.

'So good of you to come,' said Mr Wakefield. 'May I present you to my parents – Sir Everard and Lady Wakefield and Dr Hunter.

Lady Wakefield was a frail old lady who gave me a pleasant smile; then I turned to Sir Everard.

'You will forgive my not rising,' he said; and I noticed he was in a wheelchair with a tartan rug about his knees.

The doctor shook hands.

'Dr Hunter has just been making one of his calls,' said Lady Wakefield. 'If you are going to live here, and need a good doctor – which I hope you won't – you will find him excellent. Franklyn, do ring for fresh tea.'

'I have already told them to bring it if and when Mr and Mrs Herrick called.'

'So thoughtful,' said Lady Wakefield with an adoring look at her son, who said in his dignified manner: 'Pray be seated.'

'We have come to tell you that we are delighted with the Mercer's House,' I told him, 'and we want to take it.'

'Splendid,' said Mr Wakefield.

'It's time it was lived in,' added Sir Everard. 'It doesn't do the place any good to be left standing empty.'

'It's a charming old place,' put in the doctor.

There was a knock at the door and a trolley was wheeled in accompanied by a footman and a parlourmaid. Life was clearly lived in an elegant fashion at Wakefield Park.

'Mr and Mrs Herrick are looking for a house in the neighbourhood, I gathered,' said Franklyn. 'That's why they are taking the Mercer's House temporarily.'

'They are not easy to find,' the doctor warned us. 'That is, if you want a house of character.'

'We do,' I replied.

'We have noticed a charming old place,' began Stirling.

'Whiteladies!' Lady Wakefield smiled. 'A most unusual place. It's actually built on the site of an old convent. In fact some of the old convent still remains.'

'The Cardews are great friends of ours,' said Sir Everard. 'If you come here to live you will be meeting them.'

'That will be very interesting.' Stirling gave me a look which was almost a grimace and I said quickly: 'We are very intrigued by the Mercer's House and are wondering how it came to have such a name.'

'My great-great-grandfather built it,' explained Mr Wakefield. 'He was a mercer of London where he made enough money to retire to the country and build himself a house. This he did. But he never forgot his trade so he called his house the Mercer's House.'

'The family prospered,' Sir Everard carried on the story, 'and my father built this house which was better suited to his needs and Mercer's was occupied by aunts and cousins and any member of the family who needed it . . . until two years ago. A sister of mine occupied it; and since she died it has been empty. It was my son's idea that we should let it and you will be the first outside the family to live in it.'

'That's very interesting,' I said. 'I am sure we are going to enjoy it.'

Stirling said to me: 'I fancy it was this Whiteladies that we visited briefly when we were here last. We have recently arrived from Australia,' he explained to the company.

'I had a brother who went there,' began Sir Everard. I could see he was a garrulous old gentleman, for his wife, smiling indulgently at him, said quickly: 'So you were at Whiteladies . . . briefly?'

I explained the incident of the scarf and Mr Wakefield looked delighted. 'I remember the occasion,' he said.

'What an excellent memory you must have!' I told him. 'There was a lady in a chair . . .'

'Lady Cardew. She has since died. There is now another Lady Cardew.'

'And a very pretty young girl.'

'That would be Minta,' said Lady Wakefield. 'Such a dear girl!' Her indulgent smile was turned on her son. Oh yes, I thought, there will be a match between Minta and Mr Wakefield. 'She has a little half-sister now – Druscilla – daughter of the second Lady Cardew.'

'And Minta, is she married?'

Again that roguish look for Mr Wakefield. 'Not yet.'

The doctor, who had said very little, took out his watch and looked at it. 'I should be on my way,' he said.

'So many people needing your services,' commented Lady Wakefield.

'You will be going back to the Falcon Inn, I daresay,' said the doctor to us. 'Could I give you a lift?'

'It's an excellent idea,' said Mr Wakefield. 'But if you are not going that way, Doctor, I will arrange . . .'

The doctor said that he was in fact going that way, so we thanked the Wakefields and I assured them that we would be ready to move into the Mercer's House the following week when all that was necessary to be settled would have been completed.

That would be admirable, said Mr Wakefield; and soon we were rolling along in the doctor's brougham.

'Charming people,' he said of the Wakefields.

'I hope our neighbours at this Whiteladies are as charming,' murmured Stirling.

I noticed then a tightening of the doctor's lips and I wondered what that meant. He seemed to realize that I was studying him and said quickly: 'I daresay you will be able to judge for yourself in due course.'

He dropped us at the inn and when he had gone I said to Stirling: 'He was a bit odd about the people at Whiteladies. Did you notice his face when I mentioned them?'

But Stirling had noticed nothing.

I felt better than I had since the death of Lynx. I was interested in life again. I disapproved of this crazy scheme to rob its owners of Whiteladies – and indeed the more I thought of it the more crazy it seemed – but at the same time I was fascinated by these people and it was almost as though, as Jessica had said, Lynx had come back and was urging me to act against my will.

I was eager to live in the Mercer's House. I liked the Wakefield family. I had heard from the innkeeper who was a gossip that Sir Everard and Lady Wakefield had despaired of having children and that they were well into middle age when their son was born. They doted on him; and he would say this for Mr Franklyn, he was a good son if ever there was one, and it wouldn't be many more months he was sure before there was a match between the Park and Whiteladies.

'That would be Miss Minta,' I said.

'You'd be right there. A sweet young lady, and highly thought of hereabouts.'

'Then Mr Franklyn will be lucky.'

'They'll be a lucky pair.'

'And Whiteladies? I suppose that will one day be Miss Minta's – but she'll be at Wakefield Park.'

'Don't you believe it. She'll be at Whiteladies. It'll go to her – the eldest – and who'd have thought there'd be another. Sir Hilary at his time of life too! But a new young wife, you know how it is.'

I nodded sagely. He was a good source of information. I should miss our talks when we moved to Mercer's.

There were two servants attached to the place – a parlour-maid and a housemaid.

'We can't say they haven't thought of our comfort,' I said to Stirling, who agreed reluctantly. He could think of little but Whiteladies and was all impatience to approach the family.

'How?' I demanded. 'For heaven's sake be tactful. You can't exactly call and say, "I'd like your house and insist you sell it to me," you have to feel your way.'

'Don't be afraid. I'll know how to deal with it. But everything takes so much time.'

Two days before we were due to move into the Mercer's House, the landlord's wife came to my room and told me that 'a person' was downstairs asking to see me. She had been 'put' into the inn parlour. I went down and found a middle-aged woman waiting there.

'You would be Mrs Herrick?' she asked.

I said I was.

'My name's Glee – Mrs Amy Glee. I was housekeeper up at Whiteladies until Madam decided she had no need of my services.'

She could not have said anything more inclined to arouse my interest.

'Madam?'

'The new Lady Cardew,' she said with a significant sniff.

'Oh, and why have you come to see me?'

'I hear you're taking Mercer's, and I thought you might be needing a housekeeper. *I know* you'll be needing one because I've had experience of that Ellen and Mabel. They were both at Whiteladies at one time . . . and when they started getting rid of servants those two went to the Park.'

'I see,' I said.

'They'll work, but only if watched. I know their type and there's many like them. Now, madam, if you don't want to spend all your time watching lazy maids . . .'

'Were you at Whiteladies long?'

'Fifteen years, and good service I gave.'

I recognized her now. She was the woman to whom Lucie had taken me when my hand was bandaged.

'I am sure you did,' I said.

'Fifteen years and then told to go. Mind you, I was all right. I had my cousin once removed . . . down Dover way. She died six months back and left me the cottage and something besides. It's not for the need that I've come. But I'm a woman who likes to be on the go. And told to leave I was – after fifteen years. I was all right, but I might not have been.'

There was something about the pursed lips, the jerk of the head which aroused my curiosity. I decided that we needed a housekeeper at the Mercer's House.

Chapter Two

I ENJOYED settling into the house. I felt that I could be happy there in a placid way and that was what I wanted. I had had enough adventure. I had seen a man killed; I had experienced strange and not altogether understood emotions; I had been the wife of a man who had dominated me and of whom I had never known the like. That was enough. I could never know those wild joys and fears again, and perhaps I did not want to. Lynx could never come back; and I wondered whether I could ever have known real peace with him. But here in this elegant country house, built by the rich London mercer nearly two hundred years ago, I could perhaps find a new way of life. He had come to live here in peace; I sensed that. The Mercer's House would be my refuge as it had been that of the mercer. Here I would be in charge of my own destiny; I could mould my life to my own inclination. Sometimes I wondered whether I had always known that my life with Lynx would be brief. He had been so much older than I. True, I had believed him to be immortal. Often now I could not believe that he was really dead.

One thing was certain: I was fortunate to have known

him and to have been loved by him; but I had to convince myself it was over; and since I must rebuild my life, the Mercer's House was the best place in which to do it. Sometimes I felt Jessica was right and he was beside me, guiding me, urging me in that direction where he wanted me to go. I believed that he wanted me to marry Stirling and that had he not desired me himself would have arranged our marriage before he died. So I dreamed of marrying Stirling. We would abandon the crazy idea of acquiring Whiteladies. Perhaps we would buy the Mercer's House and our children would be born there. Minta should marry Franklyn Wakefield and our children and theirs should play in the lawns of Whiteladies. So after all Lynx's grandchild should play on those smooth and velvety lawns. But would Lynx ever be satisfied with a compromise?

So I dreamed.

We had not been a week in the Mercer's House when Minta came to call. She had changed little. She was very pretty and much as I remembered her. There was a certain innocence about her which I found appealing.

'Franklyn Wakefield told me you were here,' she said. 'How very interesting. Of course I remember the time you came. Your scarf blew over the wall.'

As it was mid-morning I asked if she would care for coffee or perhaps a glass of wine. She said she would like the coffee so I rang the bell.

Ellen appeared, neat and trim, and Minta smiled at her and said: 'Good morning, Ellen.' Of course the girl had worked at Whiteladies before going to Wakefield Park.

When she had left us, Minta said: 'I hope you are well looked after. Mr Wakefield was very anxious that you should be. Ellen and Mabel are such good girls.'

Mrs Glee had other opinions but Minta would believe the best of everybody.

'Our housekeeper keeps them in good order.'

'Oh yes, you have Mrs Glee.'

'I see that our actions have been well observed.'

She laughed. 'This is country life, you know. Everyone is always interested in newcomers and wonders whether they are going to enter into local affairs.'

'Is that expected of us?'

'Shall we say it might be hoped. You won't be pestered if you show you wish to remain aloof, but somehow I don't think *you* will.'

'There is my stepson,' I said.

'Oh yes.' She smiled. 'It seems so strange. You are so young to have a grown-up stepson. But I have a stepmother who is not much older than I. When we met previously I thought you were brother and sister until . . .'

'It is rather a complicated relationship. I married Stirling's father and now he's dead and I am a widow . . .'

My voice trembled. I was seeing him carried home on that stretcher. I was thinking of that immense vitality; that excitement which he had brought into my life and which was gone for ever.

'I'm sorry,' said Minta. I realized she was very sensitive to the feelings of others. I liked her, and thought what an admirable wife she would make for Franklyn Wakefield. I liked him, too. There was something worthy about them both. Nice people, I thought. Yes, that was the word. *Nice*! Unexciting but good. There would be few surprises. They were different from people like Lynx, Stirling and myself. They were lacking in our egoism, perhaps. They seemed colourless. But perhaps that was unfair when applied to such a charming girl as Minta.

I said quickly: 'It's over. One has to learn to forget.' She nodded and I went on: 'I remember so clearly the first day I saw Whiteladies. It impressed us both so much. The lawn and the kind way in which you received us. And then of course the way my hand was bandaged.'

'That was Lucie. She is my stepmother now. You will meet her. My mother died . . .' A look of sorrow touched her face. She was easy to read and one of her charms was the changing expressions of her face.

'I gathered she was an invalid,' I said.

'Yes, but . . .' I waited but she did not finish the sentence. 'Lucie has been wonderful. She has been so good to Papa. She helps with his work and manages the house perfectly.'

'I am so glad.'

'And we have an addition to the family. My little half-sister Druscilla. She's a darling. She is nearly a year old.'

'It's not really so long ago that we met for the first time,' I commented, 'and so much has happened since then.'

I was thinking: I became Lynx's wife and his widow. I must have betrayed my thoughts for she changed the subject quickly; 'You will enjoy it here, I'm sure. It's rather a pleasant community.'

Ellen brought in the coffee with Mrs Glee close behind. Mrs Glee gave Minta a triumphant: 'Good morning, Miss Cardew!' to which Minta replied how glad she was to see Mrs Glee again and then assured me that Mrs Glee would take admirable care of the household. Mrs Glee's head shook with pleasure and righteousness as she supervised Ellen serving coffee.

When she had gone Minta said: 'She really is a wonderful housekeeper. I'm glad you have her. We should never have let her go if we could have afforded to keep her.'

So it was true that they were not well off. Perhaps Stirling would succeed after all. But it was a very different matter selling a house from ridding themselves of an expensive servant.

'I daresay Maud Mathers will be calling on you soon. She's the rector's daughter. His wife is dead but Maud is indefatigable in parish affairs. She's a good, sensible girl and I'm sure you'll like her. But, please, I want your first visit to be to Whiteladies. I shall ask Mr Wakefield to join us for dinner. Sir Everard and Lady Wakefield rarely leave the Park. They are not fit for it. Now will you promise me?'

I readily gave the promise.

I was sure, I told her, that Stirling would be delighted to accept the invitation; and at that moment Stirling came in.

I said: 'Stirling, Miss Cardew has called. Do you remember?'

'But of course!' exclaimed Stirling; and I saw the excitement leap into his eyes. She noticed it, too, and she flushed prettily. 'This is a great pleasure,' he added with feeling.

I knew he was thinking he was making progress.

'Have some coffee,' I said and went over to the table to pour it for him.

'We are invited to Whiteladies,' I told him.

'I am delighted,' he replied.

She was smiling. She had become more animated since Stirling had arrived. Naturally, I thought, he seems exciting because she is accustomed to Franklyn Wakefield.

It was rather gratifying to discover what a stir we had made in the neighbourhood. We did seem rather incongruous, I supposed – a young man close to thirty with a stepmother just entering her twenties, living together in the Mercer's House. It was the most respectable of relationships; besides we had the servants as chaperons plus the presence of Mrs Glee. Stirling's rooms were on the first floor, mine on the second; his at the front, mine at the back. Mrs Glee, in black bombazine, dispelled any gossip for it was inconceivable that she would be found in any house where the slightest impropriety was practised.

She came to me every morning to discuss the menu for the day; she behaved as though we were a large household; and I realized that this ceremony was necessary to her dignity. It was only when she discussed Whiteladies that she forgot her decorum. I confess that I lured her to talk of that household which was of the utmost interest to me.

'I don't like it, madam,' she reiterated on an old theme one morning after we had decided what should be prepared for luncheon. 'For years I served Lady Cardew – the *first* Lady Cardew, that is – and I venture to say that *she* never had cause for complaint. And then suddenly I'm told my services are to be dispensed with. They could do without me. As though, madam, what I did was of such little importance that I could go and no difference be noticed.'

'I gathered from Miss Cardew that economies were necessary,' I said.

'Economies! There was money wasted in that house. Oh no, the second Lady Cardew wanted me out of the way. She wanted to run the place. She didn't want anyone there who might see what she was up to. And that's the long and the short of it, madam.'

'I daresay it had to be, you know. The expense of keeping up a place like Whiteladies must be great.'

Mrs Glee sniffed. 'I always thought there was something going on in that house.'

'Oh?' Of course I shouldn't be discussing my neighbours with my housekeeper, but the temptation to do so was irresistible.

'Oh yes,' went on Mrs Glee. 'She'd make up her mind what she wanted and she didn't want anyone there who might see through her. After all, what was she in those days? A sort of companion, neither one thing nor the other.'

'Miss Cardew seems very fond of her stepmother.'

'Miss Cardew's one of the blessed innocents. Wouldn't see what was going on right under her nose if you was to ask me.'

'She seems a very charming young lady.'

'She and her father . . . a pair of babes in the wood. Oh, you can smile, Mrs Herrick, but she was after the doctor at one time. We all thought there'd be a match there, and then her ladyship dies and "No thank you," said madam to the doctor, "I'm after her ladyship's shoes."' Mrs Glee's language became more colourful as she warmed to her subject, and I felt I must put an end to these observations which I believed were decidedly prejudiced.

'Well, I hope, Mrs Glee, you don't regret the change too much. Miss Cardew was saying how lucky we were to get you.'

'Miss Cardew was always the lady.'

'I'm sure of that. And I think we'll have the apple pie. Mr Herrick is very partial to that.'

Confidences were over; we were back to business.

Franklyn Wakefield picked us up in his carriage. Our own had not yet been delivered but Stirling already had four fine horses in the stables.

I liked the courtly manner in which I was handed into the carriage. He asked if I liked riding with my back to the horses or otherwise. I told him I had no preference.

'I daresay you rode a great deal in Australia.'

'Everywhere,' I told him. 'It was necessary. We even camped out. Do you remember, Stirling, that occasion when we rode some forty miles or so to Melbourne . . . and then back?'

I could smell the perfume of the eucalypts; I remembered

Adelaide boiling the kettle and Jagger coming close to me while I knelt by the fire. Would there always be these memories?

'You will be an expert horsewoman.'

I shrugged my shoulders, and he went on: 'I would like to show you my estate one day. Perhaps we could ride out together and I could introduce you to the countryside.'

Stirling started to talk about the vastness of the property in Australia in a rather brash, patronizing way which made me frown; and the more I frowned the more bombastic he became. Franklyn listened politely and made no effort to cap Stirling's stories which I should have been tempted to had I been in his place. It was a pity Stirling could not hide his contempt for Franklyn who, of course, completely disguised his reaction. A lesson in good manners, I would remind Stirling when we were alone.

To arrive at Whiteladies after dusk was an experience. The place looked mysteriously romantic and – in odd contrast – almost sinister. There was a lantern hanging in the porch which creaked slightly as it swung and as we mounted the steep stone steps an excitement possessed me. I glanced at Stirling. His eyes gleamed; I was aware of his tension.

Franklyn pulled the bell rope and we heard the clanging echoing through the hall. The door was iron-studded and looked impregnable; there was a grille through which we saw the eyes of the manservant before he opened the door.

Then we were in the hall; the floor was stone-flagged, the panelling intricate; candles guttered in the sconces. So it must have looked nearly forty years ago when Lynx came here to give his Arabella drawing lessons. How could I ever forget him when there were a thousand things everywhere I went to remind me of him!

Minta appeared at the staircase on one end of the hall.

'I heard the bell,' she said, descending. She looked radiant and as dainty as a fairy princess in the candle light. 'I'm so pleased that you've come.'

'We're pleased that you invited us,' said Stirling. 'It's a great occasion, I can tell you, to be guests in this house.'

Minta said she wasn't sure whether it was the house or its inhabitants that pleased him.

'Both!' replied Stirling.

'If you're interested in architecture,' put in Franklyn, 'you couldn't have a better example of the Tudor than you have here. Some of it is a little later but the house is fundamentally Tudor.'

'Living in Australia, I have had no opportunity of visiting these ancient houses,' said Stirling. 'So it's a great novelty to me. Not so Nora. She was a tenderfoot, you know. She was only out there a mere two years or so.'

'I'm fascinated by Whiteladies all the same.'

'We must show you over the house,' promised Minta. 'Perhaps after dinner. First you must meet my father and stepmother.'

Stirling started up the stairs after her, and as Franklyn and I followed he pointed out the carving which was the work of a sixteenth-century artist. He was sure of this because that particular artist always left his special mark – a nun's head. There were examples of his work in other houses in this part of the country. It might have been that his first big commission was the carving in Whiteladies and ever after he had used the nun's head as his symbol.

'As soon as one begins to delve into the past one makes all sorts of interesting discoveries,' he said.

'Do you delve into the past?' I asked.

'In a dilettantish manner. I am interested in this part of the world. We've had several discoveries. We've found old coins and jewellery belonging to the Stone and Bronze Ages.

But I'm interested in the more recent past. The history of old houses, for instance; and this one is one of the most fascinating I've ever known.'

'I find it fascinating too,' I said; and by this time we had reached the top of a staircase and Minta had thrown open the door of a room.

It was delightful with its tall mullioned windows and lofty ceiling; the cupola had been so designed to make this appear even higher than it was. I imagined that in daylight the wood carving was magnificent. There were portraits on the walls, and the furniture I judged to be early eighteenth century. It was extremely elegant; in daylight I was to discover that it was somewhat shabby, but that was not noticeable at this time.

I recognized Lucie immediately though she had changed. She had a new dignity and was striking in an unobtrusive way. She appeared to be very modestly dressed in puce-coloured velvet but the dress was beautifully cut and elegant in its simplicity. She was reserved, yet completely mistress of the occasion. Her dark hair was simply dressed but becomingly. She came forward and took my hand.

'This is a pleasure,' she said. She spoke gently but without warmth. 'I remember you well. Minta has been telling me.'

Then she turned to Stirling. 'Oh yes, indeed. I do remember. After all it is not so long ago. Come and meet my husband.'

Sir Hilary – Minta's father – came towards us and shook hands. He looked frail and had the same guileless expression I had noticed in Minta. Innocent, I thought, and quite unworldly; and then immediately I was thinking of his marrying the woman whom Lynx had loved, and it seemed incongruous that I should be here taking up the threads of Lynx's past. Here I should remember him as vividly as I had done in Australia.

'We are so pleased to have neighbours,' he said. 'Franklyn has told me all about your taking the Mercer's House. You're lucky to get it. It's a gem of a house.'

Franklyn was near. 'We're lucky to have such tenants at Mercer's,' he said.

'Ah, Franklyn, and how are your parents today?'

Franklyn said they were very lively and well; and Sir Hilary went on to ask questions about them. He was obviously interested in their ailments and comparing them with his own.

Two other guests arrived. I had already met the doctor who looked, I thought, quite ill at ease; and with him was Miss Maud Mathers, the vicar's daughter, a rather tall young woman with an outdoor complexion and a breezy manner. I was immediately convinced that she was a great asset to her father in the parish.

Dinner was served in a dining-room the same size and similar in many ways – the same type of ceiling, the same panelling – to the drawing-room. Minta mentioned that they used this dining-room most of the time although for occasions when there were many guests, such as Christmas time, they used the hall.

'In the old days we used it more than we do today,' she explained. 'We used to have a houseful of guests. I'm sure my parents didn't know half the people they entertained. Now of course we have to be careful.'

'One day perhaps it will be different,' said Stirling.

I was uneasy. He was showing his obsession with the place too clearly. There was something so honest about Stirling. I loved him for it, but I felt it would be better to hide his intentions as yet. He had no subtlety. Now Franklyn. . . . I was continually comparing the two, and everything about Stirling I loved, although I did not necessarily applaud or admire it. Now he was being almost naïve as his covetous eyes roamed about the house.

I noticed there was only one parlourmaid and the butler was the man who had opened the door. They evidently had few servants. The meal was well cooked and well served, which I imagined was due to Lucie's supervision. She had her eyes on everything and I was quickly aware that the servants were in awe of her.

Conversation at the dinner-table ranged over a number of subjects. Sir Hilary and Franklyn discussed the Wakefield estate; Stirling was asking Minta questions about the house; Lucie from one end of the table was looking after her guests and joining in here and there; I was seated next to the doctor and opposite me was Maud Mathers, who talked in an animated way about parish affairs.

'You'll love the church, Mrs Herrick. It's the same period as this house. The tower is quite impressive, isn't it, Dr Hunter?'

The doctor agreed that it was a fine old church.

'I hope you'll come along to some of our social affairs,' said Miss Mathers.

'Do you intend staying long in the neighbourhood?' the doctor wanted to know.

'It's difficult to say,' I answered. 'My stepson is enamoured of this part of the world and he has fallen in love with Whiteladies.'

'It's the sort of house about which people get obsessions,' said Maud. 'I believe one or two people have wanted to buy it.'

'I understand it's been in the family for centuries.'

'Yes, handed down from generation to generation. Not like our house, which goes with the living.'

'Miss Cardew has promised to show us round after dinner.'

Lucie joined in the conversation. 'Most people want to see over the house.'

'You must get tired of showing them.'

'I never get tired. I'm as fascinated with the place as everyone else, except of course those who are born in it, like Minta. I always tell her she doesn't appreciate it. It will be the same with Druscilla.' She smiled. 'My daughter,' she added.

'And how is Druscilla?' asked the doctor.

Lucie's smile gave luminosity to her face. Mother love, I thought, plus candle light. 'She is quite well now.' She turned to me. 'I'm like all mothers with a first child. I fuss. I call the doctor in for nothing.'

'It's called "first baby nerves",' said the doctor.

'It shows a mother's tender care,' Maud put in. 'And I'm sure Dr Hunter understands and doesn't blame any of the mothers in the parish for their over-anxiety.'

'Oh, I'm very tolerant,' said the doctor lightly.

'A necessary qualification,' added Lucie almost sarcastically.

I seemed to be sensitive that night. I was aware of a certain tension between the doctor and Lucie Cardew. Or was I imagining it? I fancied that he was very interested in her, that he admired her and she did not return his esteem. Then once again I was thinking of Lynx. There would have been dinner-parties such as this one to which the drawing-master would not have been invited. I could imagine his anger at slights, his determination that one day he would sit at the head of this table.

I came out of my reverie to hear Lucie say: 'Oh, Maud, you know you spoil her. She's getting quite arrogant.'

'She's such a darling,' Maud insisted, 'and so bright.'

'I can hear you are talking about my little sister,' said Minta. Then she told a story illustrating the intelligence of the absent Druscilla; and soon afterwards the ladies were conducted to the drawing-room and the men left at the table with their port. There Maud dominated the conversation, which seemed to be mainly about the proceeds of the coming sale of work which would help in the repair of the inevitably beetle-ridden church roof. It would be held in the grounds of Wakefield Park, which Sir Everard and Lady Wakefield had kindly placed at their disposal.

'It used to be Whiteladies,' Minta explained to me, 'but the Park is so much more suitable.'

'Is it?' I asked. 'I should have thought . . .'

'Oh, we're ancient, but the Park gardens are so much better than ours nowadays. We only have two gardeners. In my grandfather's day there were six. It means that quite a lot of the place has gone wild, and the flowers at the Park are superb.'

Another indication of poverty, but she seemed quite unperturbed by it. I wondered how Stirling was getting on at the table.

Later the men joined us and after coffee Minta said she knew that Stirling and I wanted to see the house, so she would show us now.

'Be careful of the bartizan if you go up there,' warned Lucie.

'I will,' promised Minta. She explained to us as we went out of the room: 'The stonework is beginning to crumble in some parts of the house.'

'What is this bartizan?' asked Stirling.

'It's a sort of battlemented overhanging turret on the top of the tower. Lucie's afraid it's going to collapse.'

'Shouldn't it be put right?'

'It will be one day when we can afford it.'

'But if it's dangerous . . .'

'Oh, there's so much that needs to be done. You've no idea.'

'Yes, I have,' said Stirling.

She smiled at him as though she thought he was clever. 'Most people never think that a house like this needs constant expenditure if it's to be kept in order. And if this is neglected for some years . . .' She raised her eyebrows.

'But surely it shouldn't be neglected,' insisted Stirling.

'If the money isn't available it has to be.'

'I'm sorry . . .' began Stirling.

She shrugged her shoulders. 'All my life people have been saying that Whiteladies would fall about our ears if necessary repairs weren't done. I get used to it.'

'But a house like this is a sort of trust.'

'Yes,' she agreed. 'A sort of trust. This is the entrance into the old part. These were really the convent walls. You'll be able to see how thick they are in a minute. Mind these stairs. They're rather dangerous.'

We mounted the spiral stone staircase, holding the rope banister. The steps were steep and worn in the middle.

'I've never seen anything like it,' said Stirling; and there was a lilt of excitement in his voice.

'I'm glad you find it exciting,' said Minta, who hadn't noticed the acquisitive gleam in Stirling's eyes.

Through the old part of the house we went. Minta had picked up a lantern from the walls and Stirling carried it. We followed her up winding flights of steps into alcoves that were like cells. It was very cold.

'We sometimes use this for storing things,' said Minta. 'When I was young I can remember venison and great hams being kept here. That was when we entertained a good deal and there were more servants.'

She took us back to the inhabited part of the house.

'This section was built a little later than the main part. It was in the time of Elizabeth Tudor so it is built in the shape of an E. This is the main block; there are two projecting wings on either side and this short section in between.'

'One could get lost in such a house,' I said.

'I was lost once,' Minta told us. 'They searched and searched for me. I was in what we called the studio. There's an enormous cupboard there and for some reason no one thought of looking in it. The studio was given the name when my mother had drawing lessons there.'

'I'd like to see it,' I said.

'You shall, though there's nothing special about it except that it has a good north light.'

Nothing special! When he had sat there with her, instructing her, falling in love with her!

'My mother, you know, was the daughter of the house – the only child. When my father married her he came to live here.'

'So there weren't always Cardews at Whiteladies.'

'No. We haven't been able to keep the family name going. There have been several family names. They're inscribed on the wall in the library. There have been six changes of name in three hundred years. It seems to be a feature of the family that every now and then a woman inherits. She marries and the family name is changed. That's what happened to my mother.'

'And it will to you.'

'Well . . .' She laughed with an insouciance which implied that she was completely unconcerned as to whether Whiteladies came into her possession or not. 'Before Druscilla was born we thought she might be a boy. In which case . . .'

'But she would not have been in the direct line,' insisted Stirling. 'Your father married into the family and his present wife is nothing to do with it, so . . .'

'Oh no,' said Minta quickly. 'When people marry they become the family. It has always been like that. Whiteladies is my father's now . . .'

335

'You could have lost Whiteladies!' cried Stirling, 'and you don't seem to care.'

'I should like to have a little brother. My father would love to have a son. He was so proud when Druscilla was born.'

'But if there was a son it seems you could lose Whiteladies.'

'I don't think of Whiteladies as a possession exactly. It's the family home. Whoever owned it, it would be home, always.'

'Unless,' suggested Stirling, 'it passed out of the family.'

I flashed him a warning glance. He was going too far too fast.

'That couldn't happen,' she said with a look of surprise. 'It's always been the family's house.'

'But if it were a burden . . .'

'A burden! Oh, I see what you mean . . . financially.' She laughed almost merrily. 'It's always been a financial burden.'

'If it became too heavy a one . . .'

'It's always been too heavy a one. Now this is the way to the studio I was telling you about. We have to get up this narrow flight. It's at the top of the wing . . . to get the light, you see.' She threw open a door. 'There! Look at the dust. It's not used nowadays and I suppose the servants don't often come up here. There's far too much for them to do. My mother used to come up here a lot. Oh, there's the cupboard. It's enormous . . . one of those you can walk about in. I think I must have come up here to look for her; then I wandered into the cupboard and shut myself in.'

The room was plainly furnished. There was a big table, some chairs and an easel.

'I was never any good at drawing,' went on Minta. 'Perhaps Druscilla will be. Then we can use the studio again.'

She opened the cupboard door. It was the size of a small

336

room and down one side were shelves on which were a few pencils, crayons and two drawing-boards. Minta picked up one; on it were several sketches of a horse. That was Lynx's work. I would know it anywhere. Oh Lynx, I thought, how could I ever have imagined that I would be able to forget!

'Not much to see here,' said Minta and I felt angry with her, which was stupid. How could she guess at the turmoil in my heart?

She took us to the library after that and showed us the crest and the coat of arms and the names of the family very artistically inscribed on the branches of a fig tree – Merrivale, Charton, Delmer, Berrington, Dorian and Cardew. Stirling was staring as though fascinated. I knew he was adding a new name: Herrick.

We climbed more stairs. 'This is the east wing of that E. We don't use this part now, but my mother was fond of it. When Lucie married my father she decided it would be economical to close this part of the house. Lucie is wonderful at managing things. I am sure our affairs are in better shape since she started looking after them.'

I could well believe that.

'This was my mother's room. Lucie had the furniture covered in dust sheets. The servants don't like to come up here.'

'Why?' asked Stirling.

'You know how it is when there has been a recent death . . . or perhaps you don't. Servants get superstitious. My mother died rather suddenly.'

'I thought she had been an invalid for some time,' I said.

'Well, a sort of invalid. We all thought she rather imagined her illness and then she died of a heart attack. We felt we'd misjudged her – and Lizzie, who had been her maid, started imagining things.'

'Things?'

'Oh, that my mother wouldn't rest and she believed she

was still in the house . . . her ghost, she meant. Poor Lizzie, she had been with Mamma since she was a girl. She was so sensible and practical, but Mamma's death seemed to unnerve her. Lucie is taking her in hand, though, and she's getting better.'

I looked round the room. Her room! Here she would come after the drawing-lesson to dream about him. It was in this room that they had found him with jewels in his pockets. I believed I could sense the great drama which had taken place there.

Minta was ushering us out and leading the way along the corridor. 'There's a staircase at the end of this landing,' she was saying. I was still thinking of that room. It happened forty years ago, I reminded myself. And I could feel the frustration and agony of Lynx when he was caught, trapped; and he knew he could not hope for justice. And because of this Stirling and I were here now. Poor innocent Minta! She did not know that the apparently courteous guests whom she was graciously showing round were two harpies planning to take Whiteladies from her.

I wanted to see that room again. I wanted to be in it alone. I wanted to sense the atmosphere of that tragic night when Lynx's pride was humbled. Minta and Stirling had turned a corner. I hastily slipped back into the room. It was different now. Without the lamp I could just make out the humps of furniture under the dust sheets because light from a half moon shone through the windows.

Oh Lynx, I thought, I understand your misery, but it's all over. It must be forgotten. We'll have the Mercer's House, Stirling and I – and Minta and Franklyn will be our friends. Your grandchildren shall play on the lawns of Whiteladies. That's how your dream will come true.

No! I could almost hear his scorn. He wanted revenge. I could hear his voice in my mind thundering: No!

Then my heart began to beat fast because there was something in the room. I sensed a presence. Someone was watching me.

'Lynx!' I breathed. 'Oh, Lynx, come back.'

A shape materialized in the doorway and moved towards me.

'You're Mrs Herrick.' A human voice. Not that of Lynx.

'You startled me,' I said.

'I'm sorry, madam, I'm sure. I wasn't expecting anyone in Miss Arabella's room.'

'Miss Cardew is showing us the house.' Understandably she looked round for Miss Cardew. 'They went on without me and I wandered back in here.'

She peered at me as though I were of rather special interest to her. 'You're Mrs Herrick,' she said. 'There was someone here long ago . . . of that name.'

'You must have been here a long time.'

'I was two years older than Miss Arabella. I was under-nurse when I was fourteen. Because there wasn't much difference in our ages we were together . . . a lot.'

'You're Lizzie,' I said.

She nodded. 'I was there . . . all the way through. And now she's dead and there's another Lady Cardew.'

It was eerie in this room with nothing to light it but the moon, and the odd shapes of furniture seemed as though at any moment they might take on life. I knew instinctively that this woman had known and loved him. It was impossible for anyone to be unaffected by him. She reminded me of Jessica.

'You come from Australia and that was where he went . . . this man who was here once. I know you were his wife but he had another before you. That's his son. There's a likeness, though he's not the man his father was. There's something in the air. I can feel it. It's as though he's come back.'

'He's dead,' I said sharply, 'so he can't come back.'

'He could if he wanted to. He could do anything. Don't make any mistake about that. Something's going to happen. It always does where he is . . . and he's here. I'm sure of it. I knew him well.'

I shivered. She was so like Jessica and I felt that I was caught up in some intricate pattern which kept repeating itself.

'The others will be wondering what has happened to me,' I said.

She ignored that. 'Lady Cardew died suddenly,' she said. 'We weren't expecting it. It was very strange. Sometimes I think . . .'

Fortunately I heard Minta's voice calling me.

'I'm here,' I called.

She stood in the doorway, Stirling holding the lamp behind her.

'Oh, Lizzie!' she said rather reproachfully.

'I've been talking to Mrs Herrick,' said Lizzie almost defiantly.

'Well, now we've found you we'd better continue with the tour,' said Minta. She added gently: 'Lizzie, I should get back to your room if I were you. It's rather chilly to hang about here.'

'Yes, Miss Minta,' said Lizzie meekly.

Minta turned and we all followed her. On the next landing Lizzie disappeared and Minta took us to show us the carved banisters which led up to the minstrels' gallery.

'I hope Lizzie didn't scare you,' said Minta. 'She's been rather odd since my mother died.'

'Like Jessica,' said Stirling. And to Minta: 'She's a cousin of my mother's and she went a bit queer when my mother died. *They* were always together.'

'Very like Jessica,' I agreed. 'They are two devoted people.'

340

'I must speak to her,' went on Minta. 'She mustn't go wandering round these closed-up rooms. This minstrels' gallery was put in in the sixteenth century when this wing was built. You didn't notice it from the hall because the curtains were drawn.'

We examined it and I pretended to show interest but my encounter with Lizzie had started up so many memories that my thoughts were far away. I kept imagining Lynx in this house attracting the young lady whom he was teaching – and the maid at the same time.

When we rejoined the others the doctor was about to take his leave. He had one or two patients he wanted to look in on and he said he would take Maud home at the same time. I suggested that we ought to go too and Franklyn immediately offered to drive us home. So we said goodbye and soon were driving the short distance to the Mercer's House.

'What a place!' Stirling was saying. 'I have never been in such a house.'

'I should think not,' I retorted. 'It's unique.'

'There are other houses which have been built on the site of old monasteries . . . and with some of the original stones,' said Franklyn. 'Fountains Abbey in Yorkshire springs to mind.'

'It's a pity,' said Stirling, 'that they can't afford the necessary repairs.'

'A great pity,' agreed Franklyn.

'Perhaps they'd be wise to sell it to someone who could put it to rights.'

'Oh never!' cried Franklyn. 'It's an institution. It's a tradition.'

'That sort of house belongs to posterity,' said Stirling rather pompously. 'If people can't afford to run it they should let it go.'

'If it were mine, I never would,' I said.

'And you can be sure,' added Franklyn, 'that the Cardews never will either.'

The lights of Mercer's were visible and we drove the rest of the way in silence.

We were too excited for bed. We went into the drawing-room and Stirling threw himself on to the sofa. I sat down in the armchair looking at him.

'The first move,' he said.

'Well, if you think you've made a move, I don't.'

'We've been there. We've inspected the house. My good-ness, it needs some money spent on it, and they haven't two brass farthings to rub together.'

'Exaggeration! And who wants to rub brass farthings together, which I'm sure they could easily do if they had a mind to.'

'You're becoming infected by Mr Franklyn Wakefield. That's just the sort of thing he would have said.'

'Then he'd be talking sense.'

'But, seriously, Nora, what a satisfactory evening!'

'Was it? I came away with the impression that they would never for one moment consider selling Whiteladies.'

'What will they do? Let it fall about their ears?'

'It's in no danger of imminent collapse.'

'It'll be worthless if they let it go much farther.'

'It'll always be their home. Let them enjoy it. I happen to like this Mercer's House. It's really far more comfort-able.'

'It'll do until we move into Whiteladies.'

'And when will that be?'

'In the not far distant future. I feel it in my bones.'

'I wouldn't rely on them.'

'You're determined to be pessimistic.'

'I think I see this more clearly than you do.'

'Let's be practical.'

'Yes, let's. But they are not what you would call practical people. They'll never sell Whiteladies. That's been made clear. Franklyn implied it. He would know.'

'He would know nothing. He's quite obtuse. He knows how to bow and make the sort of remark people want to hear. That's the sum total of his accomplishments. And since when have you been on Christian name terms?'

'We aren't. I only call him Franklyn privately. I think you underestimate him.'

'Listen, Nora. These people are not like us. They've been brought up to luxury. They haven't the same stamina and vitality. We're different. Think of our fathers. They had ambition, the ability to go out and get what they wanted. We have inherited that. They haven't. They were brought up in their mansions; they think they'll inherit from Papa and that's that. But if there's nothing for them to inherit, what then? I'll make a bet with you, Nora. We'll be in Whiteladies this time next year.'

'I don't think so.'

'It's the wrong attitude. You invite failure when you're certain of it.'

'Perhaps I don't think it would be such a failure.'

'It was what my father wanted,' he said. 'It's what he would expect.' And it was as though Lynx looked at me through his eyes, so that I felt I was a traitor and was silent.

Stirling smiled at me tenderly. 'You'll see,' he said.

We were invited not only to Whiteladies and Wakefield Park but to the vicarage and several other houses. We had become part of the life of the neighbourhood, Maud Mathers saw to that. I was glad to be of use, for I had taken a great liking to her. She seemed to have such good sound sense. I had a great respect for her, too. My feelings for Minta and Franklyn were to some extent affected by Stirling's attitude towards them. He seemed to despise them faintly. He was continually stressing that they weren't like us; they had been brought up in a different school. Whenever he discussed them a faintly pitying note would creep into his voice. I laughed at him for it, but it had its effect on me.

Lucie exasperated him a little. I knew why. She was more like ourselves. She had not been brought up to accept a life of luxury; she was practical and obviously doing everything she could to live within the means at their disposal. Stirling was aware of this. It hurt me in a way to see how he rejoiced in the ill fortunes of the Cardews. He had an obsession. Yet I could not entirely disapprove, for everything he did was due to his devotion to his father's memory.

On the Saturday before harvest festival I went to the church to help Maud decorate. We worked hard arranging chrysanthemums, asters, dahlias and Michaelmas daisies round the altar. There were enormous vegetable marrows, too, and tomatoes and cabbages all on display. Bunches of corn were tied up with red ribbon and set side by side with loaves of delicious crusty bread which would later be distributed to the needy.

'It's been a good year for the harvest,' said Maud, looking down at me from the ladder, on the top rung of which she was standing draping russet-coloured leaves over a brass rail.

'Be careful you don't fall,' I warned.

'I've decorated this spot in the same way for the last five years. I'm sure-footed.'

I came over to steady the ladder and hold it for her.

'What on earth would happen if you were out of action?' I asked.

'Father would have lots of helpers who would do just as well.'

'I don't believe it. And just think of the work you'd give poor Dr Hunter. He's over-worked already.'

'Yes,' she said soberly, 'he is.'

She came down the ladder then and I noticed how rosy her cheeks were. 'I've often told him he should have help,' she went on. 'Sometimes I feel anxious for him.' She bit her lip. She was embarrassed. 'He seems . . . worried. It's having so much to do.'

I was sure she was right, I told her. I'd noticed it too.

'Do you think these bronze chrysanthemums would look well with the leaves?' I asked her.

'Perfect. I do wish something could be done about Dr Hunter.' Then she started to talk about him, his selfless devotion to his cases; the good he had done to this one and that.

As I arranged the flowers and leaves I thought: She's in love with him.

I rode a good deal that autumn. Life in Australia had made a competent horsewoman of me and riding seemed the easiest and most convenient method of getting around. Stirling sometimes accompanied me. He was getting restive and making all sorts of plans. He was going to acquire land and saw himself as a local squire which, I told him, would be usurping Franklyn Wakefield's place.

'There's no reason why there shouldn't be two of us,' he would say. But the first task was to get possession of Whiteladies and he was no nearer doing that than when we had arrived.

He wanted to go to see Sir Hilary and make an offer. I dissuaded him because I was certain he would be disappointed;

and he accepted my advice when I reminded him that he might set the Cardews against him if they guessed at his motive for cultivating their friendship.

I often rode with Franklyn Wakefield. He made a habit of calling at Mercer's and suggesting he show me some part of the country which I hadn't seen before. I enjoyed those rides. We would often tether our horses outside some old inn – he always seemed to be well known in these places – and lunch off bread and cheese and cider. The food always tasted exceptionally good and I enjoyed meeting the people to whom he introduced me. I was aware of the great respect in which he and his family were held and this pleased me.

I loved the odours of autumn – the mist which was often in the air; the smell of burning leaves as we passed some garden; the nip in the air which made my skin tingle. I watched the trees gradually denuded of their leaves to make a lacy pattern against the grey-blue sky. And I learned much about the responsibilities of a country squire, for he took them seriously; I became accustomed to his rather pedantic style of speaking and grew to like it. When I was with him I forgot that slightly patronizing attitude of Stirling's which had rubbed off on me. There was something dependable about this man which I respected. I realized, too, how great was his affection for his parents. He was devoted to them. So he was to his tenants and I was astonished by how much he knew – and cared – about their affairs.

One rather warm November day when the red sun was veiled by mist, and spiders' webs were draped across the hedgerows, we rode out together. He was rather subdued that day and I asked him if anything had happened to upset him.

'It's not unexpected,' he answered. 'Dr Hunter thinks my father can only have another six months to live.'

'Oh, I am sorry.'

'He is old and his condition is worsening. I am more particularly worried about my mother.'

'She is ill, too?'

'No, but they have been so close all their lives. They were neighbours and knew each other from childhood. I can't imagine what would happen to her if my father died.'

'She will have you.'

'I don't think that would be enough. She will be so heart-broken it will kill her.'

'Do you think people die of broken hearts?'

'This would be a broken life.'

I thought of myself and Lynx. He had meant so much to me and yet here I was, as alive as I had ever been.

We rode in silence and he sensed my sympathy, I knew.

It was that day that we found the kittens. When we called at one of the farms on his estate. the farmer's wife came out from the kitchen wiping her floury arms and Franklyn introduced me as the new tenant at Mercer's.

'A fine old house,' commented the farmer's wife, 'and you couldn't have a better landlord.'

She insisted on our drinking a glass of her very own elder-berry wine and eating one of the buns which she had just taken from the oven. We sat on chairs in the kitchen and she told Franklyn about the farmer's intention to let gravel-three-acres lie fallow next year. A big tabby cat came in and, purring, rubbed itself against my legs.

'That's old Tibbles looking for a saucer of milk again,' said the farmer's wife. 'She's lost interest in her last litter.'

'How many cats have you now?' asked Franklyn.

'Well, to tell the truth, Mr Wakefield, I've lost count. I can't bring myself to destroy the little things and in next to no time they're no longer kitties and have little ones of their own. They scratch around in the barns so they don't trouble us and they keep the mice away.'

When the farmer came in he took us out to show us the new barn he was putting up and that was when I saw the kittens. There were ten or twelve cats – most of them just passing out of the kitten stage – and I noticed one in particular because she was not so pretty as the rest and was, in fact, rather thin and cowed. When I called her she came readily and I wished I had something to give her to eat.

'This one seems a little outsider,' I said.

'You get them now and then,' said the farmer. 'They're not so strong as the rest and can't fend for themselves.'

I said on impulse: 'We haven't a cat. May I have her?'

'We'd be glad for you to take any that you want,' was the farmer's answer; and I knew I was going to enjoy taking this little one and feeding her and cosseting her to make up for the hard time I was sure she had had on the farm.

We were about to leave the barn when another small cat came running up. She was tawny – much the same colouring as the one I had chosen, but much prettier though she had the same underfed look. She mewed piteously and I thought: She wants to come too. I said: 'I'll have the two. They'll be company for each other.'

The farmer's wife found a basket and the two little cats were put in it. Franklyn carried them and we rode off. On our way we called at Whiteladies as Franklyn wanted to see Sir Hilary. Minta came out and was most interested in the cats. While Franklyn was with her father we took them out of the basket and gave them a saucer of milk apiece.

'They're darlings,' cried Minta. 'And they seem so grateful, which is unusual with cats.'

'I'm sure they've had a bad time. They never had a look-in at meal times. These will be quite different from those cats who started life as pampered pets.'

I saw that she would like to have one so I suggested she should. She was delighted.

'You choose,' I said, 'and we'll name them.'

When they had licked their saucers clean they sat licking themselves.

'That one is more beautiful,' said Minta.

'The other has more dignity.'

We tried several names and at length I suggested Bella and Donna – Bella for the beauty and Donna for the dignified one.

Minta chose Bella; so I left her behind at Whiteladies.

It was only a few weeks later that we heard about the copse. Stirling came in in a mood of great excitement. The Cardews were putting up for sale the copse which was on the edge of their grounds.

'They're obviously being forced to raise money,' he said.

I heard about it from Franklyn. When he said he would buy the copse I asked if he planned to cut down the timber and build on it. He shook his head. 'No. I'll leave it as it is.' I guessed he was thinking that when he married Minta it would be as though the land had not changed hands.

I was astonished when I saw him next to learn that he had *not* bought the copse. Someone had made a very big offer for it. I began to feel uneasy when I heard this. I couldn't wait to see Stirling.

I knew before I said anything. It was what he would call making a move.

'So you've bought the Whiteladies copse,' I said.

'How did you know?'

'And,' I went on, 'you've paid about twice as much as it's worth.'

'What does that matter?'

'Not at all to our golden millionaire. Why didn't you tell me?'

'You've become very odd lately, Nora. You're getting more like Them and less like Us.'

'If you mean I try to act tactfully . . .'

'Oh, come now. What's tactless about paying a high price for something to help people out.'

'When they know it's you they'll be embarrassed.'

'They weren't embarrassed to take my cheque and get twice as much as the land's worth.'

'Sir Hilary . . .'

'Knows nothing about business.'

'Well, Minta . . .'

'She knows even less. It's Lady Cardew who has the business head in that house.'

'So you arranged it with her.'

'I arranged it with my man of business.'

'I don't think you should have done it, Stirling.'

'Why not?'

'Because Franklyn Wakefield was going to buy that land and if he had it would have remained in the family.'

'I don't follow your reasoning.'

'Then you must be blind. Franklyn is going to marry Minta, and when he does he'll be able to deal with Whiteladies.'

'It's going to take more than he's got to put that place to rights.'

'How do you know?'

'I make it my business to know. It needs thousands spent on it. Wakefield's comfortably off but he's no . . .'

'Millionaire,' I added.

He nodded, smiling. He was certainly a man with an obsession.

Minta spoke to me about the copse. 'I know now that it was Mr Herrick who bought it. He paid far more than it was worth.'

'He can afford it,' I said rather tersely.

Her eyes shone warmly. 'It was very kind of him.'

'I think he wanted it rather badly.'

'He couldn't have wanted it. There is plenty of land about which is far more valuable.'

But not Whiteladies, I thought. And I could see by Stirling's manner that he believed he already had a foot in the door.

You're wrong, Stirling, I thought. It isn't going to work out your way. You'll settle in at Mercer's or we'll go back to Australia. I knew then that it wouldn't have mattered to me either way – as long as I was with Stirling.

Christmas was almost upon us. During the week before, Stirling and I with Maud, Minta and Franklyn accompanied a party of carol singers round the village to collect money for the church. We went to Wakefield Park afterwards where hot soup was served to us. I gathered it was a custom and that long ago Whiteladies had been the setting for it. Franklyn appeared to be taking over Whiteladies' duties, and when he marries, I thought, he'll go and live there and old customs will revert to what they once were.

Seeing his father seated in his chair with the tartan rug over his knees and his mother hovering close, it occurred to me that he had delayed asking Minta to marry him because of his parents. When he was married he would be expected to live at Whiteladies and he wished to remain with his father for what time was left to him.

We all met again on Christmas morning at church and in the late afternoon went to Wakefield Park where we were to dine. The place looked festive hung with holly and mistletoe and I was reminded of Adelaide's attempts to bring an English atmosphere into our home on the other side of the world.

It was the traditional Christmas – turkey and plum pudding blazing with brandy, and gifts for everyone from a Christmas tree in the centre of the drawing-room. Toasts were drunk to our hosts, to their guests and particularly to newcomers. There were several guests besides ourselves and after dinner more called in. In a large ballroom we danced, to the music of two violins, the old country dances – Jenny Pluck Pears and Sir Roger de Coverley – and afterwards we waltzed and some of us tried the minuet. I enjoyed it all and tried not to think of Christmases spent in Australia. Franklyn's parents stayed up until the end and I noticed the old man nodding and beating tune to the music, and how his eyes and those of his wife followed Franklyn all the time.

'It was a lovely Christmas,' I told Franklyn; and he replied in his stilted way how pleased he was that I had not been bored by their old customs.

On the way home Stirling admitted it had been an enjoyable day and told me he had invited them all to the Mercer's House for the New Year.

'We must put our heads together,' he said, 'and plan something equal to Mr Franklyn Wakefield's entertainment.'

I was a little ashamed of that New Year's party. Stirling had sent for a firm of London caterers to come down and manage the whole thing. He scattered invitations throughout the place. Special plate was brought down; expert chefs came to do the cooking; and he even decided that we should have footmen in blue velvet livery wearing powdered wigs.

I laughed aloud. 'It's ridiculous,' I said, 'for a small country house like this – and appalling bad taste.'

'I wish we could have it in Whiteladies,' he said wistfully. 'Imagine that hall . . .'

'This is not Whiteladies, and what are these people going to think when they see your hired flunkeys.'

But I could not dissuade him.

Mrs Glee was inclined to be indignant. 'I could have managed very well, Mrs Herrick, with an extra maid or two and I would have known where to get them,' she scolded reproachfully. 'I hope Mr Herrick is not dissatisfied with my cooking.'

I assured her that this was not the case and that Mr Herrick had acted without consulting me. I should have planned a very different sort of party – with Mrs Glee's help, of course.

She was mollified and when she saw the decorated dining- and drawing-rooms and all the preparations, she began to take an immense pride in them. We were going to outshine Whiteladies and that meant something to her. She became quite excited, especially as she would take an authoritative part in the proceedings.

I don't know whether I could call that evening a success. At least it was memorable. Fancy lamp-posts had been fixed outside the house and red carpet laid down on the steps of the portico. Stirling had hired a band which was set up in a little room between the dining- and drawing-rooms and the players wore red breeches with white Hungarian blouses. The table decorations were a masterpiece of roses which were very expensive at that time of the year. The guests were duly impressed and faintly embarrassed in the midst of such grandeur; consequently it was not such a merry party as we had had at Wakefield Park. Stirling had arranged for a pianist to entertain us and afterwards we danced in the drawing-room which had been made ready for this purpose. It was not a ballroom such as they had at Wakefield

Park, but it was when the dancing started that the party became enjoyable. We danced folk dances which Maud led because she ran a class for them, and then everyone became more natural. At a quarter to twelve we sat down waiting for midnight to strike; and when it did we joined hands and sang 'Auld Lang Syne'. I had Franklyn on one side of me, Minta on the other; and I felt happy because I knew them.

When the last of the guests had gone Stirling and I sat down in the drawing-room and talked about the evening.

'You have made your point admirably,' I told him. 'Your friends and neighbours will no longer doubt that they have a millionaire in their midst.'

'It's rather a pleasant thing to be.'

'When it gets you what you want; but do remember money won't buy everything.'

'Name a few things it won't.'

'Those things which are not for sale.'

'You'll see. I've made up my mind I'm going along to have a talk with Sir Hilary.'

'When?'

'In a few days' time.'

'So you're waiting a few days! Tactful of you but I marvel at your sloth. Why not go along tomorrow and say: 'Sir Hilary, I've made it clear to you that I am a millionaire, an ostentatious fellow who likes to stress the point. I'm ready to pay what you ask.'

'You've changed, Nora. Sometimes I wonder whether you're on my side.'

'I'm always on your side,' I said.

He smiled, understanding. That was love between us, unshakeable, inevitable. I could criticize him; he could mock me; it didn't matter. We were meant for each other and it would always be like that. True, I married Lynx; but then

Lynx had decided that. And I was so close to Stirling that I shared his adoration of the strange man who had been his father. Stirling had had no choice but to stand aside for Lynx; and I had no choice but to stand aside for Whiteladies . . . which after all was for Lynx. But we were one – Stirling and I. After a year of widowhood I would become his wife.

As he smiled at me that night I was as certain of this as I had been during that time in the cave when we had lain close together while a forest fire raged over our heads and we thought never to come out alive. There was the same understanding between us now.

By the end of January Stirling's patience gave out and be went to see Sir Hilary. I was in the library when he came in, his face white, his lips tight and a look of blank despair in his eyes.

'What's happened?' I cried.

'I've just come from Whiteladies.'

'Is something terribly wrong there?'

He nodded. 'I've made an offer to Sir Hilary.'

'And he refused. Is that all? I could have told you it would happen.'

He sat down heavily and stared at the tip of his boot. 'He says he can't sell . . . ever. No matter what offer he had, he couldn't. "I'm saddled with the house and so is the family," he said. Those were his words. Saddled with it! There's some clause that won't allow them to sell. It was made by some ancestor who had a gambling son. The house remains in the family . . . whatever happens.'

I felt as though a burden had been lifted from my shoulders. 'That's settled it. You've done all you can and there's an end to the matter.'

'Yes,' he said, 'it would seem so.'

'You tried. No one, not even Lynx, could have done more.'

'I didn't expect this.'

'I know. But I told you there are some things which are not for sale. Now you can put it out of your mind and start planning for the future.'

'You're glad, I believe.'

'I think it's wrong to try to take from people something which belongs to them.'

'He used to talk so much about it. He was determined that we should be there.'

'But he didn't know of this clause, did he? And I never agreed with him. He could be wrong . . . sometimes. His firm intention was to be revenged and revenge is wrong. There is no happiness in it.'

He was silent and I knew he wasn't listening to me. He was thinking of all his wasted efforts.

I went to him and laid a hand on his shoulder. 'What shall we do now?' I asked. 'Shall we go back to Australia?'

He didn't answer, but he stood up and put his arms round me.

'Nora,' he said. He repeated my name and kissed me as he never had before. It was a lover's kiss – and I was happy.

I thought we would talk freely after that because we had made a tacit admission of our feelings; but this was not the case. Stirling was more withdrawn than he had been before. He was silent – almost morose; he went out riding alone. Once I saw him coming back, his horse sweating.

'You've been overworking that poor animal,' I accused, hoping he would tell me what was on his mind.

I thought I knew. He loved me, but Lynx was between

us. Lynx, his father, had been my husband; and that made a strange relationship between us.

It will pass, I assured myself. What Lynx would want more than anything would be for Stirling and me to marry. We were the two he had loved best in the world; he would want us to be together. We shall call our first son Charles after him. We will never forget him.

So I was unprepared for what happened next.

Stirling came in one late afternoon just at dusk. Ellen had brought in the lamps and drawn the curtains and I was alone in the drawing-room. There was a strange expression on his face as though he were sleep-walking.

'I'd better tell you right away,' he said. 'I'm engaged to be married.'

I could not believe I had heard him correctly.

'I've just asked Minta to marry me,' he went on.

I heard my voice then, cold, terse, indifferent almost. 'Oh . . . I see.'

'You *do* see, don't you?' he said almost imploringly.

'Of course. It's the only way to buy Whiteladies.'

'It *was* the only way . . . in view of the fact that it can't go out of the family.'

'Congratulations,' I said harshly.

I had to get out of the room or I should rage and storm at him. I should lay bare my hopes and longings. I couldn't stay in that room trying to speak to him calmly. So I pushed past him to the door. I sped up to my room and locked myself in.

Then I lay on my bed and stared at the Mercer's coat of arms on the ceiling and I wished that I were dead.

How I lived through the weeks which followed I am not sure. I had to look on at Minta's bliss. How she loved him!

I could understand that. Once she had been contented enough at the prospect of marrying Franklyn Wakefield, no doubt; and then he had come – this strong, vital Stirling who, when he wanted something, would allow no obstacle to stand in his way. Poor Minta! Did she guess why he was marrying her? Often I wanted to tell her. I had to keep a tight control on my tongue to prevent myself shouting at her; and all the time I could feel nothing but pity for her. Poor innocent little dupe! The victim of one strange man's desire for revenge and of another's tenacious need to fulfil a duty. Poor innocent Minta, who believed herself loved! She was not marrying for the sake of Whiteladies even though it would now be completely restored to its old perfection. It would be a cherished house. I could imagine Stirling's thorough assessment of the necessary repairs. No expense spared. Here comes the golden millionaire.

And what happiness would come from such a marriage, I asked myself bitterly. I was jealous, angry and humiliated. *I* loved Stirling and I had believed he had loved me. And so he did. But his duty towards Lynx came before his love for me. A voice within me said: As your infatuation for Lynx came before your love for Stirling, remember?

Lynx was still with us, ruling our lives.

If I was deeply unhappy I was determined not to show it. I think I managed very well. Stirling made sure that we were rarely alone together. He spent a lot of time at Whiteladies. He was, as I guessed, making that assessment of necessary repairs and he threw himself into the task with all the ardour a normal man might have showered on his bride.

Minta came to see me and sat in the drawing-room nursing Donna. She was so happy, she said. She would tell me a secret. She had been in love with Stirling ever since we came to the Mercer's House. No, before that really. Did I remember the occasion when we had all met for the first time? And when he came back . . . it seemed like fate.

Not fate, I thought, but Lynx.

'Stirling *adores* Whiteladies. He'll love living there.'

It's the only reason for his marriage, I thought grimly.

'He makes me see it differently. More as Lucie does.'

'And Lucie? Is Lucie pleased?'

She wrinkled her brows and I warmed towards Lucie, who, with her practical good sense, saw farther than Minta and her father.

'Lucie's worried about me. I think she has the idea that I'm a child still. She taught me at school long ago and I don't think she ever sees me as anything but one of her less bright pupils.'

So Lucie didn't altogether approve.

'And what I wanted to say, Nora, is this: If you would like to come and live at Whiteladies there will always be a home for you there.'

'Me! At Whiteladies. Oh, but you don't want your step-mother-in-law . . .' I heard myself giggle a little wildly.

'That absurd title. I know Stirling wants you to come.'

'Has he said so?'

'Well, of course.'

No, I thought. Never! How could I live under the same roof and see them together and think of all that should have been mine? And Stirling loved me. He knew it. Poor innocent little Minta, who did not understand the devious people who surrounded her.

'Well, I've grown very attached to the Mercer's House.'

'What, that big house all to yourself! Don't imagine we should live in each other's pockets. Whiteladies is vast. You could have your own wing. There are the apartments which used to be my mother's.'

'It's good of you, Minta, but I think I'll be better here for a while. I may go back to Australia.'

'Please don't say that. We should hate it . . . Stirling and I.'

And how I hated the proprietary way in which she spoke of him. My feelings were tempestuous and I was wretchedly unhappy. But I could only feel pity for Minta.

They were married that April – just as the buds were showing on the trees and the dawn chorus was at its most joyful.

Maud had decorated the church and I had helped her, which was bitter irony. How she had chattered! She was so happy for Minta.

'If ever a girl was in love that girl is Minta,' she said. And I knew Maud was imagining herself walking down the aisle on the arm of Dr Hunter, a bride. I could feel a great sympathy for Maud, but at least she did not have to see the man she loved married to someone else.

Right up to the wedding-day I kept assuring myself that something would happen to prevent this marriage; but the day arrived and Sir Hilary gave his daughter away and the Reverend John Mathers performed the service.

I sat and watched Stirling at the altar taking his vows to Minta. On one side of me was Lucie, on the other Franklyn. Lucie looked rather stern as though she feared for the marriage. And Franklyn? What were his feelings? He gave no indication that he suffered from seeing the girl who was surely intended for him marrying someone else. But that was characteristic of him.

The responses were over; they were signing the register; soon the wedding march would peal forth and they would come down the aisle together. It was like an evil dream.

And there they were – Minta, a radiant bride, Stirling

inscrutable; and the organ playing the Wedding March from *Lohengrin*. It was over.

We left the church and with Franklyn beside me, I came out into the uncertain April sunshine

Minta

Chapter One

I AM not sure when I first began to suspect that someone was trying to kill me. At first it was a hazy notion, one which I dismissed as ridiculous – and then it became a certainty. I had become a frightened and unhappy woman.

Yet on the day when I married Stirling I was, I was sure, the happiest bride in the world. I couldn't believe that this wonderful thing had happened to me. In fact, on the day he proposed to me I was taken completely by surprise. Stirling was different from anyone I had ever known. There was a special quality about him. Nora had it too. They were the sort of people whose lives seemed so much more exciting than mine; and that made them stimulating to be with. Nora was by no means beautiful but she had more charm than anyone I knew; she was poised and had a rare dignity; I felt one only had to look at Nora to be attracted by her. Her life had been so unusual. There was that marriage to Stirling's father of which she spoke very little, but I had noticed that whenever her husband's name was mentioned there was a sort of breathless pause – with Stirling as well as Nora – as though they were talking of some deity. The fact that she had been his wife elevated her in some way, made her different from other people. Stirling had the same quality. They were not easy to know; they were unpredictable; they were unlike people I had known all my life – people like Maud Mathers and Franklyn – and even Lucie whom I understood and knew so well.

I had never hoped that Stirling would care for me. I used to think that he and Nora would be well matched, and had she not been his stepmother they might have married. And then that day came and he said without warning: 'Minta, I want to marry you.' I blinked and stammered: 'What did you say?' because I was certain I had misheard.

He took my hands and kissed them and said he wanted to marry me. I told him that I loved him and had ever since I had first seen him; but I didn't dream he felt the same about me.

We told Father right away. He was delighted because he knew Stirling was rich and that when we were married I shouldn't be haunted by poverty as he had always been. He summoned the household – including our few servants – and told them the news; and he sent down to the wine cellars for the last of the champagne so that everyone could drink our health. The servants did this readily. They were doubtless thinking that their wages would now be paid regularly.

But there were two people in the house who weren't pleased.

The first was Lucie. Dear Lucie, she always behaved as though I had just emerged from the schoolroom and needed looking after. She came to my room after Stirling had gone and sat on the bed as she used to in those days when she came to Whiteladies for holidays.

'Minta,' she said, 'are you absolutely sure?'

'I was never more sure of anything. It's wonderful, because I never thought he could possibly care for me.'

'Why not?' she demanded. 'You happen to be a beautiful

young woman and I always thought you'd make a good marriage.'

'Yet you're looking worried.'

'I am . . . a little.'

'But why?'

'I don't know. It's a feeling I have.'

'Oh, Lucie, everybody's delighted. And even if I wasn't in love with him, it's good from every point of view, isn't it? He'll stop all our worries about money; and you know how you're always fretting about the house falling into ruin.'

'I know, I love this house and it is in urgent need of repair, but that doesn't mean I think you should marry because of it.'

'You're being a fussy old hen, Lucie.'

'Since I married your father I've looked upon you as my daughter. And before that, as you know, I was very fond of you. I want you to be happy, Minta.'

'But I am. Never so as now.'

'I wish you would wait . . . not rush into things.'

'You've become a gloomy old prophetess. What's wrong with Stirling?'

'Nothing, I hope, but it's all too quick. I had no idea that he was in love with you. He's never given me that impression.'

'Nor me either.' I giggled like a foolish schoolgirl. 'But he's different, Lucie. He's lived a different life from ours. You shouldn't expect him to behave like ordinary people. He wouldn't show his feelings.'

'That's the trouble. He doesn't. He certainly didn't show me that he was in love with you.'

'Why else should he want to marry me? I can't bring him a fortune.'

'He's very interested in the house. He might be seeking the background marriage into a family like ours could give him. After all, who is he? That rather vulgar display at the New Year shows a certain lack of breeding.'

'Lucie, how dare you say such things!'

'I'm sorry.' She was immediately contrite. 'I'm letting my anxieties run away with me. Forgive me, Minta.'

'Dearest Lucie. I'm the one who should ask forgiveness. I know you're worried solely on my account. But really there's nothing to worry about. I'm perfectly happy.'

'Well, you won't rush things too much, will you?'

'Not too much,' I promised. But I knew Stirling wanted an early marriage and everything now would be what Stirling wanted.

The other dissenter was Lizzie. How dramatic – and rather tiresome – she had become since Mamma died. Lizzie had to wait until I was in bed before she came in, glided was the word, with her candle held high like some ghost. She was in a long white flannelette nightdress which added to the ghostly illusion. I was aware of being too excited for sleep, and was going over that wonderful moment when Stirling asked me to marry him.

She pushed open the door and I said: 'What are you doing roaming about the house, Lizzie? You might set your night-dress alight with that candle.'

'I had to come and see you, Miss Minta.'

'At this time of night!'

'Time doesn't matter.'

'Well, I think it does, Lizzie, because I'm tired and you ought to be in bed.'

She took no notice but sat on the edge of my bed.

'So you're going to get married . . . to him.'

'I'm going to marry Mr Stirling Herrick, if that's to whom you refer.'

'That's him, all right. And the likeness is there. You'd know who he is at once.'

'Please don't speak of my future husband disrespectfully, Lizzie.'

'There's something unnatural about it. It seems a funny thing to me. His father wanting to marry your mother and now he's here and going to marry you.'

'What are you talking about, Lizzie.'

'It was his father who was here all those years ago.'

'His father! That was Mrs Herrick's husband.'

'A real mix-up,' said Lizzie. 'That's what I think's so funny about it. Your mother was mad about him and she wasn't the only one.'

'Go to bed, Lizzie. You're rambling.'

'No I'm not. What I say is true. It's as though he's come back. In a way I always thought he would.'

Events started to fall into shape in my mind. I said: 'Lizzie, do you mean that my mother's artist was . . .'

'That's right. Mr Charles Herrick. You can see his name on some of the drawings in the studio cupboard. He came here to teach her drawing, then he went away . . . sent away to Australia for theft and your mother never saw him again. She was never the same after, and now he's dead they say, but there's this other one and you're planning to marry him. Doesn't that seem like some sort of fate?'

'I don't understand it. I think you could be mistaken.'

'I'm not mistaken. There's some who don't lie down when they're dead and he's one of them.'

'You're making a dramatic situation out of a perfectly normal one.'

'I hope so, Miss Minta. I certainly hope so. But how did he come here, out of the blue? He's bewitched you just as his father did your mother . . . and others.'

'I'll ask Mr Herrick about this when he comes next.'

'You ask him and listen carefully to the answers.'

'Now, Lizzie, I'm sleepy.'

'I take the hint, but I've warned you. I can't do more than that.'

Then she picked up the candle and went out.

But I did not sleep. I was too excited. Could it be true that Stirling's father was my mother's artist? And what a strange coincidence that Nora's scarf should have blown over *our* wall. What did it mean? But did it matter? What was important was that Stirling had asked me to marry him. Was it the house he wanted, as Lucie seemed to suggest? Was it some sort of pattern as Lizzie thought it to be? And finally, what did it matter? I was going to marry Stirling.

Stirling said there was no need for delay. He was eager to become my husband.

I mentioned what Lizzie had told me.

'It's true,' he admitted, 'that my father was a drawing-master at Whiteladies, wrongly accused of theft and sent to Australia. There he quickly made good. It was a grossly unfair charge to make against a great man. When I came to England to take Nora back I naturally wanted to look at the house where my father had worked, Nora's scarf blew over the wall and we came in to get it.'

There seemed nothing extraordinary about that. It was all so logical – except of course for the fact that Stirling had never mentioned his father's connection with the house before this.

'I'm sorry about your father,' I said.

'He wouldn't need pity.'

'But to be wrongly accused.'

'It happened often in those days.'

'You were so fond of him, Stirling.'

'He was my father.'

'You have a certain reverence for him. It's the same with Nora.'

'If you had known him you would have understood.'

'Poor Nora! How she must have suffered when he died!'

He didn't speak but turned his face away. I feared I had been tactless. He never liked to speak of Nora. I thought it was because he was worried about her future so I said that if ever she wanted to come to Whiteladies she would be very welcome.

'After all, she is like your sister. I know she is, in fact, your stepmother, but that seems ridiculous. She's so attractive. I always feel unworldly beside her. I wish I were more like her.'

Stirling didn't say anything; he just stared ahead as though I weren't there. He's thinking of his father, I told myself; and I was glad that he was capable of such deep devotion.

There were so many preparations for the marriage. Maud Mathers was excited by it and envious in the nicest possible way. She immediately began working out how she would decorate the church. 'I wish it were May instead of April,' she said. 'It would give us more opportunity with the flowers.'

Lucie supervised the making of my wedding-dress. We had Jenny Callow and her daughter Flora to come in and work on it and make some other clothes for me. It was like old times because when I was a little girl before we became so poor, Jenny used to work full time at Whiteladies. Flora was a little girl then, learning her trade from her mother. I remember her standing by holding the pins. Then Jenny had to go and people used to get her to do dressmaking for them so that she could make a living.

The only person I could chatter with was Maud. Lucie would have been ideal but I couldn't bear her silent disapproval. I would have liked to talk to Nora but she kept out of the way. I was disappointed; I thought she was going to be like a sister. Maud wanted to know where we were going for the honeymoon and when I told her that we hadn't discussed this she was faintly disappointed.

'Venice!' she said. 'Sailing down the Grand Canal in a gondola. Or perhaps Florence. Strolling to the bridge where Dante and Beatrice met. Rome and the Forum and standing on the spot where Julius Caesar was struck down. I always think Italy is the place for honeymoons.'

I was surprised. I had not thought Maud so romantic.

When I mentioned a honeymoon to Stirling he said: 'Why should we go away? What could be more fascinating than Whiteladies?'

'You mean stay at home!'

'It's only just become my home,' said Stirling. 'There's nothing I'd like so much as to explore it. Of course if you would like to go away . . .'

But I wanted to do exactly what he wanted. 'There won't be a honeymoon yet,' I told Maud. 'That will come later.'

So the dresses were made and the cake baked; and Father said there was no need to consider the expense of the wedding. I was getting a handsome settlement and because of my marriage Whiteladies would be gradually restored to its old magnificence.

A week before the wedding Lucie came to my room one night for a talk.

'There's just one thing I want to say, Minta,' she told me. 'If you want to change your mind you shouldn't hesitate.'

'Change my mind! Whatever for?'

'It's all been rather hurried and there's been so much talk about how good this is for Whiteladies. But if you decided not to marry, we'd manage. We've managed so far. I don't want you to feel you have to marry for the sake of the house.'

'I never felt that for one moment, Lucie. I love the house and hate to see it crumbling away, but I wouldn't marry for it. It's just the greatest good fortune that Stirling happens to be rich and loves the house. He's going to put it all to rights. You'll be glad. I know you will. You've worried a lot about the house.'

'I'll be glad, of course, but nothing would compensate for your making the wrong marriage.'

'Set your mind at rest. The reason I am marrying Stirling is because I love him.'

That satisfied her. She started to talk about the wedding and hoped Maud would look well in the cerise-coloured silk she had chosen. Maud was to be Maid of Honour. I had hoped Nora would be but she had said it would be absurd for a married woman to take the part and had shown so clearly that she did not wish for it that I hadn't tried to persuade her. Lucie said it was a pity Druscilla wasn't old enough to be a brides-maid and I agreed. We had asked Dr Hunter to be best man. There again Franklyn would have been the obvious choice but somehow it seemed wrong to ask him because I knew so many people had expected him to be the bridegroom at my wedding. But, as I said, what did all this matter? The important thing was that I married Stirling.

And so at last came our wedding-day – the happiest day of my life. After Mr Mathers had performed the ceremony we went back to Whiteladies and the reception was held in the great hall where the brides of our family had celebrated their marriages through the centuries. On that day Stirling seemed as though he were enraptured. He loves me, I thought. He couldn't look like that if he did not.

He stood in the hall with me by the great cake and guided my hand as I cut it, and there was something about him which I can only describe as triumph.

There were the usual speeches – Father's rather rambling and sentimental; Dr Hunter's short and rather witty; Franklyn's conventional – the sort of speeches that had been made at weddings for the last hundred years. Stirling answered. He was direct. It was a happy day for him, he said. He felt he had come home.

Some of the guests stayed on to a dinner-party and afterwards we danced in the hall which made a wonderful ballroom. Stirling and I waltzed round together. He was not a good dancer but I loved him the more because of that.

'You'll find me lacking in fancy manners,' he told me.

'I know I shall love what I find,' I replied.

Then the guests left and we were alone. I was a little afraid of my inadequacy, but Stirling was kind. It was almost as though he were sorry for me and I was enchanted by his unexpected tenderness.

Yes, that was the happiest day of my life.

Chapter Two

*I*T was a strange honeymoon. On the first day Stirling wanted me to take him on a tour of the house. 'Just the two of us,' he said.

I was delighted and we went round together. He was horrified by the state of things and made a lot of notes. I remember how he probed the oak beams in some of the rooms.' 'Worm!' he commented. 'They could collapse at any moment. We'll have to get to work on them right away.'

'You're more like an assessor than a husband,' I told him.

'This is your house,' he retorted. 'It's in trust for our children. We have to see that it is kept in order.'

I hadn't realized how thoroughly neglected the house had been. 'It will need a fortune spent on it, Stirling,' I said. 'There's no need to do everything at once.'

'*I* have a fortune,' he said. I laughed because what Lucie called his ostentatiousness amused me. He was rich and proud of being so because his father had made that fortune and everything his father had done was wonderful in his opinion. 'And,' he went on, 'nothing is going to be left. I'm going to see that your house is in perfect order.'

'I wish you wouldn't say *your* house in that way, Stirling. What I have is yours. You know that.'

Then he smiled in a way which touched me deeply. He kissed me gently and said: 'You're a sweet girl, Minta. I'm sorry that I am as I am.'

I laughed at him and said: 'But that's why I love you.' He put his arms round me and held me against him. 'We're going to be very happy.' I told him, for it was as though he was the one who needed assurance then.

'Our children will play on the lawns of Whiteladies,' he said solemnly.

'A restored and beautiful Whiteladies which has lost its woodworm and whose bartizans will stand for another thousand years.'

What energy Stirling had and he spent it on the house! Within three months the rot had been arrested and Whiteladies was beginning to be a fine old house again. But he wasn't satisfied. There was still a good deal to be done. That time was what I called the Whiteladies Summer.

At the beginning of September tragedy struck Wakefield Park. Sir Everard had another stroke and died. It had been expected for we all knew that he couldn't live long, but it was a shock nevertheless. Especially for Lady Wakefield. She was lost without her husband; Franklyn was with her all the time but she fretted and a week after the funeral she took to her bed and for some weeks lay there without any will to leave it. In the middle of October she died and everyone said it was a 'happy release'.

Poor Franklyn was distressed, but he was not the man to show it. Dr Hunter told us that he had warned Franklyn of the inevitability of his father's death and the fact that Lady Wakefield had died so soon afterwards was as she would have wanted it. Dr Hunter had come to Whiteladies to see Druscilla. Lucie was always calling him. She worried ridiculously about that child. In fact where Druscilla was concerned she was by no means her usual practical self.

'She had no will to live,' said Dr Hunter. 'I've known it happen like that many times. People have been together all their lives. One goes and the other follows immediately.'

Father was upset about losing his dear friends. He insisted on going to the funeral. Lucie was quite cross about it because there was a keen east wind blowing; she declared she would not allow him to go out. Yes, she did fuss us. It was because she had never had a family before and that made us rather precious to her. Father usually gave in but he was adamant on this occasion. He said he was determined to 'see the last of his old friend'. So he drove to the church and followed the cortege to the graveside and stood there in the wind, his hat in his hand.

I was sad for Franklyn, knowing how devoted he was to his parents, and was glad Nora was there because I felt that her presence comforted Franklyn. I had known for some time that he admired her. Towards him she showed a certain aloofness but she was friendly in a way. I remarked to Stirling that it would be rather a pleasant solution for Nora if she married Franklyn, for she constantly talked as though she intended to return to Australia.

'They're completely unsuited to each other,' said Stirling coldly. 'Franklyn!' he added quite contemptuously as though Franklyn wouldn't make a good husband.

'You don't know Franklyn,' I defended my old friend. 'He's one of the kindest people in the world.'

He turned away quite angrily. Nora had married his father, of course, and I supposed the thought of anyone's supplanting him was distasteful.

Still, I continued to think how pleasant it would be if Franklyn and Nora could marry. I wondered whether the idea was in Franklyn's mind. I was sure it was not in Nora's.

❦

A few days after Lady Wakefield's funeral Father developed a cold. Lucie fussed terribly as she always did when he was ill and made him stay in bed. He should never have gone to the funeral, she grumbled.

She sent for Dr Hunter and kept him with her a long time. When the doctor left the sick room I asked him to come into the library and asked him if my father was really ill or was it just Lucie's worrying.

'It's a chill,' he said, 'but he's near to bronchitis. I hope we've caught it in time. Perhaps a few days in bed.'

Poor Dr Hunter! He looked very tired himself; and I thought of his going home to that rather dismal little house where his housekeeper might or might not be in a drunken stupor. Why didn't he marry Maud? She would look after him.

I insisted on his drinking a glass of sherry before he went out to his brougham; that brought a little colour into his cheeks and he seemed more cheerful.

'I'll look in this evening,' he promised, 'just to make sure your father is going along as he should.'

But when he came that evening, Father had bronchitis. In a few days this had turned to pneumonia. I had rarely seen Lucie so upset and I thought how lucky Father was to have such a devoted wife, for I had believed that for Lucie hers had been a marriage of convenience. I knew she had wanted Whiteladies to be her home for ever and no doubt she had enjoyed being Lady Cardew; but when I saw how upset she was I realized how deeply she cared for my father. She wouldn't leave the sick room; she was with him day and night, only snatching an hour or so's sleep in the next room if I sat with him.

'I don't trust those servants,' she said. 'He might want something.'

'If you don't rest you'll be ill yourself,' I scolded.

I sat with him but as soon as he started to cough she was up.

We waited for the crisis; but I knew Dr Hunter didn't think there was much hope. Father was old and had been failing in health for some time. Pneumonia was a serious illness, even for the young.

Father wanted Lucie at his bedside all the time and was uneasy if she wasn't there. I thought how wonderful it was to see their love for each other and I remembered how peevish my mother had always been. I was glad my father had found happiness in the end with a woman like Lucie.

We were both with him when he died but his hand was in Lucie's. I shall never forget the look on her face when she lifted it to me. It was as though she had lost everything she cared for.

'Lucie darling,' I said, 'you still have Cilla.'

I led her to Druscilla's room. It was nine o'clock and the child was asleep. Nevertheless I picked her up and put her into Lucie's arms.

'Mamma,' said Druscilla sleepily and a little crossly.

And Lucie stood there tragically straining the child to her till I took Druscilla away and put her back in her bed. It was perhaps a rather sentimental and dramatic gesture but it did some good. Lucie braced herself and I knew she was realizing that she had Druscilla to live for.

Christmas came. Last year we had gone to Wakefield Park; this year the festivities should be held at Whiteladies. They could not be as lavish as they would be next year, said Stirling, because of my father's death, but they should be worthy of the house. It must be understood that Whiteladies, not Wakefield Park, was the focal point of the neighbourhood.

Lucie had gone about like a ghost in her widow's weeds. In fact they rather became her. Druscilla was nearly two; she had become imperious and demanding, the pet of the household. Lucie loved her passionately but refused to spoil her as I fear the rest of us did. I adored her and constantly longed to have a child of my own. Stirling wanted it too. He was always talking about our children's playing on the lawns of Whiteladies.

Once I had thought I was pregnant and it had turned out not to be so. I was very upset about that and determined that I wouldn't say anything to anyone next time until I was sure. Lucie was always asking pointed questions. 'When you have a child of your own . . .' she would say. Once she said: 'Perhaps you want a child too passionately, I've heard it said that sometimes when people do they can't conceive. It's a sort of perversity of nature.'

When I told her about Stirling's ideas for taking up the old Christmas ceremonies as we used to in the past she thought it a good idea.

'Whiteladies is the great house,' she said. 'Wakefield Park is an upstart. I think your husband has the right ideas.'

I was glad that she was beginning to like Stirling and change her suspicions about the reason why he had married me.

'When you have your family you will probably want me to leave,' she said one day.

'What nonsense!' I cried. 'This is your home. Besides, what should we do without you?'

'It won't always be like that. I am just the stepmother – not really needed.'

'When have I ever not needed you?' I demanded.

'I shall know when the time comes for me to go,' she said.

'I wish you wouldn't say such a thing.'

'All right. We'll forget. But I'd never stay if I weren't wanted.'

That was good enough, I told her. She always would be.

How Stirling enjoyed planning for Christmas! A great deal of the essential work had been done on the house and he took a personal pride in it; but there was much still to be done. He had already increased the staff. Now we had six gardeners and the grounds were beginning to look beautiful. There were always workmen in the house and some rooms were out of bounds because the floor was up or the panelling being repaired.

Two weeks before Christmas I was almost sure that I was pregnant. I longed to tell someone but decided not to. I didn't want to raise Stirling's hopes. Oddly enough, Lizzie guessed. She was dusting Druscilla's room, which was one of her duties, and I had gone in to see the child, who was sitting on the floor playing with her bricks, so I knelt down and we built a house together. I couldn't take my eyes from that small face with the delicate baby nose and the tiny tendrils of hair at the brow. I was thinking of my own baby when Lizzie said in that forthright way of hers: 'So it's like that, is it?'

'Like what?' I demanded.

Lizzie cradled an imaginary baby in her arms. I flushed and Druscilla cried: 'What have you got there, Lizzie?'

Lizzie said: 'You'd be surprised, miss, wouldn't you, if I told you another baby. That would put Miss Cilla's little nose out of joint, wouldn't it?'

Druscilla touched her little nose and said: 'What's that?'

I kissed her and said: 'Lizzie's playing.'

'You couldn't fool me,' said Lizzie. 'There's always a way of telling.'

Druscilla impatiently called my attention to the bricks and I thought: Is it true? Is there a way of telling?

Christmas had come and gone. The Christmas bazaar had been held in the newly restored hall of Whiteladies; Stirling had provided lavish entertainment free of charge, something which had never been done before. It was a great success and everyone enjoyed our new affluence. We entertained the carol singers at Whiteladies and soup and wine and rich plum cake were served to them. I heard one of the elder members say that it was like old times and even then they hadn't been treated to such good wine.

We had only a small dinner-party on Christmas Day because of our recent bereavement – just the family, with Nora and Franklyn; and on Boxing Day we all went to Wakefield Park.

The new year came and then I experienced the first of those alarming incidents.

That morning at breakfast Stirling was talking – as was often the case – about the work which was being done in the house.

'They've started on the bartizan,' he said. 'There's more to be done up there than we thought at first.'

'Won't it be wonderful when it's all finished,' I cried. 'Then we can enjoy living in a house that is not constantly overrun by workmen.'

'Everything that has been done has been very necessary,' Stirling reminded me.

'If my ancestors can look down on what's happening at Whiteladies, they'll call you blessed.'

He was silent for a while and then he said: 'A big house should be the home of a lot of people.' He turned to Lucie and said: 'Don't you agree?'

'I do,' she answered.

'And you were talking of leaving us,' I accused. 'We shan't allow it. Shall we, Stirling?'

'Minta could never manage without you,' said Stirling, and Lucie looked pleased, which made me happy.

'Then there's Nora,' I went on. 'How I wish she would come here. It's absurd . . . one person in the big Mercer's House.'

'She's considering leaving us,' said Stirling.

'We must certainly not allow that to happen.'

'How can we prevent it if she wants to go?' he asked quite coldly.

'She's been saying she's going for a long time, but still she stays. I think she has a reason for staying.'

'What reason?' He looked at me as though he disliked me, but I believed it was the thought of Nora's going that he disliked. I shrugged my shoulders and he went on: 'Go and have a look at what they've done to the bartizan some time. We mustn't let the antiquity be destroyed. They'll have to go very carefully with the restoration.'

He liked me to take an interest in the work that was being done so I said I would go that afternoon before dark (it was dark just after four at this time of the year). I shouldn't have a chance in the morning as I'd promised to go and have morning coffee with Maud who was having a twelfth-night bazaar and was worried about refreshments. That would take the whole of the morning, and Maud had asked me to stay for luncheon. Stirling didn't seem to be listening. I looked at him wistfully; he was by no means a demonstrative husband. Sometimes I thought he made love in a perfunctory manner – as though it were a duty which had to be performed.

Of course I had always known that he was unusual. He had always stressed the fact that he had no fancy manners, for he had not been brought up in an English mansion like *some* people. He was referring to Franklyn. Sometimes I think he positively disliked Franklyn and I wondered whether it was because he knew that Franklyn admired Nora and he didn't think any man could replace his father.

He needn't have worried, I was sure. If Franklyn was in love with Nora, Nora was as coldly aloof from him as I sometimes thought Stirling was from me. But I loved Stirling deeply and no matter how he felt about me I should go on loving him. There were occasions in the night when I would wake up depressed and say to myself: He married you for Whiteladies. And indeed his obsession with the house could have meant that that was true. But I didn't believe it in my heart. It was just that he was not a man to show his feelings.

I came back from the vicarage at half past three. It was a cloudy day so that dusk seemed to be almost upon us. I remembered the bartizan, and as Stirling would very likely ask me that evening if I had been up to look at it, I decided I had better do so right away, for any lack of interest in the repairs on my part seemed to exasperate him.

The tower from which the bartizan projected was in the oldest part of the house. This was the original convent. It wasn't used as living quarters but Stirling had all sorts of ideas for it. There was a spiral staircase which led up to the tower and a rope banister. In the old days we had rarely come here and when I had made my tour of inspection with Stirling it had been almost as unfamiliar to me as to him. Now there were splashes of whitewash on the stairs and signs that workmen had been there.

It was a long climb and half-way up I paused for breath. There was silence about me. What a gloomy part of the house this was! The staircase was broken by a landing and this led to a wide passage on either side of which were cells like alcoves.

As I stood on this landing I remembered an old legend I had heard as a child. A nun had thrown herself from the bartizan, so the story went. She had sinned by breaking her vows and had taken her life as a way out of the world.

Like all old houses Whiteladies must have its ghost and what more apt than one of the white ladies? Now and then a white figure was supposed to be seen on the tower or in the bartizan. After dark none of the servants would go to the tower or even pass it on their way to the road. We had never thought much about the story, but being alone in the tower brought it back to my mind. It was the sort of afternoon to inspire such thoughts – sombre, cloudy, with a hint of mist in the air. Perhaps I heard the light sound of a step on the stairs below me. Perhaps I sensed as one does a presence nearby. I wasn't sure, but as I stood there, I felt suddenly cold as though some unknown terror was creeping up on me.

I turned away from the landing and started up the stairs. I would have a quick look and come down again. I must not let Stirling think I was not interested. I was breathless, for the stairs were very steep and I had started to hurry. Why hurry? There was no need to . . . except that I wanted to be on my way down; I wanted to get away from this haunted tower.

I paused. Then I heard it. A footstep – slow and stealthy on the stair. I listened. Silence. Imagination, I told myself. Or perhaps it was a workman. Or Stirling come to show me how they were getting on.

'Is anyone there?' I called.

Silence. A frightening silence. I thought to myself: I'm not alone in this tower. I am sure of it. Someone is close . . . not far behind me. Someone who doesn't answer when I call.

Sometimes I think there is a guardian angel who dogs our footsteps and warns us of danger. I felt then that I was being urged to watch, that danger was not far behind me.

I ran to the top of the tower. I stood there, leaning over the parapet, gripping the stone with my hands. I looked down below, far below and I thought: Someone is coming up the stairs. I shall be alone here with that person . . . alone on this tower.

Yes. It was coming. Stealthy footsteps. The creak of the door which led to the last steps. Three more of those steps and then . . . I stood there clinging to the stones, my heart thundering while I prayed for a miracle.

Then the miracle was there below me. Maud Mathers came into sight with her quick, rather ungainly stride.

I called: 'Maud! Maud!'

She stopped and looked about her.

Oh God help me, I prayed. It's coming close. Maud was looking up. 'Minta! What are you doing up there?' Hers was the sort of voice which could be heard at the back of the hall when the village put on its miracle play.

'Just looking at the work that's being done.'

'I've brought your gloves. You left them at the vicarage. I thought you might want them.'

I was laughing with relief. I turned and looked over my shoulder. Nothing. Just nothing! I had experienced a moment of panic and Maud with her common sense had dispelled it.

'I'll come right down,' I said. 'Wait for me, Maud. I'm coming now.'

I ran down those stairs and there was no sign of anyone. It was fancy, I told myself. The sort of thing that happens to women when they're pregnant.

I didn't think of that incident again until some time afterwards.

By the end of January I was certain that I was going to have a child. Stirling was delighted – perhaps triumphant was the word – and that made me very happy. I realized then that he had become more withdrawn than ever. I began to see less of him. He was constantly with the workmen; he was also buying up land in the neighbourhood. I had the feeling that he wanted to outdo Franklyn in some way, which was ridiculous really because the Wakefields had been at the Park for about a hundred years and however much land Stirling acquired there couldn't be a question of rivalry.

Lucie cosseted me and was excited about the baby. She wanted to talk about it all the time. 'It will be Druscilla's niece or nephew. What a complicated household we are!'

I was very amused when I discovered that Bella, the little cat which Nora had given me, was going to have kittens. I had grown very fond of Bella. She was a most unusual cat and Nora assured me that Donna was the same. They followed us as dogs do; they were affectionate and liked nothing so much as to sit in our laps and be stroked. They would purr away and I always smiled when I was at Mercer's to see Donna behave in exactly the same way as Bella did. And when I knew Bella was going to have kittens I couldn't resist going over to tell Nora.

I was a little uneasy with Nora nowadays. I hadn't felt like that before my marriage, but now there seemed a certain barrier between us which might have been of her erecting because it certainly wasn't of mine.

She was in the greenhouse where she was trying to grow orchids and Donna was sitting on the bench watching her at her work.

'Nora, what do you think?' I cried. 'Bella's going to have kittens.'

She turned to look at me and laughed and she was how I liked her to be – amused and friendly.

'What a coincidence!' she said.

'You mean . . . both of us.'

Nora nodded. 'Poor Donna will be piqued when she knows.'

At the mention of her name Donna mewed appreciatively

and rubbed herself against Nora's arm. 'So she's stolen a march on you, eh?' said Nora to the cat. And to me: 'What will you do with them?'

'Keep one and find a home for the others. I think they'd like one at the vicarage.'

So we went in and Mrs Glee served coffee in that rather truculent way of hers which amused Nora and was meant to show how much better things were done at Mercer's than at Whiteladies.

'I'm giving a dinner-party next week,' said Nora. 'You must come, Minta.'

'I'm sure we should love to.'

'It's going to be a rather special occasion.' She didn't say what and I didn't probe. I was sure it was no use in any case. Nora was the sort of person who could not be coaxed into saying what she did not want to.

While we were drinking coffee we heard the sounds of a horse's hoofs on the stable cobbles.

'It's Franklyn,' said Nora, looking out of the window. 'He calls in frequently. We enjoy a game of chess together. I think he's rather lonely since his parents died.'

Franklyn came in looking very distinguished, I thought. I wondered whether there would be an announcement of their engagement and this was what the party was going to be for. One couldn't tell from either of them. But Franklyn's frequent visits to Mercer's seemed significant. After all, I knew him very well and I was sure he was in love with Nora.

I really looked forward to the dinner-party. It seemed to me that it would be such a pleasant rounding off if Nora married Franklyn and we all lived happily ever after.

But on the night of the dinner-party I had a shock. There was no mention of an engagement. Instead Nora told us that this would be one of the last dinner-parties she would give because she had definitely decided to go back to Australia.

Bella was missing. We guessed of course that she had hidden herself away in order to have her kittens, but we had no idea where. Lucie said it was a habit cats had. I was rather worried because I thought she would need food, but, as Lucie said, we shouldn't worry about her for she would know where to come when she wanted it.

She appeared after a day and night and it was clear that she had had her kittens.

'We'll have to follow her,' said Lucie, 'and find out where they are.'

We did, and, to our amazement, Bella led us to the tower. Work had had to stop up there because some special wood was needed and it was hard to obtain. Stirling had said that there could be no makeshift so that part of the work had had to be postponed. The door leading to the tower must have been left open, so Bella had found her way up there. She had gone right to the top where workmen had left a piece of sacking and on this were four of the loveliest little kittens I had ever seen. They were tawny like Bella and I was enchanted by the little blind things and touched by Bella's devotion to them. She purred while I admired them but showed her disapproval when I touched them and she was very uneasy if anyone else approached.

'We'd better leave them up there,' said Lucie. 'She won't like it if they're moved. She might try to hide them. Cats have been known to do that.'

'I'll look after them,' I said. 'I shall bring Bella's food up here myself.'

I went over at once to tell Nora about the kittens and

where they'd been found and she said she would be over in a day or so to see them.

I went up the spiral staircase every day and I often thought of that occasion when I had taken fright. The feeling of fear had completely vanished now. The fact that Bella had used the tower for her kittens had made it marvellously normal. I made a habit of going up every morning at about eleven o'clock with a jug of cream for Bella and her food. She expected me and would be delighted each morning when I would inspect the kittens to see how they had progressed.

I was going up one morning when Nora arrived. 'To see the kittens?' I asked.

'You too,' she told me. She had become more friendly since the day I had ridden over and told her about the kittens.

'I was just going to feed them,' I said. 'Come up with me.'

It really seemed as though I had a guardian angel, for I believe that might very well have been the end of me if Nora hadn't come with me. I put the saucer on the stone ledge as I always did while I poured out the milk. It saved stooping. Nora was standing slightly behind me and as I put the saucer in its place and started to pour out the milk there was a sudden rumble. Nora had caught at my skirts and was clinging to them. The stone ledge on which I had placed the saucer seemed suddenly to crumble. I heard the crash of falling masonry. I didn't know what had happened because Nora had pulled me backwards with such force that we both fell.

Nora was on her feet first, her face ashen. 'Minta! Are you all right?'

I wasn't sure. I was too dazed. I could think of nothing but that sudden collapse and myself being hurled forward, Nora with me . . . down from the topmost point of Whiteladies as the nun had gone long ago.

'The fools!' cried Nora. 'They should have warned us. That balustrade was unsafe.' Then she was kneeling beside me. 'Minta . . . ?' I knew she was thinking of my baby. I could feel the movement of the child and I was filled with relief because it was still alive. 'I'll get help quickly,' went on Nora. 'Stay there. Don't move.'

I half raised myself when she had gone. Bella was licking her kittens, unaware of the near-tragedy which had just been enacted. I shivered and waited again for my child to let me know that it continued to live. I was afraid to get up lest I did some harm to it and it seemed a long time before Nora came back. Lucie was with her, her face strained and anxious.

'Minta!' She was kneeling beside me. 'This is terrible. Those men should be shot.'

'How are we going to get her down the stairs?' asked Nora.

'We won't,' said Lucie, 'until Dr Hunter's seen her.'

'There's something about this tower that I don't like,' I said.

'What?' asked Lucie.

'Something . . . evil.'

'You're talking like the servants,' said Lucie sharply. She hated what she called 'silly fancies'. Practical as ever, she had brought a cushion and blankets and she and Nora stayed with me until Dr Hunter came.

He made me stand up. 'No bones broken,' he said. He frowned at the balustrade. 'How could such a thing be allowed!' he demanded.

'They've been hammering away for weeks,' said Lucie. 'We ought to have thought something like this might have happened. When you think of an old place like this suddenly being knocked about . . . In any case the kittens shall be brought down. The cat may not like it but she'll have to put up with it. I'm sending Evans up to bring them down and put them somewhere in the stables.'

'You can walk down to your room,' said Dr Hunter to me. 'But I think a few days' rest would be good . . . just so that we can make sure. Feet up, eh?'

'I'll see that she does that,' said Lucie firmly.

So no harm was done but Lucie insisted that I rest. She needn't have worried. I was determined to carry out the doctor's orders, thinking of the safety of my child. But two nights later I had a dream. I was in the tower and suddenly the terror I had experienced there came upon me. I peered about me but could see nothing. Yet there was something there – some faceless thing which was trying to force me over the parapet.

I awoke with a start and for a few moments thought I was actually in the tower. Then I was aware of my warm and comfortable bed. I was alone in it. Stirling slept in another room now. He had said something about its being better for the baby.

I lay thinking and remembered that time when I had mounted the stairs to the tower and had thought that someone was following me and the fear that I had felt then was like that which I had experienced in the dream. Maud had been below. But suppose she had not been down below. I thought of myself clutching that stone balustrade, the evil presence coming close behind me . . . and no one below! This was an example of the nonsensical imaginings of a pregnant woman who so feels the need to protect her unborn child that she imagines people are trying to kill her. Why? For what purpose?

I shook myself fully awake and laughed at myself. The first incident had been pure imagination; the second an accident which could have happened to anybody. There was no reason why anyone should want to harm me.

But soon I was to discover that there could be a reason.

Stirling wanted to give a dinner-party – a rather elaborate one. He reckoned that we were no longer a house of mourning; we had been unable to entertain as he had wished at Christmas and he wanted to do something now.

I knew that he was upset by Nora's intention to leave us and I particularly wanted to please him. He planned to use the minstrels' gallery and as it was years since we had players up there I went up with two of the maids to make sure everything was in order. Later I discovered that I had lost a stone from a garnet and pearl brooch which had been my mother's and it occurred to me that I might have lost it in the gallery. I went along to search and that was how I came to be there and overheard the scene between Nora and Stirling. There were red velvet ruchings over the lower wood-work of the gallery and heavy curtains of the same material which could be drawn back when the musicians were playing. I was on my hands and knees looking for the stone, completely hidden from anyone in the hall below by the red velvet ruchings, when someone came into the hall and I was about to stand up when I heard Stirling say in a voice which I had never heard him use before: 'Nora!'

Nora said: 'I came to see Minta.'

I stood up but they didn't see me and before I could call to them Stirling said: 'I've got to talk to you, Nora. I can't go on like this.'

She answered angrily: 'Shouldn't you have thought of that before you married Whiteladies?'

I should have called to them but I knew that only if they were unaware of me could I discover something of what could well be of the utmost importance to me. On impulse

I shamelessly played the eavesdropper. I knelt to conceal myself from them.

'Oh God,' he said, and I hardly recognized his voice, so different was it from the way in which he ever spoke to me, 'if only I could go back.'

She taunted him. 'And then? You would listen to me? You would have seen the folly of marrying for the sake of settling old scores?'

I put my hand over my heart. It was making such a noise. I was going to learn something terrifying unless I stood up at once and announced the fact that I was here. I couldn't. I had to know.

'Nora,' he said. 'Oh Nora, I can't go on like this. And you're threatening to go away. How could you! It would be heartless.'

'Heartless!' She laughed cruelly. 'Heartless . . . as you were when you married. How did you think *I* felt about that?'

'You knew it had to be.'

'Had to be!' There was great scorn in her voice. 'You talk as though you were under some compulsion.'

'You know why . . .'

'Lynx is dead,' she said. '*That* died with him. I shall go back to Australia. It's the only way. You chose this marriage. Now you have to meet your obligations.'

'Nora, don't go. I can't bear it if you go.'

'And if I stay?'

'There'll be a way. I swear I'll find some way.'

'Don't forget you have to see your children playing on the lawns of Whiteladies. How will you do that? You thought it was going to be so easy. All the golden millionaire had to do was make the family bankrupt.'

'That was done before.'

'And we suspect how. It's nothing to be proud of. But it didn't work out as you thought it would. Only the family could inherit this place . . . so you had to marry into the family.' She laughed bitterly. 'All this for these stones, these walls. If they could laugh they'd be laughing at us. No. I'm going to Australia. I've written to Adelaide. You've made your bed, as they say. Now you have to lie in it.'

'I love you, Nora. Are you going to deny that you love me?' She was silent and he cried out: 'You can't deny it. You've always known it. That night of the fire . . .'

'You let me marry Lynx,' she said.

'But that was . . . Lynx.'

'Oh yes,' she said, almost viciously, 'your god.'

'Yours too, Nora.'

'If you had loved me . . .'

'You two were the most important things on earth. Of course I loved you then, and if you had loved me enough . . .'

'I know,' she said impatiently. 'But it was Lynx then, and it's Lynx now. We can't escape from him. He's dead but he lives on. You had a choice, though. When you found out you couldn't buy this place you could have come back with me to Australia. Or we could have stayed here. It wouldn't have mattered to me if . . .'

'If we were together,' he said triumphantly.

'But it's too late. You've married. You'll stay married.' Her voice was cruel again. 'You've got to see those children playing on the lawn. Remember?'

She spoke as though she hated him and I knew how deeply he had wounded her. I knew so much now. In the last few minutes everything had fallen into shape. Dominating all our lives was his father who had once lived here and who had been deeply wronged – a great, powerful man, whose influence lived on after he was dead.

'Too late,' she said. 'And you've no one to blame but yourself. When you told me . . . I wanted to die. I hated you, Stirling, because . . .'

'Because you love me.'

'It's too late. You chose. Now you must live with your choice.'

'It can't be too late,' Stirling said. 'There's always a way and I'll find it, Nora. I swear it. Promise to be patient.'

'Patient! What are you talking about? You're married. You're married to Whiteladies. This wonderful, marvellous unique old house is your bride. You can't just walk out, you know.'

'Nora!'

'I shall go on with my plans. The sooner I leave the better.'

'And you think you'll be happy back there . . . without him . . . without me?'

'I have not thought of happiness. Only the need to go.'

'I won't allow it. There's a way out. I promise you I'll find a way. Only Nora, don't go . . . don't go.'

Again she laughed at him. How cruel Nora could be! 'You're shouting. You'll tell the whole household what you have done.'

Then the door was noisily shut. I peered through the ruching and saw that Stirling was alone. He covered his face with his hands as though to shut out the sight of the hall with its dais and tapestries and vaulted ceiling – everything that had made it the wonderful old house worth the greatest sacrifice to attain – even worth marrying me in order to take possession of it.

I remained in the gallery after Stirling had gone. My knees were cramped. I had forgotten the lost garnet. I understood everything now. I should have seen it before; his sudden proposal when he had seen that there was no other means of acquiring the house; his perfunctory love-making; his moroseness when Nora announced that she was leaving. Everything fell into place.

I wished that I were worldly like Nora. Then I should know what to do. I wanted to confide in someone. If Nora had not been involved I should have chosen her. There was Lucie. I hesitated. Lucie had been suspicious of the match right from the first. Lucie was wise and Lucie loved me.

I went to my room still feeling dazed. I shouldn't have listened. Listeners rarely hear any good of themselves. How many times had I heard that?

Bella came and rubbed herself against my legs. The kitten I had kept was playing with the blind cord. I thought of that day on the tower and how the balustrade had crumbled . . . and then I thought of the occasion when I believed I had been followed up there; and I heard a voice ringing in my ears, Stirling's voice: 'I'll find a way.'

'No,' I said, 'that's stupid. He didn't mean that.' But how did I know what he meant? What did I know of him – or rather what had I known before a short while ago? At least now I knew that he had married me because of some vow to own Whiteladies. I knew that he was capable of deceit, that he had pretended to love me when what he wanted was the house. I knew that he loved another woman and that he was planning in some way to end his marriage with me in order to marry her.

How? I asked myself; and some horrible voice within me said: 'It almost happened in the tower. There was the balustrade . . . and that other occasion.' I tried not to think of his creeping stealthily up the stairs, seizing me from behind and throwing me over the tower. That was fancy. Fancy! Hadn't I heard a movement? Hadn't I sensed evil? Nora had saved me once. At least *she* was not in the plot . . . if plot there was. But I couldn't believe that of Stirling.

My head was throbbing and I could not think clearly. I don't know why I went to Lizzie's room, but I did.

'Are you all right, Miss Minta?' she asked.

'I have a headache.'

'Sometimes women get them in your condition.'

'Tell me about that artist who came to teach my mother drawing.'

'Mr Charles Herrick,' she said slowly. 'And now you're Mrs Herrick and there's another Mrs Herrick at Mercer's. And soon another little Herrick will come into the world.'

'What was he like?'

'Like your Mr Herrick but different. I never saw anyone quite like him. He stood out and above everyone else. You'd have thought he owned the place. Your mother worshipped him.'

'And you too, Lizzie.'

'Yes,' she admitted. 'And he wasn't averse, I might tell you.'

'He loved my mother.'

'He loved her for what she stood for. He was proud and poor and he saw himself as lord of the house.'

'And then?'

'There were ructions. "Get out," he was told and he went, but he came back for your mother. They were going to elope.' Lizzie started to laugh. 'He came up by the ladder. She was ready to go with him. She gave him her jewels. She had some valuable pieces. He put them into his pocket and then . . . they burst into the room and caught him . . . and that was the last we saw of him.'

'Somebody warned them.'

'Yes,' she said slyly.

'It was you, Lizzie, wasn't it?'

Her face puckered. 'You know!' She cried. 'Your mother knew. I told her on the night she died. The shock killed her. She would never have forgiven me if she'd lived. She raged at me. She said that but for me her whole life would have been different. She'd have gone away with him; he'd never have gone to Australia.'

'But he went and he made a vow and because of that, Lizzie, because of you . . .'

I walked out of the room, leaving her staring blankly before her.

I was bewildered, still not knowing how to act.

I couldn't go down to luncheon because I couldn't face anyone. Lucie came up to my room.

'Minta, what's wrong?'

'I feel ill, Lucie.'

'My dear, you're trembling. I'll get a hot-water bottle.'

'No, Lucie. Just sit by the bed and talk to me.'

She sat down and I started to talk. In whom could I confide who would be more sympathetic than Lucie, who for so many years had been closer than my own mother? I told her what I had overheard in the minstrels' gallery.

'You see, Lucie, he loves Nora. He married me for Whiteladies.'

Lucie was thoughtful for some moments; then she said: 'Nora is going back to Australia. You and Stirling will make a life for yourselves. It will be a compromise, but marriage often is.'

'No,' I said. 'He loves her and won't be able to forget her. There's a great bond between them – it's part hate and part love, or so it seemed, for Nora sounded as though she hated him and loved him at the same time. She hated him because he'd hurt her by marrying me. I've been lying here trying to think of something I can do.'

'Minta, my dearest child, the best thing you can do is nothing. This sort of thing has happened before. Stirling is married to you. You are going to have his child. Nora will go to Australia. You'll be surprised. In a few years' time he will have forgotten her and so will you.'

'He won't let her go,' I insisted. 'He said so.'

'Impulsive talk. He has no say and Nora is a wise woman of the world. She knows that nothing can be done. You are his wife. When she goes away he may fret for a while but time heals everything. He'll be reconciled. You have a great deal to offer him, Minta.'

'No, no. I've been trying to think of what I should do. I even thought of going away.'

'Where to?'

'I can't think where.'

'You are not being practical. You'll stay here and I'll be at hand to look after you.'

'But I did think of going . . . somewhere. I even started to write a letter to him.'

She went over to my desk and picked up a sheet of paper. On it I had written:

'Dear Stirling, I was in the minstrels' gallery when you and Nora were talking so I know that you love her and there seems only one thing to do. I must stand aside . . .'

I had got no farther, having paused there to wonder what I could do. Angrily, Lucie threw it into the waste-paper basket. Then she came back to the bed.

'You are overwrought,' she said. 'I am going to take care of you and I promise you that in time all this will seem nothing to you. He couldn't have been so much in love with Nora or he would never have married you.'

'You're a great comfort, Lucie, but . . .'

'You trust me. Now you're to stay in bed for the rest of the day, then you won't have to face anybody. I'll go along to Dr Hunter and tell him to come and have a look at you, shall I?'

'Dr Hunter can't help over this.'

'Yes, he can. He can give you something to make you

sleep and that's what you need really. I'll tell everyone you're resting today. You haven't been yourself since that fall in the tower.'

I shivered. I couldn't tell even Lucie of the horrible suspicion that had come to me. But merely talking to Lucie had made me feel better. She went out and left me, and I lay still, trying to believe what she had told me and failing wretchedly.

I stayed in bed for the rest of the day. Lucie brought supper for me on a tray, but I couldn't touch the roast chicken nor the cheese and fruit. She had been to Dr Hunter's, but he was out on a case and that stupid Mrs Devlin had seemed as though she had been drinking. However, she had left a message for him to come and see me in the morning. I could have one of the pills he had given me at the time of my fall. Lucie would have some milk sent up for me to take with it.

'Won't you try and eat something?' she asked.

'I couldn't, Lucie.'

About nine o'clock she sent Lizzie up with some hot milk and biscuits. Lizzie looked subdued and this clearly had something to do with her outburst earlier that day. I couldn't feel the same about Lizzie any more. Her action had had such a tremendous impact on all our lives. I looked distastefully at the milk and turned away, so Lizzie put it on my bedside table.

I closed my eyes and I must have dozed, for when I awoke my heart started to pound furiously for someone was standing by my bed. It was Stirling. I couldn't face him then so I pretended to be still asleep. He stood there looking at me and I wondered what was in his mind. Was he thinking of putting a pillow over my face and smothering me? I didn't care if he did. Who would have believed it was possible to love a man whom one suspected of murdering one. Nora loved and hated him at the same time and I loved him while I suspected him of wanting to kill me. How complex were human emotions!

He went out after a while. I lay still and the same thoughts went round and round in my mind and suddenly I was startled by a movement near the window. I sat up in bed and doing so knocked over the tray. The kitten followed by Bella came running over from the window. I realized that it was their playing with the blind cord that had awakened me. The kitten discovered the milk and started to lap noisily, so I put the tray on the floor and they finished it between them. Bella jumped on to the bed, purring, and I stroked her. After a while she jumped down and I tried to sleep. I couldn't, of course. I just lay there going over everything and finally I was so exhausted that I did sleep.

Lizzie came in. It was eight-thirty. I was usually up by this time.

'Her ladyship sent me to ask how you were this morning.'

'I'm tired,' I said. 'Just leave me. Don't pull up the blind.'

'So you're staying in bed for a while?'

I said I was. She went out and little later Lucie came in. 'Just to see how you feel,' she said.

I was half asleep, so she went on: 'I won't disturb you. A little rest will do you good.'

It was about half past ten when there was a light tap on my door. It was Mary, one of the housemaids. She said: 'Mrs Herrick's called. She wants to see you.'

Nora! My heart was leaping about uncomfortably. I wanted to see Nora, to talk to her. I was turning over in my mind whether I might tell her what I had heard. I had always felt an urge to confide in Nora. But how could I in this case?

I heard myself say uncertainly: 'Ask her to come up.'

'Shall I draw the blinds, Miss Minta.'

I hesitated. 'N . . . no. Not just yet.' I wanted to know whether I could face Nora first. My hair was unkempt; I should have washed, tidied myself before seeing her. But it was too late now. The maid was gone and when she came back Nora was with her.

Nora was wearing a grey riding habit and she looked elegant and worldly. There was a gentleness in her face. I knew that she was sorry because I was married to Stirling – not only because that meant he wasn't free for her. She was sorry because she thought I was going to be unhappy.

'Oh, you are resting,' she said. 'I heard that you weren't feeling well.'

'I didn't feel very well yesterday and since the fall Dr Hunter likes me to rest a lot.'

'I'm sure he's right.' A faint light came through the slats of the blind and she drew a chair up to the bed. 'I thought I must come and see you,' she went on. 'I shan't have much more opportunity.'

'You are determined to leave us, then?'

'I've definitely made up my mind.'

'I shall miss you. As for Stirling . . .' My voice trembled.

She said quickly: 'I always thought I should go back some time.'

'You must have been very happy there.'

She drew her brows together and said: 'Yes. I daresay you are longing for the child to be born.'

'Yes, I am.'

'And Stirling, too.'

Children playing on the lawns of Whiteladies! I thought.

'The waiting period can be irksome,' I said. 'Franklyn will miss you.'

'In a year or so you will have forgotten me . . . all of you.'

I shook my head. I had a great desire to see her face more clearly. She hid her feelings well but I thought: She must be as unhappy as I am. I said: 'It's dark in here.'

'Shall I pull up the blinds?' She rose and went over to the window. I heard her give a little gasp. She was staring at the floor. Then hastily she pulled up the blind and looked down again.

'What is it?' I cried, starting up.

'Bella and the kitten . . .'

I leaped out of bed. I caught my breath in horror. Their bodies looked oddly contorted. They were both dead. I knelt down beside them. I could not bring myself to touch those once lively little bodies which I had loved.

'They're dead,' said Nora. 'Minta, what can it be?'

I knew. I remembered the milk dripping on to the floor and Stirling standing by my bed.

'There was poison in my milk,' I said quite calmly. 'Of course it was meant for me.' Then I began to laugh and I couldn't stop myself. 'I've a charmed life. First Maud . . . then you, and now the cats.'

She took me by the shoulders and shook me. 'What do you mean?' she demanded. 'What *do* you mean? Control yourself, for God's sake. Don't touch the cats. You don't know what's wrong. Let me help you back to bed. Remember the child.'

She drew me back to the bed. I was saying: 'It's all very simple, Nora. Someone is trying to kill me. There have been other attempts. But I have a charmed life . . .'

She was very pale. 'I don't believe it,' she said. 'I don't believe it.' And she said it as though she were trying to convince herself. And I knew what was in her mind. She had heard him say it. He had said to her: 'I'll find a way.' I heard her whispering to herself. 'No . . . no . . . It's not true.'

'Nora,' I said, 'it can't always miss, can it . . . not every time?'

'You've got to get away from . . . from here. We have to think about it. I can't leave you here. You must come back with me to Mercer's. We can talk there . . . we can plan . . .'

I thought: Go with *her*! *She* is the reason why he wants to be rid of me. He wants Nora *and* Whiteladies. How can I go with her? But she had saved me once before.

'What will they say if I go with you?' I said. 'What will Stirling say?'

'We must save him . . . and you,' she answered. It was as though she were speaking to herself. It was an admission that the thoughts which were in my mind were shared by her.

There was a knock on the door. Nora looked at me in dismay. It was the maid again.

'The doctor is here, Miss Minta. I've brought him up.'

Dr Hunter was immediately behind her and he came into the room.

'Lady Cardew suggested I pop in and have a look at you,' he said. He gazed at us both in astonishment. 'Is anything wrong?'

I left it to Nora to explain. I heard her say: 'We're very alarmed, Dr Hunter. Come and look at the cats.'

She took him over to the window and he knelt down to look at Bella and her kitten. When he rose his face was ashen.

'What happened?' he asked.

'They drank the milk which was intended for Minta,' said Nora. 'Were they poisoned?'

'It could be so.'

'What should we do?'

'I will take the cats away.'

'I was suggesting that I take Minta with me to the Mercer's House.'

'That's an excellent idea,' said the doctor. He turned to me and said: 'Get up and dress quickly. Go out of the house as though nothing extraordinary has happened. Go to the Mercer's House with Mrs Herrick right away and stay there until I come.'

So he left us, taking the cats with him; and I dressed hastily and, wrapping myself in my cloak, went out of the house with Nora.

Nora

Chapter One

I SHALL never forget that journey back to the Mercer's House and the thoughts which crowded into my mind. Stirling was trying to murder his wife. That was what he had meant when he had said he would find a way. Why had I not gone back to Australia months before? I should have gone as soon as he had married her.

Half my mind rejected the thought and then I kept thinking of that terrible day which was engraved indelibly on my memory when Jagger had caught me and fought with me and Lynx had come and shot him dead. He had killed a man because he had dared touch what he thought of as his; it was not because of attempted rape. I would never forget the poor little maid Mary who had suffered through Jagger. That had been shrugged aside as of little importance. Stirling was the son of Lynx. They were ruthless, both of them. They held life cheaply – that was, other people's lives. Stirling had been determined to get Whiteladies and now that he regretted the great sacrifice he wanted to start again. He could only do this by ridding himself of Minta. No, Stirling, I thought. And Lynx, this is where your revenge has led us!

I had made Minta mount my horse and I walked beside

it, leading it. The poor girl looked as though she would collapse at any moment. No wonder! She had miraculously escaped death – and not only once, for I was sure that the crumbling parapet had been a trap for her.

I called one of the stable boys to look after the horse and took her into the house. We went into the drawing-room with its rosewood furniture and Regency striped wallpaper and sat looking at each other helplessly.

'Nora,' she asked me, 'what do you think of it?'

I couldn't bear to talk of my suspicions, so I said that the cats might have died of some strange disease. There were mysterious illnesses among animals of which we knew very little. She started to talk about animals she had had when a child and some of the things which had happened to them. But we were not thinking of what we were saying. I said I would make some tea and she said she would help. It gave us something to do and all the time we were trying to work out some plan. She must stay with me, I said. I couldn't bear her to be out of my sight. I was terrified of what might happen to her.

There was about her a surprising indifference. She had been greatly shocked by what had happened so perhaps that was why she gave that impression of not caring. I was desperately sorry for her. She was going to bear Stirling's child and I had been envious of that, but I was overcome by a desire to protect her.

We drank the tea. It was now past midday. At Whiteladies they would be wondering where she was, although one of the maids had seen us leave and I had murmured something about Mrs Herrick's coming over to the Mercer's House with me.

It was one o'clock when Lucie arrived. Her hair was disordered by the wind; she had evidently come out hastily when she had discovered that Minta was not in her room and she had learned where she was.

As she came into the drawing-room and saw Minta her expression was one of relief. 'Oh Minta, my dear, I wondered what had happened.'

They embraced and Lucie said: 'Why didn't you say you were going out? I thought you were in your room.'

'Nora came to see me and I came over with her.'

'But you've had no breakfast. You've . . .'

'We were rather disturbed,' I said. 'We found the cats dead.'

'The cats . . . what cats?'

'Bella and the kitten,' said Minta. 'They were lying on the floor near the window . . . their bodies stiff and odd-looking.' Her lips trembled. 'It was horrible.'

'Cats!' repeated Lucie, bewildered.

'Dr Hunter took them away,' I explained.

'Do please tell me what all this is about.'

I didn't want her to know. I thought: There'll be an enquiry and they'll find out. Oh Stirling, how could you! As if I could love you after that!

Minta said simply: 'I don't think the doctor wanted us to talk about it yet.' She turned to me. 'But it will be all right to tell Lucie. Lucie, the milk which was in my room . . . I didn't drink it.'

'What milk?' said Lucie.

'There was some milk sent up. You told Lizzie to bring it, didn't you?'

'Oh yes. I remember.'

'I didn't drink it. I knocked it over and the cats drank it. Now they're dead.'

'But what has this to do with the milk?'

She spoke in such a matter-of-fact tone that my fears abated a little and relief came to me. I thought: We're imagining things . . . both of us. Of course the cats' death had nothing to do with the milk!

'So the cats are dead,' went on Lucie, 'and that has upset you. I did hear that some of the farmers were putting down poison for a fox that's raiding the fowl houses. Bella's constantly roaming about.'

I looked at Minta and saw the relief in her face too.

Lucie went on to stress the point: 'What did you think the *milk* had to do with it?'

'We thought there was something wrong with the milk,' I said, 'and that because they had drunk it . . .'

Lucie looked puzzled. 'You thought the milk was *poisoned!* But who on earth . . . Really, what's happened to both of you?'

'Of course that's the answer,' I said. 'The cats were poisoned by something on the farms. It stands to reason.'

'Is that tea you have in that pot?' said Lucie. 'I could do with a cup.'

'It's cold, but I'll send for some more.'

'Thanks. Then I think we should go back, Minta. You want to take greater care of yourself. What odd fancies you get!'

I rang for tea and when it came and I was pouring it out we heard the sound of carriage wheels and Mabel came in to announce that Dr Hunter had called.

'Dr Hunter!' said Lucie. 'What's he doing here?'

I told Mabel to show him in. To my astonishment, Stirling was with him. Lucie rose in her chair and said: 'What *is* this?'

The doctor said: 'I've come to talk to you and what I have to say should be heard by all. I should have witnesses. I should have said it all before this happened.'

'Is it about the cats?' demanded Lucie.

I looked at Stirling but I couldn't read his expression.

'The cats were poisoned,' said the doctor.

'Something they picked up at a farm?' I asked, and there was a terrible fear in my heart.

The doctor said: 'I think I'd better begin at the beginning. This goes back a long way.' He drew a deep breath. 'I am to blame for a good deal.'

'Don't you think you ought to consider very carefully what you are saying?' asked Lucie gently.

'I have considered for a long time. This makes it necessary. I am going to tell the truth. I am going to tell what I should have told long ago. It was when Lady Cardew died that it started.'

'I don't think you should say this, doctor,' said Lucie in a very quiet voice. 'I think you may regret it.'

'I can only regret not having confessed before.' He did not look at Lucie. 'Lady Cardew was not really ill. She had had a disappointment in her life and brooded on it. She came to terms with life by practising a kind of invalidism. It is not unusual with some people. I gave her placebos from time to time. She would take her doses and believe herself to be helped by them. They were in fact nothing but coloured water. Then she died. I should have told the truth then. She died of taking an overdose of a strong sleeping draught. This particular drug was missing from my dispensary, and I believed I had given it to her in mistake for her placebo. I should have admitted this, but instead I wrote on her death certificate that she had died of a heart attack. She had always thought that she had a diseased heart. Her heart was in fact strong. What I did was unpardonable. I was ambitious. In those days I dreamed of specializing. To have admitted that I had mistakenly given a dangerous drug in mistake for a placebo would have ruined my career. I might never have been able to practise again.'

'You are a fool,' said Lucie sadly.

'You are right.' He looked at her mournfully.

'I would advise you to stop this silly tirade which will only bring you to disaster,' she went on.

'At least it will bring me peace of mind. Because *I* did not give her the wrong drug. It was someone else who gave it to her . . . someone who came to my house when I was absent, bringing wine for my housekeeper and drinking with her until she was insensible and then going to my dispensary and taking the drugs.'

'I think the doctor has lost his senses,' said Lucie.

'I had,' he replied, 'but I've regained them now.'

'Can't you see that he is mad?' she demanded of Stirling.

'It doesn't seem so to me,' said Stirling.

'I refuse to listen to any more,' said Lucie. 'That's if you're going on, Dr Hunter.'

'I am going on to tell everything, right to the end, right till today when I discovered that two cats died of the same drug which killed Lady Cardew.'

Lucie stood up. 'You *are* mad, you know,' she said.

'I know how the drug was obtained,' said the doctor. 'It was in exactly the same way. Mrs Devlin has admitted that you came with whisky this time. A little gift for her? Should we try a little tot? And she sat there drinking until she dozed and then you took the keys and went to the dispensary, just exactly as you did on another occasion. She has told me that she remembers it happening before.'

'I won't stay to listen to such nonsense,' said Lucie. 'I shall call another doctor. I shall tell him to get a strait-jacket and bring it here right away.'

She stood at the door looking at us. Minta stared at her incredulously. The doctor's expression was unfathomable. I fancied there was a certain tenderness in it.

'Lucie,' he said, 'you need care.'

She had gone. We heard her running down the stairs and the slamming of the door.

The doctor went on: 'It's not a pleasant story, but I have to tell it. It's the end of everything for us both . . . but at least another murder must be prevented.' He was looking at Minta. 'Thank God it didn't happen this time. You see, I was strongly attracted by Lucie and asked her to marry me. If she had . . . I believe all would have been well. But she had an obsession. It was the great house, the title. She had known great poverty as a child. She feared poverty and longed for security. She was educated by an aunt who was stern and showed her no affection, and she became a teacher. It was a precarious living; she was always in danger of losing her post and being thrown on to an overcrowded market. She was overawed and impressed by the grandeur of Whiteladies.'

I looked at Stirling and I knew he was thinking of Lynx.

'I think she was fond of me in the beginning. I believe she would have married me, but she was helping Sir Hilary a good deal and she realized how much he had come to depend on her. She saw the possibilities and was excited by them, and so this obsession was born. Lucie is a woman of great determination but the desire to possess Whiteladies unbalanced her mind – and she was tempted. Once she had taken one fatal step she was set on her path. In murdering Lady Cardew she had become a criminal and there was no limit to what she was prepared to do.'

'She murdered my mother,' said Minta. 'And she would have murdered me. Why?'

'She was Lady Cardew but that was not enough. Minta would inherit the house. When Sir Hilary died she would be merely a dependant having no control. She could not endure that. If she could have a son it would be different. But Sir Hilary was old. I was fascinated by Lucie and I did not know that she had committed murder. Druscilla is my daughter.'

There was a short silence before he went on: 'She longed for a son. Her rage when Druscilla was born was great. But she would not give up. She was determined to have a son who would inherit Whiteladies and prevent its passing to Minta. But Minta married and Sir Hilary died. There was no hope then except through Druscilla, who was believed to be Sir Hilary's daughter. If Minta were out of the way . . .' He lifted his hands helplessly. 'You see it all now. The whole sordid story. I swear I did not realize all that had happened until I saw those cats today. I knew that she had wanted a son so that she could rule the house through him. I did not know that she had committed murder and planned another. Only today did I see the complete picture. Mrs Devlin admitted that Lucie came yesterday and brought whisky and that she, Mrs Devlin, drank too much. She was asleep the whole afternoon and when I went into my dispensary I found the drug missing . . . as it had been on that other occasion. That is the story.'

I was conscious of a great relief. Stirling was looking at Minta with fear and horror and I thought: He is fond of her after all. Who could help being fond of Minta?

I said: 'What are we going to do?'

Nobody answered, but the matter was decided for us.

Minta's face creased in sudden agony, and she said: 'I think my pains are starting.'

It seemed then that reality was forcing fantasy aside, for this story of what had happened was like a fantasy to us all. It is disconcerting to discover that someone whom one has regarded as a friend, a normal human being, is a murderer. Yet I could believe this of Stirling! I excused myself. I had after all seen his father shoot a man.

There was not time to do anything then but think of Minta and we all became practical. Fortunately Dr Hunter was with us. I said: 'I don't think Minta should go back to Whiteladies. She should stay here. I can look after her.'

Dr Hunter, no longer a man with a terrible secret on his conscience, became the efficient doctor. I ordered servants to put a warming-pan and hot-water bottles in the bed in the spare bedroom next to my own; and we took Minta to it. We were all very anxious because the baby was not due for another four weeks.

The child was born late that day – a perfect child, though premature. It would need very special care and the doctor had summoned a nurse who would come to the Mercer's House solely to care for it. He himself would be in constant attendance. Minta herself was very weak. The shocks of the last weeks culminating in the so recent one were responsible, said Dr Hunter. We must take very special care of Minta.

I promised I would do this and I was determined to. I believed that if I could help bring Minta back to health I should in some way expiate my guilt in loving her husband.

I shall never forget Stirling's face when he heard that he had a son. I knew he would be called Charles after his grandfather and that he must live so that Lynx's dream could be realized – a child of his own name to play on the lawns of Whiteladies.

What a strange, unreal kind of day! Looking back on it, it seems like a dream, too fantastic for reality; but there had been other days like that in my life and perhaps there would be more.

Lucie could not be found anywhere. We thought she had run away. She was in the tower and in the morning they found her body on the flagstones below the bartizan. The wall above, which had been boarded up since that occasion when Minta and I had been up there together, was broken away.

The servants said: 'It was a terrible accident. The wall gave way and Lady Cardew was thrown to the ground.'

Chapter Two

I WAS proud of Stirling. He took on the role of country squire as though it had always been his. Lady Cardew was dead – it was an accident, was the verdict. It was explained by all the work that was being done in Whiteladies which had shaken the old house to its foundations. That, said Stirling, was the best explanation.

He asked me to talk to the doctor to make him see reason. Stirling's idea was that the entire matter should be forgotten. There was no need for anyone – who did not already know it – to know the truth. The danger was removed. Lucie was dead; she could do no more harm. Dr Hunter insisted that he had been guilty of grave indiscretion and was a disgrace to his profession. He didn't think he could allow matters to stand as they were. So the day after little Charles was born Stirling and I talked to him together.

I said: 'You have your skill. You have brought this child into the world and you know how difficult that was. If you hadn't been here Minta would have died and the child with her. Are you going to throw away that skill?'

'There are other doctors,' he said.

'But you belong here.'

'Another doctor would come and there would be no need of me.'

'And what of Maud?' I asked. 'You're fond of her. She's fond of you.'

'It's impossible,' said the doctor.

'It's not!' I cried indignantly. 'You must stop dramatizing yourself and think of Maud. Are you going to make her unhappy?'

He protested but I saw that I had made my point.

The days passed; the baby was two weeks old, still fragile, still in the care of his nurse, still needing the doctor's constant attention. They were two strange weeks. I looked after Minta. Motherhood had changed her. She seemed older and more beautiful – her features finely drawn, but there was a brooding sadness in her eyes.

Franklyn often called at Mercer's. He would sit and talk to Minta about the estate and the old days and ask questions about the baby. I thought how much more suitable than Stirling he would have been as a husband for Minta. They were of a kind, just as Stirling and I were.

Stirling came too. He would sit in Minta's room but there was an embarrassment between them. I wondered whether he knew that she had suspected him of attempting to kill her.

Once he and Franklyn came to the house at the same time so I left Stirling with Minta and Franklyn and I went to the drawing-room to play a game of chess.

As I sat there I thought of Lynx's hand stretched out to move the pieces, the ring on his finger. I treasured that ring. It brought back so many poignant memories.

And then before the game was over Franklyn said suddenly: 'Nora, will you marry me?'

I drew away from the table. 'No, Franklyn,' I said firmly.

'I wish you would,' he said quietly.

I smiled and he asked me why.

'It seems a strange way to offer marriage – almost as though you were inviting me to take a glass of sherry.'

'I'm sorry,' he said.

'I shouldn't have said that.'

'You should always say what's in your mind to me. I know I'm rather inadequate at expressing my feelings.'

'I like that.'

'I'm glad. I'm very fond of you and I hoped you might like me . . . a little.'

'Much more than a little but . . .'

'Not enough to marry me?'

'We are different kinds of people, Franklyn.'

'Does that make marriage impossible?'

'We shouldn't be compatible. You are good, precise, your life is well ordered . . .'

'My dear Nora, you overrate me.'

'I believe you would never do anything that wasn't reasonable and conventional. You are in control of your life.'

'Shouldn't one be?'

'Oh yes. It's very admirable. But hard to live up to. I can only say that we are different and I can't marry you.'

I looked into his face, but I was not really seeing him. I saw another face – a strong face that could be cruel and passionate, the face of a man who could dominate me as Franklyn never could. Even now it was impossible to analyse my feelings for Lynx. To marry him had been a compulsion. Yet I knew that now I yearned for Stirling because I had known ever since we met that we belonged together. Yet how could I reconcile this with my marriage to Lynx?

And Franklyn and myself! Minta and Stirling! We were star-crossed. Lynx like a mischievous god had made us dance to his tune and we had ended up with the wrong partners.

'No, Franklyn,' I said firmly. 'I can't marry you.'

The child was flourishing but Minta was not. Each day she seemed more wan, a little more fragile.

'She's not picking up,' said the doctor. 'She's listless.'

None of Mrs Glee's special dishes could tempt her. Mrs Glee was almost in tears when they came back untouched to the kitchen. Maud came to visit Minta bringing some of her own honey and blackcurrant jelly. A radiant Maud, this; she told me that the doctor had proposed.

'And been accepted, of course,' I said.

She nodded. 'He has told me everything and we're going to adopt Druscilla. Isn't that wonderful? And it's only right. Mr Herrick agrees.'

I told Minta about it.

'Everything is working out well,' I said. 'Now you must eat what's brought to you and try to show some interest in life. What about your son, eh?'

'You can take him.'

'I! When you are well I shall be off to Australia.'

'Are you still determined to go?'

I assured her I was. She looked very sad and I told her that I should come back in a few years and then there would perhaps be a brother or sister for our little Charles. She shook her head.

I was really worried about her and it dawned on me that there was something on her mind.

My guilty conscience set me brooding. I thought constantly of Minta. One night I was so disturbed about her that I couldn't sleep. I rose and went to her room. The lamp there was kept burning all night and as I went in I was horrified to find how cold it was; then I saw that the window was wide open letting in the chilly night air. Minta had thrown off all the bedclothes and lay there in her nightdress only.

I went quickly to the bedside. I touched the sheets and found they were damp. I noticed the empty water jug on the bedside table.

First I shut the window; then I went back to the bed.

'Who did this?' I demanded. I lifted her from the bed and seizing a blanket wrapped it round her. I made her sit in a chair, while I took off the sheets and put on fresh ones. I boiled water on the spirit lamp and filled the hot-water bottles; when I got her into bed she was still shivering. She seemed dazed and she was certainly delirious; I am sure I should never have discovered what was in her mind if she had not been.

I sat by her bed listening to her rambling. It was about Stirling, herself, *myself*. So she knew. She talked of the child who would play on the lawns of Whiteladies. That phrase which had haunted me! I would be there for she herself would be dead. It was the only way to make Stirling happy.

'It's so hard to die,' she said. 'I have to die, though, because that's the only way.'

Piece by piece I fitted it together. And during that hour of delirium she showed me what was in her mind as she never would had her mind been clear. I was appalled and ashamed by the extent of her love for Stirling since she was ready to die for him.

A great determination came to me, I was going to nurse her back to health; I was going to make her live. Stirling must love her in time . . . if I were not there. If we could grow away from this absurd obsession that we were meant for each other (for if it were true would we ever have allowed anything to stand in our way?) he would learn to be happy with Minta. Perhaps it wouldn't be the intoxicating passion which for a while I had known with Lynx, but it could be a good life; and Stirling would have the gratification of knowing that he had fulfilled his father's wishes.

Within a week Minta began to improve. I spoke to her severely. I knew what she had done, I told her; and it must not occur again. It was cowardly to take one's life.

'For others?' she asked.

'For any reason,' I replied firmly. 'Life is meant to be lived.'

She told me then how she had discovered that Stirling and I loved each other, for she had been secreted in the minstrels' gallery. I tried to remember what we had said and I knew it must be damning.

'And you love Stirling,' she said. 'You were meant for each other. You are alike in so many ways. You are strong, adventurous people.'

'Who knows what love is?' I asked. 'It takes a lifetime to discover. I believe that love at its best is not the passion of a moment. It is something that one builds over the years. You can build it with Stirling.'

'But Stirling loves you. I heard him speak to you as he never did to me.'

'One day he will. Then he will have forgotten what I looked like.'

'It's not true, Nora.'

'It is something you can prove to be true in time.'

I half convinced her. Her health was improving rapidly and the baby was getting stronger. I'll never forget the first day she was able to hold him in her arms. I knew then that she had something to live for and so did she.

I knew, too, that it was time for me to leave.

I was going within the next three weeks. I had told Stirling that nothing would induce me to stay. He had his son; he had his wife; it was his duty to make up to Minta for all the anxiety he had caused her.

He realized this. He knew that Minta had suspected him of trying to kill her. That had shaken him considerably and made him feel tender and protective towards her. It was a beginning and I told him that in time he might become worthy of her.

Franklyn came to play a game of chess.

He said: 'I've decided to go to Australia.'

'You! You'd hate it.'

'Why should I?'

'Because it's not . . . England. It's a new country. It's vigorous, perhaps rough, and things are done differently over there from the way they are here.'

'Why shouldn't I be different for a change?'

'Why are you going?'

He looked at me intently and said: 'You know why.'

'Oh no,' I protested. 'You couldn't. Not because of . . . me!'

'You are determined to go. It seems the only thing I can do is to come too. I can't lose you, you know.'

'There is your estate. What about Wakefield Park?'

'I can put a manager in. That's simple. In fact I've already settled that little detail.'

'But you *love* Wakefield Park.'

'There is something I love more.'

I could not meet his eyes. I felt ashamed.

'Me, for instance?' I asked.

'But of course.'

I stood on the deck of the *Brandon Star* and watched the shores of England recede. I was going back. Once I had stood on the deck of a ship bound for the same destination and Stirling had stood beside me.

Now Stirling was in England and I had said goodbye to him, to Minta, to the baby, to Whiteladies; and another man stood beside me.

Stirling and I were two of a kind. We had often said it. But Franklyn was with me now and Minta was with Stirling. We had despised them, mocked them because they were not like us.

No, I thought. They had a power to love which we lacked. Minta had been ready to die for Stirling; Franklyn had given up his beloved lands to come to me. What was love? Had Stirling and I understood love such as that?

'Very soon you'll see the last of England,' said Franklyn. 'Does that make you sad?'

I turned to look at him, seeing him afresh.

'Not as I thought it would,' I admitted. 'We're going to a great country, a land of endless opportunities.'

We smiled at each other; and the love I saw in his eyes was a glow that warmed me. I knew then that I wanted to learn more of his sort of love – and Minta's – that love which does not look for sensation or continual excitement, the love that is built not on the shifting sands of violent passion but on the steady rock of deep and abiding affection.

As the land slid away below the horizon, I believed that I might find it.

Mistress of Mellyn
Victoria Holt

Martha Leigh's arrival at Mount Mellyn, an eerie mansion set high on the Cornish cliffs, leaves her with a sense of deep foreboding. She is dreading her new life as a governess, particularly when she meets her arrogant employer, Con TreMellyn and his precocious young daughter Alvean.

Martha quickly realizes why three governesses before her had left that cold and brooding house. Even stranger, the sinister air that surrounds the place is encouraged by the neighbours and servants, who seem eager to give hints and fuel rumours about haunted rooms, strange accidents and past infidelities.

When Martha's resolve to stay on however, is quickened by her growing fondness for Alvean and an unwilling attraction towards Con TreMellyn, she becomes determined to unravel the mysteries that surround the family, a decision that ultimately threatens her own life.

Mistress of Mellyn is a novel of considerable power and beauty written in the great romantic tradition, a work of unforgettable suspense.

ISBN-13 978 0 00 723551 3
ISBN-10 0 00 723551 8

The Shivering Sands
Victoria Holt

When Caroline Verlaine's sister, the archaeologist Roma, disappears, Caroline is forced down to Lovat Stacy in an attempt to discover what has happened. She finds herself caught up in the drama of the ancient house and with the unusual members of the Stacy family. But it is Napier Stacy, recently returned from years of banishment for apparently killing his brother, who she is especially drawn to.

Napier is haunted by the tragedy, and Caroline becomes determined that he should put his past behind him and not allow, what she insists was an accident, to cloud his life for ever. At the same time, she becomes equally determined to solve the mystery of her own sister's disappearance.

Why had Roma vanished? Was it an accident or had she been murdered?

But as the tension mounts Caroline soon realizes that this quest to uncover the truth is a dangerous one and is marking her out as the next victim.

'For a good escapist read Victoria Holt never disappoints.'

Annabel

ISBN-13 978 0 00 723554 4
ISBN-10 0 00 723554 2